A Violent End

Best regards,

Maggie Wheeler

MAGGIE WHEELER

Published by

GENERAL STORE
GSPH PUBLISHING HOUSE

499 O'Brien Road, Box 415
Renfrew, Ontario, Canada K7V 4A6
Telephone (613) 432-7697 or 1-800-465-6072

ISBN 1-894263-41-3
Printed and bound in Canada

Cover artwork by Tim Yearington
Layout by Derek McEwen

General Store Publishing House
Burnstown, Ontario, Canada

Canadian Cataloguing in Publication Data

Wheeler, Maggie A., 1960-
    A violent end

ISBN 1-894263-41-3

    I. Title.

PS8595.H3852V56 2001   C813'.6   C2001-900249-1
PR9199.3.W4282V56 2001

Third Printing June 2004

DEDICATION

For Mom and Dad
and the pieces of you I carry with me still

and

to my daughters Anna, Evan and Lindsay
who grow like willows beside the great river

And for Robert
with whom all things begin

While the background of this novel is based on actual history, the characters and plot line are products of the author's imagination and in no way are intended to resemble real events or people, either living or dead.

MW

CONTRIBUTORS

Researching this novel was a refresher course in what "community" really means. Every door on which I knocked opened. Those who could not help me found someone who could. Without the networking, advice, resources, personal stories and/or encouragement of the following people, this novel would not have been written:

Louise Boulay—St. Lawrence College, Cornwall campus

Jim Brownell—President, Lost Villages Historical Society

Cornwall Public Library—Reference Staff

The Friends of the (Upper Canada Migratory Bird) Sanctuary   the goose people

Matthew Griffis—very patient resource and nephew

Sergeant Richard Griffis—Ontario Provincial Police (Peterborough)

Gisele Grignon—writer, friend and mentor (even without the paperwork)

George Haas—Research Associate, Institute of the Environment, University of Ottawa

Linda Halliday—Public Affairs Officer, Eastern Ontario, Ontario Power Generation (formerly Ontario Hydro)

Ellis Hancock—1st Mate, Quebec & Ontario Transportation Company (ret.)

Professor Glenn Harris—Department of Environmental Studies, St. Lawrence University, Canton, New York

George Hickey—formerly of Aultsville

Jim Hunter—Carleton Productions International Inc.

Fran Laflamme—formerly of Wales

Henry Lickers—Akwesasne, Mohawk Environmental Division

Gwen (Fetterly) McMillan—formerly of Old Morrisburg

Dr. Bob Reddoch—Chief of Emergency Medicine, Cornwall General Hospital

Rosemary Rutley—author, formerly of Woodlands, Santa Cruz, Farran's Point and Aultsville

Stormont, Dundas & Glengarry Ontario Provincial Police

Upper Canada Village Archives

and countless others who, through casual conversation and discussion of this project over the last two years, gave me the thousand tiny threads I needed to pull this all together.

Special thanks to the Lost Villages Historical Society for the material and the support.

Also special thanks to Jann and Bruce for letting me use the words to their wonderful songs.

TABLE OF CONTENTS

AUTHOR'S NOTE

When I began this book, it was only a story about a murder.

Then I chose the local backdrop of the 1950s Seaway and Power Project. In doing so, I opened a Pandora's box.

At first, the history itself was overwhelming. The word "epic" comes to mind, and in relation to those years for an area of Canada well-steeped in history, this word is not an overstatement even by modern standards. It was also very moving for me to share the experiences of many people for whom the memories of almost half a century ago remain fresh in their minds. I believe that, in the hearts of many former residents of the Lost Villages, they have never really left. Part of this story belongs to them.

However, this book does not attempt to describe exactly *what* happened, so much as how the people felt about it—then and now. This is a story of memory, perception and the human spirit. That aspect of this project belongs to us all.

As for me, I knew I would have to revisit my own past to contribute my personal vision of loss, grief and healing. While I did not look forward to reliving sad times, I was prepared to do so. What I did not expect to do was face personal issues still awaiting closure since my youth, issues of acceptance and commitment. I have spent the last thirty years of my life in the Seaway Valley. Through the writing of this book—like Farran—I have finally come home.

Maggie Wheeler

FOREWORD to *A VIOLENT END*

By JIM BROWNELL

PRESIDENT, LOST VILLAGES HISTORICAL SOCIETY

As president of the Lost Villages Historical Society, and with formative years in and around the communities of the Lost Villages, it gives me pleasure to reflect upon the life and times of an important chapter in Canadian history as a foreword to Maggie Wheeler's historical mystery, *A Violent End*. The construction of a 'new' seaway in the International Rapids section of the St. Lawrence River, and the building of the Robert Moses-Robert Saunders Hydro Generating Station at Cornwall, Ontario, were activities that captivated the attention of locals and citizens from around the world. Visitors to Eastern Ontario continue to be fascinated by the Lost Villages story.

With her skill at interweaving fact with fiction, Maggie Wheeler has captured the true spirit of those communities that were obliterated from the face of the earth in the Inundation of July 1, 1958. *A Violent End* could be set in any one of the six Lost Villages, for the community lives in each of them were very similar. In these few words of introduction, I shall reflect on moments in history as they affected the people and places of the Lost Villages.

The story of the Lost Villages is more than houses being moved, lives being turned upside down, and places from the past being covered with the waters of Lake St. Lawrence. It revolves around two great engineering projects, costing more than $1.2 billion dollars. The construction of a new seaway and the harnessing of the power created by the mighty Long Sault Rapids took four years to complete, from 1954 to 1958. These projects, the dream of engineers for over a century, culminated in a blast that was witnessed by thousands of people on Dominion Day, 1958. This blast released the waters of the St. Lawrence River behind Coffer Dam A–1, causing over 16,000 hectares of land to be covered by the headpond of Lake St. Lawrence.

On August 4, 1954, Prime Minister Louis St. Laurent, Premier Leslie Frost of Ontario, and Governor Thomas Dewey of New York

State, along with many other dignitaries and citizens from Canada and the United States of America, assembled at Maple Grove and turned the sod to begin the construction of the greatest engineering project in Canadian history.

Hydro and Seaway employees, working around the clock, fought the elements that nature forced on them, and successfully completed the engineering and construction work for the July 1, 1958 deadline. From Montreal, Quebec, to Prescott, Ontario, construction workers dug channels and built new lock systems that would allow ocean-going vessels easy passage through the International Rapids section of the St. Lawrence River. This was the bottleneck created by the Long Sault Rapids.

In the International Rapids section, the Eisenhower, Snell and Iroquois Locks were constructed, and the Wiley-Dondero Canal was dredged through glacial till on the American side of the river. Hydro engineers and construction workers, realizing that three dams were required to harness the hydro potential of the rapids, worked to create the Lake St. Lawrence headpond.

By early 1958, the dykes were completed and the Robert Moses-Robert Saunders Generating Station stood waiting for the first rush of water through the turbines. The Long Sault and Iroquois Control Dams were ready to receive the waters held back by Coffer Dam A-1, and to regulate the waters of the new lake. Citizens of two great countries stood, with visitors from around the world, in anticipation of the "big wall of water" that would sweep down to cover the lands of the Lost Villages.

Gone forever would be the site of the aboriginal community on Sheek Island, inhabited by the Point Peninsula People many centuries before. Gone forever would be the burial grounds of the United Empire Loyalists, ancestors of many who watched that day. Gone, too, would be the main streets of six communities, streets that linked them along the St. Lawrence River. As Loretta Burgess anticipated in the lyrics to *The Seaway Song* that played daily in the mid-1950s on CKSF, the Cornwall radio station, "The old St. Lawrence will have a new face, when the men of Hydro have won their race."

The villages of Mille Roches, Moulinette, Wales, Dickinson's Landing, Farran's Point and Aultsville were lost to the flood of 1958; however, the memories never faded from the minds of those who were forced to relocate to Town No.1, now Ingleside, and Town No.

2, now Long Sault. They, along with others from the hamlets of Maple Grove, Santa Cruz and Woodlands, and the farming community on Sheek Island, were the 6,500 people who were displaced.

These were the people who lived in the 531 homes that were carried to higher ground by the giant Hartshorne Brothers house-moving machines. These were the people who witnessed the "hearts" being torn out of their beloved communities. Churches were torn down and burned, schools bulldozed into the earth, and businesses forced to close or relocate.

These were the people who watched industries disappear, many of them having developed from the pioneering cottage industries of centuries past. These were the people who had to move into new towns, to say "hello" to strangers who would become neighbours, and to adjust to a new way of life in a planned town. These were the people, too, who rushed along the river's edge, following the breach of the last coffer dam, to catch one last glimpse of their former communities and property. No doubt these were the people who remember the tears shed in 1958.

Maggie has captured many key aspects of the history of the Lost Villages in *A Violent End*. Many readers, especially those who lived in the Lost Villages, will relate to the historical details presented while enjoying the mystery that unfolds around them. Many, too, in a desire to learn more about these communities, will journey to the Lost Villages Museum, three kilometres east of Long Sault, Ontario. Here, in a small, village-like setting in Ault Park, the story is told about the Hydro and Seaway projects, and the life and times of those who lived in the Lost Villages. Unlike Maggie's thoughts about a "tea party in Aultsville," you may actually find that "those Lost Village people were trying to hold a tea party. . ." under a canopy in the park.

Congratulations to Maggie Wheeler from the members of the Lost Villages Historical Society for choosing the Lost Village of Aultsville as the main site for this novel, and for doing such a superb job at mixing fact with fiction. Key elements of Lost Villages history will live on within the pages of *A Violent End*.

Part One

For some, therefore, the uprooting was demoralizing and
traumatic; for others, it was a challenge. The realization that
people were materially more comfortable helped to assuage
feelings of nostalgia. It was natural to look back fondly at the
haunts of a lifetime. But what hurt some people was the
memory of homes burnt for combustion tests, churches
demolished, caskets disinterred, memorable trees cut down,
post office equipment smashed. Settlements, on which
generations had expended their labour, were haggled over,
reduced to dollars and cents, and then covered over by the
waters of the St. Lawrence. It was a violent end to a quiet
way of life.

Clive Marin and Frances Marin
Stormont, Dundas and Glengarry 1945-1978

Chapter 1

Inundation

JULY 1-4, 1958

T̄HE BLAST was set for 8:00 a.m.

In the new house in Ingleside, Gordon Leonard sat at the kitchen table clutching a cold mug of coffee. He had not slept the night before, and when the heavens had opened at midnight he was waiting for their fury. The worst thunderstorm in a decade had shaken the St. Lawrence Valley till dawn, feeding his growing unease. His father hadn't helped matters, either. The old man—already infirm and fading—had spent the early hours wandering the house calling for his dead wife. And Hal.

Gordon would not attend the flooding. It would be best to stay home today.

Meredith Murphy was waiting on the dike in Cornwall with several thousand others. The downpour had turned the man-made hill into pure mud and many had lost their galoshes already, including her younger cousin Lynnie Holmes who was playing detective and being a nuisance as usual. Meredith listened to the updates over the loudspeaker, shaking her head. Last night's storm had been an omen, she was sure of that. You'd have to be thick as a post not to see that God Himself was cursing what they'd done to His beautiful river.

Wickedness—that's what it was, the young woman thought to herself. But then, wickedness had been here for some time.

Down in the road, young Jerry Strauss was buying snacks and souvenirs from the stands set up for the public. He ordinarily didn't have money to throw away on such things, but today his mother not

3

only allowed it but bankrolled him as well. He knew what she was doing—what she had been doing since his dad died. Trying to fill the hole she could see in her son. She didn't have to worry about that. He was taking care of it and doing a darn good job, too.

Jerry bought a Coca-Cola for his mother and began making his way through the crowd to where she stood waiting. As usual, some of the men were eyeing the beautiful widow. The boy's hand tightened around the bottle.

In the sea of people, Ruth Hoffman stood apart. Dressed in the latest fashion from her visit to Montreal, the young woman remained by the family car. The Cornwall Standard-Freeholder *had promised a thirty-foot wave after the cofferdam was breached, and no one seemed sure about much else. Her family was up on the dike to watch. They would go to Farran's Point later to say goodbye.*

She adjusted her dress and checked her pumps for mud. What a goddamn day. All she wanted to do was get on with her life. And her mother had been little help since she'd returned from the city. Out three nights in a row, as though avoiding her daughter. Maybe she was. Ruth stood in a crowd of thousands, feeling completely alone and immensely tragic.

By 7:55, excitement had reached fever pitch. The cottagers from what would be Moulinette Island in the new parkway had been evacuated just in case. Traffic along the new No. 2 Highway was halted at the junction of Power Dam Drive, for safety. The Drive itself had been jammed since early morning. Now more than 70,000 people waited along the embankment and the shoreline on both sides to see the spectacular end to four years' work. The thirty-two turbines in the new Robert H. Saunders-Robert M. Moses Power Dam stood ready and waiting, as did the thirty tons of explosives in Cofferdam A–1.

The blast came at 8:01.

As if to spite the fanfare, the explosion appeared to those on the dike as only a puff of dust in the distance. The Standard-Freeholder *would later dub it "an unspectacular whisper." The aftershock was not. One minute later, it struck. Those waiting in cars on the highway felt their vehicles lift simultaneously off the road for a few breathtaking seconds. But the big wave did not come.*

For an hour, nothing came. Then the first trickle of water appeared. Instead of one wrenching moment, the flooding would last four days. For four days, the villagers would say goodbye.

Traffic began to move along the highway again, and Lynnie Holmes tugged at her father's sleeve.

"Pa, let's go to the Point and watch the water come up."

Jake Holmes looked at his daughter with a small smile. Youth had little problem with letting go, and he understood her excitement.

"The Point won't see water before tomorrow at this rate," he said, putting his arm around her shoulders. "But we could watch a bit at Mille Roches. They'll be under today for sure. Let's get your ma. It'll take a while to get through this crowd."

It was midmorning before the Holmes' car got close to the former village of Mille Roche. Everywhere, people wandered, watching the river. Cars cruised slowly along the old highway as close as they dared, with the massive bulk of the power dam towering in the background. Except for the roads and exposed foundations, all signs of human activity were gone. As far as the eye could see, the land lay stripped and flat. Wild mustard had taken over to make a sea of yellow, except for the odd colour patch where a once well-tended garden bloomed in defiance. Thousands of stumps were all that was left of prime bush land and mature orchards. When the water came, thought Jake, it would be a mercy.

Holmes stopped the car beside a pickup truck parked in what had once been the driveway to a farm. A man stood beside the truck, which held four children. A woman sitting in the front seat did not look up. The man glanced over at the car as Lynnie's dad got out, and nodded a greeting.

"Jake."

"Ewen." They shook hands. Jake indicated the car. "Just takin' the family home from the show on the dike. Lynnie wanted to see the water coming up, so I said we'd take the river road home."

"She's got a wait, then," replied Ewen grimly. "No wave this mornin' so we came here to see it out. Mille Roche'll be the first to go, for sure, but it may take the day. You can just see the water comin' now." He pointed to the horizon, where a dark line was forming all the way down to the dam. Lynnie hung out the back window stretching to see, until her mother said to get her feet off the car seat.

"Are you stayin' the day?" Jake asked.

"Till the river's on the tires." Ewen put his hand on the truck.

The children, two boys and two girls, eyed Lynnie curiously but remained oddly quiet. They watched their father expectantly. He cocked his head toward the farmland behind them. "The farm's been in Peg's family twice back. We thought the boys would have it some day. Now we're not even farmin' anymore. I start drivin' rig next week." He shrugged. "Not much a man can do about it, is there?"

Jake shook hands in silent agreement, and got back in the car. "We'll be at the Point tomorrow, I guess. Lynnie's excited about it, but I think the two of us'll be glad to see the end of it. Time to get on with things."

A strident call made both men look up. Overhead, several small birds swooped in circles as though desperately searching for something. More could be seen in the distance where the water advanced, their calls coming bleakly over the landscape.

"Ground birds," said Ewen shortly. "Losin' their nests. Tryin' to save their young. Been doin' that for an hour now."

And in the sky, the larks still bravely singing, fly.

Jake shook his head and grimly started the engine.

When the car had pulled away, Lynnie turned to her dad.

"Why couldn't we stay there and watch with them? I could've played with those kids for a while."

"This isn't a day for play, Lynnie," he replied quietly. "Most people are sayin' goodbye to the only home they've ever known. Ewen's family don't want us there right now. They'll never see their farm again after today."

Sunday dawned. Mille Roches had disappeared overnight and Moulinette was under siege. As the deep section along the dike continued to fill, the expanding waterfront began to pick up speed. The former residents of Moulinette spent the day retreating as the water advanced. Determined to see it all, Jerry Strauss had encamped with his mother on the old highway just west of the village. An elderly man was near them, surrounded by stumps of trees near a foundation. He sat white-faced and alone, facing the water, on a set of cement steps that now led to nowhere.

"Hey, Ma," Jerry pointed, "Isn't that old man Baker? I seen him before in the Leonards' store."

Mrs. Strauss gave her son a light rap on the head with her knuckle.

"Don't stare, Jerry. It is rude. He is a person, not a sideshow. I brought you out to watch the river, not our neighbours."

The boy turned away, rubbing his head gingerly. With grownups, you just couldn't do anything right. But then, they'd been acting funny for the last four years.

Just down the road, he could see several watchers pick up their chairs and start moving away from the dark line coming in. The old man saw it, too. He rose slowly and walked over to the circle of stumps. After a minute, he looked down at them, then around the property to the foundation and driveway. Finally, he seemed to square his shoulders, turn his back to the yard and face the water.

The group on the road continued watching until the water reached the side of the old highway. Then they got in their car and drove past. The river lapped up over the side of the road and farther down made little waterfalls as it filled gutters and basements.

Mrs. Strauss put her hand on her son's shoulder.

"We had better leave before we get cut off on the road."

"Oh, all right, but what about Mr. Baker?" Jerry looked back to where the man stood, the water now only a few yards away.

Emme Strauss opened her car door.

"I think that is his truck right over there," she nodded. "He will leave when he is ready, Jerry."

The water began to come across the highway as they stepped into the vehicle. By the time they drove past the old man on the way to the road north, it was beginning to swirl around his feet and claim the tree stumps. They saw him suddenly turn away and bend over the ground. Through the open windows came the sound of violent retching.

Emme drove in silence. And suddenly, just for a moment, Jerry wanted very much to go home.

On Monday morning, the docks at the Long Sault Marina were still dry, but now the casualties had begun to mount. Mille Roches, Moulinette—gone. Workday traffic along the new highway was slow and congested as tourists and passersby watched the new town of Long Sault get its waterfront. After more than a year of sitting sheepishly in the middle of a farmer's field, the bridge to the Long Sault Parkway now spanned water.

On the river went toward Ingleside—New Town No. 1. It formed the islands that would make the parkway, covering thousands of stumps and making shallows along the new highway's edge. Dickinson's Landing gave way, and Hoople's Creek began to back up on its way to eradicate the village of Wales to the north.

Most of the older people in the new towns stayed away. They did not want to see. Some continued to follow the river along by car. One villager placed stakes daily in the ground to mark the progress of the water. Everyone found a way to get through it.

In Farran's Point, Ruth Hoffman sat on the edge of Lock No. 22 with her family and neighbours. As they had so often gathered here to watch the ships go through or have a picnic in the little park, now the people waited mostly in silence. The young woman dangled her feet over the water, which was up some from its usual mark in the lock, but didn't seem to be moving now. She wished it would start soon and be over with. She never wanted to see Farran's Point again.

Behind her, people were quietly talking. Her father stood with his arm protectively around her mother.

"D'you bide the time, Alice," he said softly, "we had our first dance in the pavilion? We saw it as so grown up, eh? But how young we were."

Alice Hoffman nodded, unable to speak. Ruth's brother ran around them in circles, making engine noises as he flew his toy plane.

"Tommy!" Ruth hissed. "Stop it. You're being a pain again." It had little effect as usual.

Ruth faced the river again. The mention of the dance pavilion started thoughts she was determined not to have today. A beautiful summer evening in the park, hanging around with her girlfriends, a fight. Hal Leonard walking through a hostile crowd to put a coin in the nickelodeon, then he and Leslie Mackenzie alone on the dance floor with every eye on them. That's how it had started. If only Leslie hadn't got mixed up with that boy. . . . If only Ruth hadn't had to leave when she did.

Dammit, Leslie, where are you?

"So where's Leslie?"

Ruth jumped at the sound of her own thoughts and looked up at Lynnie Holmes. The girl had that cat-and-canary look again, like she had a secret she'd just love to share. And almost in high school. When would Lynnie grow up? Well, Ruth wouldn't bite this time.

"I have no idea," she said, turning away. "We haven't heard from her."

"I thought for sure she'd come back for this," Lynnie persisted.

"I guess she had better things to do," said Ruth dryly.

The water touched Ruth's feet.

"Pa. Pa!" The girl jumped up and the others began to follow suit. "The water's comin' up."

As the crowd began to gather along the lock, a truck came down the north road and stopped in the park. The driver jumped out, making his way quickly to the centre of the crowd.

"I just come along the highway," he said grimly. "The Landing's gone. And Wales is almost finished. It won't be long for us, now."

This is it, Ruth thought. The end of it. It's finally happening. Suddenly, a cold wave of panic caught her off guard. For a moment she felt her stomach lurch.

Wait. Stop this. I'm not ready. I've changed my mind.

The young woman instinctively moved closer to her father, who still stood holding her mother. Even Tommy stopped for a moment to watch.

It seemed to take forever for the water to reach the lock's edge, but once over it began to roll across the grass. People reluctantly gave way before it, heading toward their cars. Ruth followed her parents, with a firm grip on her brother.

"I wanna let the water come up to my knees!" Tommy wailed as she dragged him along.

"Don't tempt me," she answered curtly, opening the car door. Turning back, Ruth caught a glimpse of some small animals scurrying across the park to find high ground. Several more had chosen the doomed tow path on the far side of the lock. It would be gone in minutes.

"Let's follow back along the street for a bit," Ruth's father suggested.

Alice shook her head.

"I've seen enough. I want to go."

"All right," he answered gently. "Let's go home."

"But this is home, Harland." Ruth barely caught her mother's whisper. "This is home."

"But I wanna see more," came the cry from the back seat.

Ruth gave the car door a satisfying slam.

At that moment in Aultsville, Gordon Leonard walked slowly past his former front yard and took a long last look around. He shook his head to himself. Everything so flat and bare. It looked as though a great fire had gone through, or a bomb had dropped. One of those atomic bombs they'd used on the Japs when he was a kid. He remembered the pictures on the newsreel. In some ways, he felt he'd been standing here when the bomb hit.

And that wasn't so far from the truth, was it?

His brother's face rose in his mind and he pushed it away.

"Gordon, are you all right?"

The young man turned to see Meredith Murphy watching him with concern. She made him nervous. He couldn't help it.

"I'm fine. I'll be better when the water comes. Get it over with, I guess." *He looked around.* "You here alone?"

She nodded. "My folks are staying with my grandparents. My grandma hasn't left the house since the flooding started. Says she can't bear to watch. So I came on my bike. Were you at the dike on Saturday? My dad took me, but I didn't see you."

"No. I stayed home. Dad was having a bad day of it. I couldn't leave him."

Gordon began to head toward the riverfront. Meredith followed beside him.

"I was thinking this morning of your ma. The cemetery will be gone soon. I'm sure that's hard on you."

"The decision was made," *he said irritably. She always had a way of sticking her finger right in it, even if she did mean well.* "Dad wanted her left here. I guess he's right. Mother's whole life was Aultsville."

"And her sons," *Meredith added. Gordon did not reply.* "Maybe it was a blessing she died before everything started to change, and Hal . . . " *She broke off awkwardly.*

They walked in silence for a few minutes.

"Has there been any word?" *she asked hesitantly.*

Gordon shook his head. He was sick of the subject.

"You'd think he'd come back for something like this, at least," *she said.*

"You seem to think my brother Hal cares about other people's feelings," *said Gordon curtly.* "Obviously, he doesn't. Why should he be here to be with us?"

They reached the old highway, which was packed with people and cars. Eric Leonard sat in a lawn chair with a blanket on his thin legs despite the sun. A few neighbours were talking to him with that forced cheerfulness one uses with the sick. It sounded even more unnatural under the circumstances.

"Something's wrong," the man was insisting when Gordon came up. "It doesn't add up. It doesn't feel right. If I could just remember . . ."

"They're flooding for the new power dam today, Dad," Gordon reminded him with a hand on his shoulder. "You remember."

"New power dam?" he said distractedly. "Already got one in Mille Roches. What do we need a new one for? And where's Hal? He said he'd be here. Has a surprise for me."

Gordon shot Meredith a worried look.

"Hi, Mr. Leonard," she broke in brightly. "It's Meredith. My folks said to say hello if I saw you here."

"I know who you are, young lady," Eric snapped back. "Your mother brought you in to be weighed on the store scale when you were born. You had a lot to say back then, too," he added.

The group laughed and Meredith flushed. But the good mood was short-lived.

"Water's up," someone called.

Jerry circled the foundation several times while his mother looked on. Then he painstakingly covered the ground around a large stump nearby.

"Jerry," said Emme with a sigh, "you checked everything before we moved, remember?"

"I know, ma, but I can't find my best baseball." The boy straightened and looked up the road. "Maybe I should look around the Leonards' old place. Hal and I played with it there once."

"Jerry, we are not wandering around someone else's property," his mother said sharply. "We should join the others at the river."

"It's not their property anymore. It all belongs to Hydro. Besides, you never know what I might find left behind."

"It will all belong to the river, soon," she replied. "And that is where I am going. With you," she added firmly.

They faced off for a minute, then the boy slowly followed his mother down the Aultsville Road toward the riverfront.

The river continued to climb past Farran's Point, digging long fingers into the shoreline to form the marshland that would soon be a provincial sanctuary. After covering Wales, Hoople's Creek became Hoople's Bay—taking out two farms to do it. Slowly, inexorably, like the hand of God passing judgement, the water moved across the land: over roads once travelled, fields once tended, gardens once loved. As any mother would at day's end, the river gathered up the toils of her children.

At last the St. Lawrence curled over the streets of Aultsville on its way to Morrisburg and Iroquois, claiming the old ferry wharf, concealing the sites of the Strauss home and the ballpark, covering the charred remains of the Fraternity Hall. Cottagers from the soon-to-be Ault Island sat buttressed against the inevitable in lawn chairs on the old highway, until the water came up to their feet.

And as the sun went down, the river filled the former cellar of the old Leonard house, the cistern last; entombing inside something that had so recently been human, head thrown back, sightless eyes trained heavenward for all eternity.

Chapter 2

Revelation

THE PHONE at the front desk of the Kingston Ontario Provincial Police detachment was ringing when Detective Inspector Jerry Strauss walked into the lobby. The receptionist waved him over.

"Sir, it's Inspector Lewis from Long Sault for you. He says it's important."

"Patch it through to my office." Strauss made his way down the hall and threw his takeout coffee in the waste can before answering the blinking light on his desk. "Strauss here, Lewis. Jesus, you can't let a guy get his coat off before you're on him," he added good-naturedly. Holidays were two days away. "What's up?"

"I have what might be a 'situation' here, Jerry." Even through the phone, Lewis sounded strained. "We got a new homicide yesterday and although technically I have enough manpower to cover it, I'm stretched. Considering the facts, I thought maybe you'd want to sit in on this one."

"Why me?"

"The remains were found in one of the lost villages, the towns that were flooded when the power dam was built. You have some background there, don't you?"

Strauss's hand tightened around the receiver. "Which village?"

"Aultsville," came the reply. Jerry felt his stomach kick. Time to cut back on the coffee like the doctor said.

After a moment's pause, he asked, "Where exactly was it found? On the sanctuary grounds or right in the old village area?"

"In the village, partially buried in an old foundation. The corpse is old; I'd say definitely there before the flooding but we won't know for sure, of course, until Toronto takes a look."

"How the hell did anyone spot it if the village is under water?"

"A good chunk of Aultsville is high and dry right now," Lewis explained. "The water hasn't been this low in at least ten years. And ever since the fortieth anniversary celebrations, there's been a real surge of interest in the whole area. The Lost Villages Society runs bus tours along there now and everything. I'm surprised no one saw it earlier this summer."

"Someone local find it?"

"No, actually the lucky couple was from New York state. Hikers who stopped on their way through the bike path. Decided to walk the old streets a little bit and see if they could find anything interesting. They weren't disappointed, I guess."

"You can't pinpoint the location yet, can you?" Strauss closed his eyes, easily calling up the old village in his mind despite having closed the door on it so long ago. And the sight of his mother standing, unbelieving, in the light of the fire as he ran screaming toward it.

"The property faces the old Aultsville Road, sits not far south of the bike path. The foundation due north of it is big, and I'm guessing with this old map that it was the Leonard's General Store. Does that help?"

The Leonards' store. The long front porch where the old men would sit every evening, waiting for the return mail on the Moccasin train. His mother, young and beautiful, walking back from the station with the mail; serving from behind the wicket in the store with her low, soothing voice that held only a trace of German accent after fifteen years in Canada. The smell of pickle brine and nuts from the barrels, the huge brass weigh scale on the counter, the backroom filled with smoke and conversation when the men played checkers around the wood stove on a Saturday night. And Hal, always ready to kid around, always smiling—even at the end when he didn't have anything left to smile about. His stomach prodded him again.

"The county road," said Jerry, opening his eyes. His office sprang reassuringly back into view.

"What?"

"We didn't always call it the Aultsville Road in those days.

Some called it the county road. The real oldtimers called it Nelson Road. And I think I know where you're saying. I grew up in Aultsville."

"I know," said Lewis. "That's the real reason I called you. I do need an extra body here, but I want someone with some background in the villages. If this John Doe turns out to be from before the flooding, it could make for a sensitive situation. I don't want our senior population all stirred up over this if I can help it. Makes for bad feeling all around. I'm taking retirement this year and I'd like to go out on a good note."

Especially since you want to run for reeve shortly after, Jerry thought to himself. His stomach was definitely unhappy with this news and he wanted to pass on it, but couldn't see how. Lewis had done him many favours over the years, and why wouldn't someone want to go back over the old times? Except himself. The past was the last place he wanted to go.

"I've got two days to kill before my holidays start, Dave. I'll come down and take a look around, help get things started. Who's the detective constable I'll be working with?"

"Wiley. He's a new guy here. A little formal but a good cop. He's out there now with the crime unit. When do I expect you?"

"Right after lunch," said Strauss, and then hung up.

Not that he'd be eating.

Gordon Leonard stared out his kitchen window on Ault Island across the mud flat that led to the back of the sanctuary. Criminal how low the water was this year, he thought. Stumps up everywhere. Boaters unhappy all the way to Lake Ontario. Wonder what the hell they're doing at the dam.

And what the hell are they doing at the sanctuary? Gordon had noticed the patrol car down on the bike path late yesterday. It was still there and now with a marked van. He couldn't make out the words at this distance. Maybe some sightseers got hurt poking around where they shouldn't be anyway. They were damn close to the old house.

Something was being put up—looked like a big tent canopy. Maybe those Lost Village people were trying to hold a tea party in Aultsville and the cops were there to get them out. A bit of a stretch, but nothing would surprise him. All this sudden interest in the villages now. In his position at Upper Canada Village, Gordon had helped many times with various events. But in his heart, he wanted the past to stay buried—where it belonged.

Yellow. A flash of colour in the sun. Yellow tape? A crime scene?

Gordon felt a sudden chill sweep over him. "Someone walking over my grave," he muttered. "More likely old age catching up with me. Good thing I'm retiring next year." Gordon looked out the window again at the cars. He could see people moving around. He set his coffee cup in the sink. Maybe his morning run should go in the direction of Aultsville, find out what's going on.

Maybe not.

"Lynnie?"

Lynn Holmes felt her heart sink. Monday morning, her desk piled with mail and press releases, one reporter very overdue with his story, and another staff meeting in one hour that did not bode well. And now a call from the only person who called her by that name anymore. She gave an inward sigh.

"Hi, Meredith. Listen, can you do me a favour? Can I call you back at lunchtime? It's a nuthouse around here today."

"I wouldn't call if it weren't important," said her cousin in her best martyr's tone.

"Of course." Lynn rubbed her forehead. Probably the president of the Ladies' League absconded with the bazaar's funds. Oh well, family was family and she didn't have much of that left. "What is it?"

"Well, I don't have anything confirmed yet, but something's up." There was a dramatic pause, and Lynn could just see the glee in her cousin's face. "They found a body in Aultsville."

"What? You mean the goose sanctuary."

"I mean Aultsville. You haven't been home yet this summer and seen the water. It's the lowest in years. Anyway," Meredith warmed up to her news, "the word is that a couple of hikers were nosing around the old streets and found a body half buried in the mud. And it's old—from our time. Don't you wonder who it is?"

"Haven't had a chance, really. But I'm sure you'll tell me."

"Well, how would *I* know? You're the reporter."

"Editor," Lynn interrupted. The voice went on heedlessly.

"I thought that the *Citizen* would be interested in an old murder, and you could come down and find out all the details."

"It's a murder?"

"Oh . . . well . . . I—I just assumed that, I guess," Meredith said awkwardly. "Why else would anyone bury someone out there?"

"Who told you how old the body was?"

"Uh . . . just a rumour, really. The papers don't confirm anything yet," the woman admitted grudgingly, "except the body and that it's in Aultsville."

"Look, Meredith, I really have to get back to work. Can you fax me the news story? I'll look at it and trace it on the wire, see what I can find."

When it came through—less than a minute later—Lynn saw that Meredith had summed it up. Nothing confirmed except a body in Aultsville. No suggestion about cause of death or gender, yet. Only the intimation that the death wasn't recent.

She got up from her desk and looked out the window at the summer day, not seeing the city before her. She was back at Lock No. 22, running through the park, eating oranges from her mother on the steps of the pavilion, hiding in trees and listening . . .

Unbidden, a face came up to her in a rush. A pretty girl with green eyes reflecting an old soul. Eyes she had not looked into for over forty years. Leslie Mackenzie had always treated the "local pest" with respect, perhaps because she, too, lived on the outside.

"You should have stayed on the outside, Les," Lynn whispered to the room. "Then everything mightn't have gone so wrong."

"Slipshod work. I always said it was slipshod work—that modern thing." The old woman sat straight in her wingback chair, hooking a rug with frightening speed. "No sense of a proper job done. Now they find a body someone left behind."

Ruth Hoffman Tremblay murmured a customary response to her mother while she put the groceries away. After a minute, she turned around.

"A body? What are you talking about, Mother?"

Alice Hoffman gave a piercing glance in her direction, rug hook not missing a beat.

"A body. Sarah said someone found a body in Aultsville yesterday. The police are there now and no one is sayin' much. Probably a grave they forgot to cover."

"It's probably some poor soul that drowned and washed up on the shoreline." Ruth closed the cupboards and put her purse in the closet. "It happens this time of year on the river."

"Sarah says the body is old. It's buried. Floaters don't bury themselves." Alice stopped long enough to change colours.

Ruth turned away from her mother. "Sarah shouldn't be getting you excited with stories about bodies," she said, putting on the teakettle. "It'll just give you bad dreams again."

"Don't be badmouthing Sarah," the old lady snapped. "If she didn't come to take care of me, you wouldn't get to trot about the way you do. You've always been that way. And look what it got you. Hangin' about with that Mackenzie girl . . . "

"Leslie Mackenzie never did anything to you, Mother," Ruth shot back, despite herself. She never won these battles. "And what did she ever do so wrong? She's been dead for forty years. Leave her in peace."

"She got sweet on that Leonard boy. And trouble followed him like a puppy." Alice put her rug aside. "I'm tired, Ruth. Where's my tea?"

The whistle sounded and Ruth jumped. She took the kettle off the burner and lifted the lid of the teapot. Tea bags. She opened the canister and put two bags in with shaking hands. "Won't be long, Mother," Ruth called over her shoulder, pouring the hot water.

There was no reply. Ruth turned to see her mother sitting back in her chair, facing the window. The old woman seemed to be talking to herself.

"Mother, are you all right?" Ruth crossed the living room and sat on the hassock in front of her. "What's wrong? Are you not feeling well?"

"It's so changed . . . all so changed," the elderly lady's chin trembled. "Why did they change it, Ruthie? It was such a pretty village before. Now you can't even see the river."

Ruth sighed. "This isn't Farran's Point, Mother. It's Ingleside."

"Ingleside? What kind of a name is that? What was wrong with Farran's Point?"

"They didn't change the name. We moved to Ingleside. Farran's Point is gone, remember? The Seaway took it."

"The Seaway? Yes. They rimracked everything, didn't they? Tore everything out. What's left of the Point? Of Aultsville?"

Ruth patted her mother's hand. "Nothing, Ma," she said gently. "Not a thing. Farran's Point, Aultsville, the Landing—all of them are under water."

"It's all gone, Ruthie?" Alice looked hopelessly at her daughter. Ruth could feel the two of them switching roles again.

"Yes, Ma," she said, turning to look out the window. "All gone."

Until now.

It didn't look good.

The corpse lay deep in the dried mud, only the head and one hand showing. What had once been the face seemed to look up—almost backwards—as if frozen in the final moment of death. Animals, water and time had done their work. The hand was missing several joints of the fingers and the head was only a skull. As Strauss stood near looking it over, something skittered out of one of the eye sockets and he tried to repress a shudder. He hated bugs.

"Poor bastard." Lewis came up from behind. "If this is as old as I think, I know I'd hate to be alone out here all these years."

Strauss made a non-committal noise. They were standing in the half-filled foundation where a house had once stood, under the tarp set up to protect the scene from the elements. The police photographer had finished just before Strauss's arrival that afternoon, and now the rest of the identification team would begin the painstaking process of a grid search. Mark the area off into squares and search it one square at a time.

Jerry looked around at the stumps, the decayed road and the mud baked hard in the sun. His father's face came to him suddenly and he closed his eyes for a moment.

"It's August," he said, turning to Lewis. "If the water's been this low all summer, why didn't anyone spot this before?"

"I don't know about Kingston, Jerry, but we had a wet July. Not great sightseeing weather." Lewis nodded toward the skeleton. "Now the earth is hard and dry. It's going to be a son of a bitch to get that out."

They fell silent for a minute. Lewis took a good look around him.

"Can you remember what it was like here? Or were you too young at the time?"

Strauss waited a moment before responding.

"I was thirteen when we moved, fourteen when they flooded. Hard to believe, Dave, but this mud flat was once a beautiful little village. Mostly stone and brick homes. Lots of flower gardens." He fell silent again.

"What was here? As you can imagine, it's taking the registry office a little longer to get back to us on this one."

Jerry looked around, remembering. "The Leonard place. They ran two good businesses just up the road, had money, pillars of the community—that sort of thing. Didn't end well, though. The mother died right before the project started, the father right after it ended. They lost one business in a fire. One son left to go sailing and never came back. The other stayed in Ingleside for some time after his father died. Now he lives over there, on Ault Island." Strauss pointed across the small bay to a large white house standing sentinel on the island's east point. "You probably know him. Gordon Leonard. Runs Upper Canada Village now. Funny thing, that's where the house ended up. The Leonards donated it to the Village."

Strauss made his way out of the foundation and over to where Detective Constable Wiley was talking on his cell phone. Seeing the older officer approach, Wiley cut it short.

"The shift supervisor just ordered some supper for everyone from the diner at the marina, sir," he reported. "I assumed you'd be staying, too."

Jerry shook his head. He wanted to get out of there, back up the old road to the highway and the present.

"I'm heading up to the office with Inspector Lewis to look things over. Have the press been sniffing around?'

"Not really, not yet, anyway." Wiley took off his hat and wiped his forehead. "The *Standard Freeholder* has been here twice. The *Morrisburg Leader* showed up, too. We didn't let them through, of course, and they left soon after."

"Good. I agree with Lewis. The less we say for now the better."

"I understand you grew up here, sir," Wiley broached with a tentative smile. "Saw the Power Project go through. You must have some interesting memories."

"That's a good word for it," Strauss said curtly, stepping over the yellow tape.

Wiley logged him out.

For three days, Aultsville had life again.

The crime scene was mapped out into the search grid; it would take two days to complete. For the second morning, the heat was almost unbearable under the rented canvas; but by afternoon the weather broke, making the tent a welcome refuge.

Strauss decided to delay his holidays until the site was reopened. At the end of the third day, he returned to watch the team remove the remains. The bones had been placed in a container with a special marker on it. One ident officer would accompany the container to the Centre for Forensic Science in Toronto and attend the post-mortem to make sure the remains arrived untouched. Following along would be samples of surrounding earth. Different bugs mean different rates of decomposition.

They lifted the gurney with its grisly cargo to take it to the OPP Crime Unit van. It suddenly hit Strauss how lonely it was out there. Lewis was right. Not the type of place he'd choose to be buried in.

Jerry stood at the water's edge on what was left of the decaying road. He looked out at the river—past the foreign tankers moving through the shipping lane with their massive engines throbbing like heartbeats to a little boy sitting on the front steps of a neat brick home, absorbed in his plastic soldiers while his parents had their Sunday afternoon fight. God, he could almost hear them. Then he shook himself. Superstitious locals swear you can hear the old voices from the villages at night when the wind blows a certain way. Better watch it or he'd end up one of them.

The detective inspector turned to see his officers struggling to get the gurney up the small embankment beside the bike path where the vehicle was waiting. Finally the remains were safely in with the ident officer and the doors closed behind. The driver started the van and carefully began the long drive up the path toward the sanctuary road, kicking up a small cloud of dust from the gravel. The security unit fell in behind him.

Strauss watched them go until they disappeared from view. Forty years after Aultsville died, the town's last resident left forever.

Part Two

Cardboard masks of all the people I've been
Thrown out with all the rusted
Tangled
Dented
Goddamn miseries

You might say I'm hard to hold
But if you knew me you'd know

I've got a good father
And his strength is what makes me cry

Jann Arden
Good Mother

Chapter 3

Prodigal

SIX MONTHS ago to this day, I learned my father's real name. It came with the news of his death—bringing down the house of cards I did not know was my world, plowing through my life like Dorothy's tornado to deposit me here. And this was neither Kansas nor Oz. I wouldn't be that lucky.

My car was one of the first in the parking lot at Upper Canada Village that late May morning. My appointment with Gordon Leonard, the general manager of the provincial museum, was for 9:00 a.m. The village would not open for another half hour. A restaurant supply truck was parked in the bus loading zone, and I watched a man in 1860s garb direct the shipment to the café beside the gift store.

I also wondered for the hundredth time what the hell I was doing here.

There was still time to stop this. I could cancel, pack my things and go home to Cambridge and the remnants of my life there. But it wouldn't work—hadn't worked for almost a year. Tragedy had hit me broadside and, like an accident victim, I would never be the same.

Now the only thing I could think of next was to come to this place my parents had called home. Someone had killed my father, and I had to find out the truth.

I was parked in the main lot across from the entrance, as most of my day would be spent in the village itself. I walked down the road to the small white administration building marked OPERATIONS and announced myself to the receptionist in the front lounge. I didn't wait more than a minute before being shown into the GM's office.

"Dr. Mackenzie." Gordon Leonard shook my hand warmly, with a Class-A networking smile on his face. "I've been looking forward to meeting you. I've read both your books. How was your trip down? A lot of construction?"

I took the chair he offered me while I sized him up. Early sixties, good physical shape, dark hair shot with grey, handsome even for an older man. Must have been a real heartbreaker in his youth. His office window was open, letting in a spring breeze.

"No, actually, the 401 wasn't too bad—except for Toronto, of course. Things will probably be quite different by the time I head back, I'm sure. And please," I added, "not so formal. My friends call me Fan."

"Okay, Fan." He gave me another brilliant smile, but I noticed he did not ask me to call him Gordon. Leonard was one of the good ones—one that could make you feel like a long-lost relative without a second thought. How ironic. "How long will you be staying? Is your study on land expropriation quite extensive?"

"Actually, the focus is on the historical significance of cultural disruption through land expropriation," I explained. "I just started my sabbatical and expect to be in the area most of the summer. There's a lot of material to sift through."

Leonard leaned back in his chair. "Well, anything we can do here at the village we're happy to do. I've talked to Sue in our PR department and she's at your disposal for any questions you have. There are also our archives right here in the Operations building that could be helpful. Have you been in contact with the Lost Villages Historical Society yet?"

"Yes," I nodded. "I'll be working closely with them as well."

"Then there is the SD&G Historical Society, the Cornwall Public Library—that's right on Second Street . . . " he trailed off in thought, his eyes on my face. "Have we met before Dr. Mackenzie? I feel as if I know you from somewhere."

"No," I could say honestly. "I've never been in Eastern Ontario before. But I will take some time to just have a look around. This area is certainly unique. Are you originally from here?"

"I've lived here my whole life. Got started with the Parks when the dam was put in and these areas became provincial parkland."

"So you were here when the villages were moved?"

"Yes." Leonard rose and came around the desk. I sensed he didn't want to go that route and our chat was at an end. "If you ask around, you'll find many people still living in the area that could tell you of those days. I apologize for not having more time today, but I leave within the hour for Toronto. I'll be gone pretty much the week, but Sue will take good care you. If I can be of help after that, you know where to find me."

I stood and we shook hands again.

"Thanks for fitting me in, then. I'm going to spend the day looking around your village. It's too nice to be indoors doing research."

"Upper Canada Village is unique. With your background in history, I'm sure you'll enjoy yourself. You'll find a season's pass waiting for you at the admissions office."

Polite creature that I am, I showed myself out. As I turned to cross the lounge, I saw Gordon still watching me from doorway of his office. I waved gamely. If this were a Christie mystery, he'd be my prime suspect for one very good reason. But I always prided myself on being a fair person, as my students usually realized over the years, and this was to be a non-partisan murder investigation. Anyone in his age group had the same chance to be considered a killer until I learned otherwise.

I had arrived in the area two days before, taking the Power Dam Drive turnoff from the 401 into Cornwall and following it right down to its namesake. Partly because the dam is the focal point of the Power Project, I thought I'd start with a peek at the big beastie before working my way down the river. And big it is.

Titanic in proportions, the R.H. Saunders–Robert M. Moses Power Dam remains, after all these years, a miracle of twentieth-century technology; a testament to the marriage of genius and hubris that rewrote North America in the post-war era. It sits hunched, Atlas-like, against the river—its thirty-two turbines generating 2,000 megawatts of electricity daily for Ontario, Quebec and Upper New York state as it has done since 1958. I could see only the Canadian half through the rain-streaked window of my car in the parking lot, but the scope of its creation still impressed me. When first built, it must have been almost beautiful.

Yet I was reminded of an aging Hollywood star, trying to hold on to a former glory. And I knew what it was to feel tired and out of place.

As odd as it sounds, for the first time in my life I was coming home.

Home, that is, to a place I had never seen and which was now mostly under water. All I had to work with were a few pieces of paper, some names, and a gut feeling that I had to find out the truth no matter what it cost me. I would question that assumption many times in the near future.

I never knew my father. In our house, his identity was never discussed and no information offered. Once, as a teenager with the house to herself, I dared to go through my mother's private drawer. I found a torn half of what I realized to be a picture of him: a blond, decent-looking young man with a shy grin standing in front of a square brick house from nowhere that boasted a distinctive oval window over the front porch. Another tiny photo lay hidden in the heart locket of my mother's gold bracelet, a delicate band she never wore. Both photos showed a man who wouldn't have been more than a few years older than I had been then. My subtle snooping efforts must have been noticed because at my next opportunity, I found both the picture and the bracelet gone. I would not see either again for almost thirty years, until I opened Mother's safety deposit box upon her death.

Somehow through the years, I learned to be satisfied with half a background, half a history such as it was. Maybe that's where I got my fascination with the past—from the glaring gap in my own. Only Freud would know. And then last year, everything changed. I was not only free to go in search of him, but impelled to do so.

I found my free season's pass waiting for me as Gordon Leonard had promised. The open area in front of the admissions office was now jammed with hundreds of school kids, everybody talking at once. I squeezed through the entrance and took a day's schedule of events from a large, cheerful woman in period dress. I walked past the watermill that was thumping rhythmically, over the little stream that flowed into the St. Lawrence. The smell of stream and fish mixed with the scent of horse, and I skirted around a wagon with a team of two waiting to give tours of the village. Another horse-drawn wagon filled with hay came by on the dirt road. Staff already roamed the streets, the women in cotton dresses in a variety of colours and patterns while the men seemed more uniform in their breeches with white cotton shirts and suspenders.

The whole scene was restful to the modern mind, borderline bucolic. I should have taken more time to enjoy it. In three weeks, I would never find that particular stretch of the village pleasant again.

It was tempting to stop and visit all the houses and shops. Obviously, a lot of time and care had gone into Upper Canada Village to get the atmosphere right. It would be nice to come only as a spectator someday. But I had my agenda, and my next target was the Lost Villages display at Crysler Hall.

Using the map the cheerful lady had given me with the schedule, I continued down Queen Street on the plank boardwalk to Willard's Hotel. The sign said no exhibits, only a working restaurant for which reservations were recommended. Another must-see, maybe for today's lunch.

Crysler Hall turned out to be the largest and most beautiful house on the property. Once the home of a prosperous landowner (the map said), the elegant Georgian building now served as a museum. I pushed open the big door and stood blinking in the sudden relief from the bright sun. Once my eyes adjusted to the dark and cool interior, I followed the signs to the exhibit that led me upstairs.

I admit I hesitated at the top of the stairs. The room was taken up with glass cases of things once used by those I called the Survivors, the people who had made a life on the river here only to lose it. I had tracked down hundreds of such exhibits in my work over the years, but this time it was personal. I didn't like the feeling.

On the wall were display boards of pictures, each headed by the name of one of the villages now gone: Moulinette, Mille Roches, Wales, Dickinson's Landing, Farran's Point, Aultsville. I slowly crossed over to the one titled "Farran's Point" and began to look at the photographs. The old canal. The dance pavilion. All these things

I had read recently in the books were now real and in front of me. Then I looked at the smiling faces of a girls' softball team . . . and found her there. Not smiling as much as the others; a little apart from them, too. As she had been with everyone all the years I had known her. But young, so young, and so beautiful. With long hair in braids almost to her waist. She seemed to hold herself differently from the others, more reserved as if on guard. I unconsciously touched her face with my finger.

"Can I help you find something or answer any questions?"

The voice came from behind me. I turned to face a tall, commanding woman with grey hair—in period dress, of course.

"Not just now, but definitely in future." I held out my hand. "I'm Dr. MacKenzie from the University of Waterloo. I'll be hanging about for a few weeks. I'm down here to do research for a new study."

The woman seemed impressed with my credentials, and shook my hand. Good grip. "How interesting. Are you a professor of history, Dr. Mackenzie?"

"Yes. I'm interested primarily in the flooding that was done here and the events surrounding it. Were you living here at the time, Mrs. . . .?"

"Murphy. Meredith Murphy. Yes, I was. I grew up in Aultsville. I've been in Ingleside ever since."

"I bet you have a lot of stories I'd love to hear. I know you're working right now, but perhaps we could talk sometime in the near future."

"Oh, I don't know that I could tell you much that you couldn't read about," she said, waving it off. "Aultsville was a pretty quiet place."

I could hear a gaggle of voices approaching outside. Any minute, we would be swamped with budding historians and tourists. I decided to go for a more direct hit.

"Didn't they find a body down there last year? One that had been there since the flooding?"

Murphy iced over immediately. "I'm afraid I don't really know much about that, Dr. Mackenzie. Do you have any family from these parts," she added, cocking her head to one side. "There was a Mackenzie family in Farran's Point in those days, but they're all dead now. Unless you're a distant relative?"

The big door below banged open. Youth was upon us. In a few seconds they would breach the stairs and flood the upper room. She turned to go.

"Are you in any of these pictures, Mrs. Murphy?" The question pushed a button somewhere, and she turned back.

"That's *Miss* Murphy," she corrected primly and then unexpectedly smiled. "Actually I am. Right there, third from the left on the girls' softball team of '54. Those were fun days. The rivalry was quite intense between the villages, you know."

I refrained from skimming over any other photographs and zeroed in on the Aultsville team. Murphy was easy to pick out, towering over the others and looking rather masculine with a solid build and boyish crop. Probably not a big hit on the dating circuit back then. Or now. But something told me she had had a good RBI.

Voices were coming up the stairs so I impulsively threw my smoke bomb to try its effect.

"If you played against the other villages, perhaps you knew my mother." I crossed over to the Farran's Point spread. "She was on this team. There she is right there at the end." I pointed as the woman came up close. "Her name was Leslie. Leslie Mackenzie."

If I was hoping for a reaction, I wasn't disappointed. Murphy's eyes and mouth opened wide and her face went white. I wasn't sure if I could catch her if she fainted, so I steered her to a chair at one of the tables. And that's how the kids found us when they arrived upstairs, her blinking and bobbing with me awkwardly and guiltily patting her hand.

When I left the power dam the afternoon of my arrival, I followed the river road. County Road No. 2, the signs said. I would soon learn that no one local used the new name. It had been the No. 2 Highway too long for that. The older people still called it the "new No. 2," as it had been built along the old CNR tracks to replace the original now under water.

The river, or rather Lake St. Lawrence—the name given to the headpond created by the dam in 1958—seemed to stretch forever along the road. The flooding had taken 22,000 acres of farmland at the time. Over 6,000 people, including my mother, had to be relocated from eight villages along the original shoreline: the six "lost" villages, the village of Iroquois, which was moved north of its original position, and the old main streets of Morrisburg along the waterfront. Six deaths, one transplant, and one amputation. Quite a score, even by today's standards. I hadn't yet been in touch with a colleague at St. Lawrence University in Canton, New York, so I was still unsure of the American body count.

The pictures of the old roads and farms with canals passing them by seemed unreal in the stark reality of the new landscape I was seeing that day. Not that I had a good chance to judge the riverfront as I drove. From outside Cornwall almost to Long Sault, the river is cut off from view by Ontario Hydro's bushland. There seems to be little access to the river until you reach the Long Sault Parkway. It must have been quite a wrench to go from living in a community based on the river to one that merely watched it from a distance. I wondered what my father had felt about the whole thing.

"Miss Murphy . . . Miss Murphy." My concern was genuine. In my mind, I had envisioned a dozen different openings to my search, but none quite this physical. The students and their teacher milled around the room uncertainly, while I helped the woman to her feet. She brushed her dress and touched her hair self-consciously, clearing her throat.

"I must get to work now, Dr. Mackenzie. We're getting busy."

I stopped her one more time. "I'm sorry to have upset you, Miss Murphy. I didn't realize it would shock you to hear that. Why would it?"

"Because Leslie Mackenzie from Farran's Point *died* over forty years ago," she answered in a low voice. "She never married."

"Leslie Mackenzie died last year. She was my mother."

We seemed to reach a standoff. I could sense that for some reason, my news was making this woman angry—though for the life of me I couldn't say why. Her mouth worked for a minute. I figured she was trying to come up with a non-crass way of asking me who my father was and couldn't do it. She gave up.

"Well . . . that's some news to pass on. I don't understand the mistake. That's very strange. Wait till Lynnie hears," she added as though to herself.

"Who told you my mother had died?"

Murphy seemed lost in thought for a moment, then shook her head and made her way to the top of the stairs.

"I'm not the person to talk to about your mother. That'd be Ruth. But wait a day if you can so I can call her and let her know first. She'll be right upset too, I know."

"Ruth? Ruth who?"

"Ruth Tremblay. She was a Hoffman in those days. You'll find her on Maple Street in Ingleside. She came back home to care for her mother. Ruth was your mother's best friend," Murphy added, and then she was gone.

I remember standing in the exhibit room for some moments, digesting this unexpected twist. People here had thought my mother dead all this time. No wonder no one had come looking for us. I would have to ask this Ruth Tremblay for more details, try to figure out where this might fit in.

And Meredith Murphy had said she would call Ruth to warn her about me, to soften the blow. I would have to change my plans for the day and drive to Ingleside now to find Ruth first. Shock value was one ace up my sleeve, probably the only one. People spill a lot more when they're rattled.

I took a quick look at the Aultsville spread before leaving. There was one photograph of Leonard's General Store with a handful of people standing in front. I spotted Gordon to one side with my father a little behind him. On my way out, I picked up the top cassette of a pile of videos near a TV with a sign advising staff help for viewing. The label said *Aultsville*. I would have to come back here soon.

On my way out, I saw Meredith Murphy talking to another group of students as they filed into the small theatre on the main floor. She looked up as I passed but turned back without nodding, obviously still unhappy with me. I had a quick premonition about having that effect on many people here during my visit.

Once outside, I decided to make one circuit of the main roads before leaving. Business was picking up in the village, and I had to dodge several families with preschoolers. In fact, I was so busy people-watching as I continued east along the Queen Street boardwalk that I almost missed it.

The Physician's Home, the guide said. A small red-brick building with a wrap-around porch, and a distinctive oval window upstairs.

I was standing in front of my father's house.

Ingleside and Long Sault (New Towns No. 1 and No. 2 respectively) were born as fraternal twins in 1955 to house those dislocated by the Power Project. Built to the direct north of Highway No. 2, umbilical streets attach them to the main road but leave them not of it. Each had been given a strip mall in lieu of a naturally formed main street or town centre, yet the malls themselves now seem detached from the flow of village life. On my first drive past two mornings before, I saw a curious mix of older (transported) homes, 1950s bungalows and newer monster houses mutating on the fringes. Despite the sight of tall trees and mature gardens lining the streets, the town still had an air of impermanence about it. Like they were all still waiting for something.

But that wouldn't be true, I remembered. In another generation, that which was now memory would become myth. History would only be housed under glass and on the walls of museums like Crysler Hall for their children's children to make school reports about, looking at pieces of where they came from—as I was doing now.

The porch on the Physician's Home looked a little different from its counterpart in the old photograph I pulled out of my purse, but it was undeniably the same house. Upper Canada Village had been formed in part from heritage homes moved out of the villages. I remembered a shot I'd seen recently of the white Anglican church being taken here from Moulinette on the back of a massive house-moving truck. This house must have been moved here, too—lifted off the same foundation that entombed my father for forty years.

I decided to take the chance that Meredith wouldn't call her friend Ruth at least until her lunch break, and it was only ten a.m. I had to see the inside of the building.

As at Crysler Hall, the darkness struck me momentarily blind when I entered. The house was quiet, except for a small group in the dining room listening to the 'physician' describe medical practices in the 1860s. I eavesdropped for a minute and decided that, restructuring commission notwithstanding, I'd rather take my chances in the twenty-first century. Then I took a good look at the house itself.

It didn't seem large by today's standards. I was in a front hall facing the stairs to the upper floor. To my left was a sitting/living room that opened into the dining room running along the back of the house. The front hallway led around the stairs to the right toward the dining room, passing a small study. Since the village physician was busy at the moment, I headed up the stairs. The second floor was no more spacious, with one central hall connecting the three bedrooms with a closet door at each end. There was no bathroom. The master bedroom with the oval window faced the front of the house, of course. The two smaller bedrooms shared the rear. I wondered which one my father had grown up in.

Naturally, the house was furnished in keeping with the 1860s period. But as I wandered back down the stairs, I thought of how many mornings that boy had raced down those same stairs for breakfast. I paused on the last step, my hand on the newel. How does one start out a regular kid and end up dead in a deserted village? It would be a challenging case of connect-the-dots, but I didn't know which end to begin with.

"You look as though you have a question."

A man in a frock coat stood smiling at me. The physician. I returned the smile.

"Just one. Did this house come from Aultsville?"

He had to think a minute. "Yes, I believe it did. This is the only one from that village, if I remember correctly. It's been changed a little, too."

"In what way?"

"The front porch was extended, I think. And they added on the back, too."

"You wouldn't know what family owned this before, would you?"

He shook his head. "Sorry. But Meredith Murphy is working today. Probably in Crysler Hall. She'd know. Meredith helped put together the Lost Villages exhibit at the Hall."

I thanked him and went back out into the sunshine and the present day.

There was only one Hoffman listed in Ingleside, and that was on Maple Street as Meredith had said. After several false starts on the wrong side of the town's central square, I stopped in front of a building marked ROTHWELL–OSNABRUCK SCHOOL. The school was an entire block long and obviously built in stages, with the west end sporting telltale 1950s turquoise panels. I asked a group of teenagers standing near the door marked LANCER COMMUNITY CENTRE for directions. Unlike many city kids, they didn't send the stranger on a wild goose chase. Maple Street turned out to be just two in from the highway. I ended up parked outside an older home surrounded by the many 1950s bungalows that lined the street, deciding how to approach my mother's former best friend.

A woman in her thirties dressed in a pale blue shift that spoke of health services answered my knock. Meredith said Ruth was home to take care of her mother. This was obviously support staff.

"I'm looking for Ruth Hoffman . . . Tremblay." I passed the woman my card. "Is she home today?"

"Not at the moment," she said, reading the card. "But I expect her home shortly for lunch."

"Well, who is it, Sarah?" a voice asked peevishly from the living room.

Sarah motioned me in. "It's a visitor for Ruth, Alice," her voice rising as younger people tend to do with the elderly. They think it makes them hear better, like talking louder to someone that doesn't speak your language. "A Dr. F. L. Mackenzie from the University of Waterloo."

"A doctor? Ruth isn't sick."

I rounded the corner in the hall and followed Sarah into the small front room. An old lady with silver-blue hair was sitting in a chair near the window, hooking a rug with surgical skill. She barely slowed down to look me over.

"I'm not a medical doctor," I explained, taking the chair Sarah offered me. "I'm a professor of history."

"History?" she snorted, her hook flashing in and out. "What do you want with Ruth? She's gettin' long in the tooth, but I'm her mother. Ask me how old I am."

"How old are you, Mrs. Hoffman?" I obliged.

"Never ask a lady her age," she snapped. "Sarah, for God's sake, offer the woman a tea. You're a long way from Waterloo, Doctor Mackenzie."

I waved off the tea with Sarah. "I'm here to get some background on the land expropriation done during the fifties when the power dam was going in." I figured I'd leave the news of my mother's death being greatly exaggerated for Ruth's ears only. After what happened with Meredith that morning, I wasn't willing to risk the old lady's having a coronary on me. "Were you here through all that?"

"Of course." Alice changed her hooking colour with nimble hands that belied their age. "We lived in Farran's Point. Moved this house from there. What a ruckus that was for everyone. And the Hartshorne people tellin' us that we didn't have to pack anything. Nothing would move. Well, I packed my china just the same. Took all the lamps off the tables, too. Harland thought he'd test them and put two mayonnaise jars on top of each other in the kitchen. Fool things were still sittin' like that when we got back in the next week."

"Did you attend the flooding?"

"Of course. My son wanted to see the big finish we'd been promised. It never came. No big wave, just dust in the air and four days of waitin'. It would have been easier to have done with faster." The old woman stopped and looked at me. "Mackenzie. We had a family by that name at the Point. But you don't look like them," she added, "and that was a second marriage anyway."

I longed to ask her so many things, but didn't. There would be a time, later perhaps. For now I needed to keep the questions general and the focus away from my lineage.

"I'll be here for several weeks, Mrs. Hoffman. Perhaps I could come back sometime for tea and we could talk about those years, if you'd like."

She didn't answer for a moment. I wondered if she'd heard me.

"What is your maiden name, dear?" came the unexpected question.

"Mackenzie—I've never married." And never wanted to—except once.

Alice put her rug down and gave me that disturbingly penetrating gaze that only the elderly can manifest. "Who is your father?"

I stared back, a pink flush exploring my face. She had me—but God can be kind even to those who don't believe.

Ruth Hoffman walked into the room.

She was one of those rare women who can look and dress with sophistication, yet keep the fresh presence of a young girl. The suit was Armani, the hair expensive, and the face made up so well it looked natural. There were a few streaks of grey allowed on her head, but she was well-packaged and looked years younger than the almost-sixty she must be. Still, Ruth swept into the room with the excitement of a teenager just asked on her first date. Despite the trappings, I suddenly liked her.

"Mother, you'll never guess who I ran into . . . " She stopped when she saw me and uncertainly held out her hand. "Hello, I'm Ruth Tremblay. I didn't realize Mother had a guest."

"She's not here to see me, she's waitin' for you," said Alice as I stood up to shake Ruth's hand. "And about time you got home, too. It's almost lunch."

"That's what I wanted to tell you, Mother. I brought home a guest for lunch . . . Lynn Holmes. You remember Lynn from the Point, don't you?"

A younger woman had followed Ruth into the living room and I recognized her immediately. Lynn Holmes—author, critic, columnist for Southham News. Investigative journalist for many years before accepting a major post with *The Ottawa Citizen*. What was someone from those circles doing in this small town?

"Lynnie Holmes?" Alice replied. "Of course I remember her. Always hidin' in trees and bushes or peepin' through fences spyin' on people. Someone told me they pay you to do that now." She addressed this last remark to Lynn, who had come up to shake hands. Ruth looked mortified, but Lynn had the grace to laugh.

"That's right, Mrs. Hoffman. They do. And thank God for it because it's the only talent I have."

"I wouldn't say that, Ms. Holmes," I ventured. "I've read your work. You're an excellent writer."

"Well, thank you, Mrs . . . "

"Dr. Mackenzie." We shook hands. "Doctor of history, not medicine. But please call me Fan."

"I'm sorry," said Ruth, "I'm not doing well with introductions today. Please sit down, Doctor. Mother said you're here to see me."

I stayed standing. "Perhaps I should come back another time. It *is* almost lunch, as your mother said, and you have company."

"What exactly is this about? You do have my curiosity."

I could see there was no way out of it without seeming rude, so I sat down and they followed suit. "I'm in the area to do research on the land expropriation that went on here in the 1950s. It came to my attention just a little while ago that we have a common acquaintance."

"Who is that?" Ruth smiled politely.

I suddenly wished I'd let Meredith call this woman to break it to her in private. I let out a deep breath.

"Leslie Mackenzie."

It was obviously the last name Ruth had expected to hear. Her face went pale and she unconsciously glanced at Lynn, who looked equally shocked. Alice Hoffman surprisingly said nothing, sitting absolutely still.

"But that's impossible," Ruth countered. "The Leslie Mackenzie I knew died over forty years ago. Probably before you were born. Are you sure you have the right one?"

"Yes," I said simply. "My full name is Farran Leslie Mackenzie. Leslie was my mother."

Ruth sat back heavily in her chair. Lynn leaned forward in hers.

"You say 'was,' Fan," she pointed out. "Is Leslie still alive?"

"No," I answered quietly. "She died last year. I had no idea when I came here that everyone thought she was long dead. As you can imagine, I have a lot of questions."

Lynn nodded. Ruth was still digesting my news. I would've given my right hand to be a fly on the wall of her brain right then.

Then Alice Hoffman broke her silence.

"I believe you never did answer *my* question, Dr. Mackenzie. Who is your father?"

I looked at the old lady, feeling that deer-in-headlights sensation again. But there it was. I'd changed my carefully thought out plans with the first blip on the screen and created this mess myself. So I gathered my thoughts and stumbled through it.

"That man . . . the one they found . . . in Aultsville last year." I could feel the anger coming back. "Murdered. Buried in the old basement." I raised my head and looked straight at them. "Hal Leonard. Hal Leonard was my father."

That moment stays clearly in my mind: Lynn Holmes half rising from her chair, her face dark and unreadable. Ruth Tremblay staring down at her hands as though they held something the rest of us could not see. And Alice Hoffman sitting sphinx-like—old, still as death, eyes trained on me with a look I could not fathom. They say that silence is golden. But the vacuum that followed my announcement that morning felt more like the proverbial lead balloon.

"Well, Doctor Mackenzie," said Alice finally, "I guess you're stayin' for lunch."

Chapter **4**

Endings

YOU CAN spend your whole life with someone and not know her.

I'm referring, of course, to my mother—Leslie Evian Mackenzie. She was my entire family for forty years and the one person I loved completely in this world, yet so much of who she was remains a mystery to me. Strangely enough, our relationship began to grow in a new direction after her death.

We lived in Cambridge, Ontario. That would be Preston, Galt and Hespeler to the generation before me. Almost three decades ago, the three towns amalgamated, pooling their resources and ethnicity. Like neighbouring Kitchener-Waterloo, Cambridge was settled by waves of Europeans particularly in the early years of the twentieth century. It still hosts a considerable German population, but its architecture stands as testimony to the other strong culture from the British Isles. Perhaps that's why Mother chose to settle there when she left the villages. In one of her rare open moments, she told me her father had been Scottish.

I have said Leslie was enigmatic, reserved and intensely private about her background. But she was also a warm and loving mother to me. I lived as the centre of her life and wanted for nothing. We had a little brick house in Preston on what was then called Water Street because it followed the small Speed River that ran through the town. During my childhood years, Water Street was the perfect neighbourhood for a kid. The street ended in a rough road leading into a farm area, so there was little traffic. And the river beckoned just down the path across the road. Turn-of-the-century homes like ours lined the street; they had begun as workers' houses and would end up the darlings of upscale Boomers looking for retro-chic. Our neighbourhood was a cultural melting pot, long before the phrase became politically charged; and we all got along.

The more I began to study the villages, the more I saw that Mother had chosen to live somewhere not so different from home.

I had a happy childhood, in many ways because Mother had somehow remained a child herself. She was the best of playmates, our home always open to the neighbourhood kids. It was not until I was a teenager and becoming wise to the ways of procreation that it hit me how young she'd been when I was born. That was when I began asking in earnest about the father I'd never known.

Mother's answers were vague and reluctant. I could see the memories gave her great pain: a young man she had loved and married, only to lose him shortly after in a car accident. A first name—Hal. No pictures, except for the ones I found in secret. I tried one night to make her tell me everything. We had a terrible fight, and I stormed off to bed. Hours later, I woke up to hear her still sitting in the kitchen, crying softly. We never spoke of Hal Mackenzie again.

Until one year ago when I came home from my apartment in Waterloo to spend Sunday with Mother, a ritual through the years we broke only when I was overseas on a study tour. That Sunday, I found the *Cambridge Daily Reporter* still on the doorstep when I arrived.

"Mom?" I called from the front hall. "You sleeping in?"

I heard her reply and followed it to the kitchen. This was my favourite room in the world, its bright and sunny air reflected in white fixtures and a yellow/white floral wallpaper laced with blue forget-me-nots. Leslie sat at the table with an empty mug and a teapot in a cosy. Even with a bare face, brushed hair and a housecoat, my mother looked beautiful. Fair skin still smooth, dark almost black short hair with just the first suggestion of grey. But that morning she seemed tired—something I had noticed more frequently of late.

"Still not dressed?" I teased. "Late night with a tall, dark stranger?"

"No, of course not." Mother rose to give me a lavender-scented kiss. "I just needed to sleep in a bit this morning. Feeling my age, I guess."

"Well, you don't look it." I gave her a hug and opened the fridge door. "Have you had breakfast yet?" When she shook her head, I pulled out some bacon, eggs and bread. "I'll make us brunch, then. Where's the milk?"

"Oh, that's right. I ran out yesterday."

"I'll run down to the corner store. Anything else you need?"

"Not that I can think of." Mother walked over to the counter. "I'll start the bacon while you're gone."

"Okay." I headed out to the front door, then scooped up the newspaper from the hall table and returned to the kitchen. The bacon was already frying and Mother was loading up the toaster.

"Here's the Sunday paper, Mom." I threw it onto the table. "Don't put my toast down yet. I'll do it when I get back. Some like it hot, you know," I added pointedly.

"You should eat it cold like a good Scot," she shot back.

"I'm only half Scot, remember."

Mother turned and gave me a faraway look I had seen on her face only a few times in my life—usually when I caught her alone and deep in thought. "Yes," she said softly. "I remember. I've never forgotten, you know."

A sudden chill went up my back and impulsively I walked over to give her another hug. "I'll be back in ten," I promised, and left.

I do no exercise, so the ten minutes to the corner store two blocks away was really closer to twenty. I was coming abreast of the neighbour's house, milkbag in hand, when I saw it. Smoke seeping out of the back door of our house. For a minute, it didn't register and I stood there, stupidly watching. Then I dropped the bag, spilling milk all over the sidewalk, and ran to the back door.

I tried to open it but it was locked. I rattled the knob, which I noticed felt warm.

"Mom!" I yelled, and pounded on the door. "Mom!" There was no reply. Squinting into the small window, I could see flames around the kitchen window and up on the ceiling. No sign of my mother. I raced to the front door and burst into the house, calling her name. Still no reply. The swing door to the kitchen was closed and smoke was coming out around the cracks. A black spot was growing on the middle of the top panel. Without thinking, I grabbed a linen napkin off the dining room buffet and held it to my nose and mouth.

The swing door was hot to the touch but I pushed on it anyway. The heat hit me like a fist and drove me back into the dining room. I paused for just a second, then pushed through again. The entire kitchen was in flames. Through the smoke, I could make out the fry pan and toaster burning on the floor, but not much else.

"Mom!" My scream was cut short as the smoke grabbed my throat and I started to cough. My eyes blurred with tears. I wiped them away with the napkin and looked once more around on the floor. No mother. A couple of ceiling tiles hit the table in flames and I fell back through the swing door.

"Leslie? Leslie!" I heard a voice call from the front door and stumbled toward it, coughing and gagging. Our elderly neighbour, Mrs. Heipel, was cautiously moving into the hallway. "Are you there?"

The smoke was beginning to build in the living room. "Call the fire department, Mrs. Heipel," I called hoarsely. "Don't come back. The whole kitchen is gone."

"Where's your mother?"

"I don't know. I have to find her."

The woman retreated and I scanned the living room. To the left of the kitchen were the bedrooms and bathroom. I checked the bathroom and my old room on the way to my mother's. Her door was closed. I heard a crash from the kitchen and panic set it. I grabbed the doorknob and turned it. It was unlocked, but wouldn't open. Something was blocking it.

"Mom!" I screamed again. "Are you in there?"

I faintly heard a moan from inside the bedroom. I pushed again, but still the door did not move. I banged on it desperately.

"Mom! Can you open the door? We have to get out of here!"

I heard a second crash behind me and felt a sudden blast of heat. Turning, I saw that the fire had breached the swing door and was toasting the upper wall and ceiling of the dining room.

"Shit!" I threw my weight on the bedroom door once, twice. I felt it give and stepped back to ram it with everything I had. When I hit the door, the centre panel caved in along with my left knee. Pain seared up my thigh, but I didn't care. The door was now open several inches.

"Mom! Are you okay?"

Another soft moan reached my ears, followed by a sudden roar as the living room drapes went up. We were cut off from the front door. I took my good leg and, placing my foot on the doorframe, pushed the door open enough to get through. My mother lay unconscious on the floor next to the bed, clutching the newspaper. I climbed over the vanity that had fallen in front of the door, blocking my entry. The only way out was the window, but it was old and narrow with the long screen held on by outside clips and inside hooks. I didn't have time to fool around. Pushing the sash up to its limit, I grabbed the letter opener Mother kept on her small secretary desk and hacked a large hole in the old screen. Then I leaned over my mother's still form.

"Mom, I'm getting you out of here. Hang on." I picked her up, newspaper and all, and carried her to the window. Far away, I could hear sirens approaching. I looked back once, only to see black smoke pouring through the opening I'd made to get in the doorway.

Somehow, I got us both out the window. Hands grabbed my mother, then me, taking us to safety across the street. I vaguely remember people gathering and Mrs. Heipel sitting with us until the ambulance arrived. I watched my one real home burn to the ground, holding my mother in my arms, rocking.

We would piece together later that Mother had suffered a heart attack right after I left. She must have knocked the hot toaster into the cooking bacon, starting a grease fire before making her way to the bedroom. Grabbing the vanity for support, she pulled it over in front of the door before falling unconscious beside the bed. They said it was a miracle that she made it out of the kitchen, and the reason she was still alive when I found her.

It did not feel miraculous to be sitting there in the ICU of the Cambridge Memorial Hospital, with only the soft squeak of the nurses' shoes breaking the sound of the machines that were marking the final moments of my mother's life. My beautiful and vibrant mother looked suddenly old and tiny in the hospital bed, and I knew I was losing her. I held tight to her hands—the soft hands that had cared for me a thousand times—and felt like stone. So many times Leslie Mackenzie had picked me up and dusted me off when I needed it; yet now all I could do for her was sit and wait and listen to the goddamn machines with my knee wrapped in cold packs.

Mother drifted in and out of consciousness. Only once, in the ambulance, did she awaken enough to talk to me—but they were dismembered thoughts that made no sense. I heard her call my father's name several times and she cried a little. When she got very upset, I asked the attendant to pull the oxygen cup off her mouth and I stroked her forehead.

"It's okay, Mom. It's Fan. I'm here. Everything is okay."

Her eyes seemed to clear for a moment and she touched my face.

"Fan." It was almost a whisper. "Father's . . . eyes." Her eyes closed and I thought she was asleep again, but she suddenly looked at me. "More . . . "

"More what, Mom?" The effort it cost her to speak made me feel more helpless.

"Moor . . . remember?"

"Moor?" I thought frantically. "You mean Blackamoor, our cat?"

She nodded slowly. "Didn't come back. Cats."

"The cats didn't come back?" I hadn't thought of Blackamoor, my childhood pet, in years. He had been a sleek, black maverick that had adopted us when I was six. For three years, he graced our home and led the neighbourhood pack of felines. Then one night he didn't come home. The cat pack disappeared from our yard, too. Three frantic days later he returned with mud dried on his usually impeccable coat. But something was wrong. Moor wouldn't go out and began to cry at all hours. Finally, we took him to the vet, where he died of internal injuries suffered somehow during his absence.

It wasn't until we buried him in the backyard that Mother realized Moor's cronies had never returned, even after he did. "They knew, Fan," she said then. "They knew he was already dead." And now she was saying it again, after thirty years. It's strange what the dying mind will grab on to.

"Yes. They . . . knew. *They knew.*" She clutched my hand and closed her eyes. This time she was asleep. After we arrived at the hospital and they stabilized her, I sat with my head on her shoulder, as I had so often before.

And that is how we were an hour later when Leslie Mackenzie died. I was told after that she suffered a major stroke, probably brought on by the heart attack. The machine went flat-line, and she slipped quietly through my clutched fingers that tried to keep her with me. They came in response to the Code Blue, firmly took my fingers out of my mother's and walked me out to the hall. I stood there like a fly in amber until a doctor came to tell me that they had done all they could.

I spent a few minutes alone with Mother in that room, the machines more terrible in their silence. I don't remember if I cried. They eventually led me away to sign papers and claim her personal effects: watch, plain gold wedding band, nightie, housecoat and slippers.

"Oh . . . and this," the young nurse said hesitantly, offering me what looked to be a crumpled page from the *Cambridge Daily Reporter*. "Your mother had it tight in her hands when they brought her in. Took some work to make her let it go, I heard. I thought it might be important."

Nodding numbly, I thanked her and scanned the paper quickly. Nothing outstanding. Taking my mother's things, I went back to my apartment.

The next day I braced myself and returned to what was left of my home. It wasn't much. The charred, brick walls still stood for the most part, surrounded by yellow tape. Official-looking people were picking their way through the black mess, and one of them came over when he saw me.

"You Miss Mackenzie?" When I nodded, he continued. "I'm Bill Marley. Fire chief. We'll be here for the rest of the day, until we have our report. I'm afraid there's really nothing left for you to look over, but you can come back later this afternoon and take a look. These older homes, the wood inside is so dry. They go up very quickly." He paused and shoved his hands into his pockets. "They called me this morning about your mother. I'm really sorry."

"Thank you," I said softly, and rubbed my eyes. "Can I walk around the yard?"

"Sure," he replied sympathetically, looking at my crutches and bandaged knee. "But don't touch anything from the house just yet. It may help us find out what happened."

He moved off back toward the taped area and I walked down the small sidewalk that had led to the back door. Mother's peony hedge looked trampled on, but her vegetable garden was untouched and in full bloom. The one elm in the corner still held my old swing and I sat in it. The black ruin in front of me didn't seem real. I could see the house as it had been just by closing my eyes. Then followed a rush of different memories all at once—picnics in the backyard, doll swimming parties with the big old washtub, sleepovers in my tent, high school graduation pictures by the peonies in bloom.

I opened my eyes to make it stop. With some difficulty, I got off the swing and back on my crutches. My smashed knee was really howling by then, but I didn't want to use the painkillers they'd given me. My knee was the only feeling I had left.

As I crossed the backyard to the sidewalk, I saw a paper fluttering in the grass. It was a piece of the kitchen wallpaper, its gay pattern framed by black edges. I silently put it in my pocket. I didn't think they would mind.

Two days later when I opened my mother's safety deposit box for her will, I found my birth certificate and a faded marriage certificate. Both had the names Leslie Mackenzie and Harold Leonard. Hal. Hal *Leonard*? Mother had gone back to her maiden name for our family name, unusual for a woman of her generation. But there was something else. I'd seen that name before, but couldn't quite remember where.

For three months, life was a blur of those details that accompany the end of a human life. Mother's funeral, attended by her neighbours and work associates from the union office. She had had no close friends. Selling the house—or rather the lot that was left after the building was demolished. And all the paperwork the lawyer led me through to close her estate. I was spared the emotional task of packing my mother's life into boxes as almost everything was lost in the fire.

I had a heavy student load at the university, and was also involved with a consultation contract. I kept busy and safely distanced from the reality of my loss. Then one day I cleaned out my car and found my mother's sweater in the back seat. I had borrowed it the week before the fire and was returning it that Sunday. I buried my face in it, letting the comforting scent of my mother carry me into emotionally dangerous territory.

That's when I remembered where I'd seen my father's real name before. In an article on the page of the newspaper the nurse gave me with Mother's things. I tore through my apartment, stereotypically messy for a history professor. It was gone, probably shot out during one of my cleaning binges that happen when my stuff reaches critical mass. I immediately drove over to the offices of *The Cambridge Daily Reporter* and made my way to the morgue. It was on the microfilm, and I read it three times before its import sank in:

CP—Ingleside, Ontario.

OPP in Stormont county confirmed Friday that the human remains found last week in an abandoned foundation are those of one Harold 'Hal' Leonard, 18, who went missing over 40 years ago.

The foundation lies in Aultsville, one of the villages removed to make Lake St. Lawrence during the massive Seaway and Power Project on the St. Lawrence River in the late 1950s.

Detective Inspector Strauss of the OPP says the remains date from that time. The boy's family had presumed he had joined a shipping company on the Great Lakes. Leonard's surviving brother, Gordon, 63, refused to comment.

At the inquest today, a severe blow to the back of the head was cited as cause of death.

The inquest resumes tomorrow.

I sat in the morgue on the swivel stool, shaking.

At the mention of lunch, I heard a sudden flurry of activity in the Hoffman kitchen. Obviously, Sarah had paused in her labours to hear my saga. If I knew small towns, that meant that my background would be all over Ingleside and possibly Long Sault by tomorrow.

"I . . . I don't believe it," Ruth said slowly. "How? Did they meet up again and marry? We thought Hal was gone sailing."

"Until his body turned up," Lynn pointed out. "I don't mean to be rude, but do you have any proof of this, Fan?"

In response, I pulled out the marriage and birth certificates from my purse. I had figured this question would pop up eventually. I handed them to Lynn, who looked them over carefully before passing them to Ruth.

"I don't have any more answers yet than you do," I said. "I was hoping we could compare notes and fill in some of the gaps. Like why you all thought my mother was dead."

"It was local gossip," Alice said brusquely. "We heard she'd been killed in a car accident."

"Who told you?"

"Good Lord, you expect me to remember that after all these years?" Alice was getting snippy—probably from hunger.

"I remember, Mother," said Ruth grimly. "You called me in Montreal to pass on the news. I think you enjoyed that."

Her mother gave her a glare that would have levelled a tax auditor, but Ruth didn't budge.

"I suppose Meredith told me," Lynn offered. "She's my cousin. She still lives here, keeps me abreast of the local news."

"Meredith. Meredith Murphy?" I hazarded.

"Yes. Do you know her?"

"I met her this morning at Upper Canada Village. We got talking about the villages at the exhibit. When I told her who my mother was, she got quite upset. Almost passed out."

Lynn shook her head. "Meredith has a flair for the dramatic. She never left Ingleside and I think she gets bored with things. She's very much like her mother was—full of energy and involved in everything. Goodness knows whom she heard it from."

"*When* did you hear about this?"

Ruth and Lynn looked at each other. Alice tidied up her wool bits and said nothing.

"Oh, I don't know," Ruth shrugged. "About a year after the flooding, I think. Mother called me shortly after I'd returned to Montreal to live."

"Is that important?" Lynn added.

I sighed and ran a hand through my hair—remembering too late that I'd actually styled it this morning for my interview with Gordon.

"I have no idea," I admitted. "I came here for answers and right now I have more questions than I started with. But your thinking her dead sure is weird." And dead in a car accident, just as Mother had told me about Hal who had been murdered. I didn't say this last out loud. They seemed to be nice ladies, but any one of them could be my father's killer.

"Farran," Ruth looked up suddenly, "does Gordon know?"

Ault Island is one of only two Canadian parcels of land on Lake St. Lawrence with private access to the river. The other is Moulinette Island in the Long Sault Parkway, known to the locals as Island 17 from its designation during the Power Project years. Initially peopled only with summer cottages moved from locations along the old seaway, both islands were now gradually becoming upscale waterfront property sporting large permanent homes. I had managed to rent one of the last surviving cottages on Ault Island for the summer, pulling every string in the book to get it. I had tracked down Gordon Leonard's address some months before and I wanted to live close by. Part of my agenda was to get to know my uncle, even if—being Hal's brother—he was my prime suspect. If he hadn't killed my father, he probably had a good idea who did.

The day of my arrival in the area, I drove onto the island across the causeway that connected it to the mainland. Except for a bike path and some old rural mailboxes, there was no sign of human life for the first kilometre. The rain had stopped, the sky breaking blue above me. The bush was green and full of birds. I saw two Canada geese standing on the grass beside the road, and they did not deign to look up as I passed. A small rabbit took off into the bush as I came into view of the mailboxes. The road split there and I went left. Just around the curve, I slammed on the brakes. A deer, young but too old to have the spotted coat of a fawn, scrambled across the road and stood nervously at the edge of the bush. An older doe, probably the mother, stood absolutely still in the field on my right. For a moment, none of us moved. Sensing the yearling's reluctance to leave its mother for the safety of the trees, the doe suddenly made a breathless dash in front of my car and crossed the road. With a flash of white tail, they were gone. Another example of a universal instinct: Protect the young.

Was that what my mother had been doing when she lied to me all those years—protecting me from something? My father's death, or the manner of it, had shocked her so deeply that she'd had a heart attack. Had she been hiding me from him only to find he'd been dead the whole time? Why?

In the months that followed my discovery in the morgue files, something began to happen to me on a deep level. I decided to let the news go for the time being, as the files said the inquest had come up with "death by person or persons unknown." I went on with my life and my work—or so I thought. A sudden case of insomnia I dismissed as a symptom of creeping middle age. I had frequent headaches and began to skip supper in lieu of liquid meals. I found it hard to focus when teaching, and research was impossible. The same colleagues that had been so supportive after my mother's death now began to suggest that I take some time off. I could scarcely blame them. I had told no one of what I had found.

Sometimes anger can keep you warm. That's when you mistake it for comfort. I realized it was time to admit that I was not coping. These events had really shaken me, and until I found closure of some kind I would not be able to let go and move on. In the late winter, I applied for a long-overdue sabbatical and spent the months left in the semester priming myself on the St. Lawrence Seaway.

And now here I was. The riverfront porch of my tiny cottage ran its length and gave me my first unobstructed view of the great river. It stretched as far as I could see to either side, grey-blue and dotted with waves from the wind that afternoon. Across the expanse on the far side of the shipping channel lay the American shoreline with trees that underlined the sky all the way east to a small gap where out-going tankers seemed to fall off the face of the earth. Geese were everywhere—in flocks on the water, eating things on my rented beach, and defecating on my lawn. They started up like a brass orchestra at my arrival, moving with a combination of dignity and speed to a safe distance out on the river. Obviously, they had not been told I was coming and seemed quite put out by it.

I put my personal things in the larger of the two bedrooms, my briefcase and box of materials in the other. It would serve as my office while here. The rest of the cottage was really one large room with a kitchenette at one end and a stone fireplace at the other. It was small and cosy despite the lack of heat. I turned on the baseboard units and flipped the switch marked 'water heater'. After a hot bath and a canned supper, I fell asleep until almost dawn.

"No," I replied to Ruth's question. "He doesn't. We've met briefly but it was in his office and I didn't think that was the time or place. I wasn't going to say anything for a week or two, just get familiar with the area. He was leaving for Toronto, and said he wouldn't be back for a few days."

Ruth got up and stood looking out the window, twisting her hands.

"He took it hard when they found Hal—your father," said Lynn quietly. "Meredith said he didn't eat or sleep for days. I wonder how he'll handle this."

"Meredith," said Mrs. Hoffman acidly, "probably fussed him off his food. Has the sensitivity of an ox."

"Lynn, does Gordon have a wife and family?" I asked. "The papers didn't say anything about other family members. What about my grandparents?"

"Gordon was married briefly in his twenties," she explained. "Brought someone home from university. She died in labour, and they lost the baby, too. A boy. Your grandmother died in Aultsville in 1954. Eric Leonard, your grandfather, died in Ingleside in 1960. Meredith could give you the details."

I'd heard more than I could digest at that point. It was time to go.

"Meredith will be calling you, Ruth, to warn you about me," I said, rising to my feet. "Here's where you can contact me." I scribbled my local number on a business card and gave it to her. "I hope I can call you sometime soon, just to talk about my mother."

Ruth took the card slowly. Then she nodded. "Of course, Farran."

"Call me if you need anything." Lynn passed me one of her cards, and then shook my hand. "Your mother was always good to me. It's wonderful to think that Les not only lived, but had a child as well."

My third morning on the river I enjoyed in peace. The bright side to insomnia is the number of sunrises you get for free. As I made the tea, I tried to shut down my brain. It was full of what the ladies had said and I wanted to just let it simmer. There was nothing to do until Gordon Leonard returned.

I looked out the window toward the road where a group of retirees were already walking briskly. It made me tired just to see them. Only if I were lucky would I reach that level of fitness in the intervening twenty years between us. I took my tea and shuffled out to the porch to take in the river.

To someone raised in the metropolitan confines of Cambridge and area, this open stretch of river seemed vast and alive. The spring morning—painted in pastel shades of pink, blue and purple—appeared twice beautiful as reflected by the river. The dew was heavy on the lawn chairs (mental note: cover them at night) so I brought out a cushion to sit on and wrapped myself in a blanket to spite the coolness. Some perennials were blooming in the flower bed and the bees had started their rounds. Out on the water, I saw a pair of loons glide by before beginning their dives for food. Soon after, the geese appeared. The flotilla was peppered with tiny yellow-brown fluffballs diligently trying to keep up with their parents.

I let the river fill my mind and wash it all away. Such a peace I would not know again for several weeks.

It is hard to describe my feelings at that point. The facts, however, were clear:

1. My mother was dead.

2. So was my father.

3. My mother had lied about his name and his death.

4. Everyone thought my mother was dead, too.

5. Everything I grew up with disappeared in the fire, along with the assumptions of who I am and where I come from.

6. Someone killed my father. I had to find out who and why.

The irony of moving from having half a history to none was not lost upon me. Still, I was firmly lodged at the "anger" phase of the grieving process. Acceptance was not even a dot on the horizon. My mother had not trusted me with her secrets—secrets that were definitely my business. Someone had cut my father's life short long before his time, and in doing so had robbed me of him. People here who were strangers to me knew my family better than I did. And almost all the places where my parents had lived, played, worked and prayed were gone forever beneath the waters of the St. Lawrence.

In retrospect, the chip on my shoulder was understandable.

I had work to do. Tomorrow, I would begin. Today, I would relax and explore the island, giving my knee a break and taking advantage of my uncle's absence to look over his house. A hot shower helped put me in gear, but the woman I looked at in the bathroom mirror was a stranger. Still the same fair hair, but no longer cut and styled. Grown down to my shoulders for the first time since college. Painstaking makeup now forgotten, still slim but suits replaced by jeans. Except for the laugh lines, I looked very much as I had in public school. Why did the past seem so much more substantial than the present?

I began my mission after breakfast, with a slow and very un-brisk walk to the other side of the island, down the road that forked to the right at the mailboxes. My side of the island was just inside the township of South Stormont, but this side lay in South Dundas. It was furnished with the same mix of houses and cottages and house/cottage hybrids as the other side. There were several newer monster homes as well.

I retraced my steps toward my cottage, noticing for the first time two century-old farmhouses along the way. The only evidence left, I gathered, that this area had once been valuable farmland. The properties to the east of the second one, including my own, were dotted with apples trees growing in equal space from each other. Former orchard. The fruit trees in the bush to the north of the road were mostly bare of blossoms, having been untended for so long. The ones on the properties, however, were in full bloom and the air was heavy with scent and the sound of bees.

My uncle's house lay at the eastern tip of the island, on a stretch of road that branched off to the river from the main drag where it curved back into the bush before reaching a dead end. Gordon would tell me later that this piece of road once led to Aultsville, the village being a healthy stone's throw from his beach. The house itself was large and white and commanding, sitting on the point as it did. The lawn was immaculate and professionally done. There was a two-car garage with both doors tightly closed to prying eyes like mine. I considered the sculpted hedge for a moment, remembering what Lynn had said about Gordon losing his wife and child. Our family wasn't what you'd call lucky.

I returned to my cottage to find the light blinking on the answering machine. It was Meredith, calling before leaving for work about stopping in to see me tonight. I could see that Lynn wasn't kidding about energy. I left a message on her machine with directions, and resolutely tackled the "office" I had to set up.

Shortly after five-thirty that afternoon, I heard Meredith's car pull up outside. She had exchanged her 1860s dress for jeans and a sweatshirt with "Lost Villages Museum" on it. Not surprisingly, she got to the point when she got through the door.

"Why didn't you wait to go over till I'd called Ruth? She's right upset."

I had a flashback of my grade three teacher. But I wondered if Meredith was ticked with me more because I'd stolen the thrill of revelation from her than anything else.

"I guess I couldn't wait. I wanted to know more about my mother's so-called death." I motioned to the room. "Come in. I have coffee made and we can take it out on the porch."

I poured two cups and turned to find Meredith staring at me. "You look like your father," she said simply. "I wonder Gordon didn't see it."

"Did you know him well?"

She nodded and took her cup. "Well enough. Aultsville wasn't a big place." She looked at my support bandage, now exposed by my shorts. "What happened to your knee?" she added bluntly.

"I ran into a door."

We made our way outside. The bees had packed it in for the day and the geese had gone, too. I opened two lawn chairs and pulled up a little table. We sat for some minutes without speaking.

"Tell me about them, Meredith," I said finally. "Tell me about my family. Were they happy? Were they good people?"

Meredith looked into her coffee for an answer before responding. "Yes, Farran, they were good people. And I think they were happy enough. Your grandfather, Eric Leonard, was a widower with Gordon to raise when he met and married your grandmother Lila. She was a good wife, and a mother to Gordon. A few years later, your father was born. The boys grew up as close as full brothers. Gordon taught Hal most things like fishing and swimming and baseball because Eric was running two businesses. They were well off." She stopped suddenly. I sensed a problem.

"But things changed?" I asked.

"Yes," she answered reluctantly. "Things changed." She turned her head to look downriver in the direction of Aultsville's remains. "I think it really started when your grandmother died."

H-BOMB TO COME IN VARIETY OF SIZES

SEAWAY BILL SIGNED—AT LAST
Work May Now Begin Says 'Happy' President
Nine Pens Use For Signing

SEAWAY JOBS NOW OPEN
The government today called for applications for engineering jobs on the navigational end of the St. Lawrence Seaway project.

GO-AHEAD ON SEAWAY IN 2 WEEKS
Plan For 5,000 Evacuees

May 1954
The Cornwall *Standard-Freeholder*

Many times in the past, Eric Leonard had offered to build his new wife a larger, more impressive house, but each time Lila had refused. "It's the only home Gordon has known," she'd explain, referring to her young stepson. And now the small, red-brick house on the County Road known as Forget-Me-Not Cottage was packed with those who had attended her funeral that beautiful May afternoon.

Just about everybody was there. Meredith Murphy picked out faces from her usual perch in the corner: Alice Hoffman and her daughter Ruth having a warm discussion over some bowls of salad in the dining room; William Strauss, foreman of Eric's lumberyard, standing with his workers and their wives; Emme Strauss (the Ice Queen) standing apart from her husband as usual, looking distant while her young son Jerry made short work of the food on the dining room table; Meredith's extremely annoying cousin Lynnie trying to listen in on some whispered adult conversation.

Gordon and Hal stood side by side across the room. She noticed, not for the first time, how much the brothers resembled each other, despite Hal being fair and Gordon dark. You'd never know to look at them they were only half brothers, but as people they were quite different.

"Hello, Meredith." Dr. Sam Burns came up smiling before she had a chance to bolt. "Keepin' an eye on the boys?"

Meredith flushed. He had brought her into this world—she was a "Burns Baby" like almost a thousand others along the Front—but she wished he wouldn't tease her like some kid. Didn't he realize she was almost fifteen? She glanced over at the boys to see if they'd heard.

Dr. Burns patted her shoulder affectionately. "Don't mind me," he said, looking at her over his half-moon reading glasses still sitting on his nose. "I tend to get worse with age."

"I'm glad you could make it, Sam." Eric Leonard, a tall and husky man, had crossed the room from the hallway, and now shook the doctor's hand. "I wanted to thank you again for all you did for Lila. I know it was great comfort to her that you were there through it all."

"I'm just sorry I couldn't help her, Eric. The cancer had spread too far. I really felt it best to make her comfortable and let you have some time together." Burns took off his glasses and polished them badly with his handkerchief before putting them in his pocket. "Lila was a fine woman. How are the boys takin' it?"

Eric turned to look at his sons. Hal was talking animatedly with a group of girls while Gordon stood white and silent. The latter was clearly suffering.

"I'm not sure," said Eric slowly. "Even though Lila wasn't Gordy's real mother, she raised him from a little boy. He feels as badly as Hal." He turned back. "And now we have the Seaway problem, too. Will you be at the meeting next week?"

Burns nodded. "Wouldn't miss it. Still doesn't seem real, though. We've heard the talk about the Deep Water Project all our lives but I never thought they'd do it. Can't imagine everything we know bein' under water. It's goin' to be tough on the old folks."

Eric was quiet for a moment. "Maybe it's a blessing that Lila won't be around to see it. She loved Aultsville."

The men moved off and Meredith made her way out to the front porch. It was filled with people so she continued down to the front *gate and on to the road. The street was lined with family homes, many of them second generation, she knew. Most were built of brick from the local brickyard and had large, well-tended gardens framed by tall trees. For the first time, Meredith really looked at the neighbourhood. It seemed so permanent. Could they really make it all disappear?*

"Market value? What the hell's market value? All your talk about floodin' all these years has drove our property values into the ground."

The shouts of agreement from the crowd made it impossible for the man in the suit to reply. Hostile men and cigarette smoke filled the township hall in Osnabruck Centre. At one end of the room stood maps and sketches of the proposed New Towns No. 1 and No. 2, plus models of the new homes that would be built. Along with the representative from Ontario Hydro was the reeve of the township—a small man with glasses who was quickly losing the reins of the evening. Meredith almost wished she'd never convinced her father to let her come with him. She craned her neck again but couldn't see . . . anything.

"You've got that right," yelled another. "Last year I needed to build another barn on my field but the bank wouldn't loan me the money. My mortgage is paid. I even offered twice the interest rate—ten percent if you can believe it—and he still turned me down. Said with the Seaway comin' he couldn't see the wisdom of buildin' something for the fish to swim in."

The crowd's volume went up again. The reeve waved his hands. "Please, please. Let Mr. Ballard answer your questions."

The man in the suit took a step forward. "My company realizes there has been an effect on real estate around here because of this project. That's why we're offering fair market value plus ten to fifteen percent in cash. Or you can take a similar residence or business location in the new towns."

Bill Strauss stood up and pointed to the models. "That's another thing—look at those houses," he said. Having arrived in Aultsville as a young man with his parents during the Depression, Strauss's voice held almost no trace of his German heritage. "They look like chicken coops. And all our houses will look the same. Nothing like what most of us have now."

"You can have a bigger home built if you want, sir."

"But it will cost me extra?"

"Yes."

"So after working my fingers to the bone for the last fifteen years to pay off my house, I'll be owing again?"

The shouting that threatened to pick up again quieted down when Eric Leonard stood up. "My concern is with the layout of the new towns." He pointed to one of the sketches. "We're designated New Town No. 1. Who decided the plans for it? None of us were asked and we have to live there."

"We had well-qualified engineers design these plans," Ballard replied. "I can't see anything wrong with them."

"Well, I can," Leonard shot back. "First off, where are the parks for the kids? And look at those streets, shaped like 'P's. I run the volunteer fire department. What if there's a fire near the neck of the street? How will people farther down get out or help get in?"

Everyone started talking at once. The reeve wiped his forehead with his handkerchief. Ballard crossed his arms and waited.

Then a man in the rear got to his feet. He stood well over six feet with shoulders to match, thick black hair and a full beard. Harper Mackenzie—the trader from Farran's Point. Meredith had seen him only a few times before, but he was someone you didn't forget.

Mackenzie looked around at the crowd as he waited to speak. One by one, his neighbours fell silent.

"To my mind," he began in a thick Scottish accent, "with all of us havin' such different properties and losin' value on them for so long, the only way to make sure we don't lose in this deal is to get full replacement value for our homes and farms."

A low murmur of agreement went through the hall. Ballard's lips tightened into a thin line.

"You tell your Mr. Saunders that we should have that," Mackenzie continued. "Our premier Mr. Frost promised a fair deal for all and we expect him to stick to that."

Pandemonium broke out with everyone shouting to be heard over the din. Meredith saw a young boy beside Mackenzie get up and go out the door, followed by one of the Leonard boys. She made her *way out the main door into the cooler air of the evening. When the heavy door swung shut, the silence beat upon her ears still humming from the meeting. The crickets were singing full force and up through the branches of the big trees, she could see the stars.*

Hearing voices, Meredith walked along the sidewalk till she saw the two boys standing in the light from a window. It wasn't until she was up close that she realized the shorter one was a girl.

"Had to get out of there?" It was Hal, a grin spreading across his face.

Meredith found her voice. "Smoke," she managed. "The cigarette smoke was gettin' to me." She stole a look at the girl. Dungarees, cap, long hair in a braid down the back, unsettlingly pretty. Leslie Mackenzie, Harper's stepdaughter.

"You're from the Point, aren't you?" Hal asked Leslie. He struck a match and lit a cigarette, never taking his eyes from the girl's face. "I've seen you with the girls' team in the park at home. You're good. So good I thought you were a boy." He dropped the match to the ground and stepped on it. "I'm Hal. Hal Leonard. This is Meredith."

"We've played ball a few times against each other," said Meredith. "You're Harper's girl Leslie, aren't you?"

"Yes." It was the first the girl had spoken. She chewed her lip for a moment. "I'm sorry about your ma," she said suddenly to Hal. The young man nodded quickly and then became absorbed with the glow of his cigarette. "It's tough," Leslie stammered. "I mean, I know how it is. I lost my ma last year. It's tough, really tough, and I'm sorry." She stumbled to a halt and stared at her feet.

Meredith had absolutely no idea what to say to rescue the moment. Then Hal looked at Leslie.

"You're right, it is tough. It's a bad deal all around. Not much you can do about it, though. And now," he added, shaking his head, "on top of all this, we have to decide whether Ma stays in St. Paul's Cemetery or we move her to the new one they're makin' on high ground. Dad wants to take her there and Gordy says she should stay here. I don't know what to think."

Meredith opened her mouth to reply but the meeting began to break up, people spilling loudly into the street. Gordon Leonard appeared, spotted his brother and strode over.

"What did you come out here for?" he demanded. "Don't you care what's goin' on in there?"

Hal shrugged. "Sure. But what difference will I make? Besides," he added, grinding his cigarette out with his foot, *"sounds like we'll all do fine anyway. I could go for paved streets, street lights everywhere. Dad's goin' to make a mint on supplyin' lumber for these guys. Maybe we shouldn't complain so loud."*

Gordon seemed to notice the girls standing there for the first time. He nodded to Meredith. "Evenin', Meredith. Who's your friend?"

"This is Leslie Mackenzie, from the Point," said Meredith. She wanted to add, "she isn't my friend" but didn't know a good way to do it. "How did the meeting end?"

"I heard what you said just now, Hal." Eric Leonard had come up behind them. He put his hand on his younger son's shoulder. "And you're right—we do stand to get good business for the lumberyard through this. But we all need to make sure we don't do anything hasty or give away too much too fast."

"Dad, this is all gonna happen anyway," said Hal. "I figure, why not play for the winnin' team? We make nice with Hydro, we get what we can while they're givin'. Nothing wrong in comin' out ahead in a bad situation."

"There is if you have to sell out your friends, Hal," said Gordon quietly.

Harper Mackenzie was standing by his pickup truck. "Come on, gal," he called over. "Time to go home." Leslie said good night and crossed over to the truck. It was a '39 Ford that had obviously been repaired many times, and struck a high contrast with the shiny new one marked LEONARD'S GENERAL STORE on the side. The others followed, and Eric came up to Harper's window.

"I liked your ideas in there, Harp. I think a few of us need to get together and come up with a firm approach for this. Are you interested?"

Harper grunted and started the truck. "Don't see what help I can be. Sharks will be in soon enough and we'll all be in the same spot."

"You think it's goin' to go that way? You said in there you expected Frost to be fair."

"I was remindin' them of their own words, which is about all we can do," said Harper. "You know as well as I do, Eric, that this here's a game and the likes of you and me ain't even sittin' at the table."

Mackenzie nodded his good night and pulled away. Meredith watched Hal watch the battered truck until only the tail lights were visible.

"Is he right, Dad?" Gordon asked finally.

"I'm afraid he might be," said his father slowly. "He never loses at cards."

Emme Strauss swept past Meredith when she returned to the store with the morning bags of mail from the Moccasin. The Ice Queen, Meredith thought as she hovered near the dry goods. Some distant relative of Bill's that had arrived as a near child bride for him just before the war broke out, Emme had never made an effort to blend in with the villagers even though few had ostracized her through the war years. Beautiful, but surely that white-blonde hair came from a bottle? And about as much warmth as concrete in January, the only person not showing the heat this sultry August morning.

"I'm really sorry to hear that, Miss Kelly." Gordon was serving an elderly lady just down the counter. "I'll pass that on to my dad when I see him this morning. I'm sure he'll drop in as soon as he can."

"Thank you, Gordon. I don't know what's to do, but a lady needs a man's advice on such things." She gathered her parcels and left.

Gordon looked over at Emme sorting mail in the postal wicket. "Train late this mornin', Em? You're an hour behind. Must be something in the water today. I need to get over and help with deliveries at the yard, but there's no sign of Hal."

"He is probably at the ceremony in Maple Grove this morning," Emme said over her shoulder in her soft German accent, ignoring his remark about the train. "The prime minister is supposed to be there, as well as Mr. Frost and the Americans, to break ground for the Project." She came out of the wicket and went around to where the brass postal boxes went down one side of her walls. She began to polish them with a soft cloth. "What is wrong with poor Miss Kelly today?"

Gordon looked troubled. "This time her problem is serious. One of the land agents came by yesterday and had her all signed up *in an hour. Now she's worried about what she settled for. That's the third one this week. First old Mrs. Henry, then the Brewster sisters, now Miss Kelly. The widows and spinsters first."*

Emme looked up from her polishing and smiled a strange smile. "That is the rule of the hunt, is it not? Single out the weaker ones first."

"That's one way to look at it, I guess." Gordon glanced over at Meredith. "Can I help you with something, Meredith?"

"I, uh, well, I'm still thinkin', I guess," she murmured awkwardly. She felt a flush rise to her cheeks. "I'll need a few more minutes."

Gordon gave her a long look and then glowered down at his cash register.

"Listen, Em," he said uncertainly, "did you ask to borrow any money from the cash register yesterday?" When the woman shook her head, Gordon said, "We're short some from the float and I thought maybe Hal just forgot to mark it down. Oh, well," he added, "we'll sort it out when he gets here. If he ever does."

"Wickedness."

I started, and shivered suddenly. The sun was starting to go down, throwing us into the shadow of the cottage. As warm spring days so often do, this one had quickly turned into a cool evening and I told myself that was the reason I felt so cold.

"What?" I asked Meredith.

She was sitting ramrod straight in the lawn chair, her mouth a thin line.

"Wickedness. I could sense even then something wasn't right." She rose suddenly and gathered her things. "But it isn't my place to say it."

I followed her to the door, unsettled. What was it Lynn Holmes said yesterday? *Meredith has a flair for the dramatic.* 'Wickedness' sounded biblical. Still, I couldn't let it go.

"It isn't your place to say what?" I opened the door slowly and stood in the doorframe. "What do you mean by 'wickedness'?"

Meredith stood for a moment, framed by the large patio door across the cottage. Behind her, the setting sun had turned the river to milk. I can see her yet in my mind's eye, struggling between dropping a bomb with flourish and stepping back from going too far. I try to use that picture now to wipe out the other, ugly memory.

Good upbringing won the fight.

"Your family didn't fall on hard times—they were torn apart. Wickedness, it was. The rest you won't hear from me." She pushed past me and was gone.

I stood in the kitchen for some time, trying to sort out what I'd heard. Even though Meredith hadn't said it, I'd sensed she'd had a high school crush on my father in the old days. Still, "wickedness" was a strong word to hold onto for forty years. My eyes fell on Lynn Holmes's card that I'd tacked onto the fridge last night. I decided to call her in the morning.

The next day, I had to be satisfied with leaving a message on Lynn's voice mail. Her recorded voice said she wouldn't be in until after lunch. Since the next thing I had to do was let my uncle know who I was, there was nothing to do until he got back.

The beautiful weather was holding, so I figured I would spend the day at Upper Canada Village and do the research I had planned before I made my detour to Ruth's place. I arrived at opening time and found it much as I had left it two days before. As I walked along Queen Street, I called the Operations building on my cell phone and was told that Gordon Leonard wasn't due back until mid-afternoon.

For some reason, it was bothering me about the rumour of my mother's death. I didn't know why, but I felt it was important. Consciously, I hadn't followed the thread all the way back to my father's murder yet, but my subconscious was kicking up a stink. When you spend a good part of your life reconstructing cultures from a handful of details, you develop a sense of what is wheat and what is chaff.

I found myself in front of Crysler Hall. Taking the hint, I went in and looked for Meredith. We met on the stairs as she was heading down to leave, dressed in a bright, red-print gown and white cap. She frowned when she saw me.

"I can't stop to talk," she said, brushing by me. "I'm on my way out just now."

"But I have a different concern today and I need your help." I followed her to the heavy front door. "It's about the rumour of my mother's death."

"I'm sorry, Dr. Mackenzie," she said firmly. "I have to meet with . . . administration. We'll talk some other time." Meredith expertly swung open the big door and vanished into the morning.

"Dr. Mackenzie?" Another gowned woman appeared, her hand offered. "I'm Jeannie Burns. Meredith told me you might be in this morning and I was to help you with your research, if you needed it."

I shook her hand warmly, exchanged some standard phrases, made an excuse and took off after Meredith. I was ticked at getting table scraps of information and my bloodhound tendencies had switched on. I wanted some meat.

Meredith was already a full minute ahead of me, but her bright red dress was easy to spot. She had taken the small path beside the hall that led to Albert Street and was just disappearing behind the Cabinet Maker's Shop. I reached the spot quickly, expecting to see her heading down the utility road that leads to the First Aid and Security building, then out to the Parks offices. Instead, she continued at a brisk pace down Albert, keeping the distance between us with her long, athletic stride—even in a gown. She never slowed down and she never looked back.

When Meredith reached the corner of Albert and Church Streets, she veered off to the footpath behind the Broommaker's Shop and headed for Beach's Sawmill. She passed several male staff in the customary breeches, shirts and hats, and a handful of tourists before going up the wooden ramp to the open door. There, she hesitated for a moment before vanishing into the darkness beyond.

I don't think I was more than a minute behind her. The sawmill sounded busy, a rhythmic thumping punctuating the air. When I was about twenty feet away from the saw mill door, I heard a scream I pray to God I never hear again. It was all the more horrible when it cut short. Everyone in the yard froze, including me. Then I ran up to the door and plunged into the dusky barn.

The miller was running down the stairs from the second floor. He made it to the central walk surrounding the massive gears that drove the saw blade upstairs, then turned away. When he saw me, he tried to keep me from looking over into the water. But I did.

Blood and foam and Meredith's horribly mangled body churned in the water around the gears. I shall see it till I die—the red print dress turning over and over like grotesque laundry in a wringer washer. And the gears slamming relentlessly, threatening to grind her in.

"Shut it off!" I screamed over the pounding. "Shut it off! Get her out!"

The miller shook me. Hard. "I can't!" he yelled back. "Nothing stops this mill. The river runs it. You'd have to stop the river." His hands dropped to his sides. "She's dead already."

"Help," I said stupidly. "I have to get help." I stumbled out through the small crowd that was gathering around the doorway. Admissions was closest so I tried to go there, but the image of blood and foam rose up in my eyes. My stomach threatened to rise with it and I went down on my good knee, fighting it.

Wickedness, Meredith had said firmly.

They were torn apart. Wickedness, it was.

Had my coming here for answers unleashed the wickedness again?

Chapter 5

Pieces

WE ARE so inadequate in the face of death.

Gordon Leonard and I sat like bookends in the chairs that faced Inspector Jerry Strauss's desk at the Long Sault detachment. Meredith had died four hours ago and the fallout brought us both here to play out the scene I had envisioned a hundred times in recent months—but never like this. Strauss had allowed us the courtesy of a few moments alone to digest each other's existence.

"So Leslie did not die?" Gordon said as though asked a trick question.

"No, not until last year."

"She married my brother Hal sometime before he died and you are their daughter?"

"Yes." I was keeping it simple, feeling it best under the circumstances.

"Why didn't you tell me when we met this week?"

I had the grace to squirm a little in my chair. "Because I didn't know you at all. I wanted some time to familiarize myself with the area and you before I loaded this on you. I wanted to see what kind of a man you were before you knew who I was. And for safety's sake, of course," I added uncomfortably.

"Safety?" He finally looked at me. "Whose safety? You come in here stirring up ghosts you have no idea of and now Meredith is dead."

"I came here for answers and . . . to see you." I faced him down. "You would have done the same thing in my shoes."

Inspector Strauss walked back in just then. He was a tall, good-looking man in his early fifties—not the movie star type of looks that Gordon had, but that rougher attractiveness like a younger James Garner. If he haunted doughnut shops, it was well hidden.

When I'd first been introduced, I found myself thinking of the father of an old school friend back home. Alison Perry's dad had been a "Reegie"—a Waterloo Regional Police officer. He'd been a good man and loving father. Freud would say he filled that space in my life to a certain extent. I grew up feeling safe around a uniform. When he died suddenly, in the line of duty, my grief was very real. Here's a tip: Never attend a policeman's funeral. The honour guard is a killer.

Strauss casually looked us over as he sat down, but I guessed he was sizing up our blossoming relationship. Somehow I didn't think I passed the test.

"We seem to be doing this a bit more these days, Gordy," he said quietly. "Last year, we sat here trying to understand Hal's murder."

Gordon nodded, but did not speak. "Did she suffer, Jerry?" he said finally.

Strauss threw a quick glance at me before replying. "I would say no. From what Miss Mackenzie says in her statement, it all happened very quickly."

"Does Lynn know?"

"I just talked to her." Strauss passed his hand over his face. "I never like giving that news over the phone."

"Meredith tried to call me," Gordon sighed, looking at the floor. "Several times. I had messages from her on my machine at home asking me to call when I returned." He rubbed his forehead hard. "I should have called from Toronto. I left it. I was busy, and I thought she was being . . . Meredith."

"Why should you think otherwise?" Strauss leaned forward in his chair. "Did she sound in distress?"

"She sounded excited, as though something were up."

"That was me," I broke in. "She probably wanted to tell you about me. But she didn't seem excited with me. Her first reaction when we met—after hyperventilation—was *anger*. Meredith was not happy to find out about me. Any idea why?"

Gordon faced my direction, but continued to look at the floor. "You said you talked to her just when she left the hall. Did she say who she was meeting?"

I shook my head. "She started to, but caught herself. Then she said she had an appointment with administration. That's why I was surprised to see her go to the sawmill."

"I don't think we should jump to any conclusions yet, Gordy," said Strauss, crossing his arms as he leaned back in his chair. "I'm treating this as a homicide because it's standard procedure to do so until proven otherwise. But this could just have been an accident. Or Meredith could have felt sick and lightheaded, and fallen over the railing. It could even have been a heart attack."

"I hope you're right, Jerry," said my uncle, but he sounded unconvinced. He rose and made his way to the door, stopping with his hand on the knob. "When you found Hal last year," he turned to Strauss, "I said then that it felt like it was all coming back again—after all these years."

"The wickedness?" I said.

Gordon shot a glance at me.

"That sounds like one of Meredith's sayings," he said accusingly.

"It is." I stood up. "We talked a bit about the old days in Aultsville, then she clammed up and wouldn't say any more. Said it wasn't her place to tell me. That my family didn't fall on hard times—they were torn apart by wickedness." I let it drop then and waited while it rolled across the floor to his side of the court.

A strange look crossed his face and he said nothing for a moment.

"Meredith could always be a little dramatic," he explained, then added, "We obviously have to talk, Miss Mackenzie. But not now. I need a little time to understand all this. I will call you." And he was gone.

We both looked at the closed door in silence. Then the inspector leaned back in his chair.

"Go easy with him, Miss Mackenzie." He spoke softly, but the warning was unmistakable. "I've known Gordon Leonard my whole life. And I can tell you he's had his share through the years. He seems to be getting it again. Go home," he added, not unkindly. "You've been here long enough. I'll have an officer drive you back to get your car. But I'll be calling you, too."

His look was inscrutable, but I knew a lot was going on behind those grey eyes. Strauss was probably very good at his job: quiet and easy-going on the outside, but missing nothing on the inside. If I were a criminal, I'd have been nervous.

I followed orders and took my leave.

The next morning I awoke thinking I heard the river call my name. But of course it was nothing of the sort, only the waves from a passing ship kneading the beach. The sun was barely up and the sky was beautiful. For a moment, I forgot the horror of the previous day. Then it all came flooding back.

I had won the battle of my stomach after I stumbled out of the sawmill, and somehow made it to the admissions office. The cheerful lady from the other day lost her smile as soon as she caught sight of me.

"What's the matter, ma'am?" A firm hand with the grip of a stevedore steadied me. "Are you all right?"

"The sawmill. An accident." My voice was shaking. "Meredith Murphy."

The woman's face went white and she whipped out a walkie-talkie from somewhere in that flowing cotton dress, calling security with the efficiency of an FBI agent. The incongruity of it was one of those strange lucid moments that stays with you long after. Maybe this was really just a play I was in.

Security appeared almost immediately. After checking with us, two hurried off to the sawmill and the other took me to the First Aid office. I waited there, feeling like I had outside the principal's office years ago. Eventually, an OPP officer came to see me.

Constable Wiley was in his mid-thirties, with a formal manner but a nice smile.

"I understand you saw the accident, ma'am," he said, pulling a chair up next to me.

"I didn't see it," I corrected him, "but I heard the scream and was the first person to get there. The miller and me, actually."

"I'm sure you've had quite a shock, ma'am, but we'll need you to come and give a full statement."

"Of course."

"Can I have your name?" He took out a small notebook and was already writing something—probably his suspicions.

"Mackenzie. Dr. Farran Mackenzie." Out of habit, I gave him my Waterloo address.

"So you're here as a tourist. I'm sorry this had to happen on your visit."

"Oh . . . no, actually, I'm staying on Ault Island for a while." I corrected my information with him.

"Visiting?" he asked pleasantly, but I sensed the questioning was already under way.

"Yes," I said hesitantly, adding dryly, "old friends of the family."

The cruiser used the utility road, so I bypassed the village. Later I would find out that the miller had immediately used a long pole to push Meredith's body away from the suction of the gears. It floated down with the current, lodging just in front of the bridge. Security blocked off the area and someone pulled the corpse out of the water, covering it with a blanket until the police arrived. Then the scene had been secured with yellow tape and the village closed for the day.

An officer was waiting for Gordon when he arrived from Toronto. I'm sure the offices were in a genuine spin when he got there, and the sight of a uniform probably warned him it wasn't good. Two hours after my arrival at the Long Sault OPP detachment, my uncle appeared to join the little party I was having with Inspector Strauss.

I could hear them trying to locate Strauss when I first arrived. I sat in the squad room directly off the lobby and gave my statement to another officer. I answered only the questions asked of me. In the midst of this, Strauss appeared at the door. I had the feeling he had been listening for a few minutes. Probably standard cop procedure.

"Finish up," he said to the officer, "then bring Miss Mackenzie to my office."

In a few minutes, I was heading down the long corridor that connected all the ground floor rooms together. The whole place was very Sixties, with light woodwork, tan brick walls and that speckled stone floor you see in so many old schools. For a big building, it seemed rather quiet. But an educated guess told me that in its heyday, when money and staff were no objects, the place had been a real beehive.

Strauss's office was at the end of the hall, with windows that looked out on the police garage in the back and Anglican-Christ Church across the road. I will note now that I did not see any open doughnut boxes sitting around. He was on the phone when I walked in and waved me to a seat in front of his desk.

"Well, you can't really in this situation. Just send it on and do the best you can in the mill. And tell Toronto we want the autopsy ASAP," he added before hanging up. "It's personal."

Strauss spread his hands on the top of his desk and looked out the window. When he did not speak for a few moments, I broke the ice.

"You knew Meredith?"

Strauss fastened his eyes on me. I tried to look like an owl. The door opened and Officer Wiley came in with a sheaf of papers that he laid in front of Strauss. While the inspector looked it over, Wiley turned to me.

"Dr. Mackenzie," he asked, "have you had anything to eat? I could get you some sandwiches from the mall."

I smiled weakly, and shook my head. "No, thanks. I—I don't think I could eat just now."

"How about a cup of coffee? It's government standard, but it's hot."

"Thank you. That would be great." We settled the fine details of sugar and cream, and he left, returning almost immediately with a steaming Styrofoam cup I accepted gratefully. After waiting for a nod from his superior, he left us alone.

"I have your statement here, Dr. Mackenzie," said Strauss, leafing through the papers, "but I'd like to hear it from you. Why were you at the village that day?"

I used the warmth seeping to my fingers through the foam cup as strength while I told it all again. This time, I coughed up the background. One look at Strauss told me I'd better be up front with him from the start.

"So I thought I'd combine business with pleasure and look up some family I didn't know I had here," I finished.

"And who would that be?"

"Actually, my parents came from here—from the villages that were lost to the Seaway," I explained, beginning to feel a little warm despite the open windows. "I thought I'd see if anyone would remember them."

"Which village?" Strauss was turning a pencil end over end with one hand in rhythmic taps, adding to the myriad of grey dots already on his desk blotter.

"Farran's Point." I cleared my throat. "My mother named me after her hometown. But my father came from Aultsville. Technically, he never left." To my horror, I felt a hysterical giggle rise in the base of my throat. I cleared it again. "Were you stationed here last year when they found his body in Aultsville, Inspector?"

The pencil froze in mid-flip. We eyeballed each other for a moment. He won. I looked away across the field to where children played around a school.

"What are your parents' names, Miss Mackenzie?" The pencil remained silent.

"Leslie Mackenzie and Hal Leonard." I released a long sigh and faced him again. "My mother raised me. I never knew who my father was until . . . until the newspapers reported finding his body."

"Leslie Mackenzie died over forty years ago, probably around the same time that Hal Leonard was killed."

"Leslie was my mother. She died last year from heart failure, brought on in part by the news about my father." My mind flashed back to two days earlier, standing in Ruth Hoffman's living room. "And so far, only one person here has been pleased to learn that Leslie Mackenzie lived a longer life. I'm beginning to wonder about the 'Friendly Seaway Valley'."

The pencil began to tap again, more slowly this time. No other sound broke the silence for several minutes. Finally, Strauss put the pencil down and leaned back in his chair.

"I assume you can prove what you're saying."

"Of course. I have the papers in my purse." I looked around my feet, realizing for the first time that I'd left my purse at the Village. "My purse is in my car at Upper Canada Village."

"Does Gordon know?"

I silently wished people would stop asking me that question so I wouldn't have to admit how badly I'd handled everything.

"No. I've been here for only a few days. I met Gordon before he left for Toronto, but that was about my research and I didn't want to tell him something like this in his office at work."

"Did Meredith know?"

"Yes. I met up with her at the Lost Villages exhibit several days ago and we ended up talking about my mother. After she got over her shock, she told me about Ruth Hoffman in Ingleside being my mother's best friend and I went there to talk to her and . . . in the discussion, it came out who my father was and Ruth told Meredith." I stopped before I blabbed how Meredith had come to see me the night before she died and that I'd gone to the Village the next morning just to talk to her. I was beginning to sound suspicious to myself.

Strauss looked into the coffee mug on his desk, didn't like what he saw and pushed it away. "Not to speak ill of the dead, but if Meredith knew, then half of Ingleside knows now. You'd better tell Gordon at your first opportunity, before he hears it from someone else."

"Hears what?"

At the sound of the voice, we both looked to see Gordon Leonard standing, drawn and tired, in the doorway.

And that was the setting when I first told Gordon that I was his murdered brother's daughter.

I have to give Strauss credit—he was quick on his feet. As soon as Gordon sat down, the inspector was out the door, muttering some composite remarks about taking opportunities and making a new pot of coffee. I sensed somehow I owed him one for that, or perhaps he did it out of kindness for Gordon. Either way, I had no more excuses.

"Why are you here, Dr. Mackenzie?" He was watching me carefully, perhaps sensing more upsetting news.

"I was near the sawmill when Meredith . . . had her accident. I've given my statement."

Gordon combed long fingers through his grey hair, looking ten years older than when I saw him last. "The police were waiting for me when I arrived at lunchtime. It doesn't seem real somehow."

"It gets worse," I said in a low voice, and looked down at my feet. "I didn't lie to you about my reason for coming here. I am writing a book on the effects of land expropriation." I steeled myself and looked back up at him. "But there's something else I haven't told you yet." I got up and faced the window. "There's really no easy way to say this so I'll just get it over with." Turning back, I looked him in the eye. " 'Fan' is only my nickname—it's short for Farran. My mother came from Farran's Point. Her name was Leslie Mackenzie." I stopped for a moment to let that sink in.

"I remember Leslie," he said slowly, watching me again. "Why would your mother's identity be upsetting to me, Dr. Mackenzie?"

"Not my mother. My father." I sat back down in the chair beside him. "Gordon, my father was Hal Leonard, your brother. I'm your niece."

I had expected almost any reaction from him at this stage—anger, disbelief, even scorn. But I never thought of laughter. The hysterical giggle that I'd squelched earlier bubbled up in him, coming in waves until he had to wipe his eyes. I wondered when Strauss would make his re-entrance.

"I'm sorry," Gordon said finally. "It's just that what you say is absolutely impossible. And the day's been hell since I got up. Early traffic in Toronto, construction all the way here. I'm full of doughnuts and greasy chicken. And Meredith is dead, and you're here telling me this." He shook his head.

"It's the truth," I persisted. "When you're feeling better, I can show you my birth certificate and tell you the background. Then maybe you can tell me about my father—and why he was killed," I added.

For a long moment, Gordon said nothing. He looked at me and saw something that seemed to change his mind. What was it Meredith had said? *You look like your father. I wonder Gordon didn't see it.* Just about then, I think he finally did.

I lay in bed that next morning, thinking it was Saturday and I had no plans. The book did not call me, so I made myself a large pot of tea and took it out on the porch. The sunrise was breathtaking. With almost nothing to disturb it from one end of the river to the other, the new sun painted its ribbons of colour right across the sky. The morning star hung dead centre. Two loons dived for breakfast just off the beach, but the goose battalion was not along yet.

I drank the hot tea gratefully, thinking back to so many mornings of Mother and me hanging over our mugs in companionable silence. *Just like a creme rinse for your mind,* she would sometimes say after her first sip. *Takes the tangles out.*

I was the only one Mother ever really relaxed with that way.

Although a beautiful woman, she never remarried. I thought she had done this for my comfort, but as my adult years went on I wondered that she never seemed to want that special relationship and the companionship it provides. But then I was one to talk. One bad apple in university and I had literally closed the doors to anything permanent. Like Mother, I never wanted for attention—but love? I had lost my taste for that particular form of self-annihilation.

Meredith had called Harper Mackenzie a "trader" and mentioned that he had the best instincts for deals and poker. I allowed myself a slow smile, remembering my mother's unorthodox rise into mediations. It had started innocently enough: Our church got involved with a local issue and Mother ended up heading the committee that stared down city hall. After that, she was asked to help with other municipal groups, and went back to school part time to get her certification. For someone who had spent years at home with me, Mother showed a talent for negotiating that training could never supply. Now I knew she came by it honestly. I would have to ask Ruth to tell me more about Harper, if she ever spoke to me again.

I sat there, wrapped in a blanket and my thoughts. The stillness was music in itself. I let it fill my mind, pushing out the memories of yesterday for a little while. This solitude, this being alone here away from what I was back home was both disturbing and healing to me. I sensed many things trying to push to the surface, things I had kept from the light of self-honesty for years. But this wasn't the time for introspection. I had come here for answers. I had to keep my focus on that.

And then the bird came, cutting across the middle sky with surgical precision. Long-necked, long-beaked, pterodactyl wings spread impervious to the morning wind, long legs thrust straight out behind with knobby knees that would have been silly on any other creature. It landed without a sound in the shallows of my beach and stood, aloof and motionless for several minutes. The goose people at the sanctuary would later help me identify it as a Great Blue Heron, possibly the most beautiful and graceful thing I have ever seen. I grew up feeding the swans in Riverside Park in Preston, but this vision faded all others from my mind.

Deciding I meant him no harm, Mr. Heron (as I grew to call him) slowly walked his way through the water to where he thought the pickings looked good and stood there on one leg imitating a plant. I admired his patience and ability to be so still. Eventually, I had to answer nature's call that is loudest after a whole pot of tea and rose to leave. He looked at me and his eyes were riveting—glittering black and bottomless. When I returned, he was gone.

I had received no answer from Lynn Holmes to my message, but that was understandable. Gordon had said he would call me when he was ready and I would leave it that way for a while. I'd tap danced on his life enough for one week. Ruth wouldn't be good to talk to until after Meredith's funeral, but I would try again. For a best friend, she hadn't been too happy to hear that Leslie Mackenzie had lived. I wondered why.

I walked out to grab my copy of the *Citizen* and waved to the healthy retirees as they power-walked past my driveway. Then I saw a jogger approaching and, just in time, realized it was Gordon. I scuttled into the cottage and watched him go by from behind the curtains of the front window until his red shorts disappeared around a bend in the road.

I read the paper while eating my low-fat breakfast of bacon and eggs. VILLAGERS THREATEN SUICIDE OVER DAM—RESIDENTS READY TO DROWN THEMSELVES IF PROJECT PROCEEDS. The story referred to the massive Sardar Sarovar Dam Project in India, but it connected in my head. The news files I had read in the last few months made little mention of protests or group action from the villages to stop the St. Lawrence Project. But I knew the answer to that one from my own work. The 1960s hadn't happened yet. Government was still seen as benevolent, progress as something you didn't stand in the way of, and big business as being good for all. Not the evil entities responsible for so many imaginative conspiracies they are today.

Evil. Wickedness. I knew one person here who would be comfortable, even pleased to talk about wickedness. I guess I had plans for today after all.

But first there was one stop I had to make.

The St. Lawrence Valley Union Cemetery sits on a rise at the junction of Highway No. 2 and Wales Road. The latter once led to the village that started as a train station for Dickinson's Landing but in 1860 was named for its most famous visitor—Albert Edward, Prince of Wales and eldest son of Queen Victoria. At the bottom of the hill between the graves and the river, I could see a few valiant pieces of the old Wales Road still holding back the weeds. Between the shoreline and a large, heavily wooded island lay a smaller island covered in bush—the only part of the village of Wales still above water.

The cemetery still looked new and immaculate, with only a small portion of very old graves. These were the ones disinterred and moved here at the time of the Seaway. As I wandered around, I saw names on the newer graves that I remembered from my research for my book: Martin, Harrison, Brown. It was building to be a hot day, but the river managed to comb a breeze through my hair.

I found the grave in the northeast section, not far from the fence that divides the main area from the Jewish burial ground. The tombstone was new, of course, and the inscription was simple:

Harold William Leonard
June 19, 1940
1958
Finally, at rest

Graves never do anything for me. Many times I sat at Mother's grave in the Woodlawn Cemetery in Cambridge, with so much to say. But there was no feeling there, no connection, no matter how hard I tried. It was just a stone in a rock garden, as was I.

That morning produced the same nothing in me—in this case, even less. I had no memories of this person, only questions. And a faded photograph of a young man less than half my age who seemed to my eyes only a boy. Certainly not someone I could call Father.

And I would always see him like that. Murder had granted him the terrible beauty of being forever young.

I turned and saw Gordon standing behind me, watching me intently. The thought crossed my mind like a tiny spider that he had followed me here, although I could see no reason why. An uncertain smile moved over his face, stopping just below his eyes.

"I come here every Saturday," he said abruptly, nodding at the grave. "I'm still trying to come to grips with this. And now you're here. I certainly never expected that."

I found myself temporarily out of appropriate replies, so I waited. Gordon looked out across the river.

"That small island in front was the site of St. David's Anglican Church. The water wouldn't have covered it, even at first. It could still be there as a tribute to the villages, but Hydro tore it down. Probably thought it would be more of a painful reminder." He turned back and gave me a long look. "I thought it was all in the past where it belonged, but here we are. You're Hal's daughter—the only family I have. We have to talk sometime. Would you come for supper in the next few days if I call you?"

I could see I wasn't the only person struggling with this situation.

"I'd like that," I said. "Thank you."

He gave me a curt nod and turned to go. "Your grandfather's grave is two rows over and down some. The older Leonard tombstones, including your grandmother's, are in the Memorial at the Village, but I expect you've already been there."

Gordon walked away, dignified, resentful, the last of my family—and still a suspect for my father's murder. If Meredith had been murdered and if it were connected to Hal's death somehow, then Gordon fell to the bottom of the list, having been on the 401 at the time. I still had no feelings toward him one way or the other, except as a link to my ambiguous past. However, he *was* my uncle and it would be nice to come out of this with someone to call family.

I set my flowers on my father's grave, a totally inadequate tribute to someone who, stranger or not, was half of me. My father's death was the big question, but the answer would come only from understanding his life.

"*Finally, at rest*," I read aloud. "Not yet, Hal. Not yet."

On this second trip to Ingleside, I was not so lost and had the luxury of truly looking around me. Names from the Lost Villages did overtime with the roads and streets here, but I was getting the hang of it. If the name ended in "Drive," "Street," or "Avenue," it was a namesake only (I must admit, "Farran Drive" has a nice ring to it). If it ended in "Road," it was the remains of the real thing. On my way to the cemetery, I had passed Farran's Point Road and Aultsville Road, both now ending where they intersected Highway No. 2

instead of leading into the villages for which they were named. Farran's Point Road led into Farran Park—a beach and campsite. Aultsville Road led into the Upper Canada Migratory Bird Sanctuary. Next week I would follow them both to see what was still left of the past, if anything.

Today I hoped to talk about wickedness with a little old lady, quietly retired in a small town and still connected with her church after a lifetime of active service—in short, an expert. I wouldn't go so far as to group Alice Hoffman with Miss Jane Marple, but she would have to do. For my part, I needed to tread carefully. The first rule of gossip is the willingness to give something as good as you get. Alice would most certainly ask me about my own wickedness. And I had to remember that Alice Hoffman could somehow be involved with my father's death through Ruth's close friendship with my mother. If Alice hadn't murdered him herself, it was still very possible that someone she knew and/or cared about did.

Luck was with me that morning. Ruth had gone for the day to Montreal to see her daughter and Alice was alone with Sarah. This the latter offered without asking when I appeared at the door after seeing that Ruth's car was gone.

"Terrible thing about Miss Murphy," said Sarah with undisguised relish. "Horrible way to die. And it must have been an awful shock for you to see that . . . "

The opening offered was unmistakable, but I didn't take it. "Is Mrs. Hoffman upset? Perhaps now isn't a good time to drop by."

"Alice?" Sarah looked over her shoulder toward the living room where you could hear the sound of a TV turned up loud. "Nothing bothers that woman. Tough as nails and always has been, my mother says. Come in. She'll be glad of the company, though she always pretends otherwise."

Alice Hoffman sat in her particular chair, enthralled with a house renovation program. I had expected either a quilting show or perhaps *World Wrestling Federation*. Maybe it wasn't on in the daytime. I was glad to see the rug hooking was nowhere in sight. I hoped to have her complete attention—if I could disconnect her from the TV.

"Alice, Dr. Mackenzie is back to see you again," Sarah said loudly, with good reason to do so this time.

"I can hear you," Alice snapped back, clicking the room into a roaring silence. "I'm only old. Not deaf."

"I'll get you some tea," Sarah returned in a soothing voice and I marvelled at her patience. "Dr. Mackenzie?"

This time I accepted the tea, and took a good look around the room. Alice waved me to a seat on the green-gold couch that was flanked on both sides by matching chairs. The lamps were ornate and the coffee table mirrored glass. With the light panelled walls and the mustard-brown carpet, the retro effect was complete. I guessed they had purchased new furnishings for the front room just after moving here and had never changed them. Yet what I was seeing was not a stagnation of life. It was an attitude I had run into many times back home in people that had either survived the Great Depression or were raised by someone who did: Buy only what you need, take care of what you have, and don't piss your money down the drain amusing yourself with new toys every week.

"Meredith's funeral is Monday here at St. Matthew's Presbyterian," Alice said, cutting to the chase in her usual fashion. "Are you up to goin'?"

"Yes, if you think it would be all right . . . considering."

"Of course it would be all right," Alice glowered at me. "Meredith grew up with your family. Why wouldn't it be all right? *You* didn't push her in, did you?"

A laugh escaped me and I shook my head.

"No, Alice, I didn't. You seem certain someone did. The police haven't ruled out an accident or heart attack yet that I know of."

She sniffed. "Accident? Meredith worked at the Village from its opening. Why would she slip and fall now? And never a heart attack. Meredith was always into sports and games. Strong as an ox."

"Still," I said, trying to hold off the memory, "it does happen sometimes out of the blue to someone you'd never think of."

For a millisecond, the woman's eyes softened. "Yes," she admitted, looking over at a picture on the mantle. "I lost Harland that way. He died in my arms."

I got up and walked over to the picture. It showed a nice-looking man in his sixties who looked very much like Ruth. I said as much to Alice.

"He was like Ruth inside, too. He understood her in a way I never did. Still don't. My son Tom is more like me. We got on with things after Harland died. But in some ways, I don't think Ruth ever did."

I sat near Alice again on the couch. The chair she sat in looked markedly older and more used than the matching set that filled the room, despite being covered with an afghan. I wondered if she'd brought the chair from Farran's Point.

"You've been a survivor your whole life, haven't you?" I asked.

"What other choice is there?" Alice shrugged. "Things happen. You go on. My family lived through two world wars and the Depression. I had Ruth when Harland was serving overseas and I had to move back with my parents till he came home. Then the Seaway took everything away. You don't get through things like that by whinin'."

Sarah brought us each a mug of tea and I thanked her. Shortly after, I heard the vacuum running upstairs.

"Tell me about Farran's Point, Alice. What did it look like?"

The old lady looked out the window and half a century back.

"It was the prettiest village, you know. One of the smaller ones along the Front."

"The Front?"

"The stretch of towns and farms between Cornwall and Morrisburg. It's all gone now, under the water. Farran's Point had one of the locks of the old seaway canal system, Lock No. 22. It was always well kept, and the biggest one on the St. Lawrence River. Everyone used to wave the boats through from the park."

"The park was beside the lock?"

"Yes. Farran's Park. There was a little pavilion up there and in the evenings there would be some kind of music. Sometimes people would play the nickelodeon, but often someone would bring their fiddle or guitar. We had our socials and picnics in the park, and Sunday School when the weather was nice. There was no real baseball diamond, but the kids played baseball there anyway. I often sold drinks with the Women's Institute. It was just a lovely little place. The pavilion ended up on the Newington Fairgrounds." The smile that had slowly lighted up her face suddenly left. "The park was where we waited for the water to come at the floodin'."

"I've seen pictures of the Longue Sault Rapids," I offered. "They looked beautiful."

Alice turned to give me a hard look. "The Longue Sault was more than beautiful. It was wild and dangerous. You had to have respect for it. It had no time for fools that thought they could outsmart the river, and most of them died tryin'. We never thought they'd really slow the rapids down, you know, and then didn't they take them away. But it took those smart engineers three tries to do it. The river kept chewin' up what they did to her."

"But they finally did," I said quietly. "It must have been strange to see them dry and empty."

"When the water was gone," Alice remembered, "people took to walkin' out amongst the big stones that had made the water white. My son Tom begged Harland until the poor man had to take him. But I didn't go. It just didn't seem right. And it was so damn quiet there after," she added, "people had trouble sleepin'."

We fell silent for a few moments.

"It wasn't a big place," Alice said finally. "But it was a friendly place. Everybody knew everybody. We had St. John's Presbyterian Church at the Point, and many people went there whether they were Presbyterian or not. Like us. And people knew each other more. Everyone would come out at night to get the evening mail from the train. Or just to watch the boats lock through. We got streets and lights and new towns from Hydro, but we lost our river. We lost our ways."

The vacuum stopped upstairs. I felt myself coming back to the present and struggled to hold onto the threads of the past.

"Alice," I took the plunge, "tell me about my family."

She looked at me but did not reply for some minutes. I wondered if she were sizing me up or deciding her strategy. Probably both.

"Your mother had gypsy blood in her," Alice began, "or at least we all thought so. And when people get to thinkin' something about you, it's as good as done."

"Gypsy?" I echoed incredulously, with visions of brightly painted wagons rolling through my mind.

"Yes. Wanderers and vagrants that used to travel through the area, along with the homeless tramps during the Depression. They'd camp in a laneway off the No. 2 for a few days, sell things, barter for food. We kept our children inside and the doors locked. The gypsies had pretty much disappeared from the Front by the end of the war, but they had moved more north and were settlin' down. We figured that's where Harper met your grandmother and married her, child and all, though none of us had the courage to ask. He'd been alone and a loner 'long as we knew him, and one day doesn't he come home from tradin' with a wife and child. No warnin'. They seemed happy, though," she admitted at the end.

"So Harper was my mother's stepfather?"

"As far as we knew," Alice said cryptically. "The old gossips used to say they weren't married at all, that she had just come to keep house for him really. Jealousy talkin', I'd say. Your grandmother Evian was a fine lookin' woman."

It was a pretty safe bet that Alice spoke of the "old gossips" from front-line experience, but gossip was what I'd come to hear. Gossip from a half century before.

"What happened to her?"

"Evie was run down on the highway one evening on her way back from the river," said Alice matter-of-factly. "They never found the driver. Leslie had stayed behind with Harper for somethin' and they found her when they left." The old lady shook her head. "I swear the whole village heard him. We all came runnin'. Big man like that, and he cried like a baby. And I can still see your ma, twelve years old, standin' there like a stone statue, lookin' like she didn't know which was harder to believe. She'd never been much of a talker, and after that it was even less. They sure seemed unlucky, as time went on."

"Was it bad luck, Alice," I asked, "or wickedness?"

Her eyes took on a gleam. "Wickedness? Why would you ask me that?"

"Meredith told me my family was torn apart by wickedness. Did she mean my mother?"

"No," replied Alice firmly. "Harper was a hard man, but a good one. He was a good father to Leslie in his own way. I'll say it now— I never warmed up to your ma, but she wasn't bad so much as grown wild. Needed discipline. She was a bad influence on my Ruth. But what they got was just plain bad luck. The wickedness . . ."

"Yes?" I prompted.

"The wickedness didn't come till your father brought it with him."

PERON SAYS ARGENTINA REVOLT CRUSHED

COMPENSATION PLAN GIVEN MIXED WELCOME
Rehab Formula To Receive Baptism In Iroquois Area

POWER PROJECT MAPS SLATED FOR TOURISTS

June 1955
The Cornwall *Standard-Freeholder*

Damn chainsaws.

Alice Hoffman's mouth pressed itself into a line grimmer than usual as she walked up Farran's Point Road to the little house on the corner. The sound of trees being cut came from a distance, a constant reminder of the full-scale destruction under way everywhere you looked. Traffic on the highway was relentless now, with work on the dam going ahead twenty-four hours a day, seven days a week. Serial numbers, too, on all the houses like they were criminals. Land agents popping up out of bushes when you least expected them, trying to catch you at a bad time. Now people who hadn't even signed their papers got up in the morning to see that Hydro had already started cutting their trees. A beautiful little cherry tree that Harland said could be taken to the new town was gone without so much as a by-your-leave. No sweet perfume through the kitchen window next spring, she thought.

Opening the picket gate, Alice breached the forbidding welcome of the funny little house with its many gables that had been added on as the years had dictated need. The house had appeared seemingly overnight on a lot empty of life for years after a destructive fire. No one knew if Harper Mackenzie had outright purchased the place— and no one had thought it prudent to ask him. Mackenzie was a black-haired Scot with a temper known through the three counties. He had a bad leg from his days in the lumber camps up north; rumour had it he'd killed a man in the fight that left him that way. Those along the Front who didn't respect him, feared him. He was called a trader to his face and a junkman to his back. It was no mind to Mackenzie either way.

Alice didn't fear Harper, but she didn't relish this conversation. Thank God she had God on her side.

Her knock was answered almost immediately. Mackenzie eyed Alice with reserve, but she could smell no whisky on him.

"Harper, we need to talk," she said without waiting for a greeting.

The big man shrugged, then led the way to the kitchen. "What's Les done now?" he asked over his shoulder.

Alice took the chair offered, quickly scanning the kitchen as she did so. It was small and simply done, but it was surprisingly clean. Better than she'd expected with no mother to look after the two of them. Leslie was just a girl, let alone a woman.

"Nothin' Harp," she replied, "but it is your girl I come to talk about. And don't brush me off," she added as he tried to speak. "I know you've countenanced no help since Evie died, but I've got something to say and I'm sayin' it."

There was a hint of a smile in Mackenzie's eyes as he poured out two coffees, but it didn't appear on his face. "Go on," he said gruffly, joining her at the table.

"I know you've been doin' good by Leslie since Evie died, and the girl's been fine, but," Alice hesitated, "but you can't be both father and mother to that girl. She's fourteen, almost a young woman. She needs an older woman to turn to for direction."

"Are you suggestin' that I get married again?"

Alice had the grace to blush. "Well, no, that is, I—I didn't mean that. Not that it wouldn't be fine for you. It's been two years since the accident. But I meant something a little simpler, Harp. Leslie should come to church."

The big man lost any trace of a smile. "I'm not a church-goin' man, Alice. You know that. And I've got nothin' nice to say to God right now. I can't tell Leslie to go."

"The church could give her some support," Alice persisted. "We have our girls' group, and the women would be happy to help Leslie find her way."

"Her way or your way?"

Alice felt two hot spots appear on her cheeks. "Leslie needs more people in her life, Harper. Ruth has been spendin' time with her at school lately with projects and what not, and Ruth says Leslie keeps to herself at school. She has no friends, and she needs to be part of a group. *Things are changin' here. In a few years, Leslie will be out on her own, maybe even married. She needs to know how to handle herself as a woman, and that's something you can't teach her."*

Mackenzie got to his feet, indicating the conversation was ending. "There's nothin' wrong with Les. She's fine as she is. Maybe I can't teach her to dance or make eyes at the boys, but she's clean and dressed. She goes to school and gets good grades. She's a good girl and she'll do just fine out there."

"Where am I goin', Harp?"

Both adults turned to look at the young girl who stood in the open doorway.

Alice thought that if she didn't know Leslie was Harper's girl, she would have thought it was a boy standing there. The girl was wearing a shirt and slacks rolled up, with no shoes, grasping a fishing rod in one hand. Her hair was completely tucked under a baseball cap, and she was generally covered with mud.

Evie had been a great beauty, and it was clear that Leslie was taking after her mother. Alice thought of Ruth with a pang of envy. Leslie hung up her cap and thick, black hair fell past her waist in high contrast to the short bobs all the other girls sported these days. Very fair skin set off two green eyes that always made one feel as though she could look right through you. Leslie was tall for her age, but graceful, especially on the baseball field in the park.

She looked suspiciously from her stepfather to Alice.

"Are you sendin' me somewhere?"

"No, Les," Mackenzie reassured her. "Mrs. Hoffman stopped in to ask you to join the girls' group at the church. Says it would be a good social outin' for you, with people your own age, and older ladies you could talk to about . . . things."

Leslie looked at Alice, with mutiny in her eyes. "Thank you, Mrs. Hoffman," she said politely, "but I have friends at school. And I talk to Harp about things."

Alice nodded and got up from the table. "Well, think about it, Leslie. We could use your help at the church."

Leslie smiled thinly and said nothing. She took the fish she had caught to the sink and began cleaning them silently. Alice looked at Harper, who shrugged.

"Have you signed your papers yet, Harper?" she changed the subject.

"No, and I don't see to in the near future," he said. "I want replacement value. They haven't come close yet."

The land agents didn't know who they were up against in this case, Alice thought with a small grain of satisfaction. If anyone in the Front could stare them down, it would be the old trader himself.

Harper unexpectedly walked her to the front gate, then paused as if he had something on his mind.

"Alice, I meant what I said about I'm takin' good care of Les," he began.

"Of course. You're doin' your best," she said soothingly. "Anyone can see that."

"But if I was gone, she'd be alone. If that ever happened, you'd look after my girl, wouldn't you?"

"Well, I . . . of course I would," Alice said.

"Promise me?"

His tone was serious enough that she looked hard at him. There was more being left unsaid than spoken here, and she wanted to ask him what was going on. "Promise," she said simply.

He nodded, satisfied, and opened the gate. As Alice left, a red truck pulled into the yard. Gordon Leonard got out on one side, Hal on the other.

"Dad said you wanted this scrap iron, Mr. Mackenzie," said Gordon, wiping his forehead. "Where do you want us to put it?"

"Back there in the far corner," came the curt reply. "Tell your pa I'll settle with him first of next week."

Gordon looked for Hal to help him, and found him on the porch talking with Leslie.

"I'll have a delivery next week again," the boy was saying. "Why don't you come with me to see it for yourself?"

"Hal," called Gordon testily. "Work first, play after." He shot a glance at Harper, whose mouth had formed a thin line. Leslie flushed.

No, thought Alice, not good. That boy was getting off track without his mother there to keep him in line. Heard about troubles with the cash, and troubles with Bill Strauss's wife. Wouldn't want him around Ruth. Now Gordon, on the other hand, was a prospect.

"Evenin', Gordon," said Alice. "How's your pa keepin' these days?"

"Just fine, Mrs. Hoffman. I'll tell him you asked."

"With a house full of men, you must miss a woman's meal," she purred. "We'll have to have you out for supper sometime soon."

"Thanks, ma'am," Gordon replied hurriedly. "That would be nice." He hopped into the truck and drove to the far side of the yard. Hal reluctantly joined him and they piled the scrap in a heap before leaving with a beep and a wave.

"Ruth and her friends will be at the park this afternoon, I think, Leslie," Alice said as she moved to leave. "I'm sure they'd be happy to have you join them." The girl nodded without reply. Oh, well, they couldn't say Alice hadn't tried. She'd tell Ruth today that she'd done her best.

Alice was a few houses away when she saw a strange figure coming up the road toward her. It was an old man with a white beard and black cap, wearing a long black coat. He walked slowly but steadily with his hands in the large pockets of the coat, as dignified as an Anglican priest.

"Stewart Cassidy," she muttered in disbelief. She hadn't seen him in town for years, although it was said that he came over from his home on Croil Island for supplies sometimes—in his little canoe at the worst hours and in the worst weather. An old-school river rat who never worried about getting by, Cassidy was one of only a few that ever survived shooting the Longue Sault Rapids. Probably helped that he was stone drunk and passed out in the bottom of his boat that was being towed home. The boat cut loose and Cassidy woke up on the other side of the south channel that had chewed up so many other small crafts.

Alice nodded to the man as he passed, and sniffed to herself. She'd seen him last three years ago when the Ladies' League had gone berry picking on Croil Island, and they'd wandered into Stewart's claimed area. Then she'd seen more of him than she liked when he stripped himself stark naked and chased the lot of them back to their boats. Margaret McLaren had lost her new sun hat in the rush and steadfastly refused to go back for it.

And then for just a moment, Alice felt a twinge of pity for the old man. The river was his whole life. What would happen to him when the Deep Water Project was finished? Where would he go? He was too old to change now. She turned to watch him go on and was amazed to see him turn in at the gate to Harper's house. She looked with open curiosity as the old man knocked on the door and was let *inside. Moments later, Leslie came out and headed for the road. Seeing Alice standing there, the girl headed in the opposite direction.*

The woman turned and marched indignantly down the road. That was fine with her. She'd wash her hands of the girl and be done with.

Unless something happened to Harper. But it wouldn't.

"Vroom. Vroom." Alice could hear her son playing construction in the living room. Busy packing food for the family dinner at her sister's, she waited for the inevitable.

"Tommy, why can't you do that in your room?" came Ruth's voice impatiently.

"Vroom. Bang. Can't. Not enough room in there. You'll have to leave the area, Miss. You're on eggsprodiated land."

"Mother!" Ruth flounced into the kitchen, movie magazine in hand. She was a tall, slim girl with fine features, but no beauty. Still, Alice took comfort that her daughter wore her homemade copies of the latest fashion with grace. "Why did you ever get him that Seaway construction set for Christmas? Every time I turn around, I'm trippin' over dams and rivers and houses. When do we get the living room back?"

"Now, Ruth," said Alice practically, "every boy in the county wanted one of those. I was lucky to get one. It's educational for him. Helps him understand what's goin' on."

Ruth rolled her eyes. Harland came in from the back yard with a newspaper in his hand.

"So what do you think, Alice, about movin' our house?" he said.

"It sounds so incredible," she answered. "Do you think they could move this house?"

"I don't know." He scratched his head. "Seems not all houses can be. But we'll look into it, if that's what you'd want."

"What are you talking about?" Ruth asked.

"Movin' our house to New Town No. 1, instead of takin' cash and buildin' something new," said her father. "Hydro's got a new idea about movin' people's homes as a fair way to keep what you've got."

"How can they do that?"

"A company from New Jersey," he answered, spreading the newspaper out on the table. There was a picture of a large truck with a house on its back. "They've got this huge monster that will pick your house up as gentle as a baby and set it down the same on the new foundation." Harland smiled expectantly.

"But I thought we were going to build a new house," Ruth blurted out, "and get rid of this old place."

"You mind your tongue, Ruth," said Alice curtly. "Your grandfather built this 'old place.' It's been the only home your father has ever known. And you might be helpin' us more for the dinner instead of keepin' your nose stuck in those silly magazines."

"Ruthie," her father cut in gently, "it won't just be a new house or a new street. This whole area is goin' to change. We can't imagine it yet, even though we've seen the maps. It might be a good thing to have something familiar to call home when it's all said and done."

"You just don't understand," the girl said, suddenly near tears. "I want change. Big change. I want to live in a town that's shiny and new—not like this place. Or this house." She turned and ran from the room.

Alice moved to follow her, but Harland placed a hand on her arm.

"Let her go, Alice. It's hard enough bein' that age without all this goin' on. She doesn't mean it."

Alice didn't go after Ruth, but she was unconvinced. Her daughter was getting harder to deal with all the time. And after the summer, she would move on to the Continuation School in Aultsville—at least until the town was moved. The woman went quietly to the door of the kitchen and watched her son play construction. At least her boy was still her boy, young enough to see it all as great fun. As for the rest of us, she thought, I have no idea what the future holds.

"Vroom." Tommy picked up speed with his bulldozer, plowing it into one of the toy block houses. It scattered the pieces to the far corners of the room.

It was a perfect June evening. Harland was working the evening shift at the Howard Smith paper mill in Cornwall and wouldn't be home until after midnight. Alice served cold refreshments from the

Women's Institute stand, watching her son run around Farran's Park with the pack of neighbourhood boys. Ruth was dolled up as usual, standing around the dance pavilion with her friends trying to look bored. Someone had brought a fiddle and some couples were dancing gamely to the music. In the distance, she could see a canal boat approaching the lock. Nothing could disturb this kind of peace.

Hearing a murmur, Alice looked over to see Leslie Mackenzie coming through the small crowd alone. She was wearing a plain red shift dress, but it was a dress. Her hair hung loose down her back, and she held her head high like royalty being lead to execution. Her feet were bare. Ruth saw Leslie and left her friends for a moment. The two girls spoke, then Leslie shook her head and continued down to the river. Ruth shrugged and walked over to her mother.

"Leave it be, Ruth," Alice said, pouring her daughter a lemonade. "You're a good girl to try but she isn't worth it. She'll be a loner like Harp. Not really one of us, anyway. Her kind's not from around here."

"When you talk like that, Mother, I understand how she feels," Ruth retorted.

"Now there's someone to talk to." Alice raised her head to look over Ruth's shoulder. "Isn't that Gordon Leonard? I always think how he looks so much like that Tony Curtis you're so fond of."

Ruth rolled her eyes and turned around, then straightened. Gordon was crossing the park with his brother Hal. Alice shook her head. Imagine the nerve of that Hal to come here after what happened with that cheque. The Bank of Montreal spent two days a week at Aultsville and two at Farran's Point. Whispers in the village spoke of forgery and Eric Leonard maintaining it was a misunderstanding with the bank. Possibly, but Alice didn't think so.

The boys came up to the stand, Gordon seeming reluctant to be there.

"Evenin' boys," said Alice to Gordon, as she poured their drinks. "You remember my daughter Ruth?"

"Yes, ma'am," said Gordon, digging for change. "Evenin' Ruth."

"I've got it." Hal flashed a smile at Ruth and dropped some coins in her mother's hand.

"Make sure he pays cash, Mrs. Hoffman," a voice said behind them. "Don't take anything on paper."

A group of young men stood with arms crossed, staring defiantly at Hal. Alice recognized the one that had spoken as Desmond Shaler, whose father ran a gas station on Highway No. 2.

Hal set his drink back down slowly. "And what might you be meanin' by that, Shaler?" he said quietly.

"You know what I mean. When I heard about the problem at the bank, it didn't surprise me any. The cheque you wrote for last month's bill bounced on my dad. He had to go callin' your dad for the money."

"That's a lie. Why would it?"

Desmond shrugged. "You tell me. All I know is that you've been up to no good for the last while, and soon you're goin' to go where your dad's money can't buy you out."

Hal made a move toward the boy, but Gordon stopped him.

"Come on, boys," said Alice. "We don't want no fightin' here tonight."

"I've got no fight with him," said Desmond, looking at Gordon, "but I don't want the likes of this one here after him passin' bad money around town."

Alice noticed Leslie coming near out of the corner of her eye. The fiddle music had stopped and people were starting to listen.

Hal thrust his chin up and glared at the boy. "This is a public place, Shaler. I can come here if I want."

"Let's just go, Hal," Gordon murmured. "Maybe this wasn't such a good idea."

"If you're here," said Desmond, taking a step closer to Hal, "it's just to cause trouble. Aultsville not good enough on a Saturday night?"

"I'm here and I'm stayin' to do what I came for."

"And what is that?"

Hal looked around and his eyes found Leslie, standing apart from the others. "I guess I came to dance," he said quietly. Then he pushed past Shaler and headed for the pavilion.

"Then you came for nothing, Leonard," Desmond called after him. "Ain't no one goin' to dance with you here."

Hal didn't reply. He walked past the couples that stood uncertainly on the small dance floor and put a coin in the nickelodeon. After a minute, the golden sound of Nat King Cole's Mona Lisa filled the evening air, but no one moved to dance. Hal

came down the steps toward Ruth's friends and passed them,
stopping in front of Leslie.

"Miss Mackenzie, will you dance with me?"

Leslie's face flushed red, obviously taken off guard. Ruth
glanced at Gordon, who looked distinctly nervous. Desmond and his
friends snickered.

Leslie looked down at her feet. "I—I can't. I'm not dressed for
it."

To her horror, Alice saw Ruth lean down and pull her sandals
off. "Ruth!" she hissed. "Stay out of it."

Ruth ignored her mother and handed the shoes to Leslie, who
didn't move. "Go on," she said. "Dance."

Leslie looked at Hal, the boys behind him, and Mrs. Hoffman.
Then slowly she took the sandals and slipped her feet into them. Hal
led her to the empty dance floor, and took her easily in his arms. She
seemed unsure at first, but quickly learned to follow his lead.

She danced with her chin up, eyes cast down. Hal never took his
eyes off her. And every eye in the place was on them both.

The music faded. I was back in Alice's living room on the green-
gold couch.

"That's how it started," she said, as though to herself. "My
Ruth became Leslie's best friend—and look what it got her. Leslie
took up with Hal Leonard, never mind the rumours. All these years
we thought it bought her an early grave. Now we find out it's the
other way around."

"Whatever happened to Stewart Cassidy?" I took a sip of my
tea that had grown cold.

"No one really knows," Alice shrugged. "He made himself
even more scarce during the Project. Someone said they saw him
once in Ingleside when they were still movin' houses in, but I don't
believe it. Something would have to be awfully important to take
him that far from the river. After the floodin', he was never seen
again."

Probably went back to what was left of Croil Island to die in
peace, I thought sadly. Single-handedly survived everything life sent
him—and then the Seaway came.

"Do you have any children, Dr. Mackenzie?"

The question caught me right off guard. I felt a slow flush creep over my cheeks as I struggled to word my reply. Shooting a glance at Alice, I saw she was pleased with the effect and already had her answer.

"I think I told you," I stumbled. "I've never married."

"As we both know," she returned primly, "that isn't always necessary."

"I've never had the pleasure of raising a child," I said guardedly.

Sarah saved my behind by marching in, teapot in hand. "Refills?" she chirped.

"No," I said, rising. "I've been here long enough. I don't want to tire Mrs. Hoffman."

I took my leave, promising to attend the funeral.

I had an early supper that day, and spent the evening walking my share of the beach. The water and sand were still quite cold, but it was beautiful nonetheless. I thought I saw Mr. Heron commuting eastward at the end of his day, but he didn't stop. The geese were everywhere.

At first I picked up only interesting rocks. Then I took a closer look at what else was there.

Bricks. Old bits of terra cotta house bricks worn smooth by the river. And pieces of old blue and white china with the pattern intact. Although everything had been razed to the ground during the Project, I knew that people back then didn't use dumps. They burned and smashed their waste in backyard piles. I glanced over at the old farmhouse several lots away, and then back to the shards in my hand. Small pieces of lives long gone.

Pieces are all we are really given to go on. A lifetime spent with my mother had left me looking for pieces of who she really was. And in my search to understand my father's death, I was now trying to find enough pieces of Hal Leonard to bring him back to life.

"Will I ever really know you, Hal?" I asked the sunset.

The shriek of an evening train whistle brought me back to earth. The sun was going down and the night's chill approached from the river. I curled my fingers around the blue and white shards, inexplicably feeling I'd received an answer to my question.

I brought in one large piece of brick and made it a centrepiece for the kitchen table. The shards I placed in a bowl on my nightstand. Perhaps because they were real, because I could hold them in my hands, these pieces gave me the first feeling of hope about this personal excavation I was trying to pull off. I knew colleagues that spent years looking for a site before hitting pay dirt, and remembered how they'd all said that you always seem to find that one trinket, one shard, one bone just when you are ready to give up on the dig.

Alice's question about children came back to me as I drifted off to sleep. Somewhere out there was another large piece of me, not lost but given away. Was she even now searching for pieces of me?

I slept with a strange serenity all night and awoke with the sun.

I guess I came to dance, the river whispered in my sleepy ear. I rolled over, and what I had not grasped the night before came to me as a morning revelation.

The train whistle.

I sat bolt upright and ran it through my mind. The small tourist train at the Village shuts down at 5:30 p.m., not sunset. Other sources? A factory? But a train steam whistle is quite distinctive. Trains use horns now, as they have for over thirty years. The crazy thought bubbled to the surface before I could push it away.

The Moccasin?

Chapter 6

Dusk

MEREDITH'S FUNERAL was at eleven o'clock Monday morning. I scraped together some decent clothes and tried to do something with my hair. I knew I'd be a conversation piece for anyone who attended.

I hadn't heard from Gordon yet, but I would see him there. Lynn had never returned my call, so this was an opportunity to touch bases, grim as it was. And perhaps, over egg salad sandwiches at the reception, Ruth and I could set a date for a heart-to-heart.

My mind chattered away to me, trying to muffle the whispers of my guilty heart. I hadn't heard any news on Meredith's autopsy, but wasn't holding out any great hope that she had keeled over from a heart attack. Alice assumed Meredith had been pushed—and I did, too. I remembered the horror and the nausea that day, and the certainty mixed with them that my questions had caused the woman's death. Someone was killing again.

I made it to the church with the stragglers, arriving at the same time as Inspector Strauss. He had traded his uniform for a suit, making him more attractive and formidable at the same time.

"Good morning, Dr. Mackenzie," he said, waiting for me at the bottom of the steps. "Gordon didn't come with you?"

I flushed a little, and shook my head. "We haven't really talked yet, but I've been asked for supper later this week. Alice Hoffman wanted me to come today. Said I should, being a Leonard."

Strauss smiled unexpectedly.

"Alice is right, as usual. You can sit with me, if you'd like."

I nodded and we started up the steps. Strauss took my arm. It was an old-school gesture—and I didn't mind the touch—but I felt like a criminal being led away at the end of a TV show. The church was full inside, but we found a place at the back. Heads began to turn as I sat down. I looked around and found Gordon near the front. He seemed surprised to see me, but nodded a greeting.

I went for small talk with Strauss.

"Has there been any news on the cause of death?" I whispered. He didn't reply for a moment.

"The tests came back negative," he said finally, keeping eyes front. "As far as Toronto is concerned, Meredith was healthy and in control of her senses when she went over the guardrail."

"And an accident seems unlikely," I mused quietly. "So we're left with foul play."

"You seem intent on that, Mackenzie. I find that interesting."

"Call it a gut reaction," I replied. "Alice Hoffman is certain of it, too, and you just said she's usually right. I find *that* interesting."

At that, Strauss turned to me and our eyes met.

"Did I mention that you're not to leave town without letting me know?" he whispered, face unreadable.

The service started. When it finished, the coffin was brought out to the waiting hearse. There would be a short prayer service at the graveside in the Union Cemetery. We filed out of the church and broke into groups on the sidewalk. The bell tolled mournfully, reminding me that I'd read how it was brought from St. John's Presbyterian in Farran's Point. It had probably tolled for my grandmother half a century ago. Strauss moved off to talk with Constable Wiley, who emerged from the crowd. Lynn followed the coffin to the hearse and did not look up. Ruth stayed with her. It was Alice Hoffman who rescued me from my solitude.

"Dr. Mackenzie."

I looked around to see her standing with a walker, surrounded by other elderly ladies. She waved me over.

"I want you to meet some other people from the old days," she said, indicating her friends. "This is Annette Leger, Pauline Martin, Janet Brown, and Nellie Harrison."

There were smiles and handshakes all around. Annette Leger spoke for the group.

"We asked Alice to introduce us, Miss Mackenzie. Except for Nellie, we all lived in Farran's Point. Knew your family quite well. We just wanted to say welcome home."

I felt a lump rise in my throat suddenly—and I am not a throat lumper by nature. Welcome home. What a thought.

"Thank you very much," I managed. "Where are you from, Mrs. Harrison?"

"Aultsville," she said. "I lived just down the road from your grandparents. They were both fine people. If you want to talk about the old days, dear, you call any one of us. That's all we seem to talk about these days, anyway."

"I'd like that," I replied honestly. "Especially about my father. I'd like to get to know the kind of person he was."

There was an uncomfortable moment's silence, until Alice wheeled her walker around.

"I'm goin' in for tea and lunch," she said over her shoulder. "I'm too old to be standin' around cemeteries."

She disappeared into the church and the others followed suit. Nellie was the last to go and she turned back to me before leaving. Her gnarled old hand gripped mine suddenly with surprising strength.

"Your father was a good son to his mother," she said firmly. Then she was gone.

"What have the Weird Sisters been telling you?"

I turned to see Gordon standing there.

"They were quite nice," I protested—being up on my *Macbeth*—and added pointedly, "They welcomed me home. Said I could see them to talk about the old days any time."

He glowered at the church door.

"They seem to forget how their gossip was a big part of Hal's problems. I won't." When I did not reply, he pointed to his car on the road. "If you're going to the cemetery, you can have a lift with me both ways. Are you staying for the lunch?"

I agreed to both and we were soon covering the short trip in silence. This time it felt more companionable than awkward. Perhaps we were getting used to each other.

"Gordon," I said abruptly, "the Village train."

"Yes?"

"It stops its run at 5:30, when the park closes. Do they ever run it in the evening, say for repairs or something?"

He looked understandably confused.

"No, at least I don't think so. Why? Is it important?"

"Not really," I mumbled. "I just . . . wondered."

We stood together through the prayer service for Meredith, a little behind Ruth and Lynn. When it was over, they came up on their way to the cars.

"Lynn, I'm so sorry," I said, feeling the inadequacy of the words. I'd heard the phrase so many times after Mother's death, and each time wondered who I had more sympathy for—the bereaved or the speaker.

"I'll be at the car, Lynn." Ruth flashed a half smile at me and moved away.

"I appreciate your coming, Fan." Lynn looked tired. "I did get your message the other day. I was on the road that morning. But with everything . . . "

"No, no, of course not," I said hurriedly. "It wasn't anything important. I just wanted to talk about the old days with you."

"Of course." She looked around the cemetery. "I remember standing here at Harper's funeral. Leslie looked so horribly alone that day. I wanted to protect her."

"Protect her? From what?"

Lynn glanced at Gordon self-consciously.

"I don't know. Just life, I guess. She had no family left then, and it was a very uncertain time for all of us."

She began to walk to the car, and I followed. Gordon stayed put.

"Meredith came to see me the night before . . . before she died." I explained. Lynn stopped to look at me, and I continued. "She talked about my father's family, but wouldn't go into details. Said it wasn't her place, but she used the word 'wickedness'. Do you know what she meant?"

Lynn hazarded another look at Gordon, but did not reply. We started for the cars again, and I also stayed silent, hoping for an answer.

"I'm here until tomorrow," she said at last. "I have plans for tonight, but I'll be free in the afternoon after the lunch. Will you be home?"

I said yes and gave her directions. When Gordon dropped me back at the church, I passed on the lunch after all. Lynn was coming to the cottage, Ruth was actively avoiding me, and I wasn't up to small talk. Not even for church-lady-style egg salad sandwiches.

Lynn Holmes wore her age well. I judged her to be about Strauss's age—early fifties—but she could have passed for closer to mine. She had brown hair with natural curls that kept falling into her startling blue eyes. While Ruth looked well through good packaging, Lynn simply seemed younger all round. Ruth was silk and linen; Lynn was polyester crêpe.

I offered her a stiff drink as soon as she sat down, figuring she could use one by then. Lynn accepted gratefully. I poured two brandies, put ice in mine, and we sat out by the river. I planned to nurse mine, but when Lynn shot hers back, I followed suit and refilled us both.

"It's been a good forty years, Fan," Lynn began quietly, "and somehow it all seems to be real again. As though it never ended, just waited."

"Because of me?"

She nodded. "Yes, that's part of it. But it's more than that. Ever since your father's body was found, I've been living with one foot in the past, running it all through my mind again. I have the memories of a young girl, but now I'm looking at them with age and experience. It was a big thing that went on, but it seemed pretty straightforward at the time. Now I'm not so sure."

I wasn't sure if she meant the Project or my parents, but I didn't interrupt to ask.

"For instance," she continued, waving her glass at the river, "all this. It's beautiful, but it's synthetic. *It's not real.* I know that what I see is not natural, and maybe that's why I've never accepted it. I was about ten when it started and for kids it was the greatest show on earth. But it came to me just recently that all this time I have only tolerated the changes, as though it's only temporary. Fan, I sit here and I see that the water covers Farran's Point now, but the village is still more real to me than anything in front of my eyes. And I was thirteen when I left. It must have been terribly hard on the older people."

"I've seen mention a few times that many of them didn't live through their first winters in the new towns. The change was too much for them."

"Yes. I can think of three elderly neighbours who caught the flu or developed pneumonia and never recovered. It could have been coincidence, but these people were tough as nails from living hard lives. I remember old Miss McLaren. She was always doing something at the Point. After they moved her house to Ingleside, she just sat day after day on the front porch, looking in the direction of the river. My mother noticed that she didn't put up any preserves that year, for the first time in her life. It was as though she knew she wouldn't need them. Poor lady died right after Christmas."

"How did your parents feel about it?"

"My mother came from Ottawa. She moved to the Point when she married my father, so the ties weren't that deep. My dad was a different story. He grew up there. Loved the rapids, the canal, the lock, the park. It was hard on him, though I don't remember him ever saying anything. He worked at the Howard Smith paper mill in Cornwall, like Ruth's father, so the changes didn't affect his work. Still, he became a little withdrawn, not so ready with a laugh after that. I didn't really think about it at the time."

"How did my mother handle it?" I asked. "I know she wasn't from the area, but in the end she lost her home too, right?"

"Leslie had a lot on her plate through those years," Lynn answered. "She was still getting over losing her mother when the Project started. Then they started tearing everything up. Harper got sick—cancer, I think. She cared for him right through school. He died in . . . the summer of '57. Some business partner came and claimed the house, and Leslie moved in with the Hoffmans. I guess I can understand why she took up with Hal, in spite of the rumours."

"Tell me about the two of them, Lynn. Did they love each other?"

Lynn emptied her glass and I refilled it.

"Leslie loved Hal, of that I'm sure. But I couldn't get a bead on your father." She turned to look me in the eye. "I'll be straight with you about Hal because I know that's what you want."

"I'd appreciate that," I said simply.

She stared into her brandy.

"I was just a kid and I didn't really know your father that well. He was older—and a boy—so I had little interest then. But Leslie was my friend. She never treated me the way the other older kids did, like a pest. I probably *was* a pest, in all fairness. Since we shared the last name, I fancied myself a distant relative of Sherlock and was always spying on people. But Leslie never minded. I think she understood what it felt like to be on the outside looking in."

"Alice said my mother kept to herself, didn't hang out with others her own age. Why do you think my father got involved with her?"

"I don't know," Lynn shrugged. "Maybe the challenge attracted him. That sounds crass, I know. But remember that your mother was becoming a beautiful young woman." She was slowing down on the brandy, taking small sips. "Hal Leonard was an unusual boy, hard to read. The grapevine was very healthy back then so you knew what people were up to, but when you met up with Hal you couldn't help liking him. He had a way with him. Gordon had the looks, but Hal was the one with the girls lined up around the block. Even Meredith liked him, I think. I used to tease her about that." She fell silent.

"Did my father do the things they say he did—steal money from the store, forge cheques?" I asked quietly.

"I think he did," Lynn replied, looking out at the river. "You know, one or two misunderstandings and you can give someone the benefit of the doubt. But Hal's troubles continued to spiral and I was afraid he'd take Leslie with him. That would have been bad enough, but he was involved somehow with Emme Strauss, Jerry's mother. She worked in the store with him. Bill—Jerry's dad—was much older than his wife, I remember, and she was probably lonely. Still, it wasn't right."

"Was that the wickedness Meredith referred to?"

"Probably. I think it hurt her when she found out. She never admitted her crush, but she was always finding excuses to hang around the Leonard boys. And Meredith never liked Emme. I remember now. She was very upset."

EISENHOWER TO RUN FOR SECOND TERM
Senator Discloses Decision During Press Conference

**UNEARTH INDIAN VILLAGE ON SHEEK
ISLAND BLUFFS**

**NEW TOWN 2 REHAB MOVE SET FOR START
ON JULY 16**

July 1956
The Cornwall *Standard-Freeholder*

"Poppa says they're goin' to build bridges to connect the islands that are left and make them into parks. Call it a parkway." Meredith walked like a schoolteacher, just ahead of Lynnie who lagged behind as usual. "It's goin' to cost one million dollars. Can you imagine?"

Lynnie did not reply. Aultsville was starting to look strange, with no trees and many houses missing. She was hot and bored, and mad at Meredith for dragging her along to the store when the place to be on a great July day was swimming at the wharf. Only the promise of penny candy brought her out. She picked up a stick and began to picket.

"Why can't we go to Millers' store?" she asked for the tenth time. "They're just down the highway. It's too hot to walk up to Leonard's."

"I don't want to sit around at home," Meredith glowered at her. "Grownups are boring. I thought I'd do you a favour and take you for a walk."

"You just want to stare at Hal," said Lynnie accusingly.

Meredith turned on her cousin.

"That's not true. And don't you be sayin' anything while we're in the store, or I'll throw you in the river myself."

Lynnie said no more, knowing she was no match for the older, athletic Meredith. The girls made their way in silence up the County Road. Leonard's General Store stood north of the village, near the CNR line and Leonard's Lumberyard. The yard was busy when they passed.

Saturday regulars were camped out on the store's front porch but inside was quiet. There was no sign of any Leonards, only Emme keeping watch behind the counter.

"Oh, great. The Ice Queen," Meredith whispered. She walked slowly up to the food bins and ordered five pounds of sugar. After it was bagged, Lynn picked out her penny candy with agonizing precision. Meredith hung back, impatiently waiting while her cousin discussed the merits of different candy with Emme. At last, the little paper bag was full.

"I thought you'd be there forever," she grumbled as they headed for the door. "I can think of better places to be on a Saturday afternoon."

Lynn opened her mouth to say the obvious, but replied instead, "Like the lumberyard?"

"The lumberyard?"

"Yep. I told the Ice Queen I had a couple of Hal's fishing lures he lent me and I wanted to give them back. She took the story hook, line and sinker," Lynnie giggled. "Anyway, Mrs. Strauss says the boys are both working at the lumberyard today because they're behind in their orders."

Meredith said nothing, but when they reached the porch, she detoured to the large red Coca-Cola cooler sitting at one end. Leaning over, she slid the lid open, put in two nickels, and pulled out a cold drink for each of them. Popping the tops with the opener on the side, she handed one bottle to Lynnie.

"Here. I still think you're a brat, but sometimes you can be okay."

Sometimes Meredith could be okay too, thought Lynnie as she took the frosted drink. "I've never seen the lumberyard," she said.

"Then that's why we'll go," her cousin replied firmly.

"Hey, I heard Ma say they're goin' to start movin' dead people now," said Lynnie with undisguised relish. "Goin' to dig up the cemeteries and pull them right out of the ground."

"Lynnie! Ugh."

"Well, they are. Ma was tellin' Mrs. Leger that the new cemetery on high ground will be for everyone. And if you want your people moved there, you have to file papers and stuff to get it done."

"Gordon says they aren't movin' his mother," said Meredith quietly. "Says he and his dad want to take Lila to the new cemetery, but Hal won't have it. Can't understand him about it."

"Well, Leslie says they aren't movin' her mother, either. Harper says it goes against nature," the younger girl said firmly. After a minute, she asked, "Lila was Hal's mother, not Gordon's, right?"

"Well, yes, but Gordon's real mother died when he was little. Lila was the only mother he ever knew. I think he loved her as much as Hal did."

The lumberyard was busy and the smell of freshly cut wood was everywhere. The girls could see Bill Strauss in the distance, directing a truck to a load.

"We can't go wanderin' around there," said Meredith. "Let's go to the office."

The office was at the far end of the yard, along the road. There were two small benches in front, in the shade of a large silver maple. It was tempting to sit this out on one of them, but Lynnie didn't want to miss anything good.

When they reached the door, Lynn and Meredith stopped just inside. Hal was there, standing with his back to them. Gordon seemed not to notice them—he was clearly facing off with his brother.

"Just don't expect me to cover for you anymore, Hal," said the older boy stonily.

"I never asked you to. I don't need your help. Maybe if you'd stop bein' so helpful all the time, I wouldn't have these troubles," Hal replied darkly.

Gordon shot a look out the back door.

"What am I supposed to do, sit by and watch you hurt Dad? This isn't just about you, you know. Every time you mess up, it hurts the family."

"I haven't done anything wrong," said Hal quietly. "I didn't steal any money and I never forged any cheques. You know I wouldn't do that."

"What I know is that I looked like a fool cashin' those cheques you gave me. How could you set me up like that? I've always gone to bat for you. I kept the cash shortage quiet as long as I could."

"It wasn't me and that's all I can say," Hal shot back angrily. "My word used to be good with you and Dad, but I see it isn't *anymore. Maybe I'd better work out in the lumberyard for now. Kind of hard to steal lumber."*

"If you do, you'd better keep your head low around Bill." Gordon looked out the door again. "Dad says it's hard enough to face him now as it is."

"What the hell does that mean? And what's out the back door?"

"I don't want anyone hearin' what we have to say." Gordon faced his brother squarely. "Hal, don't you think people are talkin' about you and Emme Strauss?"

"Why would they? There's nothing to talk about."

"You walk her home every night and stay a while."

"So I walk her home. Bill always works late, and the whole place is crawlin' with strangers because of the Project. I don't think she should be walkin' home alone. And then I have a coffee on the front porch or pitch some ball with Jerry, for Chrissakes."

Gordon looked away.

"Gossip says you're keepin' time with a married woman. That puts Dad on the spot with Bill at the yard and you know it." He suddenly seemed to lose his patience with Hal, and raised his voice in anger. "I don't care what schoolgirl you're chasin' but stay away from Emme. It makes trouble we don't need."

The timing couldn't have been worse. There was a noise at the back door, and everyone turned to see Bill Strauss standing in the doorway.

"Oh, no," whispered Meredith. Biting her lip, Lynnie held her breath. Then a strong hand grabbed her arm and pulled her through the front door.

"Time for us to go," her cousin muttered grimly. Lynnie considered protest, but let it go. The girls walked home in silence, and though they finally made it to the wharf, Lynnie felt more or less on her own. Meredith remained lost in thought the rest of the day.

It wasn't until a month later that Lynnie thought about it all again. She saw Leslie heading out one evening with her fishing rod, making for the canal. By the time the younger girl was able to escape home in the same direction, she could see a small bonfire down on the bank. Leslie was with Hal, both fishing.

Drawing close with rod in hand, Lynnie meant to ask to join them, but decided to listen a bit first.

"I don't know, Les," Hal was saying, "You're the only person I feel comfortable around these days."

"What about Emme Strauss?" Leslie asked, emotionless.

"Emme?" Hal laughed. "God, I've known her since I was kid. She's okay too, I guess."

"You're not a kid anymore," said the girl flatly. "People have been sayin' things about you two. Even Pa asked me about it."

"People always have something to say," he replied and tossed his line out farther. They sat in silence for some minutes.

"Is it true?" Leslie asked finally. Good question, thought Lynnie.

Hal turned to look at her. "You mean, am I keepin' time with Emme?"

"Yes." Lynn could barely hear her.

He looked back out at the water, and the gathering dusk.

"I started walkin' her home a bit back because of the strangers we got nosin' around with the Project and all. We just talk a bit on the porch before I go—with Jerry, usually. Doesn't seem like a big deal to me."

"What do you talk about?"

"Stuff," Hal shrugged. "The kind of things I used to talk about with Ma." He turned to looked pointedly at the girl. "I guess that's the reason I hang about some. In some ways, Emme reminds me of my mother."

For a moment, Leslie concentrated on her fishing. Don't fall for that old line, thought Lynnie. She almost spoke it out loud.

Obviously, 'that line' was the right thing to say. Leslie slowly turned to face Hal, their faces only inches from each other. Then Lynnie saw the dark between them disappear, and there was only the sound of the water lapping in the canal.

A fish tugged at the line. Lynnie used the sudden activity to slip away.

"Maybe it *was* innocent," I ventured.

"Maybe." Lynn didn't sound convinced. "But it went from bad to worse. Gordon should tell you about that." She put her empty glass on the patio table and rose to leave. "Thanks for the break today, from everything. I needed it. Meredith was the only family I had left. Everyone is being so kind, and that somehow makes it worse."

I nodded with first-hand understanding.

"Lynn," I hesitated, "I really am sorry. I keep thinking that if I'd been faster and caught up with Meredith, none of this would have happened. Strauss hasn't ruled out an accident yet, but I can see he doesn't think it likely, either. I just came here to . . . to find out about my father. I never meant for anything to go so wrong."

She looked at me hard.

"You mean you think you caused this? By asking questions? That it's somehow connected to Hal's murder?"

"I don't know . . . I mean . . . Yes, I guess I do. That's the feeling I have and I can't shake it. I think Gordon feels the same way," I added. "He said something to me about coming here and stirring up ghosts I had no idea of. Maybe that's what I've done."

Lynn chewed her lip as she walked to the door.

"I don't know if that's true," she said finally, "but if it is—if someone is killing again, you'd better be careful yourself."

I hadn't thought of that, but she had a point. Then I remembered one question I needed to ask.

"Lynn, about the rumour of my mother's death," I broached. "Can you remember for sure who told you?"

"I'm sure it was Meredith," she said. "I left this area right out of high school and never looked back. Meredith was the one who kept me in touch with the local news."

I thought for a moment.

"This might seem like a funny question, Lynn, but . . . you know how you told me that Meredith had a flair for the dramatic?" She nodded and I continued, praying I could word this right. "When she told you something, did she ever add to it or change it as a rule?"

Lynn smiled a small smile.

"If you're asking me if Meredith was a liar, I'd have to say no. She loved gossip and the chance to spread sensational news. I'd even say she would embellish a little here and there if it didn't hurt anyone. But Meredith had a good heart. She didn't lie."

When Lynn had gone, I wandered around the cottage a bit until I saw the box of papers I'd brought with me. I felt a surge of guilt, grabbed the car keys and headed for Cornwall. Time to put in some time on local research and earn my sabbatical.

The Cornwall Public Library sits at a major intersection in the city, facing Second Street with parking access off Sydney Street. I didn't think I had a hope in hell of finding parking late in the afternoon, but miraculously a car pulled out of a slot right in front of the back entrance.

The building is large and airy, having started life as the Cornwall Post Office in the 1950s. With decentralization, the posties deserted their post and the building was up for grabs. The library saw a good thing and transformed it into a beautiful working facility, capable of handling resources for a bilingual population and providing community access for the Internet.

Unfortunately, I was not heading for those modern conveniences. The files I wanted were stored on microfilm—a necessary but diabolical and unbalancing method of storing old reference materials, such as back copies of *The Standard Freeholder*. If you're wondering at my malice, just spend an hour or two winding away through the months of old issues and you'll see what I mean.

Luck was with me. I was asked if I had booked my time for one of the machines and guiltily admitted I had not. However, no one seemed interested in the past except me that afternoon, so I had my pick of the machines.

I pulled out the box labelled "MARCH TO JUNE 1958" and began skimming through for interesting headlines. Somehow, I find that reading material from finish to start makes it much clearer. I found a few that piqued my interest and one in particular touched me with its poignancy after forty years:

BIG BLAST TO SEND DEBRIS A MILE HIGH AS I-DAYS LAUNCHED

June 16, 1958

An earth-shattering roar and mile-high explosion, which will send some 27,000,000 cubic yards of earth and water rising into the sky, will herald the creation of the giant 35-mile-long international powerpond on July 1.

Thirty tons of nitrone, contained in some 3,120 separate cans, located in groups and buried in 25-foot holes throughout the 600-foot long cofferdam, will be set off in intervals of a few thousandths of seconds apart.

The explosion will be the biggest single shot of the whole seaway-power project on which 21,000,000 pounds of explosives have been used so far.

Immediately following the big bang, a 30-foot high wall of water will rush onto dry land, spreading out like thin icing on a cake. This onrush will be the start of 180,000,000,000 gallons which will cover the 34,000 acres to be inundated.

I tried to imagine 70,000 people waiting for a wave that never came.

I hung in there, headlines spinning as fast as my stomach was starting to. The old pictures were beginning to blur together. I was glad when the library closed, but made a booking for later that week.

I headed up Sydney, admiring the blocks of Victorian homes. Sydney is one of the few streets that shows its age. While Cornwall is one of the oldest cities in Ontario, it lacks the abundance of heritage buildings of other cities and towns much younger. Many were lost by fire, or in the flurry of modernization that plagued urban centres until historical preservation became stylish.

When Sydney became Thirteenth Street, I followed it out to Vincent Massey Drive. There was a plethora of fast food restaurants here so I had my choice of soul food. I ate my meal slowly, trying to appease my stomach—which was really still back at the library.

I thought about Meredith and the story of my mother's death. For some reason, I couldn't drop that bone. It meant something, but I didn't know what. Meredith didn't lie, but Meredith passed the story so she must have believed it to be true. She must have heard it from an unshakable source. But who? And why tell such a whopper to her anyway?

I finished my meal and headed out to Highway No. 2. When I had travelled the river road before, it had been daylight; what had impressed me then was the sense of being cut off from the river until just outside Long Sault. Now dusk was falling rapidly. With the trees lining the river, the darkness seemed heavier, more acute. It was a lonely stretch of highway between Cornwall and the village. *Be careful*, Lynn had warned.

Right about then, something deep in the back of my brain started to tap me on the shoulder. I had heard something today that I needed to pay attention to. What else had Lynn said?

It all seems to be real again . . . as though it never ended, just waited.

Leslie loved Hal . . . I couldn't get a bead on your father.

No, that wasn't it.

When you met up with Hal, you couldn't help liking him.

Not that either. I shook my head impatiently. I guess I'd have to sleep on it and hope to wake up to an answer.

The trees gave way and I passed through Long Sault. I found the lights cheering at the intersection, as I passed the entrance to the Long Sault Parkway that had cost only $1 million a lifetime ago. After stopping to get some milk at the convenience store on the corner, I headed on to Ingleside and stretches of open river, but the dark was swallowing it up.

It went from bad to worse. Gordon should tell you about that.

Ever since I had arrived, the tale of Hal Leonard got more and more grim. I wasn't sure I wanted to hear the "worse" part. Maybe everybody along the Front had reason to kill him. Maybe I was beginning to understand why Mother never spoke of him.

Now I watched the river, wrapped in the night. Lake St. Lawrence was clear to the islands of the parkway. From Long Sault to Ingleside, the lights of homes broke the darkness on my right, but on my left there was almost nothing. On Ault Island, I had my neighbours along the waterfront and the American lights of Wilson Hill Island. But along the river road, along the new shoreline of the old Front, not a sign of human life graced the river's edge on either shore, wrapped as it was in a shroud of black.

Chapter 7

That Good Night

GORDON AND I had The Dinner two days later.

It was a nondescript day of chill late spring wind, so I found it easier to hole up and grind away on my project. I was beginning to see a problem of personal involvement. I had considered this before, but had always been able to separate myself from my subjects in the past. This time, however, the more I talked to people, the more their voices began to overlay the facts like a transparency. Clearing the acres was now Alice Hoffman losing a favourite cherry tree. Caskets disinterred had become my grandmother's being left for the waters to cover. Dissecting Farran's Park meant losing my parents' courting grounds. Croil Island was Stewart Cassidy. On and on.

Before I had added modern history as my second concentration, my professional focus had been the ancient worlds. Now I could see why—my subjects were dead and dust and unlikely to complicate my life.

That afternoon, I bundled up and walked to the home of my major complication. Family, information source, suspect. If the Leonards were well off in the 1950s, maybe there had been a sizable inheritance that my uncle decided not to share with his half-brother.

I decided to be magnanimous about it when Gordon opened the door to the big white house and the waft of something delicious hit me in the face.

"I hope you like turkey," he said, taking my coat shyly. "Not all the trimmings, but most of them."

Good-looking *and* a cook, but unmarried. Go figure.

"Sounds great," I said, offering my bottle of wine. Thank God for wine. I've never become more than a short-order cook, although I can beep and fry with the best of them. "I haven't had a meal like that since--" I stopped.

"Since?"

"Since Mother died. I used to visit her at least once a week and she'd always have a big meal ready for me." I smiled, remembering. "Mother was an excellent cook."

"As I remember," he said quietly, "your mother was a very capable woman."

We moved into the living room, which overlooked the small bay between Ault Island and the sanctuary. It was too windy for much bird action out there, and it just looked bleak.

"That land you see there is all that's left of Aultsville," Gordon said, moving over to a small bar. "Can I get you something?"

"Brandy on ice, thanks."

"Ice? You're kidding, of course. Kills the taste."

"That's the point," I said.

He shrugged and filled the glass. "Where you see the gravel bike path was once the County Road. Our store was closer to the old CNR line that lies under part of the sanctuary road. So was the lumberyard. Our house was just south of the bike path that now parallels the river."

"That's where they found him?" I asked quietly.

"Yes," he said, coming over to hand me my drink. "Right out there. I was in the kitchen here and could see the cruiser and the yellow tape going up. Never in my wildest did I think it was Hal."

"It must have been horrible for you," I said softly.

Gordon took his Scotch and we sat down. "It certainly wasn't one of my best days," he replied dryly. "I was at work when Jerry came to see me. I'd heard he was in town but didn't connect it with the investigation. At first it was just to let me know that the remains were in our old foundation and, of course, ask me if I knew anything about it. When the autopsy report came in, Jerry came with another constable to see me here." He took a long drink and stared out the window. "He was in some kind of bag, nylon, a sleeping bag they think. It had rocks in it to weigh him down." Gordon stopped, fighting with something inside. "Hal was only eighteen," he managed finally.

We sat together in silence for a moment, sharing only anger but at least it was something.

"How were they able to identify him after all this time?" I said.

"The police tracked down the old dental records in Morrisburg." Gordon got up to refill his glass, offering me the same but I refused. "There was no dentist in Aultsville, so we used to drive to Morrisburg when we needed one. They started on Hal's trail when they found the picture in his wallet."

"Picture?"

"An old family photograph that was wedged in his leather wallet, in a back pocket. It was mostly intact. Jerry gave it to me after the inquest was over." He walked over to a captain's desk in the corner and opened a drawer. "It's only half a picture, though, and he didn't have the other half on him."

When Gordon placed the photograph in my hand, I felt an odd chill run down my back. The picture was old and there were signs of mould on it, but it was otherwise clear: A young Gordon Leonard with an awkward smile standing in the front yard of a small brick house with long front porch. I knew where the other half was. I pulled it out of my wallet where I store it for safety and placed the two halves together. Something was coming full circle after a long, long time.

I handed them to Gordon. "The other half was in my mother's safety deposit box. I believe it was one of only two pictures she had of him."

Gordon held the two halves for several minutes, with a strange look on his face. I couldn't read his thoughts, but they didn't seem pleasant. Finally he handed my half back.

"We have a few minutes before dinner. Why don't I show you around? I have a few things in the garage you might be interested in, from the old days. It's hard to talk about sad times on an empty stomach."

The house was beautiful and immaculate. I thought of my condo in Waterloo, with stacks of papers on chairs and boxes sitting in the living room. He must have had a cleaning service. The furnishings and decor were very modern, unlike Alice Hoffman's house. Also unlike the Hoffman home, there were no relics of the past. No antique furniture, no conversation pieces, not even a photograph.

"My relics are in the garage," he said, as though reading my thoughts. "I'll get your coat."

The garage (also immaculate) was the size of my cottage, with the silver Mercedes we had taken to the cemetery taking up space alongside a fairly new Ford truck. Gordon had done well for himself, with a good job and no family to spend it on. Still, the question of inheritance flittered through my mind.

"I've heard that your father ran two businesses in Aultsville," I said. "It must have been a lot of work for the family."

"It was." He pulled out something long and flat from behind a cupboard. "But it was also a good life. We'd never heard of stress, even though everyone worked from dawn to dusk. You made your way in the world and got by on your own hard work. In a way, I guess, your life was more your own back then," he added, taking a clean rag to wipe the dust off the long, flat thing. "You got out of life what you put into it." He turned it around. It was a large sign that read LEONARD'S GENERAL STORE. Impulsively, I reached out to touch it.

"The house went to Upper Canada Village," he continued. "With Dad ailing, I knew we needed a small, modern bungalow in Ingleside. The old house is the Physician's Home now."

I nodded. "I went there. I recognized the front from the photograph."

"We sold just about everything from the store, gave some fixtures to the little general store in the Village. I kept this."

"What happened to the store itself? Was it moved?"

He shook his head. "Many buildings couldn't be moved because of their foundations. The store was one of them. It was destroyed during the Aultsville Burn."

The Aultsville Burn. I remembered the pictures in the books of houses being set on fire while being filmed. Something to do with heat tests and flashpoints. And people standing, watching their homes go up in flames.

"What about the lumberyard? You must have kept that in full operation until the last minute."

"We fully intended to," Gordon said grimly, turning away to replace the store sign. "We lost everything in the fire." He walked over to something draped in a blanket. "I hadn't thought of this in years, and it popped into my head the night I called you about dinner. Do you have children, Farran?"

"I'm on my own, I'm afraid," I said, pulling out another technically honest reply. "I've never married."

He pulled the blanket off, revealing an antique baby carriage made for a doll. It was in great shape, and must have been the pride of some little girl once.

"This was my mother's when she was a girl. I thought I'd give it to my daughter or granddaughter, but I...have no family."

I remembered what Lynn had told me at our first meeting. "It's beautiful, Gordon."

"I . . . I thought, perhaps, that it should go to you. I mean, it should be passed on."

The enormity of the gesture was not lost upon me. I flushed. "I would be honoured to have Lila's carriage, Gordon. Thank you."

"*Catherine* is my mother's name," he said quietly, covering the carriage up again. "Lila was my stepmother."

Trying to get my foot out of my mouth, I changed the subject. "Meredith said you were more of a father to Hal than your father was, his being so busy with the two businesses. That you brought him up, were very close."

"My father was a solid family man, but he was gone a lot when we were little," Gordon admitted. "I was four years older than Hal, so I taught him all the manly tricks in life—how to change a tire, how to play baseball, how to spit, how to bait a fish hook." He unexpectedly gave me a real smile. "Fishing was our favourite. The old river was full, especially sturgeon. It was nothing back then for your mother to holler at you that she needed some fish for supper, and you'd go down to the wharf and within the hour you'd have supper."

"And now? Do you still fish?" We headed for the door.

"No. I never did after the Seaway was finished. It wasn't the same." Gordon snapped the lights off. "And it's been years since anyone caught a sturgeon in these parts."

"So there have been environmental repercussions from the power dam?"

"I'm not the person to talk to about that, Farran, but if you need that information for your study, I can give you some names. There were studies done in the 1980s, and the University of Ottawa did an independent study about three years ago. They published the findings in the *Citizen*, and it wasn't good news. Maybe Lynn could get you copies." The wind had picked up so we scuttled quickly to the back door and dove into the warmth and smells of supper.

"If you want my two bits on the whole thing," he said, taking my coat, "it's just another case of science catching up with old wives' tales. The older people here have been swearing for forty years that the weather has never been the same."

We were having coffee post-feast in the living room. I had given Gordon a pencil sketch of my life to date (with a few erasures), and he was responding in kind.

"I lost Dad about a year after the flooding. He'd been ailing for some time. We lost the lumberyard in the fire, and then the store began to suffer—partly because of our problems and partly because the area was leaving. Dad couldn't make up his mind about setting up shop in Ingleside, and we lost a place in the mall. With Hal gone and Dad sick, I couldn't tackle it alone, so that was the end of Leonard's General Store. I got a job with the Parks. When Dad died, I started night courses with the University of Ottawa. It was a long haul, but eventually I went into business administration with the Parks. I've been there ever since."

He made no mention of his dead wife and son, and I certainly wasn't going to ask him.

"What did my grandfather die of, Gordon?"

"Heart disease, they told me. I think he just lost the will to live. I look at it now as an older man myself and I can see it, you know. The Leonards had lived in Aultsville for three generations. The store was one of the biggest in the area, and my father bought the lumberyard himself and doubled its business. And he had two sons to hand them down to. Dad had a lot to be proud of." Gordon looked into his coffee for a moment. "Then it all seemed to slip away," he continued. "First Lila, then the lumberyard, then Hal, the store, and finally Aultsville itself. I would say my father died of a broken spirit."

"The Project changed so many lives," I said. "Would you say it changed you personally?"

Gordon shot me a glance, and then smiled.

"I'm beginning to feel like a subject of your study, Farran."

"Well, yes and no," I admitted. "I did come here to get people's feelings on it. But with you, of course, the issues are personal."

Gordon offered more coffee, this time with cognac.

"The Power Project changed the direction of everyone's life and that always changes you as a person," he said finally. "But the reality is that life is going to do that anyway. It's just that this was a Big Thing, like war or the Depression. The change happened to everyone, all at once."

Gordon looked out over the little bay.

"I know what people are dealing with today. We were the group that was gung-ho about changes, modernization, technology. We thought we were building a brave new world, much better than the old one—that our parents were old fuddy-duddies about it. But now we're older, we've taken their place, and we're not so sure. My age group is retiring; we have grandchildren. We'd like to go home to retire, or at least take our grandchildren there. Show them our old playgrounds, our homes and churches, our schools. Tell them what we did and who we were. Pass it all on. But none of us from the villages can do that. We can't go home. It's a bitter pill to swallow at this age."

"Is that what you feel about it now?" I asked. "Do you resent how it was done?"

Gordon shook his head.

"No. Nothing is ever perfect, Farran. You know that. And the enormity of the project meant that some things would fall through the cracks, not be handled the way they should.

"But look at what they *did* do. An international agreement between two countries and two power authorities. They changed a river, moved 6,500 people and over 500 buildings. Re-routed rail lines and highways, built two towns from scratch. And they did it all on schedule and on budget. Even if you could appease the environmentalists and the human rights activists, it still could never be done today."

"But it wasn't the shot in the arm for the economy here everyone thought it would be, was it?"

"No," he admitted. "It changed everything. Cornwall lost its locks to Massena halfway through the project, and that hurt. The new Seaway created an economic tunnel from Cornwall to Iroquois, and the area lost all the spin-off industries that the riverfront provided—hotels, restaurants, marinas. Except for the Long Sault Marina, there were no longer clear access points to the river in that entire stretch. And the counties lost the waterfront tax base. The Parks did well in the Sixties when the baby boomers were young and gas was cheap. But it's been a struggle since then."

"So the people that gave up the most got the least for it?" I said dryly.

"That might be a little harsh," Gordon said, setting his cup down, "but not entirely untrue. However, the ironic twist to forty years of recovery is that this has given the area an unexpected advantage."

"An advantage?"

"Yes. You see, after all the workers left and the dust settled, we more or less waited for Big Brother to come back and save us. Needless to say, we were among the first to realize that wasn't going to happen. Then, to add insult to injury, we lost a lot of our manufacturing sector when Free Trade came in. So, when everyone started scrambling for cover with downsizing and restructuring, we did too; but the Seaway Valley had already been working toward recovery for years."

He leaned forward and refilled our cognacs.

"Listen to me rattle on," he said, shaking his head. "You'd think I was at a conference. Let's get back to my brother. I'm sure you have a thousand questions."

I didn't reply for a moment. Then I raised my eyes to his.

"Only one for tonight," I said quietly. "Tell me about the wickedness."

FRENCH TRACE PLANS FOR SUEZ CANAL
**Would Be Managed By International Authority,
With Egyptian 'Owners'**

LAUNCH CONSTRUCTION A-ENERGY PLANT
**See Heavy A-Power Demand.
Economical Plant Will Come Later
(Chalk River, Ontario)**

OVER 10,000 ATTEND MAYOR HOROWITZ
PICNIC
Premier Frost Special Guest
(Cornwall)

UNVEIL CRYSLER MEMORIAL PARK MODEL,
PLANS
Plan Autumn Start On Major Project
Consultants' Work Lauded By Commission
(Morrisburg)

August - September 1956
The Cornwall *Standard-Freeholder*

"You can't come up with a better explanation than that?"

Eric Leonard and his sons stood in the small kitchen, still in
their clothes from church. Hal shrugged at his father's question.

"How can I? I don't know where the money is goin' any more
than you do. And I don't believe Emme would do that, even if she
had the chance—which she doesn't because when I'm there, I'm
there. I'd see her."

"So where is it goin'?" Eric ran his fingers through his hair. "I
thought we had this all cleared up months ago and now it's startin'
again. Are you lendin' money to friends? Do you owe someone and
haven't told me?" He threw his hands up in the air. "I just need to
know what's goin' on. We can't let people know it's happenin' again.
We finally have things smoothed over from the last time."

"I'm not stealin'!" Hal shouted angrily. "Why can't you just
believe that?"

"Don't you think I want to? But it's always your cash that's
comin' up short again. And with everything else . . . If you're in
trouble, son," Eric pleaded, "tell me. I'll help you."

Hal's face was like stone. "I'm not in trouble," he said flatly,
"and I'm not stealin' from you, Dad. My word used to be good
enough, but I guess that isn't true anymore." The boy grabbed his
coat and headed to the back door. He turned to his father for a
moment. "Ma would have, you know. She would have believed me
no matter what." He slammed the door behind him.

Gordon came to stand behind Eric, putting his hand on the man's shoulder.

"I know how it looks, Dad, but I can't see Hal doin' it. Why would he? After all the trouble last time and with the cheques . . ."

Eric turned to his older son. "Before I would have agreed with you, Gordy. But not now. He's . . . changed somehow. He seems closed off and strange. His work at the yard has gotten careless. He doesn't do half what he's supposed to. I know you've been coverin' for him."

Gordon walked over to the window and said nothing. Eric sat down heavily at the table. He rubbed his chin thoughtfully.

"I know about that fistfight last week with Jeff Wilson over Jeff's girl. Hal and Jeff have been friends their whole lives. What is he doin'?"

Gordon did not turn from the window. "I tried to stop them," he said briefly, then shook his head. "Boys will be boys, Dad."

"But the money, Gordy. Doesn't he understand what this could do? People around here haven't forgotten about the last business, just chalked it up to bein' young and stupid. But if it starts again, they'll start questionin' the honesty of our business. It's tough enough tryin' to handle people startin' to leave Aultsville now. We don't need to drive them away. And I don't want to tell Hal that he can't work with us anymore. He'd never forgive us."

Gordon turned to look at his father. "Maybe he's coverin' for Emme. They are . . . good friends, I think."

Eric made no reply. He obviously wasn't happy about that, either.

"This all started after Lila died," he said finally. "Losin' his mother has been hard on him." Eric saw a look pass over Gordon's face. "I'm sorry, son. I know it's been hard on you, too. I guess the squeaky wheel still gets the oil sometimes."

"I'm goin' down to the wharf, Dad," Gordon replied, putting on his jacket. "He's probably there. I'll try to talk to him."

Steam locomotive CNR No. 5008, the Moccasin, pulled into Aultsville station on its return run from Montreal. The September evening was warm and fair, and the store was full of wanderers coming in for a forgotten purchase or late mail as an excuse to fit in a quick game of checkers at the back with the men. Others hoped to catch some of Hockey Night In Canada *on the new television Eric Leonard had had the foresight to buy for his business rather than his home.*

Emme Strauss came into the store, laughing with Hal who carried the mailbag. The checker players looked up from their game at the couple and then over at Gordon behind the counter. Gordon ignored his brother until Emme was safely behind the wicket, dealing out to a handful of people. When Hal came behind the counter, Gordon pulled him down to the far end.

"Do you have to make an entrance like that with her?" he whispered. "Everybody in the store was watching you."

Hal shook off his hand. "Don't be stupid, Gordy. I took the parcel to the Moccasin like you said and I carried the mail back for her. That's all."

"Well, try to keep your distance for a while, okay? We just got things quiet here again."

A group of schoolgirls entered the store and approached the counter.

"What can I do for you, ladies?" Gordon asked.

A blonde girl with a Doris Day crop and an obviously new pink sweater and skirt hesitated.

"Ah, well, I . . . I'm not sure . . ." She looked over where Hal was restocking the shelves. Gordon took the hint.

"Hal," he sighed, "you have a customer."

The girls giggled as Hal walked over to them. Gordon gathered up a few small boxes and took them to the shelves beside the mail wicket, now empty of customers.

"That bothers you?" Emme leaned toward him with a smile.

"He has work to do," Gordon replied briefly, not looking at her.

"All work is not healthy for a young man," she said knowingly. "You, too. Why don't you have a nice girl to walk about with?"

He turned and looked her full in the face for a moment. "Same reason Bill's not home much these days—too busy keepin' things runnin'. But maybe that's okay with you."

She flushed. Jerry came through the door with some friends who ran over to the television.

"Hey, Ma," he waved. "Can I watch some before we go?"

"Just a little bit, Jerry. Your father will want something to eat when he gets home."

The girls had gone and Hal was adding up the cash. Gordon stopped behind him and looked at the money.

"I thought you were goin' to take the cheques to the bank today?"

"It was busy. I forgot," Hal waved Gordon off and continued counting. The store was beginning to empty. Emme locked up the mail stall and hoisted a pile of magazines into her arms.

"Jerry," she called over, "we need to go home now."

"Ah, Ma," the boy whined. "It's a tie game."

"Well, come straight home when it is done, then." Emme put the pile on the counter for a minute. Jerry reluctantly left the television, waving goodbye to his friends.

"Okay, I'll go. Poppa made me promise to walk you home every night from now on."

Emme looked embarrassed and unconsciously turned to Hal, who was taking his apron off. He grinned at Jerry.

"Smart man, your pa. Lots of strangers around now with the Project going on. Shouldn't let pretty ladies like your ma walk about alone at night. Tell you what," he added, looking over to where Gordon was putting covers on a couple of displays, "I'm done here for the day. Why don't I help you carry that stack of magazines home? Looks like a two-man job to me."

Jerry brightened as Hal gave him some of the books before taking the rest in his arms.

"Can you stay and throw the ball around with me?" he said.

"Well, we'll see." Hal felt Gordon's eyes on him as they headed for the door. "It's gettin' dark faster these days."

"Poppa never has time anymore," Jerry complained. "He's always at the yard."

Hal stopped to shift the magazines into a more comfortable hold. "Everybody's got more on their plate these days, Jerry. Everything's changin'. My dad relies on your poppa to keep up with the extra orders. I'm sure he'd rather be throwin' the ball with you." He hoisted the bundle again. "You really read all these things, Em?"

She shrugged and smiled a little, holding the door open. "Yes. It is, well, something different than . . . this." She waved her hand at the neighbourhood outside. A neighbourhood that would soon be gone.

Gordon was washing his hands in the kitchen after supper when Hal burst through the back door.

"Gordy!" The young man grabbed his brother. "Where's Dad?"

"Hey, calm down. I think he's at a meeting in the Hall. What's wrong?"

"Fire," said Hal tersely. "At the lumberyard." He snatched a jacket off the hooks and put it on. "You get him, Gordy. I'll round up the others. Meet us there with the fire truck."

Gordon pulled his own jacket on and left by the front door. Far up the road, he could just make out a glow in the direction of the lumberyard. A brisk October wind was starting up. They'd have a job on their hands.

He ran down to the No. 2 and then along to the Fraternity Hall, calling "Fire!" as he went. Lights started going on along the road, with people coming out on their porches.

"Where, Gordon?" someone yelled.

"Lumberyard," he called over his shoulder. He knew people would move quickly. Even though Aultsville still had a volunteer fire department, all available hands were expected to help. And now half the people were in the new town.

"Dad!" Gordon burst through the front door of the old hall and looked around. Hearing voices, he ran up to the second floor. "Dad!"

The men in the room started getting to their feet, hearing the urgency in his voice. Eric crossed the room in three strides.

"What's happened, Gord?"

"Fire, Dad," Gordon caught his breath. "At the lumberyard. Hal told me. He's gone to get the guys and meet us there. We need to get the fire truck out."

"Christ," someone muttered. "Not the yard. That'll go up like Victoria Day."

"Okay," said Eric, thinking quickly. "We'll need help. Jack, get Shirley on the exchange to Morrisburg—and Cornwall. Anyone she can find. Tom, you ring the church bell for five minutes, then get on over to the new town and find anyone who can help. Everyone else come with me."

It took twenty minutes to get the 1918 gasoline-powered pump engine in full throttle and out of the warehouse. Then it had to manoeuvre around people and cars heading north to see the fire. The flames could be plainly seen now, with only a few houses and no trees to break the view.

Eric jumped off the truck when they arrived. Men had already started two bucket brigades, but the fire was moving quickly in the wind. Piles of lumber blazed all over the yard, and the office was beyond saving. The heat was almost unbearable.

"Hal!" Eric called. His son left the line and came over, his face and hands dark with smoke and ash. "We've got help comin'. Get two guys and take the engine over to Murphy's well to fill the tank. Thank God Hydro's not too fussy about closin' wells. Where's Bill? Is he here yet?"

"I haven't seen him, Dad." Hal shook his head, then wiped his eyes with a streaked handkerchief. "There was no answer when I knocked earlier." He started toward the fire truck, then stopped. "Dad, there's Em and Jerry."

Eric looked around, and headed in their direction.

"Emme, where's Bill? I need him to direct the men on the other side."

She looked confused for a moment. "What do you mean, Eric? He's here."

"We can't find him. When did he find out about the fire? Maybe he went to the new town for help."

"No," Emme shook her head, pulling her son close. "The truck is at the house. No one told him about the fire. He's been here all evening, working on the books."

They looked over at the office. At the same moment, the men nearby gave a shout and moved back as the roof caved in.

"He's working on the books," she repeated tonelessly. Jerry broke free of her hold and started to run.

"Poppa! Poppa!" he screamed.

Hal made dive for him before he got too close and they hit the dirt together. Jerry struggled, but Hal held firm.

"We don't know he's in there, Jerr. We don't know," the young man yelled over the noise, trying to keep his voice calm. "He might have gone to get help." The boy became still and they sat together in the light of the inferno.

Gordon went over to them. "Don't worry," he said. "We'll find him."

"We found him."

The men stood grave-faced just inside the kitchen door. The table was covered with food picked over by those who had kept vigil all night with the Leonards. Miraculously, the fire had not jumped the road and the worst was over by midnight. By the time backup arrived from the neighbouring towns, there was little they could do. The lumberyard was gone. In the early morning, when the ashes had cooled somewhat, some of the firemen had taken a preliminary search of the office remains. It did not take long to make the gruesome discovery.

"Are you sure it's him?" Hal asked.

"The police will have to check, probably by dental records," Jack Harrison said, rubbing his forehead. He tried to stifle a yawn.

"The police?" Gordon looked up from his cold coffee.

Eric nodded. "They'll have to look into it. Maybe Bill accidentally started the fire and couldn't get out. Maybe he caught someone doin' it and they left him there."

"That would be murder," said Hal quietly. "What about Emme and Jerry," he added, turning to Jack. "Have you told them?"

"No, we figured that should come from your dad. I can get my wife to come sit with her, if you think that'd help," he added to Eric.

Eric sighed, and stood up. "That's a good idea. I'll go over now. I think everybody else should go home and get some sleep. It's been a hell of a night."

"So where were you before you spotted the fire?"

The OPP officer sat carefully on the ornate sofa in the front parlour, and opened his notebook.

"I was comin' home from the Second Creek. I was gettin' some last fishin' in before it got too cold." Hal crossed his arms. "I already told you this when we gave our statements last week."

"Yes, Officer," Eric moved to stand behind his son's chair. "We're happy to help, but why are we goin' through this again?"

"We're trying to clear up reports that this young man was seen at the lumberyard shortly before the fire was discovered. Were you there?" he added to Hal.

"Who says I was?"

The officer gave him a look. "It's just a rumour at this stage, but we'll pin it down. How well did you know the deceased's wife?"

"*Emme? Since I was born. She's worked for my dad that long, I think. Why?*"

"*Were you two . . . close?*"

"*Another rumour,*" Gordon interrupted from where he'd been standing silently. "*Also one you'll have to pin down. But you won't. You never do with gossip.*"

"*Just what direction are you takin' with this, Officer?*" Eric asked. "*What happened was a terrible accident. Are you sayin' Bill Strauss was murdered?*"

"*Not saying anything, Mr. Leonard.*" The officer got to his feet. "*Just looking at all the facts. You have a good day now.*"

When the three were alone, Eric sat down heavily.

"*Did anyone see you at the creek that evening, son?*"

"*No, but Gordon knew where I was. I also asked Jerry to go with me, but he had homework.*" A look dawned on his face and he stood up. "*Do you think I had something to do with this?*"

"*No,*" said Eric hesitantly, "*but I'm afraid of what . . .* "

"*You do,*" Hal spoke softly. "*Or at least you're not quite sure.*" He shot a glance at Gordon.

"*Hal, it's talk we're afraid of,*" said Gordon. "*People know that you and Bill had words over Emme. And no one found the gun in the fire,*" he added.

"*The gun?*"

"*Dad's gun he brought back from the war. The Lilliput. We didn't find it or anything that looked like it in the ashes.*" Gordon hesitated, then turned away. "*We haven't said anything about it, either, to the police.*"

A few seconds later, Gordon and his father heard the door slam.

The biting November wind whipped Leslie's hair into her face as she hung onto Hal's arm. The sun was going down, adding to the chill. Gordon caught up to them at the canal just as the rear gates of Lock No. 22 closed behind the Lake Emerald.

"*You don't have to do this, Hal.*" Gordon looked at Leslie. "*Tell him, Leslie.*"

"*Gordon's right, Hal,*" the girl agreed. "*Bill's death was an accident. The coroner said so. Don't go.*"

"*Gordon's right about something else,*" said Hal grimly. "*Everybody around here thinks I'm guilty.*"

"*What I meant was you have to give them time to change their minds, now that the inquest is over,*" *Gordon explained.*

"*They won't change their minds—they never do. I thought I could handle it, but I went to see Jerry after the inquest. He said he believed me, but . . .*" *Hal looked at Leslie, cupping her face in his hand. "I could see it in his eyes, Les. He thinks I killed his father."*

"*He's hurt and confused,*" *said Leslie. "He doesn't know what to think. Don't leave."*

Hal shook his head. "He's not the only one confused. I don't know what to think anymore. I have to get out of here for a while."

"*Hey, you two.*" *A burly sailor in dungarees leaned over the railing. "Which one is comin' on?"*

"*Me.*" *Hal grabbed his duffel bag and hoisted it to his shoulder.*

"*You got yer papers? They're gettin' fussy about that now.*"

"*All here.*" *Hal patted his jacket, then turned to Leslie.*

"*Don't go,*" *she said softly.*

"*I have to, Les. I'll be back. I promise.*" *Hal pulled Leslie close with his free arm and kissed her.*

"*Give 'er one for me, boy,*" *said the sailor with a grin. "Hey, Bick," he called to another crossing the deck, "would you go sailin' if you had to leave the likes of her behind?"*

The other sailor just shook his head and waved.

Hal turned to Gordon and stuck out his hand. "I guess this is it, big brother. Take care of Dad for me. Things should get easier on him with me gone."

Gordon shook his hand slowly. "What'll I tell him?"

"*Tell him I'm sorry. Tell him whatever you feel is best. You'll think of something, Gordy. You always do."*

Hal climbed the rope ladder and followed the sailor to the cabin. Shortly after, the lockmaster opened the front gates of Lock No. 22 and the Lake Emerald *began to move out into the canal. The sun was very low now, shining bleakly into their eyes, making it hard to see the boat. As it moved away, Hal came out on the deck and waved goodbye.*

They watched the Emerald *until it faded from view. Then Gordon turned to Leslie, whose face was streaked with tears.*

"*Leslie, I . . . If I . . .*"

The girl looked down, then shook her head. Without a word, she turned and began the walk through the dying village toward home.

"And you never saw him again?" I had remained motionless the whole time, and suddenly needed to get up and walk around.

"I saw him almost a year later, the summer of '57," said Gordon in a strained voice. "He turned up at Casselman's Dance Hall in Morrisburg. We were all there—Ruth, Leslie, me, even Meredith—as if she knew he'd be there. He didn't have to catch up with his ship until midnight, so we spent the evening together. It was awkward, but your mother was happy to see him. I tried to get him to see Dad, but he wouldn't. Still too angry, I guess."

"And he never tried to contact my grandfather?"

There was no reply. Gordon seemed lost in thought, hands gripping the armrests.

"Gordon?"

"I saw him once after that." My uncle spoke almost in a whisper, as though to himself. "Hal called, said he was in town and wanted to see us. I asked him to meet me away from Ingleside. I didn't want talk and I didn't want Dad upset. So we met in Aultsville that night. He said he wanted to see what was left of the place."

The wind was still howling around the corners of the house. Darkness had fallen, completing the effect, and my dinner sat heavily in my stomach.

"Did you meet?" I asked softly.

"Yes. We walked the dead streets together at first, and he asked about everybody. Couldn't believe how desolate it all was. There wasn't a soul around that evening.

"I asked him if he knew where Leslie was—she'd left Ingleside a few months before. He seemed to get angry. Said she'd been with him for a while, then suddenly left. Hadn't heard from her since."

"Did he say they'd married?"

"No. And I've wondered about that since you arrived. You see," Gordon ran a hand through his hair and dropped his eyes. "You see, Hal said he wanted to see Dad, mend fences, make peace. It's what I'd hoped for—but he seemed angry, volatile. I felt as though he were in trouble and maybe just needed money. I was afraid to take him to see Dad because our father was so ill. If they fought, the upset could have killed him. So I asked him to give me a few days to prepare Dad, and give me a number I could call him at. He refused that, but said he'd call me. I never heard from him again."

"When was this?"

There was a long pause, with only the wind as accompaniment.

"If you blame me, Farran, I'll understand," Gordon said finally. "I never told anyone before because it was a family matter. After they found him, I felt too guilty and ashamed. I'll have to call Jerry about it tomorrow and explain, come what may."

"Explain what, Gordon?"

"We met *only a few days before the flooding*. Do you understand what that means? Someone killed him shortly after. If only I'd trusted him one more time, brought him home that night, Hal might have lived. Farran, I . . ." He hid his face in his hands. "I'm sorry. Sorry to Hal for letting him down. Sorry to you for letting someone take your father away."

The wind seemed to drop suddenly, and I could hear my heart beating. Connected to this man by loss and little else, I didn't know what to say. And my pain and anger were real but quite new. My uncle had been bleeding from this wound for a long, long time.

"I'm the one who should say sorry, Gordon," I began awkwardly. "I'm sorry for the way I handled everything about finding you. And I don't blame you for my father's death," I added. "You were trying to do the best you could with a difficult situation. Besides, why should you think that someone was going to kill him? You couldn't know, and you couldn't control that choice."

Gordon did not reply. It was late so I took my leave, thanking him for everything. I looked at him in the chair and saw how he suddenly seemed aged and frail, despite the physique. If you don't stop the hemorrhaging, it will kill you.

I said I'd show myself out and left him still sitting there, alone with his self-made demons whose faces I could only imagine.

Chapter 8

Entropy

(T)HE LOST Villages Museum stands located on Highway No. 2 east of Long Sault, about halfway into Cornwall. Rather than a single building with displays, it is a collection of small houses saved from the villages and later donated to the site. The former Moulinette train station, the Manson-Lapierre Grocery Store from Mille Roches, and the Zina Hill Barber Shop sit in their former glory with several other buildings on Fran Laflamme Drive, the road named after the driving force behind the Lost Villages Historical Society.

I rolled in there the weekend after my dinner with Gordon. Aside from sending him a thank-you note for the supper, we had not been in contact. To say I was suffering from mixed feelings was an understatement. Gordon had survived, but his life had been destroyed, too. By the time Eric Leonard had died, everything Gordon had grown up with was gone, and he'd had to start over. And Hal had been murdered. If I didn't know better, I would think someone had set out to destroy my family back then.

But I didn't know better, did I? And who would want to destroy an entire family? And why?

I switched off the car and sat for a minute. The day was beautiful and the museum was already busy. Cars pulled into the small road and passed me, heading off into Scout Camp Tsotahoteh. Parents and kids doing the quality time thing, I guess. I thought of my parents, of a windy night so long ago when my father left his home to escape what he'd become. Of a young girl left behind to cope with the world being torn apart around her. I didn't know what I thought about my father at that point, but there was a big piece of the puzzle missing. I needed to know more about who my mother had been before I could decide about Hal.

And I knew just who had the piece I was looking for. I was going to ask for it now, even if I had to be rude.

Ruth Hoffman was behind the counter in the gift shop, giving some background to a customer when I walked in. She turned to smile, saw it was me and forgot what she was saying. I browsed quietly until we were alone in the store.

"Have you come to do research, Fan?" she said, deciding apparently on the offensive approach.

"Yes," I replied, "but not so much with the museum today as with you. I called your house this morning and Alice told me you were here. I came to ask when we could sit down together and talk about my mother."

She had the grace to flush. "I'm sorry. I should have called you long before this, but I . . . I'm still working this out, I guess. It seems like so much has happened since we heard about the body in Aultsville. But I guess that's true for you, too, isn't it?"

"You could say I've had a busy year," I said dryly. "Are you working here all day?"

"No. We have students that work here for the summer. I just come in to cover for someone if they need it. Julie had an appointment this morning, but she should be in shortly. Can you wait?"

I nodded. "I'll take a look around for a while."

Along with the three buildings, the museum hosts a pioneer cabin, a blacksmith shop, and a red school house beautifully restored with maps of the old river on the walls. The white church was not open yet to visitors, and I watched several people working inside it.

It was close to eleven o'clock when I saw a young girl arrive and make her way into the gift shop. Ruth appeared outside a few minutes later. We walked over to a bench not far from a barbecue pit and sat down. She handed me a Styrofoam cup with coffee in it.

"Milk and one sugar, right?" Ruth said with the first smile I'd seen since I'd introduced myself ten days ago. "I remember from when you stayed to lunch that first day."

"You have a good memory," I said taking the coffee. "Thank you."

"I think my memory has improved a little since I came back here and got involved with the society," Ruth smiled into her coffee. "I get asked so many questions about the old days that it makes me really think about it all again. And then it all seems real to me once more, but at the same time like a movie I saw long ago. I remember the girl I was back then and I can't recognize her."

"Alice said you two locked horns a lot in those years."

"We still do," she laughed, and then shook her head. "But back then it was much worse. Adolescence hasn't really changed much over the years. All I wanted was out—someplace new to start a new me. The idea of a brand-new town and a bright future with the Seaway really appealed to me then. Now after all these years, the angels are chuckling because I'm back here and all I want is to go home again.

"I have three grandchildren. I'd love to take them to Farran's Point, show them the park and the canal. My old school. And I can't do that." We fell silent for a moment, exiles both.

"You *did* get out, though, didn't you?" I asked finally. "You said you lived in Montreal after the flooding."

"Yes. I had an aunt there, and she'd enjoyed my company when I stayed with her for a while when she was ill. When I left, she said I could come back and live there when I was ready to look for work, if I wanted to. As soon as I was finished school, I did just that. Mother put up a fuss, but I was going to the big city to find my fortune."

"And did you?"

"Yes, I guess I did. I went to secretarial college and then worked for a few years with an insurance company. That's where I met my husband. We married; I raised four children. Only one of them stayed in Montreal, and I can't say as I blame them. It's hard to make a future for yourself there now with the political unrest. Anyway, my husband and I divorced about two years ago and I came back to care for Mother."

"I'm sorry."

Ruth shrugged. "The prodigal always returns home, right? I don't mind. It gives me time with Mother and she's not getting any younger. My brother lives out West and hardly ever comes home. I think it helps her to have me here, even though we squabble a lot."

"Family is important," I said briefly. Then I turned to look her straight in the eye. "Since I came here, I've heard some bad things about my father. It doesn't look good for the relationship he had with my mother. So it's even more important that I talk to you. I need to know what kind of a person my mother was back then so I can try to judge what really happened between them. Will you help me?"

Ruth looked away for a moment and I wondered where she was. "I'll tell you what I know," she said finally. "Up until she left the area, we were very close friends."

"How long did you know my mother?"

"Almost ten years. Leslie was eight when Harper brought her home to the Point with her mother. She was very withdrawn and kept to herself. It didn't help matters when the other kids used to tease her about being a gypsy, saying their milk at school curdled because she looked in it."

"What?"

"Old superstitions, Fan. I remember the gypsies parking in the fields just out of town from time to time when I was small and my mother dragging me indoors to keep me safe. But by the time Leslie showed up, they had disappeared from the area. Still, old beliefs die hard and children, as you know, can be cruel."

"Sounds like something out of a book," I said curtly.

"Did Leslie never tell you any of this?"

I shook my head. "Mother always said to leave the past where it belonged—in the past. For all intents and purposes, her life began when mine did. Only once in a blue moon did she ever let anything slip about the old days. Maybe that's one reason I have a passion for history. I always lacked one of my own."

"Actually, that sounds just like Leslie. For someone with gypsy blood, she was excruciatingly practical about things. Until the last little while, when everything was coming to an end."

"And about my father," I offered. "He was becoming one of the bad boys in the area, yet she spent time with him."

Ruth's face took on a look I could not fathom. "Yes," she said softly, "Leslie loved Hal completely. She didn't say much when he left, but I knew her well enough to see she was hurting badly over it. I think she felt that he'd run out on her."

"Did he?" I asked. "Gordon told me about the fire at the lumberyard and Bill Strauss's death. Was it really so bad for my father or did he just use it as an excuse to get away?"

"The talk was bad, Fan, even though nothing could be proven. In many ways, that's even worse than hard evidence. You're tried and convicted on gossip. And Les told me Hal had had a bad fight with his father over it. I guess he felt he couldn't stay on here."

"Not even for my mother?"

Ruth sighed. "Maybe he thought he was doing Les a favour by breaking ties. Although, looking back now, I think if Hal had known what hard times your mother would face the year after, he would have stayed. He shouldn't have let her go through it alone. Especially after making sure she'd lost her heart to him."

Summer 1956 (continued)

"Absolutely not."

Leslie and Ruth, both in dungarees and tie-waist shirts, pitched a softball back and forth under the hot sun in Ruth's backyard. It was treeless like everywhere else, so shade was out of the question unless you went inside. Being restless, they had opted for pitching practice instead

"I absolutely will not cut my hair. That is where I draw the line." Leslie underlined her thoughts with a firm throw.

"Ow. Take it easy." Ruth shook her hand out of the glove and wiggled the fingers. "Okay, leave the hair. But we're going to make those dresses just like Marilyn is wearing in the picture."

"Fine. And wear them where?" Leslie deftly caught her friend's pitch and gave her a speed ball.

"I don't know. What about Casselman's in Morrisburg?"

"Harp wouldn't let me go. And your mother wouldn't let you go, either."

"Who says she has to know?" Ruth gave Leslie a grin. Leslie sighed. A horn broke in, leaving the plans for later. They turned to see Hal Leonard watching them, leaning against the side of a lumber truck that carried a full load. He took a long drag on his cigarette and flashed them a smile.

"When you weren't at home, I figured I'd find you here. Hi, Ruth," he added with a nod. Ruth shyly returned the greeting as Leslie walked over to the truck. "I'm on my way to the power dam *with this load. I know you haven't been to see it yet, so I thought I'd see if you wanted to come with me today. It's pretty spectacular."*

"I don't know if I really want to," Leslie replied. "Besides, I'm here with Ruth."

"Bring her along. It'll be cosy, but there's room." Hal put his hand under her chin. "Ignorin' it won't make it go away, Les. And you really should see this thing before they fill it with water."

Leslie turned to Ruth. "Want to go for a ride to Cornwall to see the dam?"

Ruth dropped the ball and glove. "Absolutely," she said, giving her friend a pointed look. The three piled into the cab of the truck, with Leslie in the middle. Ruth hung out the passenger window for a cooling breeze. Pat Boone played on the truck's radio, and life suddenly seemed full of possibilities.

"Have you seen the dam, Ruth?" Hal called to her over the music.

"My dad's taken me a couple of times now," she said. "He has to take my brother almost every weekend. Tommy is just crazy about the whole thing."

"Seems like everyone is," Hal replied. "They had the president there last week, you know." They had passed the section where work was beginning to empty the rapids, the cottages of Woodlands and Santa Cruz (slated for what they said would become Ault Island), and were now passing through Dickinson's Landing. Hal beeped at a man pumping gas at the station. The road, already heavy with trucks going to and leaving the site, was becoming clogged with sightseers driving slowly along or parked on the side of the road, wandering about with cameras.

"Damn nuisances." Hal looked at Leslie. "I hear Harper had a run-in with one of them last week."

"Uh, huh. Found the guy wanderin' around the yard, goin' through the stuff. Harp asked him if he was lookin' to buy or trade something, and the guy said he was just takin' a few things for souvenirs. Said he wasn't goin' to pay. Not when the water would take it anyway. Harp changed his mind about that, let me tell you."

Hal smiled to himself and shifted gear. Then he quietly put his hand on hers.

"Mother had the same problem a few days ago," Ruth offered. "Came out to hang the laundry and saw a couple pokin' around

our garage. She asked them what they were doin' wanderin' on
private property and they said it wasn't anymore. Everything
belonged to Hydro."

"What did she do?" Hal asked.

"Chased them off with the broom." Ruth slid a quick smile in
his direction. "Mother's real good with a broom."

The Landing gave way to Moulinette and then to Mille Roches.
With no trees to break the view, they could see the dam looming up
in the distance.

The Cornwall dam was massive beyond belief. A monolith of
concrete and scaffolding, it rose like a vengeful god from the
landscape—dwarfing the Mille Roches power station that had
supplied electricity to the area for the last fifty years. It gave Ruth a
strange feeling to look at it, a mixture of awe and dread in the pit of
her stomach.

"I have to bring this into the work area and it's busy, so stay in
the truck," said Hal. He drove slowly along a service road at the
base of the dike, stopping to be waved through several times. The
place was like an anthill, full of workers all doing a hundred
different things. Most of the men had their shirts off in the heat, and
while many of them were older, Ruth managed to pick out some who
were younger and quite good-looking.

"God, Les," she whispered when Hal was getting directions,
"it's like Christmas around here. Look at that one over there.
Doesn't he look just like Rock Hudson?"

"Ruth, you're hopeless." Leslie shook her head.

"Easy for you to say," Ruth shot back, miffed. "You have
yours."

While Hal was outside directing the unloading of the wood,
Leslie leaned out of the window and craned her neck for a better
view to the top of the dam. There were ladders and platforms still all
over it and she could see men working across its face like spiders.

"Hey, Beautiful. What's a girl like you doing in a place like this?"

A young man in a hard hat sidled up to the truck and grinned
at Leslie. She rolled her eyes and sat back in the cab. Ruth leaned
over to look at him.

"Hey," he said, leaning in at the window, "How come I haven't
seen you at any of the dances here? I make the rounds every
Saturday night, and I remember the pretty girls."

"I guess you've just missed us," Ruth broke in brightly.

"We don't go," said Leslie coldly. "We're not allowed."

"Can I help you with somethin'?" Hal came up and put his hand on the door.

"Just making small talk," said the man. "Being friendly, you know."

"Jackson!" someone yelled. The man looked up and turned to go. "Hope I see you around sometime, Miss," he said to Leslie, touching his hard hat. Then he was gone.

Hal got into the cab and slammed the door. "Was he botherin' you? Maybe I shouldn't have brought you with me."

"No," Leslie reassured him. "I didn't really give him a chance." But Ruth said nothing, and remained quiet for the rest of the trip. Hal brought the truck around carefully, skirting the dike again and then approaching the dam from the Cornwall side. They got out and climbed to the viewing station, looking out over the dam and the old and new parts of Mille Roches on either side of the river to the west. In the distance to the east could be seen the tall cement pillars that would one day hold the International Bridge. People were lined up for the telescopes that Hydro had put there to use free of charge.

It was spectacular.

"Kinda takes your breath away, doesn't it?" Hal offered Ruth a cigarette and when she accepted, lit them both. Leslie stood silent, taking in the view, her hair blowing in the wind.

"Seems like the end of the world," was all she said.

STRIKE TIES UP CPR TRAINS
Trains Come To Halt All Across Canada
Locomotives 'Put To Bed' In Shops And Roundhouses

NEW IROQUOIS NEARS COMPLETION

January 1957
The Cornwall *Standard-Freeholder*

"I'll never get this algebra," Ruth sighed, running her fingers through her carefully styled hair. Now it stood up like a rooster. She took a fresh sheet of paper and started again. The snow was coming

down too heavily to do much else, so the two were studying at the Mackenzie house. Leslie set two mugs of tea on the kitchen table, then sat down to her notebook. She did not pick up her pencil.

After a minute, Ruth sensed the silence and looked up at her friend.

"Les? Les." She waved at her. "Yoo hoo!"

Leslie came back across the miles and focused on Ruth. "What?"

"You're not doin' your math. Not that I can't understand that reluctance, but I don't think that's it." The girl took a sip of tea. "This isn't about Hal, is it?"

"No," said Leslie. Then she added defiantly, "Not that I don't think about him. I do. I know you and Harp think I should just forget him because he's gone, but I know he'll be back. And I think he'll need me more than ever then."

Ruth said nothing, drawing doodles in her math homework. Now she'd have to start over, again.

"Ruth," Leslie said suddenly, "Dr. Burns was here when I got home from school yesterday. I think they were arguin' about something—something important enough to bring the doctor here. I heard him say to Harp something about 'If you can't do it for yourself, then at least do it for Leslie.' Then they saw me and clammed up."

"Did you ask Harper about it?"

"Yes, but he gave me a story. Said the doctor came by to let him know his new address in Morrisburg and they got arguin' about Harp still not sellin' the place."

"Maybe that's all it was, Les."

She shook her head. "Harp's never gone to the doctor as long as I've known him. Why would Dr. Burns bother? Besides, I heard he's retirin' when he moves."

"So what do you think it is, then?" Ruth finished a large doodle of two hearts entwined. She put her name in one and a question mark in the other.

"I think Harp's sick, Ruth. I've been wonderin' about that for sometime." Leslie stirred her cooling tea. "When you know someone real good and something's not right, you just know it. Little things that change. He goes to bed early every night now, and the other day

I had to wake him up. It was 7:00 and he wasn't out of bed. He's always been the first one up, even when Ma was alive."

"Les," Ruth said gently, "remember he's gettin' old. Harp must be at least over fifty by now."

"Maybe that's all it is." Leslie sounded unconvinced. "But I don't think so. Something's wrong."

Ruth got up and helped herself to another mug of tea, topping off Leslie's too.

"Did I tell you that we got our movin' date?" she said brightly, changing the subject. "The Hartshorne people are movin' our house to Ingleside June fifteenth. I wish Harper would sell soon so you could get a lot near ours. They're startin' to sell quickly now."

"I think Harp will sell soon. He's gettin' tired of the game."

"You said this house couldn't be moved." Ruth looked pensively at her friend.

"No. They'll tear it down—or burn it." Leslie looked around at the small, neat kitchen warmed by the woodstove. "This is the last place my mother lived, Ruth. I still remember when she picked out the wallpaper. She loved the yellow and white with the blue forget-me-nots. Said it was cheerful. She's still so much here. It'll be like losin' her all over again."

The Reverend James MacDonald cleared his throat again and looked out at the packed church. Despite the inclement February weather, St. John's Presbyterian in Farran's Point was full for its last service. Over half his parishioners were now coming in from Ingleside and the Point was becoming a ghost of its former self. Still, almost a century should count for something, not just be wiped out like this.

Oh, they were going to save the bell, but the rest of this beautiful little church would be destroyed.

Ruth sat with her family, looking around at her neighbours. St. John's had always been open to anyone of any faith, such as themselves. But the new big churches that were going up in Ingleside seemed much more formal. More organized. She realized suddenly that she'd miss this quiet country church she'd started turning her nose up at. Some of the women had handkerchiefs to their eyes already, and Reverend MacDonald was having a hard time starting this last service. Ruth almost felt sorry for him.

The reverend rubbed his forehead and took a drink of water.

"But God led the people about," he began, "through the way of the wilderness of the Red Sea: and the children of Israel went up harnessed out of the land of Egypt.

"And Moses took the bones of Joseph with him: for he had straitly sworn the children of Israel, saying, God will surely visit you; and ye shall carry up my bones away hence with you.

"And they took their journey from Succoth, and encamped in Etham, in the edge of the wilderness. And the Lord went before them by day in a pillar of a cloud, to lead them the way; and by night in a pillar of fire, to give them light; to go by day and night."

The door to the church suddenly opened, and two bundled figures came in. MacDonald gave them a glance as he warmed to his subject, then suddenly faltered to a stop. People began to turn in their pews. Ruth craned her neck to see and felt her mouth hang open. "Well, I never," she heard her mother say.

Harper Mackenzie stood in the aisle with his hand on Leslie's shoulder. He slowly took off his hat and gave the reverend a nod. Speechless, MacDonald gave him one in return.

As Leslie helped her father find a seat, Ruth noticed how pale the big man looked. Maybe Leslie was right.

"We welcome our friends and neighbours, Harper Mackenzie and his daughter Leslie, to our final service here today," said MacDonald with emotion. "We are all of us from the villages of Farran's Point and Woodlands, and though these will soon disappear, we will continue to be friends and neighbours. Together, and with God's guidance, we will face the future—no matter what it brings." He picked up his songbook. "If you will turn to page 158 and rise, we will join together in song."

The little church rang with the voice of its flock on that last morning. Carry Me Across the River floated out across the snow and curled around the stillness of the few nearby houses, only to vanish in the roar of trucks on the highway headed for the dam.

"I'm sorry, Leslie." Dr. Burns took off his half-moon glasses, putting them in his vest pocket. Then he sat next to the girl and patted her hand. "I didn't want to be the one to tell you. Harper said he would the last time I came to see him. He is a very sic. man."

Leukemia. Chronic lymphocytic leukemia, a type that only adults get. Ruth stole a glance at Leslie from her corner of the front room. She had stayed with Leslie since her friend had arrived, panic-stricken, at the Hoffman home early that morning. Alice had called Dr. Burns on the telephone when Leslie explained that Harper could not get out of bed. Then the three of them had returned to sit with the man until the doctor arrived.

Now Leslie sat still as death on the old sofa, seemingly in shock. She did not speak.

"How far along is he, Doctor?" said Alice.

"He's been sick for months," Burns replied. "It's a wonder he didn't collapse long before this. He won't go to the hospital for treatment to prolong his life. He won't take any heavy medications." He turned to the girl beside him. "You're his next of kin, Les. He's incapable of takin' care of himself any more. Won't you let me take him to the Cornwall General where he could get treatment? At the very least, they could make him comfortable."

For some moments, Leslie didn't reply. Then she slowly looked up at Dr. Burns.

"I know you mean well, Doctor, but I can't. If Harp doesn't want to go, I won't make him. He'd die in a hospital. The only place he'll feel comfortable is in his own home."

Burns fumbled with his glasses, polished them with his handkerchief and finally placed them on his nose. Peering over them, he gave Leslie a stern but compassionate look.

"Your father is dyin' now," he said quietly. "And between now and then, he'll need a lot of care. Harper is goin' to have night sweats and fever, bruising, and pain in the joints. He'll start losin' weight and can pick up any infection that comes along. Eventually, his bone marrow will fail. He'll need you here all day, every day—right to the end."

Leslie raised her chin. "I'll be here," she said. "Where else would I be when he's so sick? Harper is the only father I've ever known."

"I'll help you, Les," said Ruth suddenly. "Whatever you need. You just tell me what to do."

Leslie looked over at her best friend and gave a slow smile.

Burns was unconvinced. He looked at the two of them for several minutes in silence.

"That's right, Dr. Burns," Alice added unexpectedly. "They'll be movin' our house in June, but until then we're just down the road. We can certainly help out a bit here when Leslie needs it."

"Very well." Burns rose to leave. "I'll be droppin' by to check up on you both several times a week. I'll also be back tomorrow with something for his stomach. Maybe the first thing Alice could do for you, Leslie, is show you how to change the sheets around a sick person."

Burns left and Leslie went upstairs to sit with her stepfather. Ruth came over to her mother.

"What you said about helpin', Mother," she said awkwardly, "well, thanks."

"Don't thank me," Alice curtly replied. "I made a promise and I always keep my promises."

At the sound of the knock, Alice wiped her hands free of flour and opened the kitchen door. Startled, she gave a small scream. Ruth came running in to see her mother helping Harper Mackenzie to a chair.

"God, man," Alice exclaimed, "sit down. What the devil are you doin' out of bed? Where's Leslie?"

"I sent her on an errand," said Harper. "I need to talk to you alone."

Ruth pumped a glass of cold water and set it in front of him. Harper picked it up carefully in shaking hands as pale as a ghost's. His face was drawn and lined, and his clothes hung on him. The once black beard was shot with grey, his eyes ringed with shadows. Many times of late, Ruth had spent the afternoon with Leslie, but she had mainly helped with the cleaning and brought lessons for her friend who could no longer attend classes. This was the first time she had really seen Harper since the day they'd called Dr. Burns, and the difference in him was shocking.

"I could have gone to your house, Harp," Alice scolded him. "Can I get you a cup of tea?" When he shook his head, she turned to her daughter. "We're okay, Ruth. Leave us be, now."

Ruth went out, then quietly climbed the stairs to Tommy's room. She sat down next to the grate in the floor. It commanded an excellent view of the kitchen below.

" . . . no matter what happened," Harper was saying. "I've always thought the best of you, Alice."

"And I you, Harp. I hope you know that."

He placed a frail hand on her strong one.

"This damn thing—I'm not afraid of death. But now of all times. Les is too young yet to be on her own, especially with everything so strange." He turned to Alice. "You made me a promise last year. I'm here to hold you to it. I need to know that someone will look out for my girl. Someone that I trust. Will you do that for me, Alice?"

"My word still stands." Alice took the frail hand in hers, but did not look up.

"For old times' sake, eh?" Harp said softly. "And those were good times."

"Yes," Alice whispered. Ruth could barely hear it. "For old times." The woman raised her face to meet his eyes, with a tenderness of youth at first love. Ruth had the uncomfortable feeling that she was seeing her mother for the first time.

Harper reached out to touch her face, pushed a strand of hair away from her eyes, then rose heavily from the table.

"I'll help you back, Harp," said Alice gruffly, following suit. But he waved her away.

"Best I go back alone," he said, and was gone.

When Ruth came down a few minutes later, she found her mother still at the table—lost in thought.

"Mother?" Ruth sat down beside her. "Are you all right?"

"Of course, Ruth." Alice wiped her eyes and got up to finish her cake. "Can't say the same thing for Harper Mackenzie. And not a word to Leslie about this visit, mind. What's done is done."

"Maybe he's gettin' better for a while. Dr. Burns said that happens sometimes. How else could he get out of bed and come here?"

Alice shook her head. "No, Ruth. What you saw was sheer will," she said over her shoulder. "Harper Mackenzie is a dead man walkin'."

The truck had HARTSHORNE HOUSE MOVER emblazoned across the front. It was massive, with a tractor up front that moved on wheels higher than a man. The flatbed itself was rigged up with a series of levels and pulleys that would instantly balance the house *once the lift picked it up. The lift, a huge, two-pronged affair, was slowly backed under the house through pre-made openings at the building's base. All pipes and wires had been disconnected the day before. When the lift was properly placed, the order was given to hoist. With a sickening screech, the house separated from its foundation, slowly rose, swayed, then righted itself as the levels went to work. Then the men secured all fasteners.*

"See, lady?" said the foreman to Alice Hoffman, standing with her family. "Just like I told ya. Ain't no mother on the St. Lawrence gonna handle her baby better than that machine will your house."

"I still packed my mother's china," Alice sniffed. "And I took all the lamps off the tables. I would have done more, but when you come three weeks early and give a body one day's notice . . ."

The foreman shrugged. He was getting used to the complaints.

"I just get my orders every day from the main office, and we move the houses they tell us to move. You'll have to move back now. We're gonna pull out."

He turned and signalled the driver. Harland took Ruth's arm and grabbed Tommy's hand firmly. They moved over to stand with the neighbours that had come to watch.

"You're goin' early, aren't you?" said one.

"Three weeks," Harland replied. "And we got the call yesterday. It was like buggin' out in the war."

"Be glad it was only three weeks," said another. "My uncle got moved two months ahead, right in the middle of harvest last year. They had to finish it after movin' out, and they lost some equipment out of their barn what with not bein' there. And they had to give their animals away with no time to sell."

The house mover roared into gear, and slowly began to trundle forward. The people gave way before it, still entranced with the act of moving a house off its foundation of several generations. Gradually, the Hartshorne pulled out onto the road and the Hoffmans watched their house start its journey to Ingleside. When it was out of view, they walked back to the gaping foundation.

Ruth had a funny feeling in the pit of her stomach, despite the excitement of moving to a new town.

"Well, Tommy," said Harland, "what did you think of that?"

"It was really neat. Can we go watch them put our house down in Ingleside?"

"*Of course. We shouldn't miss that.*" *He turned to his daughter.* "*Ruth, you're rather quiet. This is the big day.*"

"*I . . . I don't feel well. Maybe I'm comin' down with the flu or something.*"

Harland looked at Ruth carefully, but said nothing. He changed his gaze to watch Alice, who had not moved after the truck left. She stood looking at the houseless property, at her gardens, and at the neighbourhood—ravaged as it was by the same machine.

"*They can take it all away, Harland,*" *she said simply,* "*but the Point is still home.*"

"*Les?*" *Ruth found the kitchen deserted, the front room ominously, too. The windows were open for the breeze on this hot August day, but no sign of meals was in the sink.* "*Leslie? Are you home?*" *She didn't want to call out too loud and disturb Harper. Still receiving no reply, Ruth climbed the stairs and stood at the top, listening. It was 10:00 a.m. and Leslie had been expecting her. Something was terribly wrong. She wished her father had stayed for a moment when he dropped her off on his way to work.*

After a minute, Ruth thought she could faintly hear the sound of muffled sobbing coming from the big front bedroom that Harper used. She quietly picked her way down the hall and looked in the door. The man was asleep on the bed. Leslie sat on the floor beside him with her face in the bedclothes, holding his hand. She was still in her pyjamas.

Ruth came up and put her hand gently on Leslie's shoulder. The girl jumped and turned around, showing a face bloated with crying.

"*Les, what's wrong?*" *Ruth wasn't sure she wanted to hear.*

"*I can't wake him up, Ruth. I tried all morning, but he won't answer me. He's breathin' but he won't wake up. I didn't know what to do except wait for you.*"

Ruth looked up at Harper lying in the bed. He seemed so diminished, like a life-sized doll of himself. He was as white as alabaster. But he was still breathing.

"*We need help, Les. There's still a phone at the corner store on the highway. I'll go down and call Mother. She'll know what to do. Go wash your face and get dressed. When I get back, I'll make you something to eat.*"

Ruth ran out of the house and down the road to the river. Harper's house was the only one still on the street. There was little else left other than stumps and foundations with steps leading nowhere, and one or two houses boarded up waiting for demolition. Without anyone to care for them, the once beautiful gardens had grown wild—except for old Mrs. MacGillivary's. She got her son to drive her down each week to care for the gardens she'd spent her life building. Until the water comes, she said once to Alice, they're still mine.

But no one was there today. Ruth was the only person as far as she could see right down to the highway. The town she'd known since the day she was born now seemed alien and eerie. Like a ghost town—except there was little town left.

There were strangers in the store, stopped off to get drinks before heading to the dam for sightseeing. Ruth went straight to the phone and called Alice. When she went to leave, Mr. Winters handed her two cold soft drinks.

"Take these for you two girls, Ruth," he said. "I heard what you said there. Come back if you need anything else. I'll be here."

I'll be here. The words cut into her after the walk on the deserted streets, with Leslie hanging on to Harper for dear life in the one house still standing there. Tears welled up. Embarrassed, she wiped them away with the back of her hand and thanked him.

It was only an hour but it seemed forever before Alice arrived with several women from the church. They came in like a well-trained army, restoring order for the time at least. Death was an old acquaintance to them all.

"I called Dr. Burns," Alice told Leslie. The girl had washed and dressed as Ruth suggested, but refused to leave Harper and eat some lunch. "He'll be here within the hour."

"But he's retired," said Leslie dully.

"Men like that don't retire," returned the woman sharply. "And when he gets here, he'll need to see Harper alone, so you come down and eat something then. You need to keep your strength."

Ruth sat with Leslie until the doctor arrived. They could hear the women downstairs washing dishes and starting the wringer washer. Someone was sweeping and shaking rugs. Do the ordinary while you wait for the unthinkable. Keep life going in the face of death.

Soon the screen door slammed and they could hear the deep voice of Dr. Burns. In a few minutes, he appeared in the doorway. Amazing how it always felt that anything could be fixed by him, Ruth thought. Fifty years of doctoring. Maybe he could take on death and win, too.

Burns took a glance at Harper, then turned to Leslie.

"I'll need to see him alone, Les," he said gently. "The ladies have something for the two of you in the kitchen. Go eat. I'll be down presently."

For once, Leslie did as she was told. With Ruth's hand on her arm, she slowly made her way down to the kitchen. The table was set for two, with sandwiches, cake and a pot of tea. Leslie picked at her food while Ruth guiltily wolfed hers down. The ladies still moved about with busywork, talking quietly amongst themselves. From time to time, one would place a hand on Leslie's shoulder in passing.

Finally, they heard Dr. Burns on the stairs. Leslie rose from her chair, everyone else stopping to wait expectantly.

He'd taken his jacket off and his sleeves were rolled up, glasses on the top of his head. It was one of those rare times when the old doctor actually looked his age. He must be over seventy, Ruth suddenly realized. Burns sat down beside Leslie who returned to her seat, and someone poured him a steaming cup of tea. He placed a gentle hand on her head, making her instantly seem a small child. She probably felt like one right now.

"He's goin', Les," said Burns simply. "And what we have to do now is let him. Right now, he's slipped into a coma. Keep him comfortable. Let him know you're there. A day, maybe two, maybe a week—he'll just slip away. And it's time. I don't think he's got any more fight left in him."

Leslie nodded without speaking, tears spilling down her cheeks. Ruth swallowed hard, eyes downcast.

"She'll need help keepin' vigil, Alice," the doctor said over shoulder. "Will you ladies be helpin' her with that?" There was a murmur of agreement behind him. Burns nodded to himself, then sighed. "Harper assured me that he'd made arrangements for you after he's gone. You're sixteen now and the law says you can make up your own mind, but do you have somewhere to go?"

Ruth managed to speak up. "She's movin' in with us, Dr. Burns—when the time comes."

"Okay." The doctor rose to go. "I'll be back after supper tonight. I'll come by twice a day as long as you need me, Leslie. I wish you had a telephone here, but it can't be helped now. I guess we'll do fine without it." He picked up his jacket and slapped his vest pockets. "Now where are my glasses?"

"On your head, Dr. Burns," said Ruth with a small smile.

He found them, gave a small grunt of approval and headed out the door to his Oldsmobile.

"Well, ladies," said Alice briskly, "let's split up the days and nights."

The vigil lasted four days. On the morning of the last one, Ruth was eating cold cereal with Leslie while Mrs. Martin sat upstairs with Harper. Suddenly, the latter appeared in the kitchen.

"It's Harper," she said breathlessly. "He's callin' for you."

The girls jumped up and took the stairs two at a time. Harper's eyes were open and he seemed feverish. His lips were moving, but it was hard to make out what he was saying.

"Harp. Harp." Leslie put her hand on the sunken chest and looked closely into his eyes. "Harp, it's Leslie. I'm here."

He turned his head but could not focus his eyes on her.

"Les," he whispered. "Les, don't worry, gal. I've made sure. Made sure." The effort seemed to cost him and he closed his eyes.

"Made sure?" Leslie spoke loudly. "Harp. Made sure of what? Harp!"

His eyes flew open. "The stacks, gal. I kept the stacks. They're yours, Les. I made sure. Made sure of that, at least."

"Harp," she said desperately, "I—I don't understand. Just rest now. Tell me later."

"Cass. They're safe. Remember that—no matter what happens." The eyes turned to a corner of the room. "See, Evie? I took care of our Les."

Ruth couldn't stop herself from looking at the corner, too. She felt a cold shiver run down her arms.

"Harp," Leslie said again. "Rest now. I'm fine. The Hoffmans are lookin' out for me. The ladies from the Point are helpin' right now, too. I'm okay. Do you understand? I'm fine. Don't worry about me. Rest."

Harper tossed about for a minute, then seemed to look right in her eyes. "The stacks, Les. Don't forget. Wait for 'em. They're safe." His eyes closed again, his voice dropping to a whisper. "The stacks. I took care of my gal."

When he had dropped back into a deep sleep, Leslie looked up at Ruth and then at Mrs. Martin standing in the doorway.

"I don't understand," she said miserably. "He was tryin' to tell me something important and I don't understand."

She dropped her head to the quilt and started to cry. Ruth could see Leslie was near exhaustion, physically and emotionally. How much more could she take?

"Les," Ruth came up behind her, putting her arm around Leslie's shoulders. "Let's take a break from this and go for a quick walk. Get out in the sunshine for a few minutes. We won't go far."

Leslie shook her head. "Listen to his breathin', Ruth. It's changed. It sounds funny. Something's happenin'. I'm afraid," she added. "I'm really afraid. I want Dr. Burns."

"Perhaps we should track him down," Mrs. Martin agreed.

"All right." Ruth stood up. "I'll go to Mr. Winters' store and call Mother. Try to relax, Les. We'll find him."

It was a Monday morning. The streets were deserted, except for the still constant flow of traffic on the highway going to and from Cornwall. A few holidaying stragglers sat on the store's steps while across the way, some had crossed the park to see a boat go through the lock. For a moment, Ruth looked over at the park—or rather where it had once been. She thought of the day, a million years ago, when Hal and Leslie had danced in the little pavilion. It was now in the fairgrounds at Newington, Hal was gone, and Leslie was watching her father die.

She brushed the thought away, along with tears that threatened to come again and pulled the store's door open. Crossing the floor quickly, she rang the phone exchange.

"Shirley, it's Ruth. Get me Mother in Ingleside. Quick."

"Hang on, love," came the reply. The old switchboard would operate for a few months more, then shut down forever. How odd it would be to have no one to talk to while placing a call.

The phone at the other end rang and rang. Then she heard her mother answer.

"Mother," Ruth cut her off, "somethin's wrong with Harper. He's breathin' funny and talkin' nonsense. Leslie thinks he's dyin'. Can you come? Can you get Dr. Burns?"

"Calm down, Ruth," came the sensible reply. "We know he's dyin'. You stay with Leslie and tell Mrs. Martin that I'll be there shortly. I'll see if I can find the doctor."

Ruth rang off and ran all the way back to the house, not even bothering to glance at the foundation of her former home. She burst in the door and ran up the stairs. In the bedroom, no one had moved. Harper's breathing was becoming hoarser and shallow. Leslie held both his hands in hers, watching his chest rise and fall.

"They'll be here soon," said Ruth, taking the chair nearest Leslie. Her friend did not reply.

Mrs. Martin came up to give Leslie's shoulder a squeeze. "You stay here with her, Ruth. I'll go down and put on the kettle."

Ruth found herself watching Harper's breathing with Leslie. As they waited, the breaths seemed to become more irregular, until she noticed she was holding her own breath waiting to see if his next one came. From time to time, Ruth stole a glance at Leslie, but the girl's face was like stone. Unreadable. As though the act of facing the unthinkable took every ounce of who she was to do it.

Minutes ticked by on the old clock beside the bed, the only sound besides Harper's laboured breathing. Would they never come? Ruth went to the window and strained her ears for the sound of a car, but heard nothing. And then she realized that she heard nothing but the clock.

Ruth turned horrified eyes to the bed. Harper lay absolutely still, eyes closed. His chest no longer rose. She stared at it for a full minute, as though to will it into motion again. Then slowly, as if the silence might shatter into fragments on the floor, Ruth moved over to Leslie still sitting on the bed, fingers entwined with Harper's.

"Les. Les." Ruth knelt down and looked up into her friend's face.

"Harp." Leslie's eyes welled up with tears. "Oh, Poppa. Poppa," she whispered to him. "Did you have to leave me?"

Ruth put her head into Leslie's lap. Leslie remained on the bed, silent tears falling onto the quilt. Neither moved for what seemed like forever. Even Time must stop in the presence of the dead. And then suddenly, there were footsteps on the stairs.

"Lord bless us," came Alice's voice.

Ruth raised her head. "Ma? He's dead, Ma."

"Come with me, Ruth," said her mother, gently pulling her up off the floor. "The doctor is here, too. He'll need to get in here."

They left the room, but Ruth stayed by the door. Dr. Burns walked briskly in and took a close look at Harper. Then he turned to the girl, placing a gentle hand on her head.

"He's gone, my dear, but I think you know that. I'll need some time alone with him before I write the death certificate. Why don't you go down and get something hot to brace you up? Speakin' of bracing'," Burns looked over at Ruth and her mother in the doorway, "if memory serves me correct, Alice, Harp kept a bottle or two of good Scotch in the cupboard over the icebox. Leslie could use a little of that right now."

"What about me, Dr. Burns?" said Ruth.

Burns gave Ruth a hard stare, but couldn't fight the trace of a smile. "Yes, you too, Ruth," he said finally. "I'm sure it's been hard on you as well."

Alice made a noise in the back of her throat but said nothing. Ruth went over to Leslie, who had not moved.

"Les," she said, putting her arm around her friend's shoulder, "let's do what the doctor says. I'll come back up with you later if you want to sit with him a spell."

When Leslie still made no move to go, Ruth looked up uncertainly at the doctor.

"Come, Leslie," said Burns quietly, slowly helping her to her feet, "it's time to let go." He gently pulled the dead fingers from the living.

"And if a man die, shall he live again? All the days of my appointed time will I wait, till my change come. Thou shalt call, and I will answer thee: thou wilt have a desire to the work of thine own hands. For now thou numberest my steps: dost thou not watch over my sin? My transgression is sealed up in a bag, and thou sewest up mine iniquity. And surely the mountain falling cometh to nought, and the rock is removed out of his place. The water wear the stones . . ."

They were gathered in the new cemetery on the hill. Ruth stole a glance at Leslie beside her. The girl was as she had been since Harper died—stone silent and dry-eyed. Despite Ruth's best efforts this morning, the toll of the past few weeks clearly showed on her friend's face. The dark circles seemed to underline the eyes that looked so empty.

The sun was hot but a cool breeze blew in mercifully from somewhere. The Hoffmans stood behind Ruth and Leslie; Reverend MacDonald faced them across the casket. Around them stood many of the families from Farran's Point—the Martins, the Legers, the Browns, the Holmeses. The same people that filled the Mackenzie house with food and hushed conversation during the wake.

Slowly looking around her, Ruth also saw some men that she didn't know. Must be business associates of Harper.

"And as we release the soul of our friend and neighbour Harper Mackenzie to the care of the Lord our God, we also commit his body to the ground. Leslie?"

Leslie was holding a single red rose. Silently she started to walk forward, but stopped and put out her hand.

"Ruth," she hissed. "Help me. Can't see."

Ruth looked into her face and saw eyes suddenly brimming with tears. She took Leslie's hand and led her to the casket. The girl put her rose on the lid. From somewhere in the back, a bagpipe began to play and the strains of Amazing Grace *drifted out over the field. Ruth wiped her own tears away and helped her friend back from the casket. Leslie gave her hand a squeeze.*

When the music ended, Reverend MacDonald came around to take Leslie's hands.

"My dear child," he said with a sad smile, "he's at peace now. His suffering is ended. I hope that gives you some comfort at this difficult time."

"Yes, Reverend," she answered, barely above a whisper.

"You have a heavy burden to bear at your young age, but I truly believe that God never gives us anything He thinks we cannot live up to. Harper was your father in the true sense of the word. You get your strength from him. Remember that."

"I will."

"And remember one more thing," he added, turning her around. "You are not alone in this world. We are all here to help you any way we can."

Leslie looked around at the faces standing with her in the cemetery and gave an uncertain smile. From somewhere in the distance, Ruth seemed to hear a church bell tolling. It couldn't be from Ingleside—that was too far away.

"You're all welcome to join us for coffee and sandwiches at our house," Alice announced. The crowd began to break up, people making for their cars. Some stopped to give their regards to Leslie before heading home. One man stood at the edge of the crowd, watching.

"Who is that, Mother?" Ruth asked in a low voice.

"Don't know," said Alice. "Never saw him before. Looks like no good to me. Well, ladies, let's get in the car and get home before our guests do. Where's Tommy?"

"I'm sorry, Mrs. Hoffman, but I can't do any more today. I'm just goin' to go home." The girl spoke in low tones, eyes to the ground. Her chin looked set, though.

"What do you mean?" said Alice briskly. "Your home is with us now. You can't go on livin' alone in that house with no one around you. It isn't safe with all these foreigners around workin' on the dam."

"I just want to go home," Leslie returned softly. "Besides, if no one is in the house, someone might break in. You know there is no security out there now."

"We're goin' to board things up but it has to wait for tomorrow."

Leslie shook her head at Alice. "Then I will come to Ingleside tomorrow. I can't leave the house open like that. I'm sorry." She started to walk away.

"Ruth, say something," Alice prodded.

"Les," Ruth ran to catch up, "how are you goin' to get there? Walk? It's a long way in this heat. And Mother's right—it isn't safe for a girl to be alone now."

Leslie did not reply or slow down.

"Les! Come on, Les. Be reasonable." Ruth gave up. "Dad!" she turned to her father.

"Leslie," Harland called over. Leslie stopped to look at him. "I'll make you a deal. You, Ruth and I will drive down to the house, and I'll board it up with what I can find good enough to hold it for a few days. While I do that, you pack a box of important things you want to keep with you. Maybe more clothes than what Ruth put together for you today. But when we are both done, we'll all go to Ingleside and you'll get settled in there."

For a minute, Leslie didn't answer. Then she nodded and came back. "Thank you," she said.

"Alice, you and Tommy get a ride with the Martins," Harland continued. "We'll meet you back at the house presently."

Alice opened her mouth and shut it again without reply.

The girls got in the front seat of the car and Harland joined them. They started down Wales Road toward the river, passing through the remains of Wales itself. One of the houses still left there was being burned to the ground, with people standing nearby. One woman held a handkerchief to her face while her husband stared stonily at the sky. Ruth looked at Leslie and knew she was thinking of her own house at the Point. It was only a matter of time.

As they continued south to Dickinson's Landing, traffic seemed to congest until they were at a complete stop. Harland got out of the car and began talking to the man parked in front of them, while the girls stood out on the road trying to see what was holding things up. The distant sound of a tolling bell was now close by.

"Look," Ruth grabbed Leslie's arm. "There's a steeple comin' along. They must be movin' a church."

Harland came back. "We can't get to the Point this way, girls. The road is blocked for Christ Church Anglican they're movin' from Moulinette today. It's so big it's takin' up the whole road. We'd best turn around."

But Leslie was walking forward through the crowd to the edge of the highway. The old church could be seen plainly now on the Hartshorne mover, on its way to the new museum called Upper Canada Village. Ruth moved in beside her to watch.

"That's the only church they're goin' to save," someone said behind them. "All the others are goin' to be destroyed."

"It's just not right, you know," another answered. "No matter what you want to say about progress. They're tearin' down the churches and diggin' up the dead. They goin' to move God out of here next?"

Ruth suddenly thought of Leslie's words at the dam that day last year: Seems like the end of the world. Unconsciously, she took her best friend's hand.

The church drew abreast and began to pass the crowd. Instinctively they moved back, even before the police escort waved them away. Everyone fell silent, watching the white frame building *with its tall spire rolling gently side to side like a ship at sea. Torn from its roots of more than a century, the old church looked tired and beaten. Over the sound of the Hartshorne's great motor, the church bell tolled mournfully as though at its own passing and was gone.*

Chapter **9**

The Edge of the Wilderness

⊖HE SOUND of the tolling bell faded in my mind and I realized that Ruth had fallen silent. I hazarded a glance and saw her face wet with tears. Instinctively, I put out my hand.

"God, I'm sorry, Ruth. I didn't mean to upset you."

She took out a handkerchief and wiped her eyes. "It's not really your fault, Fan. It's mine. I shut it all away for so many years, you know. I lost touch with your mother, I moved away to start a new life, I buried it all. Even after they found your father last year, I refused to think about it. The past was the past and that's where it belonged."

"And then I showed up."

"Yes. The most disturbing thing about it was finding out that Leslie had been alive all these years and never contacted me. I've missed her over the years, and now I've lost her all over again."

"Do you have any idea why she wouldn't?"

Ruth gave me a look. "I was hoping you could tell me."

"Mother kept no contact with this area at all," I shrugged. "It's something I have to figure out, too. She rarely talked about her childhood and almost never about my father. Something must have happened that scarred her so badly she closed the door on it all forever. But I'm still wondering why everyone thought she was dead," I added. "Did you remember who told Alice?"

"It must have been Meredith," she answered. "Why is that important?"

"I'm not sure," I said truthfully, "but it keeps gnawing at me." I finished my coffee and looked around at the grounds. "This is a nice setup here. I think it's great that the villages are kept alive this way."

"It's been a lot of work. And it's taken time. The Lost Villages Historical Society was formed in the Seventies. We had a celebration for the thirtieth anniversary of the inundation and another for the fortieth, but it seems that in just the last couple of years there's been a surge of interest about it all again."

"Interest and controversy," I commented. "A lot of arguments back and forth about whether it was done right or should have been done at all, from what I understand." I smiled. "I know what your mother thinks—she made that very clear. How do you feel about it all now?"

For a few moments, Ruth didn't answer. "I guess I see the point is moot," she said at last. "It was all over and done with a long time ago. And hindsight is always twenty-twenty. You teach history so I don't have to tell you that. But I remember my dad saying once that a lot of the difficulty then was that Hydro didn't really know how to cope with people and people problems. When it came to time, money and things, they were very efficient. But they treated people like things instead of realizing you can't move memories, and that's all we've got when we're older—our memories."

The sun went behind a stray cloud, putting a tinge of grey around us.

"After Harper died, did things settle down for my mother?"

"No, I'm afraid not, Fan. She had a few more surprises to cope with. And then, just when the dust began to settle, your father came back."

GIANT A-BLAST ROCKS NEVADA
Canadians Watch Biggest Blast since Hiroshima

MOHAWKS HOLDING COUNCIL, OLD HUNTING GROUND CALLS
St. Regis, Caughnawaga Braves Hear Call; Irked with Seaway

AMERICAN 100,000th VISITOR TO PROJECT

MORRISBURG PLANNING BIG NEW CIVIC CENTRE

Late August 1957
The Cornwall *Standard-Freeholder*

"I'm afraid it looks legitimate, Leslie." Harland Hoffman rubbed his forehead. "Of course, we'll have a lawyer look at it, but I'd say Mr. Taylor is tellin' the truth."

"Sure, I'm tellin' the truth," smiled the man Ruth had first seen the day of the funeral, at the cemetery. He reminded her of the Cheshire cat. "I don't want to cause trouble, mind, Harper bein' dead and all, but I paid good money for the property and it's mine."

"I don't believe you!" Leslie blurted out, rising from her chair. The four of them and Alice were seated at the Hoffman's kitchen table. Alice put a hand on her arm. "Harper wouldn't sell the house out from under me like that."

"Well, he didn't exactly sell it, Miss. He used it as collateral for a loan." Jeremy Taylor sat back in his seat and crossed his arms, his eyes fixed on Leslie's face. "About five years ago, Harper come to me and said he needed money—several thousand dollars. I loaned it to him and he signed the house as security. He made payments until about a year ago, when he said he needed more cash. I gave him the full value of the house, what with the Project comin'. He never made a payment after that. I finally come down to see what was what."

"Harp would never borrow money," said Leslie stubbornly. "He would never be beholden to anyone."

Taylor shrugged and rose to his feet. "All I know is the property is mine. I'm sorry to come here when you've just lost your father and all, but I need to clear this up and get what I've got comin' from Hydro. There isn't a lot of time left."

Harland showed him to the door. "We'll have to see a lawyer first, Mr. Taylor, but after that we'll call you."

"Don't take too long now," Taylor smiled again. "Like I said, not a lot of time left." In Cheshire fashion, he vanished.

"I don't like that man," Alice said bluntly. "Now he looks familiar to me. Where have I seen him before, Harland?"

Hoffman got to his feet. "I don't know, but it'll come to me." He turned to the girls. "Why don't you two get out and get some fresh air? Tommy's out watchin' that new house goin' up down the street. Go see the new high school you'll be at in the fall. Just keep busy and don't worry, Leslie. Everything will be fine."

Leslie nodded and smiled, but Ruth knew she wasn't convinced. They went up to the room they shared to get changed into shorts. Ruth put her finger to her lips and motioned to the floor grate hole *in Tommy's bedroom. Soundlessly, they crossed the floor and knelt down to listen.*

" . . . to say anything in front of Leslie. After the fur flyin' the way it did, I'm real surprised to hear that Harper had anything to do with the man since. He'd always felt he'd been cheated."

"That was one thing about Harp," said Alice softly. "He was honest. Traders like Taylor give the others a bad name. Do you think this loan story is a lie?"

"Well, I wouldn't put it past him, but the paper looks legal. Why would Harp do such a thing? He was always smart about things like that. I don't know," Harland shook his head. "There's something not right about it all."

Ruth quietly got to her feet and then went to her closet. "You'll have to finish unpackin' tonight, Les," she said in a loud voice, pointing to the floor. "Hard to find anything." She stifled a giggle and was gratified to see a genuine smile on her friend's face.

They changed and headed outside into one of the last summer days. Every mother in Ingleside was blessing the hot, dry weather. With not a front lawn in sight, rain meant a sea of mud with only the boardwalks to cover it. Kids from Aultsville, Wales and Dickinson's Landing were appearing at the new strip mall as the communities began to meld in the town. Rothwell Public School was almost finished one block north of the mall, but Osnabruck District High School right beside it was behind schedule. They would return to the Aultsville Continuation School for the first few months.

September brought rain (and mud) and news that the loan papers were in order. The house now belonged to Taylor. Due process of estate and transfer of land would take time, but with the lien on the property much greater than its value, Leslie was told she would have to turn over the furnishings for resale. All personal possessions Leslie would be free to take.

On a particularly cheerful September day, Leslie went with Ruth and Mr. Hoffman to pack up her things. She stood for a long moment in the quiet kitchen, darkened by the boarded windows. Even the sprightly yellow wallpaper seemed somber. Yet it still felt as though Harper would come through the front room doorway and fill the kitchen with his presence, as he had a hundred times in the past. But only the silence remained.

"Let's get to it, Leslie," said Harland kindly. "There's nothing more depressin' than a deserted house. The sooner we're done and back out in the world, the better. It isn't good for you to be here, wrapped in the past."

Leslie sighed. "All right, Mr. Hoffman. Let's get it over with it."

The knock at the door made them jump. Ruth opened it to Jeremy Taylor, hat in hand, smile in place.

"I hope you don't mind my bein' here for your packin', Miss Mackenzie," he said cheerfully. "I have to wait for a land agent to come and work on the price, so I thought I might as well kill two birds with one stone."

"We don't need a chaperone, Taylor," Harland replied darkly. "We're honest people."

"Oh, absolutely, absolutely," Taylor concurred heartily. "It's just that 'personal possessions' is such a vague idea. You just forget I'm here and I'll only help if there's something we're not sure about." He almost managed to swish a tail. Ruth wished he would disappear. This was hard enough on Leslie as it was.

Leslie gave him a hard look and then pointed to the front room. "You might be more comfortable on the davenport, Mr. Taylor," she said smoothly. "This may take a while."

"That's very gracious, Miss." He studied her face and the curves of her summer dress as he passed through to the other room.

"What are you bein' nice for?" Ruth hissed. "He's creepy."

"I'm not," Leslie shot back under her breath. "The davenport is Victorian. It's as comfortable as a bed of nails. I'm goin' to start in my room, Ruth," she added, speaking up, "if you want to help me there. Then I'll do Harp's room alone. Maybe then you could just check the upstairs closet for my extra clothes."

They moved upstairs, passing Mr. Taylor who sat on the edge of his seat, the picture of discomfort. Doing Leslie's room took close to an hour, but the closet only a few minutes. Ruth waited outside Harper's room. At last, Leslie opened the door, eyes red. She ran a hand through her hair and put the box of things on the hallway floor.

"Well, that's over." She squared her shoulders. "I want my mother's china in the front room."

"Uh, oh," Ruth grimaced. "Taylor time."

"Don't let him bother you," said Leslie as they went downstairs. "He enjoys that."

Harland was nowhere in sight when they reached the kitchen. Taylor slowly got to his feet when the girls entered the front room.

"Stiff," he said ruefully. "Must be gettin' old. Your father went out to the car, Miss. I asked him to get me the receipt for the scrap sold after the funeral. I understand it got a good price."

Leslie turned her back to him. "I guess. You'll get your money, Mr. Taylor." She walked over to a small china cabinet in the corner of the room and opened its doors. "All I want in here is my mother's china."

Taylor slid over and took a plate from her hand. "Looks valuable," he said, turning it over. "Might fetch a good price, too."

Leslie flashed dangerous eyes at him. "It was my mother's, Mr. Taylor. The only thing she brought with her from her home when she came here. It's mine by birthright."

"Well," he said silkily, glancing over his shoulder at Ruth before placing a hand on Leslie's arm, "you're as beautiful as your mother ever was. I'm sure we could work something out."

Leslie stiffened as Ruth felt her cheeks grow hot. "Taylor," she said, looking him straight in the eye, "nothing on heaven or earth is worth that to me. I'd rather see these dishes in pieces. You know," she added quietly, "that's not such a bad idea."

Ruth watched her nervously as she crossed over to a closet near the door and took out her baseball bat. Leslie stepped up to the cabinet and wound up to swing.

"Stop!" he yelled, hands out. "You can't do that!"

"Can't I?" She gave him a strange smile. "What's done is done. Ruth and I would say it's vandals' work and who would believe you? Maybe I'll just do everything in the house right now. Maybe we'll say that's how we found it today. Our word against yours." Leslie started to swing.

Taylor's yell brought Harland running in.

"What's goin' on?"

Ruth and Leslie started talking at the same time until he waved them quiet. Then Taylor broke in.

"She's crazy," he said, pointing to Leslie. "Says she's going to smash up the place rather than let me have it."

"Leslie?"

She put the bat down. Ruth grabbed her father's arm.

"He made a pass at Leslie, Dad."

"What?" He glared at Taylor, who threw up his arms.

"That's nuts. She's been around this one too long. And this one's crazy." He moved toward the front door. "Blood tells, you know. Old Harper was loco, and she's loco, too." He stormed out and slammed the door.

"Look," Ruth pointed out the bus window, "the Leonards' house is gone."

It was a beautiful fall day, and where the trees still stood in the bush areas along the shoreline, the leaves were in full turn. Aultsville had been stripped of that beauty last year. Now almost a ghost town, it was flat and bare with only boarded houses slated for demolition breaking the trail of abandoned foundations along deserted roads.

The school bus was headed north on the county road to the new No. 2 Highway and on to Ingleside with its load of teenagers from the Continuation School. Most of them were talking or singing, immune to the devastation around them. Earlier today, another house had passed the school on the great machine, but no one ran to look. It was just another day on the Front.

Leslie turned in time to see a gaping hole in the earth where the red brick house had once stood. Ruth bit her lip, watching Leslie's face and wishing that she'd let it pass unnoticed. But maybe it was okay—the girl's face was expressionless.

"I saw Gordon at the mall the other day," said Leslie absently. "He seemed friendly enough so we talked a bit. I asked if he'd heard anything from Hal and he said no. Got upset for a minute, I think. Then asked me if we'd want to go to the dance at Casselman's Hall tomorrow night."

"I think that's a great idea," said Ruth enthusiastically.

"So do I." Meredith's head came up from behind. The girls turned around.

"I thought you didn't go for that sort of thing," said Leslie.

"Well, there isn't much else to do around here anymore with everything half gone." Meredith shrugged. "Maybe we should all go. I can ask Gordon to drive us. He has a car."

Ruth nudged Leslie with her shoulder. "I think so, too. Why don't we? We could use a night out."

"I don't think your mother would like the idea," said Leslie. "The new Elvis movie is in Cornwall at the Capitol and she won't let us see that, remember? Says he moves too much. Besides, it's not in Osnabruck Township. They sell liquor there."

"Not in the hall, only in the hotels—but most of them are probably closed. If we don't go soon, we never will. The whole block is bein' demolished next spring. And my mother will love the idea," Ruth added with a giggle. "She's been tryin' to set me up with Gordon for months now."

Leslie shook her head. Meredith, other than a sigh at the mention of Elvis, remained silent.

"Our house is now in Upper Canada Village," Gordon said over the car radio. The weather was fine and the windows were rolled down, the girls having their kerchiefs tied tightly. "I didn't really know what to do and Dad isn't much help. He's pretty frail these days. Sometimes I'm not sure he knows where he is. Everything that happened . . . well, it hit him pretty hard, I think."

Meredith sat in the front with him, Ruth and Leslie in the back. "The store is still open?" she asked.

"Oh, yes, until the winter. I haven't sold it yet, but I'm working on Dad. He's too confused to give me a straight answer but I don't want to legally take it out of his hands. It would hurt him too much. But Hydro is losin' patience. It's tough right now." He looked in the rearview mirror. "I'm sure Leslie understands that, after everything with Harper."

Leslie returned his gaze for a moment. "Yes," she looked down at her hands, "I do."

"So have you gone to the dance hall before, Gordon?" Ruth asked brightly, changing the subject. "This is our first time."

"Once or twice," he shrugged, "but until lately, I always worked at the store Saturday nights. Now we close because no one comes around at night. I'm just as glad, though. It's pretty desolate out there in the daytime, let alone at night."

Gordon pulled off the highway and turned onto the No. 31 south, into the heart of Morrisburg. They parked on Main Street, where shoppers continued their Saturday ritual of evening browsing between the highway and the post office. While Main Street and

Front Street were slated for demolition in the spring, most of Morrisburg would remain intact, buying the stores time with their customers.

Some of the hotel lounges were open for business, but with the weather still warm, most people killed time in Canal Park watching the ships lock through. The four headed in that direction, but found most of the park stripped of its finery.

Leslie walked up to Lock No. 23 and sat on a bench to watch the latest boat go in. Ruth looked at her, knowing she was thinking of Hal. Where had he gone without a trace? You kept expecting him to slide in on a boat and jump off with his usual grin like nothing had happened. Maybe Gordon felt the same way. She hazarded a glance at him and saw him watching the ship's crew carefully, nodding his head to what Meredith was saying.

The light was fading fast, so they made their way along to the lighted street still filled with evening shoppers enjoying one of the last warm evenings.

"The orchestra doesn't start till nine," said Gordon, looking at his watch. "It's eight-thirty, but let's wait until we hear them before going up. Even in September, the hall gets warm quick up there."

'Up there' was the third floor central section of a large building that housed the Casselman Shoe Store and the York Five and Dime on the street level. Young people in party frocks and suits already lingered around a small door between the two stores. Some went in ahead of the music.

Ruth and Meredith perused the shoes in the Casselman window. Gordon stood with Leslie, hands in pockets.

"You look very nice tonight, Leslie," he said awkwardly.

"Thanks," she murmured absently, patting her red dress. "This is Ruth's dress. I don't have anything this fancy of my own, yet. Money's a little tight right now."

"I heard about the trouble with that Taylor fella," Gordon said to the pavement. "I'm sorry things turned out that way."

Leslie shrugged. "What's done is done. I just wish I could figure out where the money went so I could pay him off and keep the house. But the river's goin' to take it anyway soon enough, I guess."

The sound of musicians warming up began to fill the air. Shortly, the noise became the strains of In the Mood, drawing the loiterers into the small doorway with the power of the Pied Piper.

Gordon and the girls moved in with them, squeezing through the door frame into the wide, old staircase that allowed four abreast with no traffic moving down yet. At the top was a door on the left, leading to the next set of stairs. Once up, they paid their admission and got their hands stamped, moving into the hall with the flow of the crowd.

The big room was packed with young people from all over the area. The fading evening light came in from two sets of three large windows, framing the hall on the north and south sides. Halfway down the east side sat the band, playing to a fair number already dancing. Single girls clustered around the south window near the ladies' washroom, single guys in the opposite corner, the space between taken up by official couples. The girls hesitated, unsure where to go.

"I'm going to freshen up a bit," said Meredith, heading for the safety of the bathroom. Leslie looked at Ruth and Gordon standing together and excused herself also.

The next song was a waltz and Ruth felt her cheeks get warm. Gordon watched the couples move out on the floor and chewed his lip.

"Hey, Gordy!" A young man with a tight suit and highly polished shoes came up and slapped Gordon on the back. "You're becomin' a regular here. And you finally brought your girlfriend."

"Uh, no," stammered Gordon. "Ruth and I are just friends. Ruth, this is Ernie Black. Ernie, Ruth Hoffman."

"Just friends, eh?" Ernie smiled as her pumped her hand. "Well, then, Ruthie, would you like to dance?"

"I'd love to. Thanks." Ruth tossed her head for Gordon's benefit and moved out on the dance floor. She watched him as she kept up with Ernie's interpretive dancing and flowing narrative. Gordon moved over to talk to friends in the group of guys huddled in the corner, not unnoticed by the girls standing near the washroom. Leslie and Meredith emerged from the bathroom at last, saw Ruth dancing and stayed near the wall. Several of Gordon's friends looked over at them with practised casualness, then huddled with Gordon who glanced over his shoulder and shook his head. Leslie would have a full dance card tonight.

The band picked up tempo with the next song and many of the couples parted. Ruth made her way over to her friends, Ernie close behind. With introductions, he shook hands all around, lingering a little with Leslie.

"Gordon wasn't kidding about it getting hot up here," Leslie commented. "It's already warm. I wish they sold refreshments here."

"Nope, not a thing," said Ernie cheerfully. "They keep it simple. Guys and gals and tunes. The band takes a break around ten. We could slip out for a cold one then."

"The band is good," said Meredith wistfully, watching the dancers. "Where are they from?"

"A little all over, these guys," Ernie explained. "Mostly from Winchester, but the tall guy with the trumpet comes from Iroquois. And wait'll you hear his solo."

Gordon appeared at Ruth's other side. "Ernie keepin' you entertained, ladies?"

"Good thing someone is," Meredith said sourly. Gordon flushed a little, shooting a glance at Leslie.

"All the guys have been askin' me about you girls," he said with a shrug. "I don't think you'll be standin' around much tonight."

"Not if I can help it," Ernie grinned.

The band put down their instruments and loosened their ties. The dance floor began to clear, and a number of people headed for the door.

"Band's takin' a break already?" asked Ruth a little skeptically.

"Naw," Ernie replied. "Just a quick breather between sets. Next song will be a waltz. I should get my buddy over here to pick up the slack so we can all get out. That's if Gordy's going wake up and live a little," he added teasingly.

Gordon turned to him, but the retort died on his lips. He froze, eyes locked somewhere over Ernie's shoulder in the direction of the door. Meredith stiffened with a gasp, her hand unconsciously reaching for Gordon's arm. Leslie had followed their gaze and seemed turned to stone, face white as a ghost. With a very bad feeling, Ruth turned to look.

Hal Leonard stood in the middle of the empty dance floor, searching the crowd. He wore a suit with the jacket over his arm, tie pulled to one side. His hair was slicked back and his face had lost most of its boyish looks. He seemed thinner, yet stood with a sense of strength. A second man patted him on the shoulder and moved off toward a couple of girls.

"My God," Ruth muttered.

"What's wrong?" Ernie looked at their shocked faces.

"Long story," she said briefly.

Then Hal spotted them, his eyes resting on Leslie. He straightened his tie and smiled hesitantly before crossing the floor. When he spotted Gordon standing nearby, Hal's face darkened.

"Well, big brother," he said with a forced grin, "don't look so happy to see me."

Gordon recovered himself with an effort. "Takes gettin' used to, Hal. Like so many other things you've done. Ernie, this is my younger brother Hal," he added to his friend.

"Pleasure," Ernie said, shaking hands. "Well, that takes care of our third man. Now we just need the band to get on with it."

Meredith studied the floor, Ruth studied Leslie. The girl had not taken her eyes off Hal since his entrance, her face moving from disbelief to joy to anger. When he turned to her, she turned on him.

"Hi, Leslie," Hal said quietly. "It's real good to see you."

"Just like that? You disappear for almost a year with no word to anyone and then waltz in here like nothing happened? What are you thinkin'?"

Hal stepped back from her fury as heads began to turn in the crowd. Then he gathered himself.

"I'm thinkin' of you, Les. I heard about Harper when I was on the East Coast two weeks ago so I made sure I could come home for a bit when I got here. A friend of a friend picked me up at the Point and drove me to Ingleside to look for you. And no one was home— not you or Ruth or Dad or my brother here. Thank God Lynnie knew where you'd gone.

"I've only got a few hours. When the Emerald leaves Morrisburg tonight, I have to be on it. What with everything lookin' so strange and everyone gone, I . . . I started feelin' I wasn't goin' to see you again."

There was dead silence. Leslie looked unhappy, but the fire had died in her eyes.

"I had to see you, Les," he added softly. "I had to know you were okay."

"What about seein' if Dad is okay?" Gordon said cuttingly.

The band swung into Mona Lisa and the couples filled the floor. Ernie took Ruth's arm.

"Good time to dance," he said brightly. Ruth looked from Leslie to Hal uncertainly before letting herself be led away. She heard Gordon ask Hal why he really was here.

"Hell, I don't know, Gordy," Hal said over the music as he tossed his jacket on a chair. "Guess I just came to dance." He turned to take Leslie's hand. "They're playin' our song, Miss Mackenzie. Will you dance with me one more time?"

Leslie started to cry. Hal took her in his arms and they disappeared on the floor. Gordon stood looking like thunder till he realized that Meredith was waiting quietly beside him. They joined the couples, Gordon watching his brother over Meredith's shoulders.

From time to time, Ruth spotted Leslie and Hal dancing deep in conversation. When the band swung into a dance tune, they continued waltzing for a few minutes, oblivious to the people around them. Whatever he was telling her, she would shake her head. Finally, she put her face on his shoulder.

"I think it's time to take a break outside, Ruthie," said Ernie, wiping his face with his handkerchief.

"Let's get everyone together, then," Ruth suggested. She didn't like the turn the evening had taken. From the looks of it, neither did Leslie or Gordon.

Hal was his usual cheery self, either oblivious to their feelings or working on them. Ruth couldn't decide.

Meredith never took her eyes off him.

They joined the stream of other dancers feeling the heat and pooled at the street door. All the restaurants were still open, business as usual right up to the end. But the signs of the end were unmistakable. Boarded windows above the stores, empty shop fronts where someone had already moved to the new strip mall that faced the new No. 2 Highway, an air of decay and disrepair settling over it all without the need to maintain the properties. Soon enough would come the actual demolition. But for now, the shoppers continued to stroll the street, kids played in Canal Park, and lovers held hands as the ships locked through on another warm September evening in Old Morrisburg.

"I got off at the Point and I almost didn't know where I was," said Hal quietly, as though reading Ruth's thoughts. "It's all so changed. Everything is gone. Aultsville's a ghost town. It's like I went away for years." He lit a cigarette and took a long drag. "I *hope they know what they're doin'." He looked at his brother. "The house is gone, but it's not in Ingleside. Where is it?"*

"At Upper Canada Village," came the brief reply. "It'll be part of the museum."

"That was okay with Dad?"

"I had no choice, Hal," said his brother tersely. "You were gone, Dad dragged his feet about sellin', and he got so he couldn't use the stairs anymore. I took the offer when it came."

"Dad's sick?" Hal seemed surprised.

"If you'd have let us know where you were, I could have told you that months ago."

"Hey, why don't we walk down to the Coffee Cup and buy some soft drinks?" Ernie broke in nervously. "I sure need something."

"Yes, let's go," said Ruth, catching Leslie's arm. "Meredith?"

Taking the hint, the girls went with Ernie, giving the brothers time to talk alone. Meredith hesitated, looked back at the two Leonard boys arguing, and then followed. When they got back with the bottles, Gordon was silently leaning on his car. Hal stood chatting with a couple of girls Ruth recognized from school sport meets. One of them turned to Ernie as he came up.

"I thought it was you, Ernie," she said stiffly. "I thought you weren't coming here anymore."

Ernie shrugged and stared at his drink. "Just here with some guys, Janice."

"Well, don't just stand there," Janice replied sarcastically, looking at the girls beside him. "Introduce me to the guys."

"Janice," Ernie said irritably, "knock it off. You were the one who said we shouldn't go steady anymore."

"Maybe I changed my mind," she shot back peevishly. Then she looked over at Hal with a smile. "Maybe not."

A chill descended, no thanks to the drinks.

Finally, Ernie said, "We'd better get back before the band takes their break." He followed Janice and her friend up the big stairs, the others right behind. Ruth saw Hal quietly take Leslie's hand. She pushed him away once, but made no move the second time he tried. When they joined the dance floor, Janice spirited Ernie away and they saw no more of him. Leslie stayed with Hal for the next half hour, while Gordon danced with Ruth and Meredith. When Ruth took her turn, he was as talkative as a rock.

Finally at ten p.m., the band took its break.

"We're going to play you one more song before we break for a little while," said the bandleader as he wiped the sweat from his face. "It's an oldie—but I grew up with this man's music, and this song's always been one of my favourites.

"Before we do, I just want to let you know we finish our summer dates here next week. Now ordinarily, we'd be planning to come back next year. But as you all know, the dance hall won't be here by then. We don't know yet where we'll be next year, but we hope that all of you will come and see us there, too. Me and the boys have played here for five years, and we just wanted to say we've enjoyed every single night. Just in case we don't see you next season, best of luck to you all."

He picked up his trumpet and played Glenn Miller's Moonlight Serenade. *Even those who were making their way to the door before the crowd did stopped to listen. Something was passing, like the letting go of an old love. For all its shiny promise, the brave new world had no room for memories and they knew it.*

When the song ended, the crowd moved en masse to the door and the stairs beyond. Ruth fought the wave of people and made her way to Leslie. Hal walked over to Gordon.

"So what's goin' on with you two?" Ruth asked quickly. It was the first chance she'd had to talk with Leslie alone since they'd arrived.

"I don't know," Leslie shrugged. "His ship will lock through around midnight and he wants me to spend the next while with him. Says we need to talk."

"You're not goin', are you?" When Leslie looked at the floor, Ruth sighed. "Oh God, you're still in love with him, aren't you? Haven't you learned? He left for months without a word and then just comes back out of the blue. Besides, Mother will have a fit if you're that late and how will you get home?"

"Hal says the guy he came with and his girlfriend will pick me up at the lock. They have friends on board, too."

"I don't think you should, but it's your life I guess." Ruth said shortly.

"First Ernie, now Meredith," said Hal, coming up with Gordon trailing behind. Then he grinned. "Maybe it's my personal charm."

"Why? Where's Meredith?" Leslie asked, looking around.

"She went home with a couple of school chums," said Gordon. "Said she wasn't feelin' well."

"We're goin' to make ourselves scarce, too, Gordy." Hal stuck out his hand. "I'm sorry things didn't work out tonight, but no hard feelings."

When Gordon slowly reached out to shake hands with his brother, Ruth realized she was holding her breath and let it go.

"Will you be home after you lay up for the winter?" Gordon asked casually.

"I don't know," Hal replied. "I couldn't afford it last year. But maybe this year." He turned to Leslie. "It depends on whether I'm wanted back or not, I guess."

Leslie did not meet his eyes, but let him take her hand once more. "I'll see you at the house later, Ruth," she said.

Hal and Leslie crossed the dance floor and disappeared into the stairwell.

"If you came home late, too, it isn't my fault, so why are you mad at me?" Leslie hissed at Ruth across the desk aisle, where the girl sat wrapped in her coat and her thoughts. It was the first really cold day of the fall and the Continuation School had had its heat disconnected, not expecting to need it again. Some students wore thin gloves to keep their fingers warm.

"I'm not mad," Ruth shot back. "I just wish you wouldn't have gone off alone and left me with Gordon."

"What's wrong with Gordon?" Meredith joined in from behind Leslie. The teacher looked over and the girl dropped her eyes.

"You're no better," whispered Ruth hotly. "If you hadn't just up and gone the way you did, you could have helped me talk her out of it."

"I'm glad I went," Leslie said stubbornly. "We did need to talk. We straightened everything out." She touched a gold bracelet on her wrist. It had a beautiful heart with engraved flowers on it that opened to reveal a picture of Hal. "He's comin' back for me as soon as he saves enough money." She turned to Ruth. "If you're not mad,

why have you been so quiet? You had the flu after the dance but that was two weeks ago. Even your mother is wonderin'."

"Miss Hoffman, is there a problem?" asked the teacher pointedly.

"No, Miss Rosemary."

"Then finish your reading quietly."

The girls fell silent. Ruth tried to push all thoughts out of her head, but couldn't. Being grounded for a week after the dance, avoiding Gordon, avoiding questions about Hal, hearing the news about Jeremy Taylor's unpleasant surprise. At least that had been a small ray of sun in the bleak landscape.

"The sly old fox," her father had said. "He never owned the land. It was squatter's rights only. Now the real owners have come forward so everything's in an uproar with Hydro."

"So he paid Taylor back in the end and saved Leslie the problem of provin' ownership." Alice had shook her head. "Still the best poker player in these parts, right to the end. Only question is, where is the money?"

Well, that was Leslie's problem. If her friend knew anything, she wasn't saying. The lawyers for Hydro had come to see them, saying that Taylor had backed out and written off his debt with no idea of pursuing Leslie for any more assets. The rightful owners, people from up North, had settled with them. Leslie had to sign off any further claim as well, and she did without protest.

Ruth put her hand over her eyes. Now if only they had never gone to Casselman's Dance Hall . . .

The teacher rang the big brass bell for recess and everyone filed outside.

The bright sun did little to warm the girls and they huddled near the building out of the wind. Leslie tried small talk, but gave up when Ruth did not respond.

"How come so glum, ladies?" Desmond Shaler strolled up to them, smiling from ear to ear. A red flag popped up in the back of Ruth's mind. "Thought you'd be happy from seein' your long-lost sailor again. I heard he'd turned up again like the bad penny he is."

"Shut up, Des," Ruth snapped. "We're not in the mood."

"My, aren't we testy, Ruth? And here I just came over to be friendly and tell you the news." His eyes were bright. It must be bad news. Ruth decided to ignore him and turned her back.

"What news?" she heard Leslie say.

"My dad's working with the demolition guys for now," he replied. "Your old house is goin' today, Les."

"That's a lie! It's too soon," Ruth turned back to face him.

"Nope. It's today. My dad shows me the list every week. They won't start full demolition until next spring, but now they're burnin' down any old barns, shacks, that kind of thing. You know, anything that burns well." He smiled beatifically at them.

"Oh, God!" Leslie's hands flew up to her face. "God, no. Not today." She started to walk away, pushing through other students standing in the old schoolyard. Then she broke into a run.

"Les!" Ruth screamed. Everyone turned to look. "Les, where are you goin'?"

"Home!" came the faint reply. "I've got to get home."

Ruth sprinted after her, to where Leslie disappeared around a corner of the building. She could see her friend headed toward the river, and her shoulders sagged. She couldn't let Leslie go there alone.

Ruth turned back to see the other kids looking from Desmond to her uncertainly. "You are so bloody pathetic!" she yelled at him. "Did you know that? No bloody brains at all!"

Miss Rosemary was coming out to see what the noise was about. Ruth spun around and took off after Leslie who was now far down the road.

"Les! Les!" she screamed, but the girl did not hear. Something beyond human strength was fueling Leslie Mackenzie, and Ruth had to give up. She walked and jogged for twenty minutes before a truck that she recognized came along and offered her a lift. He left her just down from her old home at the bottom of the road on the old highway.

Ruth walked up the hill, her chest still hurting from the athletics. Then she saw a small plume of smoke rise into the air, and began to run. At the top of the hill stood the old house, marked off by safety rope. Smoke came from its windows. There were several men moving around it at a safe distance. Leslie stood alone in the centre of the road, watching, as still as Lot's wife.

As Ruth came up, a young man walked over from the house to where Leslie stood. He pushed his hardhat back and rubbed his head.

"I really don't think you should stay, Miss," he said kindly. "Especially not alone. Most folks find this upsetting."

"I'm stayin' until it's done," she said flatly. "It's the only home I've ever known. Where else would you want me to be?"

He seemed unsure what to do, and then brightened when he saw Ruth approach.

"Are you with this lady, Miss?"

"Yes, not that she made it easy." Ruth glared at Leslie, then sighed. "He's right, you know. You oughtn't to have come. It's only goin' to hurt you."

"I had to, Ruth. You would have done the same thing."

The young man still looked uneasy, but he returned to the house. Visible flames now licked at the walls through the windows. A few cars had pulled up, attracted by the smoke from the highway. One man took out a camera.

"Freeholder might want these," he said to no one in particular. "One of the first houses to go up. Who used to live here?"

"Harper Mackenzie." Leslie's voice seemed to come from far away, and the heat made her shimmer in Ruth's eyes. "My father."

The man turned to give her a curious look, then moved around to get a shot of the house with Leslie standing near. Ruth gave him a dirty look, but Leslie remained oblivious.

Within a few minutes, one of the men gave a shout and they fell back as one of the walls gave in. They could see the old front room and Leslie's bedroom above it. Ruth tried not to think of what Desmond had said about things that burn easily. It seemed to be happening very fast. The heat came in waves and drove them back to the far side of the road. Leslie did not move.

The men gave way but stayed around the parameters of the building. The young man who had come over before made his way back to Leslie.

"You have to move back, Miss," he yelled over the noise of the flames. "This thing is going to collapse any minute and it'll send out a shower of hot sparks. You could get burned."

Ruth saw Leslie shake her head, so she came over to pull her away.

"I'm okay, Ruth," said Leslie tonelessly. "It won't hurt me."

There was a sudden crash as the roof gave in, sending embers and burning bits of material into the air. Ruth dragged Leslie to the far side of the road and they watched the remaining walls cave into *themselves. Within minutes, the only thing standing was the old stovepipe from the kitchen.*

With the show over, people began to move on. The man with the camera stopped as if to speak with Leslie, but thought better of it and left. Soon the two girls were the only onlookers left on the street. They walked over to the safety rope.

The young man came over again and looked at Leslie's impassive face. "Nothing left here now, just some cleanup, Miss," he said to Ruth. "You'd best take her home, I think."

Ruth watched Leslie reach down and pick a charred scrap of paper off the road. It was yellow and white with blue forget-me-nots on it. Les carefully put it in her pocket and looked back at the smoldering ruins.

"I think it's too late for that," Ruth replied.

REDS TO FIRE 2nd SPUTNIK
New 'Moon' Bigger, Better
Pick Nov. 7th As Tentative Launching Date

U.S. SEAWAY LOCKS NEAR COMPLETION

MOULINETTE SCHOOL CLOSES ON FRIDAY
The Cornwall Township Public School Board announced today that the Moulinette school will close on Friday. Children attending the school will be transferred to the Mille Roches school until completion of the new public school at Long Sault.

October 30-31, 1957
The Cornwall *Standard-Freeholder*

It took a minute for the girls to realize it wasn't a costume. The person on the doorstep was genuinely old—very old—with long white hair and beard under a well-worn black cap. A long black coat with big pockets covered black pants and boots. Despite the size of the coat, Ruth got the impression that it was no match for that cold Halloween night.

"Would you like to come in, sir?" said Leslie hesitantly.

Ruth squeezed her arm. "Just shut the door. He might know that Dad's workin' and Mother is out with Tommy and his friends."

But the man made no move to come in, just looked carefully at Ruth, then Leslie with sharp blue eyes.

"Are ye Harp's girl?" he said suddenly to the latter.

"Ye . . . yes, sir."

"We has to talk alone. I got somethin' for ye."

"Not a chance," Ruth muttered under her breath. Then she saw a small tin box under his arm. "Les, he might have a gun," she whispered.

"Ruth," said Leslie finally, "this is Stewart Cassidy. He's an old friend of Harper's. Won't you come in for just a moment, Mr. Cassidy?" she added to the visitor.

The old man took a careful look down the front hall before coming inside. He stood just inside the door, hat in hand, running the brim through fingers as brown as earth. When Leslie closed the door, he put his back to it.

"I just come to give ye what's yours. Harp give it to me last year, said to keep it safe for ye. I was to wait a full season after the funeral before I find ye. It's been a season so here I am."

Ruth heard Harper's voice from that bad summer day a lifetime ago. The stacks, gal. I kept the stacks. They're yours, Les. She looked at Stewart Cassidy. Cass. They're safe. Remember that.

"He has the stacks, Les," she said quietly.

Leslie looked doubtfully at Ruth, then her face cleared.

"My father said something about 'stacks' when he was dyin', Mr. Cassidy. Is that what you have for me?" She looked at the tin box, which he now held forward.

"Yep. Harp said they was valuable, but I can't see it if it ain't money. But I made a promise, and I kep' it." Cassidy placed the box in Leslie's hands, then turned to go but stopped.

"Yer pa was a good man." The piercing blue eyes looked right into hers. "As good as they come. That Taylor's a liar and a thief from way back. What Harp did, Taylor had it comin' in spades. Just so ye know."

"Trick or treat!" came the cry as he opened the door. A group of goblins, ghosts and superheroes held their bags out to him. Startled, the old hermit stepped back into the house.

"Okay, guys," said Leslie, while Ruth got the bowls of candy. The small marauders made quick work of the loot and ran off to the next house. It was only after they were gone that the girls realized

the hall was empty. The old man had vanished as suddenly as he had come.

"Quick, Les," Ruth collapsed on the green and gold couch in the living room. "Before the next batch of kids gets here. Open the box. I'm dyin' to know what the 'stacks' are."

"Are you sure you're not just plain dyin', Ruth?" Leslie looked concerned as she sat next to her friend. "You're as pale as a ghost, and you sure haven't eaten much this week. You're not dieting again, are you?"

Ruth waved her comments away. "Open the box."

"Okay, okay."

The old tin box had no lock, but the clasp on the front had seen better days. It took several minutes with a strong kitchen knife to pry it open. Finally, the box agreed to reveal its contents—a stack of papers.

"Certificates of some kind. Some go back five years." Ruth looked at one closely, then grabbed Leslie's arm. "Not certificates— stocks. Harper wasn't sayin' 'stacks', he was sayin' stocks. Dad has a few of these. They're worth money—if the company is worth money."

The stocks read POWER AUTHORITY OF THE STATE OF NEW YORK.

"Jesus, Les," Ruth whispered, "I think you're rich."

"So that's why Mother never had to work when I was young."

The sun had inexplicably found the only cloud in the sky. The coffee had turned cold in my hand.

When Ruth did not reply, I hazarded one more question.

"So what made it end between you two? Didn't she say where she was going when she left?"

A door slammed shut somewhere deep inside Ruth and she stood up, brushing her dress absently. "I went to Montreal shortly after for what was to be a short visit with my aunt. It turned out she was sicker than we thought and she had no one else, so I stayed the winter. When I got back, your mother was long gone, sometime around Christmas."

"Didn't you stay in touch all that time? Did she say my father came back?"

"No . . . no. I was very busy with my aunt, and Mother didn't say anything about it. Speaking of Mother, I really should get home."

Ruth excused herself and moved quickly across the lawn toward the cars. A gold mine of information barely scratched, and a minefield of unanswered questions. I wondered what I'd said that had set her off.

Chapter 10

Undertow

𝕴 DIDN'T sleep well that night, trapped in my borrowed memories. As luck would have it, someone close by was listening to an oldies show on their radio, and the sound of Nat King Cole (in the original mono recording, no less) drifted in through the windows as I finally drifted off. I dreamed the stories again and again, until I suddenly realized that it was me—not my mother—at the dance hall. But when I looked into my father's face, it wasn't there. Just an empty form with no features.

It depends on whether I'm wanted back or not.

I opened my eyes, happy to see the early dawn. The mornings were becoming hot much faster as June took its toll on the season. The geese now came with little fuzzballs that were quickly becoming smaller versions of their parents. I hadn't seen much of Mr. Heron, but hummingbirds darted around my flowers. Small boats began to dot the river, too. Seasons and cycles seem much clearer on the St. Lawrence.

My anger readings were up again that morning, too. It took me several cups of tea on the porch before I could put my finger on it. It wasn't Ruth's evasiveness at the end or the idea of what my mother went through as a teenager. It was more about Mother not sharing all this with me, all the hard memories and the pain. I knew it never left her because I knew the kind of person she was. Why not let me know? Did she think I couldn't help her come to terms with it or just that I wouldn't care?

Maybe, said my heart of darkness, maybe she knew that you walked away from someone who needed you and never looked back. Maybe she thought you would turn away from her, too.

I stood up to end my thoughts, and he came back.

Swooping low over the river, the heron folded his prehistoric wings and landed easily on the beach. He looked right at me, holding something in his mouth and giving it a little shake. It was a small fish—breakfast—and it was very much alive. He raised his beak skyward and snapped the fish around. At one point he lost it, but with a speed and skill that was beauty in motion, the great bird plucked it out of the water and slipped it down his throat. Then he looked at me again with those black, soulless eyes, and I found myself feeling sorry for the fish.

My beautiful killer.

Having shown me his technique, the Great Blue Heron left me in search of more fish and I was alone again with my thoughts. I purposefully turned them to the time gap I had about the last few months before the flooding. Ruth had said she simply wasn't there. Gordon said the last time he saw his brother was that night they secretly met just before the murder. But Gordon was living in Ingleside then, and I hadn't asked him what he knew about my mother in those final months. And Lynn would know what there was to know, if she'd tell me. I wished I'd had more time to talk to Meredith that day. Whatever she told me would have been the real scoop.

But someone had killed Meredith. Maybe that was why.

Therein lay an important question I had not so far fully explored: Why kill Meredith? Had she seen something or known a secret that someone was afraid I'd find out? But they had found my father almost a year ago now. Wouldn't she have spoken up then? Or was she covering for someone? Would she do that if it were about murder?

I doubted that, unless she cared very much for him--or her.

It was turning out to be a bacon-and-egg day. I decided to avoid dishes (as there were plenty of them already in the sink) by getting dressed and heading to the Long Sault Marina diner for breakfast. Then I could head right over to the police station across the highway. Strauss had been ominously silent since our first meeting, but I knew better than to think he was finished with me. Perhaps he was having me watched to see if I conveniently witnessed any more deaths during my holidays here.

At any rate, I hadn't had a chance to ask him about the investigation into my father's death and the discovery of his body. It would make a good excuse to see where I stood on the suspect spectrum at this point.

The diner is one of the very few waterfront businesses between Cornwall and Prescott, and it works its location well. The restaurant is small but well kept, with three large windows giving you a total view of the St. Lawrence. That day the tables had filled with boaters and some local traffic, I guessed. The bacon and eggs were worth the trip.

The OPP receptionist told me that Strauss was out for the morning, so I decided to leave my number and go home to work. Officer Wiley came out from the back office just behind the front desk where I had given my statement, and smiled when he saw me.

"Dr. Mackenzie, right?" He shook hands. "Are you here to see the Inspector?"

"I wanted to but he's out right now. I guess I should have made an appointment."

"Is it something I can help you with?"

"Only if you were involved when they found the body out in Aultsville last year."

"As a matter of fact, I was." The officer passed a stack of brown envelopes to the receptionist.

"I only read what was in the papers, and I wanted to know a bit more about what was found and where it stands now." When he hesitated, I added, "The man they found out there was my father."

Wiley nodded slowly and I realized that of course he would know that. Strauss would have put that in my file. "Come with me," he said, indicating the hallway I had taken to Strauss's office that other fine day.

We ended up in a long room with several desks in it. Wiley pulled a chair up to the first one and we both sat down.

"I can't let you read the reports because it's technically still an open investigation, but I'll try to answer your questions."

"God, where do I start?" I sat back in the seat, not easy to do in a 1950s oak office chair. "Who found him? Why wasn't he found before this?"

"The remains—sorry, your father—was found by two hikers from New York state. It was the fortieth anniversary celebration that summer, and we had lots of sightseers come into the area and browse around the old sites. Now, July was really wet, lots of rain. People came for the celebrations but the walking tours didn't really get started till almost August."

"Why not years before this?" I persisted. "Surely people wandered around a bit in the early years after the flooding."

"I'm sure they did," he agreed, "but we figure the corpse was covered with dirt back then, plus the water. Over time the water worked away the soil and the body came to the surface. At least the top part. It was wrapped up in what we believe to have been a nylon bag of some sort, like a sleeping bag." He cleared his throat. "There were rocks in it to weigh the body down."

I tried not to think about that too much, and circled back.

"How did they spot the body in the water?"

"It wasn't in the water by then. Last year, the water levels in the Seaway reached a ten-year low for some reason, despite the rain we experienced. People around here had twice the beach area off their property, and in the case of Aultsville, which is a shallow area to begin with, the old streets and foundations came up much more than usual."

"Can you sketch me a map to the place you found him?" I asked, suddenly realizing I had been putting off this part of the pilgrimage.

"I can," he smiled apologetically, "but it won't help you much now."

"Why not?"

"The water is not only back up this year but higher than usual. Seems they have low water problems in Lake Ontario, so they're slowing down the drainage here to help it get back up in the lake. God only knows how long that will take."

I fell into a disappointed silence. Sensing my thoughts, Wiley said, "It must be very strange for you to come here about something from the past and all the markers are gone."

I looked up into a pair of genuinely sympathetic eyes, and nodded.

"Stranger than you can imagine. I make my living trying to reconstruct and interpret history, but this is something else. It's like grabbing spider webs." I sighed and looked out the window at the public school. "People I've talked to have been helpful with their memories, but perspective is everything." I turned back. "If I could just get a grasp of the context to put it all into."

"If you mean get a better idea of what life in the area was like back then, maybe this would help." The officer reached up on a shelf over his head and pulled down a small blue book: *Voices from the Lost Villages*. "Local writer who grew up on the Front. Have you read it?"

"No." I took the book with interest.

"In the Seventies, the Lost Villages Historical Society taped interviews with former residents of the villages about their lives and the Seaway days. Rosemary Rutley uses them and her own experiences to give you an idea of the lifestyle back then. You can borrow it if you want."

"Thanks," I said sincerely. "I'll start on it right away." The inside had a childish signature, DIANA WILEY. "Your daughter?" I asked.

"Yes. Diana did a study project on the villages for school last month. I've lived here for two years, but it's only been since I spent that time in Aultsville on the old streets that I really started to read up about it."

"Do you ever talk about it with Inspector Strauss?" I asked coyly. "He knew my family."

Wiley shook his head. "Nope. He doesn't like to talk about it."

I made an appreciative noise. "I'll return this as soon as possible," I added, holding up the book.

"Not to worry. Tomorrow I start my holidays for three weeks, but you can drop it off here when you're done."

"I'll do that." I rose to go. "Just one more thing, constable. Where does the investigation stand now? Do you have any solid leads or anything like that?"

He opened the door to the hallway. "I'm afraid not. As I'm sure you can understand, the time gap is the big problem. Many people who lived there have since died or are too old to remember clearly. We talked to a lot of people, but no one saw your father back in the area in the weeks before the flooding." I thought of what Gordon had said. "It's still an open case, but the chances of solving it aren't very good."

"But now Meredith Murphy has died, and probably because I came here and stirred things up."

Wiley suddenly became very official. "I'm afraid I can't comment on that, Dr. Mackenzie. You'll have to talk to the Inspector."

"I understand. Please tell him I was looking for him, if he could give me a call. Probably later this afternoon," I added. "I'm on my way to Upper Canada Village right now."

I hadn't been back to the Village since that horrid day of Meredith's death, and I really didn't want to go. But I was chewing on the mystery of my mother's movements in the last months she spent here. I wanted to see Alice Hoffman about it. I knew, however, I'd used up my welcome there for at least a few days with Ruth. So back to Gordon and then maybe a quick phone call to Lynn. I also had to finish up with the Lost Villages exhibit—work that was really never begun when my own past started getting in the way.

I drove straight to the Operations building this time, waiting to let a covered wagon and team pass me before pulling into one of the few slots marked "Visitors" in the small, dirt parking lot. When I got out of my car, the thump of the sawmill came to me, turning the bright day momentarily dark.

Nothing stops this mill. The river runs it. You'd have to stop the river.

I shook my head and walked into the front lobby. Gordon stood there, talking with a tall man dressed in a summer suit. They both turned at my entrance. Gordon faltered to a stop and the other man stared, seemingly puzzled.

"Oh . . . Farran," said Gordon uncertainly. "Did we have an appointment?"

"No, no," I put my hand up. "I'm sorry for just walking in but I'm headed for the Village today for research and there were a couple of things I wanted to ask you. If you're busy, though," I added, smiling at the visitor, "I can wait."

Gordon remembered his manners.

"Jim," he turned to the other man, "this is Dr. Farran Mackenzie. She's with the University of Waterloo, doing a paper on the effects of the Seaway on the people moved. Farran, this is James Bickman. He was with the Parks Commission for years."

Bickman shook my hand firmly. I guessed he was in his early seventies, clean-shaven with grey hair and eyes framed by laugh lines. He returned my smile, but the scrutiny stayed.

"Have we met before, Dr. Mackenzie?" he asked politely.

"Not that I know of, Mr. Bickman."

"Actually, Jim," Gordon said slowly, "Farran is my niece. She's Hal's daughter, and we've just recently found each other."

Bickman's face cleared. "Hal's daughter. My God. That's why you look familiar. You look so much like your father—except you're much prettier, of course."

I had to give him another smile for that one. Gordon unconsciously shifted his weight from one foot to the other.

"Farran," he broke in, "I have to be in a meeting in a few minutes and then I'm on the road today. Can you drop by tomorrow evening?"

"Absolutely," I said, turning to go. "It can wait. I'll track down Alice Hoffman again in the meantime. Nice to meet you, Mr. Bickman."

"I'm on my way out, too, Dr. Mackenzie." Bickman moved to hold the door open. "Can I walk you to your car?"

As we took our leave, I saw concern in Gordon's eyes. I wondered why. I'd have to ask him about that, too.

"How did you know my father, Mr. Bickman?"

"It's Jim—or you could call me Bick. That's the only name I went by in my sailing days and I don't hear it too much anymore. Your dad called me that when we sailed together."

I felt a flutter in my stomach. "You sailed together? On the *Lake Emerald*?"

"Yes, for over a year. Is this your car?" he added as we stopped. "Mine is in the main parking lot over there. Why don't I walk you to the Village entrance if you're going that way?"

"That would be great," I said. I wanted a chance to hear about those missing months in my father's life. I couldn't believe my good fortune at having them fall into my lap.

"We took your dad on in the fall of '56," Bick continued as we headed out of the parking lot. "He came aboard one night when we lost a deckhand in Cornwall. When I started shipping, we used to just ask around for a replacement and, more often than not, someone was hanging around looking for a job. But the union was putting an end to that, so we called the hall and asked for a deckhand. We got your dad at Farran's Point."

"Why the Point? Why not Aultsville?"

"Freighters didn't stop at Aultsville. We'd bypass it by going between Steen and Cat Islands. They're shoals in the river, now."

"Did you see him come aboard that night?"

"Yes, but I didn't meet him till the next day. You didn't do Farran's Point at night so we were trying to beat the sunset. I was third mate back then, and the run through the Point kept everyone busy. Lock No. 22 was one of the shortest in the old system so you had to hop to it."

"Why?" My professional training made me hazard getting off track.

"Well, with the other locks, you'd simply pull in and the lock gates would shut you in. But the Point had a strong current and a long pier. You had to land at the pier and then slowly check into the lock. Then, because it was a short lock, the guys would have to tie the winch wire on the dock to the stern and move the boat first to one side, then the other, so they could close the gates. It was a bit of job, but it gave us time to make eyes at the girls on the bank watching us work." The laugh lines deepened and I had to smile, too.

"So my father worked as a deckhand," I said.

"Well, he had no training so it was either a deckhand or a fireman—in the engine room," Bick added, noting my blank expression. "But he was a hard worker and a smart kid. The Old Man could see that. So by the time we were heading back to the area in the spring, Hal was training to be a wheelsman. And we were sad to lose him after. With that you either have it or you don't, and you have to start young or it doesn't come at all. Hal would have grown into a good one."

We were quiet for a moment. A school bus roared past us in the exit lane beside the sidewalk.

"Did you get to know him well, Bick?"

It was a loaded question and we both knew it. But he answered right away.

"Farran, those boats weren't big by today's standards. The old system wouldn't allow it. And shipping became your life for anyone who didn't run seasonal, like your dad and me. You got to know a fella pretty well, even the ones who were running from something."

"Like my father."

"Yes." He looked at me kindly. "Not that Hal was the only one. And he kept his nose clean, so the Old Man had no trouble with him."

"The Old Man?"

"The captain. And back then, it was definitely the captain's ship."

"Did he ever talk about what went on back home?"

"A little bit, now and then. Talk was okay, but you didn't ask too many questions. Your dad and I did many nights on the bridge towards the end. He had asked my help once in the summer to go see his family and a girl I sensed he'd left behind. I got a pal of mine in the area to loan him some street clothes, drive him around for the day and get him back to the ship on time that night. He'd been excited about it when we set it up, but got real quiet again after that for a while, like when he'd first come on. I figured things didn't go well."

I thought of Casselman's Dance Hall, and the two brothers standing apart, silent, on the street.

"Did he take a leave again after that?"

"No. Well, yes, but it ended up being for good." He looked down at the brick walk leading to the admissions booth. "Hal had something up his sleeve when he left at the end of the season. He said he wouldn't be back till the old seaway shut down in July for the flooding. There would be no traffic moving then, and the *Emerald* would be laid up in Cornwall. A bunch of us were going to cross over to see the *Humberdoc* be the first to use the new American locks and I expected to find your dad on board when we got back. But he wasn't."

Bickman shoved his hands in his pockets and looked at me. "You know, I haven't told a soul this in forty years, but Hal borrowed some money from me before he left. Something he'd never done before. Said he had some important things to do that couldn't wait anymore." All traces of a smile were temporarily gone. "When he didn't come back, that was one thing. But when he never tried to reach me and pay the money back, I always had a funny feeling about it. That wasn't Hal. Something was wrong. Then I found out last year how wrong. I can't tell you how sorry I am about your dad, Farran."

I nodded slowly. "I never knew him, Bick. My mother raised me in Cambridge and you just didn't ask about the old days. I found him when the report of his body being discovered was in the papers. It's been a difficult situation, to say the least."

"But you also found your uncle. That must be some help."

"Yes," I admitted. "It's been awkward at times, but we're working it through. Have you known Gordon a long time?"

"No. I met him professionally a few years ago at my retirement, but never connected the name. Hal didn't get specific about his family. Then I saw Gordon in the paper about your dad, and I made a point to go see him. Tell him what I knew. I just dropped by today to congratulate him on his retirement."

"His retirement?" I asked, surprised.

"Yes. He's handing over the wheel at the end of this month. Didn't he tell you?"

"No, but I probably haven't given him a chance," I admitted. Poor Gordon. A prodigal niece with bad timing. "When did you quit sailing to join the Parks?"

"Not long after the Seaway opened. Once the big ships took over, a lot of jobs were lost in shipping."

"I thought the extra traffic would make more jobs?"

"It did for the support services—stevedores, tugboats, things like that. But the big ships carried more cargo. Fewer lakers were needed, fewer men to crew the ships. It was a natural fallout, I guess. A lot of us took it as our cue to find something ashore." The laugh lines came back. "I found a job with the Parks and a good woman."

I smiled and shook his hand. "I don't want to keep you any longer, Bick. I really appreciate your talking with me about all this."

Bickman dug out his wallet and gave me a card. "Any time you want to talk again, Farran, you just call me. Nothing an old sailor likes better than to yarn about the past. And just let me say," he added, taking my hand in both of his for a moment, "it somehow makes up for a lot knowing Hal left a child behind."

I took his card with thanks and watched him move away to the parking lot. Hal's child. I certainly didn't feel like it. Hal Leonard was a man who had once lived and helped create me, a man I was cheated from ever knowing. But any connection beyond that hadn't come.

I squared my shoulders and headed on in to work. The sun was hot and high in the sky as I made my way down the Queen Street boardwalk. Willard's Hotel crossed my path before Crysler Hall and my top priority—food—cheerfully displaced my work ethic. It was nearly lunchtime and how could I expect to work on an empty stomach? I went in the front door.

I stood there for a moment, temporarily blinded by the dark. It provided cool relief from the heat and sun. A hostess in period costume greeted me and, after ascertaining that I was indeed a single, asked if I preferred a table in the main dining room or one on the outside patio. The upper balcony held a private reception.

"Main dining room, thanks," I said, not wanting to give up the coolness of the old house. We bustled (well, she did) down the pink hallway a bit and entered a door to the left. The room was done in beautiful early Victorian decor, right down to the authentic pictures of Victoria and Albert on the wall. The green walls held a pastel floral print, with white trim and curtains, dotted with electric lights hidden in tin candle sconces made by the Village tinsmith. It was like walking into a river.

I sat down at the offered table near the old fireplace, and considered my condo in Waterloo. White walls, bookshelves, historical conversation pieces on unremarkable furniture. Perhaps a redecoration was in order, after I cleared up this mess. If.

"I can recommend the Welsh rarebit," said a voice my heart recognized before my head did. I looked up from my menu and locked eyes with Inspector Strauss. He had a brown envelope in one hand, hat in the other. He still looked good in his uniform. "May I join you?"

"Oh . . . yes, of course," I faltered, setting down my menu and knocking over my water glass. Thankfully, it was empty. As if on cue, a waitress (in costume, of course) appeared with a Blue Willow pitcher of water, pouring us each a glass before setting it down and leaving Strauss a menu, too. He sat down and we diligently studied them.

For me, it was a toss-up between the rarebit and the bangers & mash. I had developed a fondness for them both years ago while a student at Oxford.

"The rarebit, eh?"

"Yep."

"Fine." I put the menu down as the waitress returned. "I'll have the Welsh rarebit, please."

"Make that two," said Strauss, handing over his menu.

"What's your soup of the day?" I asked, as an afterthought.

"Creamy tomato and rice," she said.

Maybe it was being back in the Village finally getting to me. I don't know. I had a sudden visual rush. Red foam. A red and white print dress. I put my hand to my eyes to blot it out.

"No . . . thanks. I'll stick to the rarebit." I opened my eyes. The waitress was gone and Strauss was giving me one of his X-ray looks.

"Something wrong, Mackenzie?"

"No. No." I took a deep breath and tried to smile. "I'm fine. What brings you here, Inspector? Just in the neighbourhood or are you following me?"

He smiled back. "If I were following you, Doctor, you'd never know."

I didn't doubt it.

"Wiley told me you'd been in to ask about the investigation we did into your father's death," he continued. "So you know that it's still open officially and I can't tell you much about it."

"Right."

"But I can show you this." Strauss handed me the brown envelope. "The report on the findings at the inquest. Public record now. That's a photocopy you can keep."

"Thank you," I said sincerely, taking the report. A busgirl with a frilly white apron brought us bread and butter, both I would later recognize from the gift store as Village-made. I set the envelope aside, knowing I wasn't up to those details just then, and lathered a slice of bread with the butter. "I know from the newspapers that my father died from a blow to the head. Any chance it was robbery?"

"No," he said, following my lead with the bread basket. "Hal's wallet was still intact. He had a large amount of money in it. Also, his wedding band was found in the nylon bag where it came off his finger."

"Gordon has those things now?"

Strauss nodded.

"I want to go see where you found him," I said, then held a hand up to the coming protest. "I know it's under water again. But I want to see the area. It's something I have to do."

Strauss gave me a look, then started to draw a map on the brown envelope.

"You take the road into the sanctuary and follow it down to where it branches off to the east. You'll see an old road leading straight ahead at that point. If you take that, you'll end up on a gravel path across the water that connects to another path at a right angle. To the east is the sanctuary, to the west is Ault Island. Straight ahead, into the water, is what's left of Aultsville. We found him about thirty yards south of that point."

"The water has come up that far?"

"It's very shallow there. It doesn't take much."

The waitress brought two plates of rarebit, perfectly done with a creamy yellow sauce, also on Blue Willow. Oxford would have been proud.

We dug in, and I found myself struggling for small talk. Murder is a subject best saved for dessert and coffee.

"I noticed Willard's is open Friday and Saturday nights in the summer for candlelit dinners," I said casually. It would work well with the intimate setting of the dining room. "Have you ever tried it?"

"No," came the deadpan reply. "I wouldn't mind, but I don't think Wiley would be into it."

A first joke across the bow. I smiled into my lunch and then shot him a look.

"I meant with your wife."

"I'm not married. Never made the mistake of trying to do this job and raise a family. What about you?"

"No. Never met anyone I wanted to spend that much time with." I speared a piece of my garden salad and let the sweet dressing drip off. "I was always looking for someone to play with and they always were looking to break my toys."

Strauss actually let the ghost of a smile slip out for a moment.

"Any children?" I followed up.

He raised his eyebrows. "I just said I never married, Mackenzie."

"Just asking. I was recently reminded by Alice Hoffman that marriage is not always necessary."

Now that got me a real chuckle.

"Alice is a one-of-a-kind lady, for sure," said Strauss, putting his empty plate aside.

"She reminds me of a neighbour we had in Cambridge when I was growing up," I mused, sitting back. "A real lady, but a real survivor, too. Came over from Germany with a young family to get away from their Depression in the late Twenties, just before ours hit. Didn't speak a word of English. Husband kept the family going and eventually built himself a small business. Then the war started. She was ostracized here for being German, while losing family in the war over there. And in the middle of all that, her husband suddenly died, leaving her alone with two teenagers." I crossed my arms and looked up at Victoria. "But she kept going, made it through. And I'll tell you something, that lady would have been the last one to complain about life. Life was life and you just got on with things." I looked back at Strauss and found myself getting another X-ray sweep. But this time, it didn't feel dangerous.

"Sounds like Alice, and a lot of the people I grew up with. It's too bad that attitude isn't more in style today."

"Speaking of Alice," I remembered half to myself, "I need to drop in again soon. The one thing we didn't get a chance to cover is the last few months my mother lived in Ingleside. It seems to be a gap in everyone's memory, but Alice will know. Did you see much of Leslie in those days, Inspector?"

He shook his head. "I didn't know your mother very well, except through Hal. We didn't cross paths much after Hal left, with her in high school and me only in eighth grade. Gordon should know something. I saw them together a few times at the mall, where all the kids would hang around. She must have talked to him. And ask Lynn Holmes, too. Lynnie had a good case of hero worship where Leslie was concerned."

"You did know my father well, though." I moved in carefully. "I was hoping that sometime we could talk about that. I'm not asking for clues to his murder. I'm asking as his daughter. I need to know who he was."

Something dark passed over the man's face and I sensed our buddy time was over. The waitress came to take our plates, and Strauss held up two fingers.

"Two lemon syllabub, with coffee, please."

She whisked off and he fell silent. I opened my mouth to protest, having wanted to ask what the daily selections were, but changed my mind. The spoon began to tap ominously on the table in a familiar fashion.

"I know you have some very important loose ends to tie up around here, Mackenzie," said Strauss after a minute, keeping his eyes on the spoon, "and I couldn't say I wouldn't do the same in your shoes. But we are talking murder here." He slapped the spoon down and looked at me.

"Lemon syllabub." The waitress cheerfully served up two frothy concoctions in wine glasses with cinnamon on top, and two steaming cups of coffee. We glared at each other until she left.

"I already have a forty-year-old killing on my hands and now an old friend is dead, too," he continued in a low voice. "I don't need you, good intentions or not, getting in my way."

I flashed him an X-ray of my own. "So you *do* think the two deaths are connected."

The Inspector sidestepped that. "That's not the point. The point is, if you really want me to find out who killed your father or Meredith, write your paper and let me do my job." He drove his spoon into the dessert. "Not to mention that, if someone is killing and it's connected to Hal, you could be next."

I studied the white tablecloth in (I hoped) a dignified silence. The dining room had become quiet. With seating for under thirty and tables close together, heads did not have to turn for me to feel the curious interest.

"Eat your dessert, Inspector," I shot back quietly. "This isn't doing much for my PR around here. Besides," I added, "I can take care of myself."

"Famous last words," he muttered, having the last word.

We had another eyeball wrestle and this time I won. But it didn't cheer me much. Our blossoming friendship had gone sour. The syllabub was fabulous, though.

We finished in a cold silence. Then Strauss grabbed his hat and rose to leave.

"Remember what I said, Mackenzie." Surprisingly, he returned my haughty glance with a touch of concern. "I don't want to be fishing you out of the river next. And while I don't see you flipping middle-aged ladies into sawmill gears, you haven't been ruled out completely. If you turn into a loose cannon around here, I'll lock you up."

I didn't doubt that, either.

"It's been fun, Inspector," I waved as he left. I finished my coffee, trying to sort out the backwash of mixed feelings he'd started. God, men can be a pain—even in uniform.

I tried to pay my bill, but the waitress told me Strauss had taken them both. Great. Now I owed him as well.

The upper floor of Crysler Hall was cool, the heat unable to penetrate the thick old walls. But by midsummer, it would be hot. I wondered if the women still wore their knickers by then. I had noticed some videos in the display of the Lost Villages last time, and asked the interpreter if I could watch the one titled "Aultsville."

She popped it into the VCR and I settled back on the student chair.

The dead village materialized on the screen, filmed on a home movie camera starting in 1954 when the camera's owner knew for sure the Seaway would come through. For over an hour I watched it—shaky images of people, some now long dead, and children now grandparents themselves. This was the aspect of my work that never ceased to entrance me. Visual evidence that ended lives had beginnings and middles, too. That they were once just like us, with mortality safely under a drop sheet. That someday someone would watch me and wonder who I had been.

A narrator explained what the camera tried to capture: The Colonial Coach bus stop on the old Highway No. 2, river freighters coming up from Farran's Point, a well-attended church supper at the United Church. A shot of the highway leading out of the village moving west and the old farmhouse near my cottage in its heyday. An orchard where the cottage now stands. Dr. Sam Burns making a call in his Oldsmobile. St. Paul's Anglican Church where my grandmother Lila was buried, and still remains under the water.

Up a long road past brick homes and flower gardens everywhere. A red brick house with a distinctive oval window. And then a store with a group of people sitting on the front porch. LEONARD'S GENERAL STORE. Someone went into the store and brought out a man who looked very much like Gordon does now. Eric, my grandfather, I guessed. He had his arm around a young man who grinned and waved happily at the camera. I felt my chest tighten up. Hal. My father walked to a truck parked near the porch with the company name on it, saying something over his shoulder and pointing to the camera. A young and handsome Gordon appeared and made his way to the truck, giving a reluctant wave.

And then a boy ran out and hopped into the truck's bed before the two brothers pulled out. I wasn't sure, but when I saw the woman who came out after him, I knew. She was blond and beautiful, like a young Kim Novak. The boy was Jerry Strauss.

Emme said something to Jerry and he sat down. Then she stuck her head into the cab on Hal's side before returning to the store. She did not wave. The Ice Queen. The truck pulled out with Jerry waving from the back. I froze the frame, then played the sequence again.

Focusing on history and people long gone makes for uncomplicated relationships. But this time there was no such reprieve. And the more I discovered, the more I mourned the loss of those years. Busy, full human lives now for the most part only on film. Not even the stage left standing after this production.

Our lives are brief pinpoints of light in the universe, a blink in the eye of God. Why, then, whispered that dark corner, have you lived your life as though you have a thousand years to get it right?

I snapped off the VCR and thanked the interpreter on my way out. The bright sun, on its way to the last part of the day, did little to dispel the gloom I was in. Perhaps Strauss was right. I should just go home and let him call me with any news. Problem was, I wasn't sure anymore where I would call home.

I drove the one minute down the highway and turned in to the causeway. Tomorrow I would see Alice, Ruth or no Ruth, and fill in those last weeks my mother spent in Ingleside. They were becoming important in my mind. Did she leave with Hal? Is that why he borrowed that money from Bick? Wouldn't they have let Gordon know? And why run away anyway?

I would be very interested to hear Alice's no-holds-barred interpretation on that.

The car in the cottage driveway was unmarked, so I didn't get the bad feeling right away. Then Jerry Strauss unfolded himself from the front seat when I pulled in.

"Inspector," I said brightly, feeling my nerves kick in. "Should I be flattered or worried? We really shouldn't keep meeting like this."

"I don't mind the meetings, Mackenzie," he said grimly. "I just wish they weren't always about death."

The earth shifted and I leaned on my car for support.

"Death? Another death?"

"I'm afraid so. And after what you said today, I thought I should come and tell you myself." Strauss sighed, and his big shoulders drooped. "It's Alice. The call was waiting for me when I got back to the office. Alice Hoffman died this afternoon."

Chapter **11**

Legacies

S TRAUSS REFILLED the brandy glass and set it down in front of me.

"Alice didn't wake up after her nap today. It looks as though she died of heart failure in her sleep," he said, taking the chair facing me across my kitchen table. "She was in her mid-eighties. These things happen. I don't see how you could be responsible."

"It was my fault," I repeated dully. "I came here and woke up a sleeping murder. I go to see Meredith and she's killed; then I plan to see Alice again and she dies."

"Mackenzie," the Inspector used his official reasoning voice, "you came here because the murder was already discovered. You didn't 'wake it up.' And in both cases, you'd already talked to these people, so why would anyone kill them to keep them quiet?"

"In both cases, I was going back to ask a specific question— something I have a hunch is very important, but I don't know why. And now I'll never know. It's as though someone is reading my mind."

Strauss grunted. "Careful," he said, draining his own glass. "Next thing you'll tell me you've been hearing the voices from the villages at night."

It penetrated the fog.

"Voices? What voices?"

"A local legend, nothing more," he dismissed it as he rose to look out the patio door to the river. "This is a very old part of the country, settled by the Iroquois many centuries ago. They say that the change in the river disturbed the spirits, and that even the villagers mourned the loss of their land so much that their ghosts return to the old sites after death. If you listen at night and the wind is right, you're supposed to be able to hear the old voices from the Front come across the water."

I felt a chill run down my arms in the afternoon heat. I remembered the steam whistle, my father's words one early dawn, and even the old music last night. I said nothing.

"I know you liked Alice," he said unexpectedly, "and I'm sorry."

"I'll have to go and see Ruth." I wasn't looking forward to that.

"I tried to call Gordon but they said he was out of town for the next two days." Strauss rejoined me at the table. "Do you know where he is?"

I shook my head. "No. I talked to him for just a minute this morning, and he said only that he was on the road for the day."

"How is it going between you two, if you don't mind my asking?"

"Okay, I guess," I shrugged. "We had dinner last week and talked about things a bit. I can tell that having all this literally dug up again has been hard on Gordon. But he's being a gentleman about it."

"Raised in the old school," he mused aloud.

"How old are you, Inspector?" I asked without thinking. Then I tried to recover. "I . . . I mean, how old were you when the Seaway was put through, when you last knew my father?" The flickering image of a happy boy in a truck bed skittered through my brain.

"I knew your dad my whole life," Strauss replied. "Both my parents worked for your grandfather. Gordon was too much older to put up with me, but Hal always let me tag along. I guess I thought of him as an older brother, being an only child. I was thirteen when he left town."

"Were you upset when he did?"

"Yes. I'd just lost my dad in a fire at the lumberyard, so it wasn't a happy time for me. Then Hal left, and the only person I felt I still had was my mother. But it was hard on everyone," he added, "especially your family."

"I know he left on bad terms."

"That was hard enough. But with Hal gone, the responsibility of the store, selling the properties, and taking care of Eric all fell to

Gordon alone. He was only a young man himself. I think it was too much for him at times."

"Gordon sold the store and gave the house to Upper Canada Village," I said. "He had a bungalow built in Ingleside and moved there with my grandfather. I heard he got a job with the Parks a short while after that. Was there no chance to save the business?"

Strauss crossed his arms and sat back in his chair. "According to Gordon, there was no business left to save."

NEW YORK'S MILLIONS ROAR NOISY WELCOME TO QUEEN
Like Giant Gala Picnic; Queen's First Visit To City

U.S. ROCKET 4,000 MILES INTO SPACE
Still Compiling Exact Data After Six-Test Series

SPUTNIK CREATES WIDE INTEREST IN T.V. SERIES

CONFERENCE TOLD POWER DAM AREA MAIN TOURIST ATTRACTION

October 1957
The Cornwall *Standard-Freeholder*

"Let's see," said Gordon, checking a list, "Bart Miller picked up the drink cooler yesterday. The scales and the glass counter went with the museum fellas. The register is at the house. So we just have to take down the sign and give the old place one last once-over and we're done."

His voice echoed in the empty store. After signing it over to Hydro last week, Gordon had held a sale to empty it of what little stock remained. He'd never seen the shelves so bare.

"Do you have to sound so damn cheerful about it?" grumbled the man in the corner chair. Gordon looked at his father stonily.

"Would you rather I ranted and raved? Just trying to perk you up a bit. And I'd really rather leave that chair here for the wreckers, Dad. It's so old."

Eric gripped the chair's arms solidly. "I've watched my Saturday night hockey in this chair for years. I don't intend to stop now. It goes to Ingleside, or you can leave me here with it."

Gordon rolled his eyes and made a 'don't tempt me' face at Jerry, who sat on some packing boxes. The boy gave him a conspiratorial grin.

"Don't worry, Dad," the man sighed. "I promise I'll throw it on the truck before we leave."

"We have to get back soon," said Eric sharply. "Hal might call."

The name fell into the silence of the room and lay there. Jerry looked at his shoes. Gordon went to the dry goods counter and began checking the drawers.

"Hal isn't goin' to call, Dad," he said over his shoulder. "You need to accept that."

"Of course he will," Eric replied firmly, getting up to pace around the room. "He said he'd come back and he didn't, so he'll call. He's a good boy."

"If he's such a good boy, Dad, why did you send him away?" Gordon said irritably.

"I did not send him away." The older man's hands shook as he wiped his mouth with a handkerchief. "I would never send my boy away. I don't know why he left."

"You mean you don't remember?" Gordon turned to face his father, then glanced at Jerry. "Let's drop it, Dad," he said in an even voice. "Fightin' isn't going to change things."

"Where is he, Gordy?" Eric shuffled back to his chair and sat heavily. "Why doesn't he come back?"

Gordon's face flushed red. "How do I know, Dad? He's off doin' what he wants to do. I'm not my brother's keeper, you know."

The door swung open, the fall day outside framing Emme Strauss. She looked at the three of them, moved to give her son a kiss and then headed for the mail wicket.

"What are you doing here, Emme?" Gordon said after her. "We haven't seen you since they opened the post office in Ingleside."

"I decided that you might be right about being here for the last day," she said, disappearing behind the counter and coming up with the old polish cloth in her hand. "Besides, I thought I would pick Jerry up myself. I am sure the truck will be full."

She came around and began to polish the empty postal boxes.

"What are you doin' that for, Ma?" Jerry came over to watch. It had always seemed so fascinating to make the brass glow, and now this was the last time. He looked at them with new eyes, unable to think of them as ever being gone. They were no match for the neat steel boxes in the lobby of the Ingleside branch, but their age gave them an air of establishment he somehow knew the steel ones would never have. Jerry spun the brass knob on one and peered through the little glass window. KELLY, it said. BREWSTER, said the one beside it. Name after name of the former residents of Aultsville. Kinda like tombstones all lined up, he thought.

"I'm looking for Gordon Leonard," said a voice. They all turned to see a man holding a clipboard standing just inside the door. His overalls had ONTARIO HYDRO written across the back.

"That's me." Gordon walked over to him, brushing off his hands. "You're here for the keys?"

"That's right," he said. "Have you got everything you want out of here?"

"I think we do."

"Except the damn chair, Gordon," Eric hollered.

"We're takin' that chair," Gordon sighed. "And the sign off the front outside. Do I sign something?"

The man passed him the clipboard. "And we'll need the keys, Mr. Leonard."

Gordon signed, handed back the clipboard, and dug the keys out of his pocket. Hesitating, he held them out to Eric but his father slowly turned away. Gordon shrugged and gave them to the man from Hydro.

"I guess that's a wrap then," he said quietly. "We'd best be goin', everyone."

Jerry followed the Hydro man out the door, with Eric leaning on Emme right behind him. Gordon brought up the rear with the chair. He tossed it into the back of the truck, then turned to Jerry.

"I think I'm goin' to need your help to get the sign down. Can you do it?"

"Sure," the boy replied eagerly. They borrowed a ladder from the utility truck and went to work. Ten minutes later, LEONARD'S GENERAL STORE lay in the truck with the chair.

"*Put that sign up myself in '33,*" *Eric said quietly.* "*The year I married your mother.*"

Gordon didn't reply.

"*That's everything,*" *he said to the man with the clipboard. The man turned and waved to a couple of guys waiting in a truck parked on the road.*

"*We'll board it up then, after the boxes are done,*" *he explained.* "*The wreckers will get here when they do.*"

"*The boxes?*" *Emme came over from her car.* "*What boxes?*"

"*The postal boxes, ma'am,*" *replied the man, looking her over.* "*Government can't let them sit around or be sold.*" *The two men from the truck moved past her and went into the store, crowbars in hand. Emme grabbed Gordon's arm.*

"*What are they going to do?*"

"*Emme,*" *he said soothingly,* "*you know the store is going to be torn down. The postal wicket and the boxes have to be destroyed, too.*"

"*No,*" *she said, moving toward the door. The sound of smashing started inside.* "*Not my nice boxes. Not that, too.*"

The Hydro man caught her by the arm and Jerry ran up to hold her hand.

"*Best not to go see, I think, ma'am.*"

Something glass hit the floor inside the store, and the smashing continued for a few more minutes. Then silence. Emme closed her eyes and began to cry softly. Holding her son's hand, she walked past Gordon to her car. Eric helped her in and slammed the door.

"*Hey, Ma, Gordon's here.*" *Jerry ran to open the front door.*

"*Hi, Jerry. Is your mother home?*" *Gordon took his hat off and stood in the hall, an envelope in his hand.*

"*Yah. She's comin' in a minute. Sit down,*" *the boy waved at the living room.*

"*How is she since the other day?*" *Gordon sat in Bill's favourite chair.* "*Has she gotten over it?*"

"*I don't know, Gordy.*" *Jerry shoved his hands in his pockets.* "*She hasn't said anything about it all week. But Ma's that way anyway.*"

"*I am what way, Jerry?*"

Emme entered the room and Gordon stood up.

"How are you, Emme? I hope that business the other day didn't upset you too much. I thought you knew they would come for the boxes like that."

"I guess I really didn't think about it," she replied evenly.

"Well, I came across something I thought you might like to have." Gordon passed the envelope to her.

Emme sat down and pulled out some photographs. They showed happier days at the store, with the Leonards and the Strausses sitting on the front step, Eric behind the counter talking with a neighbour, Emme working in the mail wicket. Jerry saw tears form in his mother's eyes. Then a small picture fluttered into her lap from the bottom of the envelope. Jerry looked over her shoulder.

It was a shot of Gordon and Hal in better days, standing near the porch of the red brick house. She passed it over to Gordon.

"You must find your brother and tell him to come home," Emme said simply.

Gordon shot her a look.

"It's not that simple."

"What else can you do? You need him to help get the business going again."

"We can't," Gordon explained. *"The losses we had in the last years with the money missin', business droppin' off with the village movin', Dad forcin' me to take a low price for the store, and then losin' the lumberyard . . ."* Gordon trailed off and looked out of the corner of his eye at Jerry.

"That is why Hal must come home," Emme maintained. *"His family needs him."*

Gordon slipped the picture into his breast pocket. *"Don't forget,"* he said quietly, *"there were good reasons why he left."*

CUT 500-YEAR-OLD ELM IN MOULINETTE
SECTOR
Tuesday, December 19th, 1957

A tree that was a sapling before Columbus discovered America was cut this week in the Moulinette area as part of the clearing in connection with the flooding for the St. Lawrence power project.

A stately old elm, the tree was 10 feet in diameter and nearly 100 feet high. According to an unofficial ring count, the tree was estimated to be more than 500 years old.

The elm was a familiar sight to residents of the former village of Moulinette, seven miles west of Cornwall. It stood near the bank of the Cornwall Canal just south of the Lion Hotel on old No. 2 Highway.

The Cornwall *Standard-Freeholder*

Jerry scooted by the man reading the newspaper at the mall, then stopped to read the headline.

"Beat it, kid," said a familiar voice. "Get your own newspaper."

Jerry looked up to apologize and met the laughing eyes of Hal Leonard.

"Hal! Hal." He swung at him playfully. "You've come home."

"Shh!" Hal put his hand over Jerry's mouth. "Don't tell the neighbourhood. I'm not here to stay, just makin' a scheduled pickup."

"What are you up to, Hal?" The boy looked his old friend over. "Look at you. New coat, new suit." He sniffed. "What's that, perfume? Still tryin' to impress the girls, huh?"

Hal grinned. "I'm just flush right now." He looked at his watch. "Speakin' of girls, I've got an hour before the bus comes. Let's go see your ma."

They started down the mall sidewalk. Jerry stole a look at the man. New duds, he thought, but same old Hal.

We sat at the table, supper dishes and memory fragments between us. Sunset was well under way, and I knew Strauss would be leaving soon. I had offered dinner and managed to whip up my one good meal. Even cooks with eleven fingers have one good, no-fail meal they can fall back on. Mine was beef stroganoff.

I had two big questions I wasn't sure I dared to ask, but I needed the answers to. Very important pieces I had to find. I decided to warm up to it.

"What did my father talk about when he went to your house that last time?"

Strauss stirred his coffee slowly. "What you might expect. He asked how we were doing, if my mother had found work and were we keeping all right. He even talked about my father. He wanted to know that we didn't think he was guilty. That's when my mother started trying to convince him to come home."

"Did she?"

"I sensed he already wanted to. He seemed happy about something and positive about the future. But he said he couldn't come home till he cleared something up."

"What was that?"

"Wouldn't say." Strauss went to take a sip from his mug, but froze halfway. Then he slowly set it down. "God. I'd forgotten that."

"What?" I leaned forward.

"Something he said before he left. It didn't mean much then, but with what's happened . . ."

"Strauss?" I'm no good with anticipation.

"Sorry." He shook his head. "I just remembered your father telling us that he'd been to the old neighbourhood again, what he could see under the snow. I guess he spent some time standing where the house had been, remembering. He smiled and said something like 'That night I left there, I never thought I'd want to see it all again so much. That I'd want to come back to Aultsville to stay.' He meant then just to have a chance to go back and change things, I think. But what hit me now was that's where we found him. He did go back to stay."

I sat silent for some minutes, then broached the first question. "It sounds as though you two were still friends, Inspector. Did *you* believe Hal was responsible for your father's death?"

It was his turn to sit silently while I waited. He picked up the coffee spoon and started that tapping thing. Not good. Finally he looked up at me.

"I wish I could give you a definite answer to that, Mackenzie. I know it must be very important to you. But I'm still not sure why my father died. I've spent personal time while on the force going over the old records, trying to use my training to find what everyone else missed. But I can't. And even though at the time things looked really bad for Hal, I remember I could never hold a grudge against him. All through it, as more things went wrong for him, he never changed. He was always my friend. He was always just Hal.

"Besides," he stood up suddenly and walked over to watch the sun set. "Maybe it was partly my fault. I think my dad was jealous somehow of my friendship with Hal. He worked a lot and didn't have much time for father-son things. Maybe he felt Hal was trying to take his place with me and that kept them at each other's throats. Maybe it all just blew apart."

I felt my cheeks get hot. *You?* I wanted to yell. *You were just a boy. What about your red-hot mama The Ice Queen who didn't keep her distance from my father, even when it threatened her marriage? A woman who didn't bat an eye when she thought her husband had burned to death but got misty when they smashed her old workstation, for Chrissakes.*

But for once I had the sense to keep my big mouth shut. This man and I were two strangers, only brought together for the moment by the tides of the past. My burden was new and had blown away the world I thought I knew. His, on the other hand, had been his personal millstone for forty years. I guess as parents our legacies cannot avoid our children—even if we do. No matter how you twist the kaleidoscope, the pieces fall on someone.

I tried not to think of the pieces I'd let fall on my own child.

"Is your mother still alive, Inspector?" I asked quietly.

"No." He turned back from the window. "She died some years ago."

I gave up on the second question. Even though it involved my father, it was too personal. At least for now.

"There's more chocolate cake. Can I cut you a second piece?"

"I'd like that, but I'll have to pass, thanks." He found his hat and managed a smile. "Seconds are deadly for your figure at my age. And I really should check in at the office before I go home."

"Did Hal tell you my mother was dead when he came back that time?"

"No. Your mother was still with the Hoffmans then, I remember. But it was shortly after that that we heard she'd left. Maybe they left together." His scheduled pickup.

I got up to walk him out. "Will there be an autopsy on Alice?" I said as casually as possible.

"There usually is in the case of unexpected death," he replied evasively. "But remember what I said today, Mackenzie," he stopped on the bottom porch step. "This isn't some Christie book, with a happy ending waiting for you. I know you want answers, but there's nothing more dangerous than an amateur Sherlock Holmes running around, stirring things up. A killer hesitates only the first time. After that, it comes easy."

"I realize that," I said peevishly, looking down at him from the top step.

"Then ask about the past but don't cross any lines."

"That's easy for you to say," I retorted. "It wasn't your father out there in the mud."

"I lost my dad, too," Strauss reminded me gently. "I know what it feels like to have those loose ends, to be cheated of your time with him."

Maybe the chocolate was hitting my bloodstream. Something was getting under my skin and I couldn't stop it.

"Well, I didn't lose mine," I shot back. "I never had him to lose. And it wasn't just his life that ended, either. My mother's did, too. She turned her back on her life here and never came back."

Never came back. The words froze me where I stood.

Moor. It seemed to come from the breeze off the river. *Remember, Fan? The cats didn't come back. They knew. They knew.*

They didn't come back because they knew Moor would die.

And then the Pandora's box of the unthinkable I had held shut all these months blew open.

My mother never came back.

"Mackenzie, what is it?" Strauss's voice seemed to come from far away, though he took a step toward me. "You're as white as a ghost."

My mother never came back because she knew my father was dead. She knew and she was afraid.

Why?

"Oh, no . . . no," I mumbled as I moved to sit down. I felt Strauss take my arm as the porch rushed up at me, followed by the most terrible question of all.

Did my mother kill my father?

Chapter 12

Shattered

$\mathcal{I}$T HAD been raining and everything was wet. A mist had settled in the trees, making it hard for me to see where I was going. My feet kept squelching in the mud. My legs felt like lead.

Fan! Fan! The voice came from behind me. *Fan. Don't wander off. You have to play in the yard.*

I stopped and turned. "That's where I'm going, Mother. I'm going home."

Squelch. Suck. I slowly plowed through the mud and overgrowth, looking for the road.

"It's here," I muttered. "It's got to be here. It can't all be gone. There has to be something left." I started to cry. "There has to be."

Suddenly my foot hit something hard and a paved road appeared out of the mud. I gratefully stepped onto the dry surface and started toward the river. Deep in the trees I could see houses and gardens, with people moving around inside. No one seemed to notice me. Within minutes I reached the end of the road, where it disappeared into the water.

Farran, said a new voice. *Don't stop. You're very close now.*

"Dad?" I called. "Dad, I can't reach you. The river won't let me."

Just a little bit more, Farran. You're almost there.

I hesitantly began to move forward, feeling my way along the road in the water. I seemed to hear no sound now except my heart pounding in my ears like a water crank. The water stayed only up to my ankles, and I tried to see down into it. I could just make out

211

the form of something large and square and deep not far from the edge of the road.

And then a rotted hand grabbed me by the ankle.

Welcome home, Farran.

I screamed but no sound came out. Paralyzed, I watched a skeletal head and shoulders come up out of the water, covered in slime and insects. It began pulling my ankle toward the edge of the submerged road. I tried to scream again and struggled to get free. It was no use.

Then the Thing turned its grisly face toward me, eye sockets pleading, jaw bone slack.

It was Gordon.

I woke up and sat up, all of a piece, sucking air. I was soaked with sweat, and then the shakes started.

"Jesus. Jesus." I hugged my covers, as happy as Scrooge after his look at the future to be safe in bed. "Oh, hell."

The luminous dial on my travel clock read 3:42 a.m. Well, a farmer's start to the day. I sure as hell wasn't going back to sleep. I considered a brandy to settle my nerves, but nixed the idea. Alcohol isn't the friend it was in my youth, and it probably was the wine and after dinner drinks that gave me the bad dream.

Wine. Dinner with Strauss. Alice was dead.

The remembering felt like hearing the news again. For a week after Mother died, I would wake up with only the sense of something not right, a heaviness on my chest I couldn't quite name. Then the reality would set in again, with the pain and disbelief of the first time.

It's my fault. I threw the bedclothes off, snapped the lights on and stormed into the shower. On my way, I made sure all the windows were closed, despite the delicious breeze coming in off the river. I wasn't up to any old voices at that particular moment.

After showering and dressing, I spent my frustrations on the cottage. I vacuumed, I dusted, I scrubbed the toilet, I washed every single dish. And I let my own voice rant on in my head.

I would have to wait for Strauss to tell me for sure, but my guilty conscience told me that Alice had not died a natural death. She'd been a fighter her whole life. I just couldn't see her lying down and dying meekly like that. She would be the one to rage against the dying of the light for months—I could see her chasing nurses with her wheelchair in the Ingleside nursing home. But why kill her?

And why kill Meredith? What could either of them have told me that wasn't local gossip by now? And why wait until after I'd seen them both already?

Work backwards. Isolate the facts. Who *could* have killed them? Remove the impossible, Holmes once told Watson. Whatever is left, however improbable, must be true.

Where was everyone the morning Meredith died? I changed heads on the vacuum and turned ruthlessly from the dust bunnies on the floor to the spiders hanging out in the ceiling corners. Ruth, I had no idea. Lynn had not been in her office. It had taken time for Strauss to locate her after the fact. Could she have driven down from Ottawa? Yes. And Gordon was somewhere on the 401—or so he said. Even Strauss had not been in when I'd first arrived with Wiley.

And Strauss knew I intended to speak with Alice again soon. So did Gordon, for that matter. And Ruth. Now Ruth might heave Meredith into the gears without batting an eye, but would she kill her own mother?

I snapped off the vacuum and put it away.

The other thin thread I could hang onto was that if the killings were connected, then it was less likely that my mother killed my father. If the guilt lay that close to home, there would have been no further murders with Mother dead.

Unless it was me, seeking revenge somehow. Now that would hold water, especially to a trained police officer. No wonder Strauss was watching me like that.

When I'd sat down on the porch last night with his help, I'd managed to wave off his concern. Said it was my knee giving me grief again, that I would have to give in and have it looked at soon. Smelling a rat, the inspector gave me the old fish eye but took his leave without comment.

The cleaning done, I set to making the bed, putting things in order and (honest) unpacking my boxes and suitcase. My condo back in Waterloo had the same problem, long before Mother's death spun me out of orbit. While Leslie Mackenzie ran an orderly house, her daughter lived in a tolerable swirl of books, papers, clothing and boxes of stuff I told myself I would get to as soon as my life settled down. But it never did—it never does.

Now more than ever, I was seeing that I needed to make a real home of my own somewhere. With our lifestyles the way they are, it is easy to discount the need for it. But the truth is home is our only survival now and we must continue to draw a square on the earth as our own, even if it feels like setting up a tent in the wind.

I had things I would do today. I had played phone tag with a colleague and old friend across the river in Canton, New York, for a week now. It was time to pin her down. I needed to go to Aultsville and Farran's Point to see what was left of them with my own eyes. I had to see Ruth to give her my condolences about Alice. I wanted to call Lynn, first to see if she had heard about Alice and then to ask some questions of my own. Subtly, of course.

Most of all, I wanted to make contact with Gordon. The dream had disturbed me deeply, and I wondered what it meant. I had a bad feeling growing in my stomach and my head kept telling me to find my uncle.

But it was only 5:30 in the morning, so I had several hours to kill before I could reasonably start calling people. I remembered Wiley's book was still in my purse from the day before so I made a pot of tea and settled on the couch, quieting my unhappy knee.

> The Lost Villages [Rutley began] is the name given the
> small riverside towns and hamlets that were uprooted
> and destroyed by the building of the St. Lawrence
> Seaway. They made up the front of the townships and
> were the first to be settled in 1784 by United Empire
> Loyalists seeking safety and a future for their families on
> the shores of the St. Lawrence River. Lost was an
> unredeemable wealth of historic and scenic beauty . . .

At nine a.m., I called Lynn at the *Citizen*. She picked up right away.

"Lynn, it's Farran Mackenzie. I hope I haven't called at a bad time."

"No, not at all, Fan. I'm actually having a quiet moment. How are things down there?"

"Actually, not so good, Lynn." I told her the news about Alice Hoffman. "Strauss came by here yesterday afternoon to tell me. It looks as though she died peacefully, in her sleep."

Lynn did not reply for a moment. "That must be what he called me about," she said finally. "There was a message on my machine late yesterday, but I haven't returned it yet. Poor Ruth. I'll have to call. Has the funeral been arranged?"

"I don't know. I plan to see Ruth sometime today, and I can call you tonight, if you'd like."

"Thanks. Seems that's all we do these days—go to funerals."

"Yes, this must have a real sense of déjà vu for you," I said sympathetically. "Weren't you at work when they called you about Meredith?"

"I . . . don't remember," she said slowly. "I think I was on field work that day."

Baloney. Those moments in life remain crystal clear.

"I hope you weren't alone when you answered your pager."

"No. Uh, I was in my car. But I waited to call back until I got to my office."

"Thank God for that," I said feelingly. "I won't keep you from your work. I just thought I'd see if you'd heard. I'll call back when I hear about the arrangements."

I rang off and punched in Gordon's number. The machine picked up. I told him I needed to talk to him and asked him to call me when he got home. I would be out most of the day until suppertime.

Finally, I put in the long-distance number to St. Lawrence University in Canton, New York, adding the extension number of Professor Leah Shadbourne. I scored two out of three when she answered in person.

"Mack, is that you?" She's the only one who still uses my sorority nickname.

"Hi, Shad," I replied. "It's good to hear your voice. How's the family?"

We spent some minutes catching up on personal things, common friends and associates, career news. Amazing how good the mundane can feel after spending so much time with the macabre. Finally, Shad turned it back to me.

"We need to have dinner together while you're in the area, Mack. You won't recognize the kids. John's the same but a little less hair." She giggled, sounding more like sixteen than over forty. "How's the book going?"

"Slowly," I admitted. "What have you got for me?"

"A couple of studies I thought were relevant. And another I worked on last year on the local impact of the Seaway."

"The flooding wasn't as extensive on the American side, was it?"

"No," Shad agreed. "Only 18,000 acres. Over 6,500 Canadians had to be moved, but only 1,100 Americans. They built a lot of dikes to protect the populated areas here, something Hydro didn't want to get into."

"Were the Americans more sold on the idea at the time?" I asked.

"At the time, I think so," she answered. "People here were convinced of the economic and population booms that the Seaway would bring."

"Booms that never came."

"Right. So that set the stage for resentment. Many people here say the river lost so much of its beauty, and some fine old landmarks were torn down, only to escape the flooding in the end. Not to mention Akwesasne."

"The Mohawk community?"

"Yes. They lost a sacred burial ground, and important hunting and fishing areas that had supported them for generations. Many ended up working in the factories that sprouted up at that time along the Seaway. A real cultural shift. I guess it's not surprising that some bitterness remains even today."

"After forty years, you'd think it would all be over," I murmured, "but it isn't."

"I made a file for you. Do you want it by fax or e-mail?"

"Neither. I'm roughing it right now." I gave her my mailing address.

"Sounds like you're really out in the sticks, Mack."

"Farther than that," I smiled. "I'm on an island. Ault Island. It was made during the Power Project. I've rented a cottage for the summer."

"It's probably a good vantage point," Shad conceded. "And the isolation must be good for writing."

"I wish," I sighed. "Actually, I've got some personal loose ends here that keep distracting me."

"Ooh. Sounds like A Man."

"Sorry." Strauss popped into my head, but I let her hopes die. "It's a little more complicated than that." When I'd finished with my thumbnail sketch of the situation, Shad was uncharacteristically quiet.

"Mack," she said slowly, "this is kind of weird."

"What?"

"I was one of the hikers that found the body."

Now it was my turn to be silent as I let this sink in. Strauss had said two hikers from Canton, New York. But the chance of it.

"You and John found my father?"

"No. I was with Randy."

"Who's Randy?"

"A part-time teacher in the computer science program. He's also a fitness trainer on the side. And it shows," she gushed. "The shoulders . . . "

"I don't want to know, Shad," I cut her off. "Tell me what happened, what you found."

Her voice grew serious. "That's easy enough. It gave me nightmares for weeks after. We were . . . hiking . . . and we decided to check out what was left of Aultsville. I knew where it was from the study I'm sending you. I also had heard that the water was really low. When we got there, you could see where the water was supposed to be and then how far it had receded.

"So we walked out a bit on the road, looking for old things. Getting a feel for what it had been like. Randy didn't want to go far. The footing wasn't good because of the decay. But you know me."

"How did you end up looking into the old foundation?"

"The police asked me that, too," Shad sighed. "I didn't really have an answer for them, either. Just said I was professionally nosey. But it . . . he . . . was right beside the front wall," she continued. "Something told me to take a closer look at that foundation. We were close to the water by then and everything was slippery from growth. I had Randy hold my hand while I looked over the edge. And he was right there, down in the shadow beneath my feet. I thought it was an animal at first. Then we realized what it was. I couldn't get out of there fast enough. I'm sorry."

I assured her that I wasn't offended, then backtracked to one of her comments.

"You say something told you to go in for a closer look."

"Yes, you know, when that voice in your head starts whispering?"

"What time of day was that, Shad?"

"Late. Not evening, but after supper sometime. The sun was starting to go behind the trees. Why?"

"Just curious."

We both said nothing for a minute, then she asked, "Promise me something, Mack?"

"Sure. What is it?"

"Give me a call once a week while you're here and let me know you're okay?"

"I can do that. Why?"

"Because that skeleton was *real*. Someone needed your father dead and they killed him. If there's an aging homicidal maniac still around and you're asking too many questions, you could be next. Or," she added the cheerful thought, "if the hate went deep enough, they could kill you just for being who you are."

"Are you trying to make me paranoid?" I tried to joke.

"Yes," Shad said solemnly. "In this situation, paranoid is a good thing to be."

By midmorning, I was on my way to Long Sault. Traffic on the highway was light and I should have enjoyed the beautiful day, but Shad's warning bothered me. *If the hate went deep enough*. How deep does hate go? And the bad feeling from the dream stayed in view, like a smudge on a lens. I tried Gordon's number on my cell phone but got only the machine again. Then I called the Village and left a message with the Operations receptionist. She said he was expected back soon.

There was someone selling flowers in the mall parking lot when I passed it and it made me think of Ruth. I couldn't go there empty handed. I swung in and stopped at the stand. The lady was serving two women dressed in tube tops and short shorts. I eyed their red toenails with secret envy.

"Well, good for you," said one. "It's his loss."

"That's what I say," replied the other. "A year since our first date and not so much as a card. I deserve these. He said he'd ordered me a gift but it hadn't come in yet. Imagine thinking I'd fall for that."

The first one made a sound of disgust. "That belongs with 'the cheque is in the mail' and 'I was sitting with a sick friend.'"

"Yah," giggled her friend, "or that you can't get pregnant the first time."

They took their change and moved off. I picked out a nice spray of roses and carnations. Then I headed for the police station.

I was about to turn into the parking lot when I spotted Wiley striding across the field toward the church. He veered off and headed down the street beside it called Kent Crescent. I looked at Diana Wiley's book on my front seat, idling with indecision on the side of the road. Then I followed him.

There were four houses opposite the churchyard, but only one with a police cruiser in the driveway. It was a small stucco house with cement steps and a large maple tree in the front yard that probably dated from the town's birth. I caught Wiley just as he was going in the door.

"Dr. Mackenzie," he said with surprise, then noticed the book in my hand. "You haven't read it already?"

"I couldn't sleep last night," I explained. "I thought it was a good opportunity to catch up on my reading. It helped very much, thanks." I held it out to him. "I'm making the rounds on my way to see Ruth Hoffman about her mother, and I thought I would drop it off."

"Come on in for a minute," said Wiley, taking the book. "I'm just here to check on Diana before I head out."

"I thought you were starting your holidays?" I followed him into the small hallway, and he indicated a chair in the living room.

"I was supposed to, but I'm on call at the detachment today. There's a real mess on the 401 near Morrisburg and we're several hands short. Di?" he called to the kitchen.

Almost immediately, a girl of about ten entered the room, blond and slim-featured like her father. Diana Wiley was girlhood in full stride—that brief peak before the long fall into the abyss we call adolescence. Some of us don't resurface until forty. Others, like me, take that long to figure out that the centre didn't hold in the first place.

Wiley put his hand on her forehead, while she rolled her eyes to the ceiling. "You don't feel warm, but stay inside and rest."

The girl looked pointedly from me to her father.

"This is Dr. Mackenzie, Di," he explained. "She's returning your book on the Lost Villages. Her parents both came from there but this is her first time in the area."

"I hear you did a study on the villages for school recently," I broached. "I'm doing some work on them, too, for the University of Waterloo. Maybe we could compare notes sometime?"

Diana looked unsure. She had remained silent until that point, but suddenly disappeared into the kitchen. Coming back, she handed me a binder.

"I'll have to leave you ladies to it," Wiley said, grabbing his hat and giving Diana a kiss. "Your mom will be home early," he told her, "by three, I think. Be a good host to the doctor and keep the doors locked after she leaves."

"Yes, Dad. You're a worrywart." Diana broke her silence with a gruff voice, rolling her eyes again.

"I'm a dad. Your safety is my business. And get some rest with that cold."

He went out the door whistling, and we heard the cruiser start and pull out.

"Home sick from school?" I asked.

Diana cleared her throat and smiled. "More sick *of* school," she said.

"Is it hard to have a police officer for a father?" I asked Diana.

"Sometimes. He's paranoid from what he works with." She shrugged. "I guess it works both ways. I worry about him, too."

"You're lucky to have him. I never knew my father. But," I added briskly, "you were going to show me your research."

I opened the binder and found the work deserving of the 'A' it had received. A short history of the villages was accompanied by a time-line of work done during the Power Project, along with a list of final statistics:

Construction: 53 km of road (37 miles)
                        64 km of CNR (40 miles)

Cost of Project: $600 million

People relocated: over 6500

Villages lost: 6—Milles Roches, Moulinette, Dickinson's Landing, Wales, Farran's Point, Aultsville. Plus the hamlets of Woodlands and Santa Cruz, part of Morrisburg.

Villages created: 3—Long Sault, Ingleside, and Iroquois (moved north)

Land flooded: 10,000 hectares (22,000 acres).

The project finished with photocopied pictures showing various stages of work throughout the Power Project. I recognized the church from Moulinette being moved to Upper Canada Village and had a flash of my mother and Ruth watching it go by. That picture was taken the day of my grandfather's funeral. I quickly flipped on.

"The last year is when it got interesting," said Diana, with the youthful lack of sentimentality. "The last building was moved in December of 1957, so in January of '58 they started the mass demolition. Anything standing went. Buildings, trees, all the bush along the river—you name it. They had 18,000 structures to tear down." She pointed to a picture of some men with equipment standing by a house in flames. "That was taken during the Aultsville Burn. Some research guys from Toronto came and did tests for smoke detectors with some of the empty houses. They burnt the school, too."

Beside that were two shots of the old Main Street in Morrisburg, one before demolition and one during. The windows of the dance hall could be seen boarded up, then staring like haunted eyes from the building's shell.

It depends on whether I'm wanted back or not.

I closed the binder. "It looks as though you did a thorough job, Diana."

"Thanks." She flashed a smile at me and added shyly, "If you think you could use it for your book, you can borrow it."

"Thank you, I will. I guess I should get going and let you get to your lunch," I added, looking at my watch.

"I'm not into lunch," she said. "But Mom left some chocolate chip cookies for me. Want some?"

I couldn't refuse. We went into the kitchen, a long room with small windows over the sink. Except for the countertop, the entire kitchen was original 1960s fixtures. The remodelling had been put off so long that it was all back in style—the retro look. The Wileys had even managed to find a chrome set of table and chairs. Diana crossed to the far end and opened the fridge.

"Iced tea or lemonade, Dr. Mackenzie?"

"Iced tea. And my other colleagues call me Fan for short," I added.

Diana tried not to look pleased. She put a mass of thick cookies on a plate, poured two glasses and brought everything to the table.

"Did you do these pictures?" I asked, wandering over to the refrigerator. There were three good drawings with biblical themes: Noah's Ark, Ruth and Naomi, and the Prodigal Son. Noah didn't have much choice about relocation, either.

"Yes. I'm in the Junior Auxiliary at the church. And I help with the little kids at Sunday School."

Did kids still go to Sunday School? In my cloistered, secular world of science and disbelief, I had always assumed that ritual to have died out in the Seventies. Another reminder that life was not what it appeared to be.

"Sounds like you enjoy doing lots of different things," I said, joining her at the table.

"Did you, when you were my age? Or did you always like old things and history and stuff?"

The cookies were delicious. I envisioned a dangerous woman— successful career, good mother, excellent housewife. Someone I could never be friends with.

"I liked a lot of different things," I remembered. "But I did like history the best. My friend Alison and I used to do some pretty creative stuff with our projects, like plays and displays." I suddenly smiled. "One year, we set up an entire pioneer home in the woods, crude but fun. Our teacher had to take the class out to see it."

"Wow, just the two of you?"

"No, that time we had help. Jeanie Ross worked with us. She was the resident tomboy, good with hammer and nails and such. Thank God, because Alison and I certainly weren't."

Jeanie Ross, T-shirts and jeans, short hair and glasses. Absolutely no time for the boys (the feeling was mutual). Then high school, a massive hormone spurt and Jeanie went wild. One day she left school and rumours flew about an unwanted pregnancy.

That you can't get pregnant the first time.

God, Jeanie, I hadn't thought of you in years. Where are you now?

But the flower ladies wouldn't go away. *I was sitting with a sick friend.*

Ruth and Naomi. *My aunt was sicker than we thought so I stayed the winter. When I got back, your mother was long gone.*

"Oh." My glass froze in mid-air. "Uh oh." The realization hit me like the wake from a freighter. "*Oh my.*"

"What is it, Fan?" Diana looked at me curiously. "Is something wrong?"

I set my glass down slowly. "I'm not sure," I replied honestly. "But I'm going to find out."

The woman that answered the door in Ingleside was a younger version of Ruth. One of the four offspring, I concluded.

"Hi, is Ruth home?" I asked. "I'm Farran Mackenzie. I just thought I'd stop in and see how she was doing."

The woman hesitated, looked at the flowers, and then motioned me in.

"I'll tell Mom you're here, Mrs. Mackenzie. Nan's friends from the church just left. Won't you have a seat?"

I sat on the green gold couch and looked over at Alice's chair. Even without its occupant, the chair seemed to hold her energy. My throat tightened up at the sight of a partly hooked rug on the floor nearby.

"Fan." Ruth came in, extending her hand. "It's thoughtful of you to come by. I know you didn't know Mother that long."

I shook her hand, feeling like a shit about my plan. Ruth was taking Alice's death very hard. Her face was drawn, eyes puffy, skin pasty white. I shoved the flowers at her.

"These are for you. I hope it all isn't too hard for you," I said sincerely.

"Mother was hard to live with," she said, taking the flowers and smelling them. "But I'll miss her. I try to remember that she had a good life."

A little boy ran in from the kitchen and threw himself at her. She gathered him up and sat down.

"This is my grandson, Tom." Ruth gave him a kiss and he wiggled free. "Both my daughters are here. My sons will be here tomorrow, along with my brother. I can't remember the last time we were all together," she added. "Unless it was for my father's funeral."

"I called Lynn this morning and told her. She asked me about the arrangements and I said I would ask you. She's going to call you soon."

Ruth smiled wanly. "The wake will be held Thursday, here in town. Jerry asked for time for an autopsy. The funeral is set for Friday morning at the church."

"Strauss told me yesterday. He said Alice died in her sleep, just didn't wake up from her afternoon nap. So she didn't suffer."

"No," Ruth twisted her hands together, "no, thankfully, it was peaceful."

The young woman that I'd met at the door came in, looking for the boy. "Come on, Tom,' she said, holding out her hand. "Let's go outside and leave Gramma with her friend. I'll take these for you, Mom," she added, taking the flowers. When they left the room, I stood up.

"I shouldn't stay too long, Ruth. I just wanted to see how you were, and let you know how sorry I am. Your mother spoke her mind, but maybe that's one reason I liked her."

"Thank you, Fan." Ruth slowly got to her feet, looking like a truck hit her. She must have been close to Alice, arguments notwithstanding. I felt another twinge of guilt and tried to squash it. I would have only one chance.

Ruth saw me to the door. I said my goodbye and then stopped halfway out, propping the screen door open with my body. I checked behind her that we were alone, then fired my first shot.

"Oh, Ruth. By the way, I've been meaning to ask you. When you left to go to Montreal, was your aunt really sick or did you leave to have a baby?"

God, the nerve of it when I think about it now. Ruth turned whiter than before, stepping back as though I'd physically struck her.

"What?" she blinked. "What did you say?"

"And another thing." I fired the second, another heart shot. "Was Hal Leonard your baby's father?"

Instinctively Ruth glanced over her shoulder, and then turned fear-filled eyes back on me. Her mouth worked.

"Damn you!" she spat out. Then she slammed the door in my face.

Well, I got what I deserved—but also what I needed to know.

To say my thoughts were in a whirl after that would have been a serious understatement. This enlightenment about Ruth put a whole different spin on things, and I needed to sort it all out. I also needed lunch.

The diner in the Ingleside mall was quiet, the lunch crowd gone. I gratefully took a seat and ordered my favourite treat meal—a club sandwich with a chocolate milkshake. Real food for thought.

When the waitress had gone, I flipped the place mat over and went to work. This was my list:

WHO KILLED HAL LEONARD?

1. Leslie Mackenzie—desertion?
2. Ruth Hoffman Tremblay—deception/baby?
3. Alice Hoffman—because of Ruth? Then . . .
4. Harland Hoffman, ditto.
5. Emme Strauss—spurned lover?
6. Jerry Strauss—revenge for father?
7. Meredith Murphy—unrequited love/jealousy?
   Well, then . . .
8. Lynn Homes—revenge for hurting Leslie? Don't forget . . .
9. Gordon Leonard—man on the spot? One of the last to see Hal alive. MOTIVE?? $$??

The thought of Gordon made me dig out my cell phone for another try. I got the answering machine again, but the lead-in beeps were gone. He had at least checked his messages. I called the cottage. There was one message for me, but from Strauss not Gordon. Checking up on me. Sounded grumpy.

The food was great and did a lot to put my brains back in my head. I went back out into the sunshine, feeling ready for my next stop.

Farran Park. Branching out into the river from Ingleside's west end, the beach and campground area is all that remains of my mother's hometown. I drove around, finally parking in the gravel lot on the east side and walking to the river. There wasn't much left to see. I found a piece of old road going into the water that had been turned into a boat launch ramp. And what looked like old sidewalk led me to a set of cement steps a little way into the bush. I could just make out the foundation outline behind them. I thought of my dream and scuttled away.

The whole park was busy, and three trucks were waiting to use the boat ramp. I found a stump beside the river at the quiet end of the boat area and sat down, pulling out my list from the diner.

Ruth's secret pregnancy explained a lot. I should have seen that story about the sick aunt as the time-honoured excuse it was. And now I understood why, after all they had shared, Ruth cut off communication with my mother. Especially if Hal were the father of her baby—and why should Ruth be immune to his charm? Was this a motive for murder? Very possibly. Ruth had been a teenager at the time and young emotions run deep. Hal comes back before the flooding, Leslie calls Ruth, Ruth secretly meets with Hal to tell him what she went through, he doesn't care. She kills him.

This would also explain Alice's enmity toward my mother. Leslie encouraged Hal the black sheep, Ruth hung out with Leslie. Therefore, Ruth's problem was Leslie's fault. Typical mother logic. A motive for murder? Could be. Leslie returns with Hal, calls Ruth, Ruth lets it slip to Alice, Alice forbids her to see Leslie but manages to meet with Hal and kills him for ruining her daughter's life.

This scenario would fit with Ruth's father, too. Perhaps more so. He was a quiet man, but Ruth was Daddy's little girl.

I looked at the next name on the list: Emme Strauss. Beautiful, enigmatic. Loving mother. Wife to a much older and unappreciative man. Takes a young lover—the boy next door who has the girls lined up around the block. What a balm to a resentful ego. Kill Hal? Why? Because in the end he left her, coming back for a younger woman he ultimately married. The Ice Queen. Cold. Dangerous. It fit.

Jerry Strauss. He'd called Lynn's friendship with Leslie a sort of hero worship. What if that applied to Jerry and Hal as well? He ignores the growing rumours about his hero and his mother. But then the fire and the terrible discovery. And the talk about Hal being there. Strauss said he blamed himself. Maybe he didn't. Love—worship—can run deep, too. And love can so easily turn to hate.

Meredith. Lonely, following Hal around and getting nowhere fast. Taking jibes about it from Lynnie and probably others, too. Did she reach a breaking point? Or had she, with a gossip's instinct, figured out Ruth's secret, spilled the beans when Hal resurfaced, offering to help because she loved him, only to have him laugh it off? Was the wickedness she spoke of a cold and selfish young man?

And what about Lynn? Could she have killed him for hurting

her hero? For what she saw as leading Leslie on? But Hal married Leslie in the end. Lynn was a young teenaged girl then. Could she not have been attracted to him, too? Perhaps she killed him out of jealousy. A new thought entered my head. Lynnie Holmes, neighbourhood nuisance and amateur spy. What if she stumbled onto something about the fire? Something incriminating about Hal? She tells Leslie out of concern for her friend. Leslie later lets it slip to Hal. Maybe that's what he had to "clear up." So he comes back before the inundation, lures Lynn out to Aultsville, and then she ends up killing him in self-defense. Leslie leaves in fear and never returns.

And Gordon. He saw Hal during that last visit. What if he begged Hal to come home and help the family but Hal refused? No, that didn't work. Strauss said it seemed that Hal had wanted to come home at the end. And the family's fortunes had taken a nosedive for the last three years, so greed over inheritance didn't float, either. Still he was one of the last people to see Hal alive and I couldn't forget that.

Or that Mother was probably the person with the best motive and opportunity. According to Gordon, Hal had said that he and Leslie had parted ways. But I was here now. What if Hal deserted his new wife, taking her money and leaving her alone and pregnant? Not a pleasant thought, but not impossible. Leslie could have followed him here. My mother had learned her strength and her smarts from Harper. Had she also learned his temper?

But I couldn't accept that. I knew Leslie Mackenzie—or thought I did. Perhaps she had had skeletons in her closet she'd kept secret, but I knew her as a person. She couldn't murder anyone.

I looked out over the river, to the islands beyond. Somewhere out there, my mother's life had played out as she found her footing as a woman while the world she knew was torn apart. So much I'll never know.

Why, Mom? I opened the locked door just a little. Why couldn't you have shared that with me? We could be here together now and I would listen to the stories while you pointed out the pieces that are left.

I would hear your voice. I miss your voice. I miss you. I love you.

A solid mass of grief worked its way up inside my chest and I couldn't breathe. For just an instant, my eyes prickled with the tears

I had given up on long ago. Then I forced it all back down, slamming the door of my heart.

My brain I let ramble on. The list of suspects changed when you added in the deaths of Alice and Meredith. But that was presuming they were both murdered and that it was all somehow connected. Either one might not meet that criteria, and I had a feeling Strauss wouldn't help me out with that.

If I'd been in the athletic mood, I could have walked the bike path that stretched west from the park to the sanctuary, coming out near where Shad had found my father. But I returned instead to the comfort of my car, snapping on the radio to drown out the discouraging voices in my head.

Cardboard masks of all the people I've been, sang Jann Arden, putting her finger on it with me as usual. Here I was trying to see under people's masks while I held firmly onto my own. Who was I kidding? Them or me?

But if you knew me you'd know . . . I've got a good father . . . and his strength is what makes me cry . . .

I snapped it off again. I've always liked the way Arden cuts to the bone, but this time she was too close to home. I needed a good father and didn't have one. My mother, Ruth, Emme, even Meredith who never married. What a body count, and those were just the ones I knew of. God knows how many he added during his year of shipping. And all before the age of nineteen.

What kind of a man *was* Hal Leonard?

The Upper Canada Migratory Bird Sanctuary covers 9,000 hectares along the shore of Lake St. Lawrence. It officially opened in 1961—the same year as Upper Canada Village—and continues to welcome over 20,000 visitors at the Interpretive Centre each year, who come to use the nature trails in the summer and the skiing/hiking trails in the winter. The way in is a winding dirt road with enough potholes to make even city speed impossible. I followed it until I reached the deep curve Strauss told me to look for. I could see the old road continuing straight toward the river. There was a chain but it was down in the grass, so I slowly drove forward along the narrow, overgrown path until I went over a rolling hill and parked in a small wayside where the gravel causeway started.

I had wanted to come here since I'd arrived in the area, but now—thanks to my nightmare—my heart pounded in my chest as I made my way down the gravel road. There was water on both sides so I stayed in the middle in case something tried to grab my ankle. In about five minutes, the road ended where it connected with the east-west bike path.

Here I saw only water. To my left was more sanctuary and bush. To my right was the eastern tip of Ault Island, dominated by Gordon's house. Well, straight ahead to the river. I poked around in the bushes and found a small piece of the old road leading into the water. This was the road they had used to get to the murder scene. Taking a deep breath and forcing all thoughts of skeletons and rotting hands out of my mind, I pushed my way through into a corridor of weedy trees and bushes.

It was surreal to think I was walking the same road my father had, probably many times on his way to the lumberyard. But my excitement was short-lived. After only fifty feet, the road vanished into the river. The mud and slime on the road under the water made it impossible for me to continue even a couple of yards. It looked like primal ooze, and the end of the world. I was cut off.

I would have to accept that it was all gone. A mammoth engineering project and almost half a century in human years stood between me and the truth. What did I have to work with anyway?

A flash of memory, like a goldfish in the sun. A visit to a salt farm on the island of Aruba years ago. We'd finished the tour and I was standing on the rock parapet overlooking the salt flats, thinking about the last farmer's young European wife coming to such a beautiful but desolate place. Without warning, waves and waves of grief had swept over me, almost bringing me to my knees. I had steadied myself on the fence until it passed, then went back to ask the tour guide about the young wife's fate. She hadn't stayed. Her homesickness had bedridden her for months; then she'd taken the first ship out after the spring storms.

I'd never mentioned this episode to anyone, not being one to read into such things. But today, I was grabbing at straws. I stood at the end of the road and relaxed, opening my mind, thinking about my father. I listened. I waited. Nothing. Nothing but the water lapping at the road.

This stupidity was the last straw. I turned and stormed back along the road and up the embankment. There was no housework out here, no safety valve for my anger and I finally let it rip.

Everywhere I turned, I was cut off—either by the river or by time and distance. Maybe I should take the hint. What kind of an idiot was I, thinking I could just come here with nothing and solve a forty-year-old murder? What the hell was I doing anyway? If Mother didn't want to let me in on the scoop, so be it. I had my life and it was time I got back to it. Let the past stay in the past where it belonged. I couldn't change anything now anyway.

I stomped up the causeway full tilt, muttering to myself and probably looking like a crazy person. Maybe the shoe fit. My knee, already complaining about its lack of rest, began a background chatter into my thigh. As I neared the end of the road, it struck me that Gordon might be watching me and wondering what the hell it was all about. I turned involuntarily to look at the big white house. Sure enough, I saw the curtains in the patio window hastily close. Great.

As I stepped off the gravel path, I noticed something I'd missed the first time. It was another small road branching off to the west into the trees. I tried to place it in my mind and realized I was somewhere near the site of the old lumberyard. The road didn't go far in, turning into badly overgrown dirt ruts, but I could make out where there had been buildings once. My eye for it was getting better with practice. I found myself in a grove of silver maples, many small ones clustered around a giant mother to them all. The big one clearly dated from before the Power Project, probably saved because it would be in the sanctuary. I walked around it, noticing that one side had no branches and faded black bark, as though struck long ago by a great calamity. The grove was beautiful and cool, with the sun dipping below the tree line and the evening breeze picking up off the river.

And then I knew Someone was watching me, and had been for some time.

It hit me full body and I froze, skin-listening. Whether I heard or saw—to this day I don't know. But it was Something. The prickled hairs on the back of my neck were not from the river's breeze. I tried to write it off as nightmare fallout, but my survival systems were switching on. Not far from where I stood, my father had spent forty years with the fish—courtesy of someone who could still be very much alive and with me now.

Lynn, Strauss, Shad—they'd all warned me. I cursed myself for being so stupid as to go out there alone.

I remained absolutely still for some minutes, unable to move. There was no sound. The wind picked up, giving the trees a menacing sway. And then I heard them—whispers that seemed to come from the trees all around me.

Run.

I raised my head, trying to decide if they were real or my panic talking. But again, stronger.

Run, child. Run.

I could see no one, not even the Watcher. This time unmistakable, many voices, urgently.

Danger. Go.

My body took the initiative, bringing my brain along for the ride. I spun around and ran as fast as I could over the unstable terrain, now barely visible in the deepening shadows. Ignore the knee. Make the car. Unlock. Check back seat. Lock. Start. Reverse. Go. Somehow I swiftly backed the car up the narrow hill and out to the safety of the sanctuary road, nearly colliding with a passing van. I swung hard around in a U-turn and headed out to the highway in a cloud of dust. By the time I cleared the woods, I was soaked with sweat and probably needed at least a front-end alignment.

I should have waited to see who followed me. If I had, maybe things would have turned out differently. But the cold knife of fear was right up in my ribs, so I beat it back to the cottage, locking the door and windows, shutting the curtains, and sitting in the gloom until I returned to myself.

After a time, I got up and poured myself a stiff shot. I considered whom I could call, other than Shad—who would first give me hell for putting myself at risk like that and then insist I drive to the States for a few days. Not to say the idea didn't sound good just then. But mixed in with the steel drum beat of my knee was the continued niggling about Gordon. It felt bad. He was home and I needed to see him.

That's when I saw the blinking light on my answering machine.

The voice was almost a whisper and horribly strained, but unmistakable. Ruth.

Fan . . . Fan . . . I . . . Oh, God. (Long pause) *Fan, I'm sorry. So very, very sorry. Please believe that. I never meant for it to happen.* (Another long pause. I prayed the tape would last. Then sniffling as though crying.) *Fan . . . I never meant to take your father away.*

She hung up. The machine clicked off and rewound. Trance-like, I played it again. No mistaking it. A confession. And a woman walking the edge.

I popped the tape out, then picked up the phone to call the Long Sault detachment. I asked for Strauss.

"I'm sorry, ma'am," the voice said brightly. "It's after hours. This is Central in Kanata. Do you need assistance?"

"No!" I yelled, panic and frustration running neck and neck. "I need goddamn Strauss!" Slamming the phone down, I reached for the phone book. No Strauss. Must be unlisted. I found Wiley in Long Sault. No answer. On holidays?

Then I thought of Gordon. I called, but this time the machine did not pick up. Neither did my uncle. Not good.

Checking carefully around outside and then again in my back seat, I started the car and drove down to the end of the island. I met no one coming out. My headlights picked up a cat, two rabbits, and then Gordon's garage in the dark.

The whole place was dark. The garage door was open and both vehicles were inside. It was extraordinarily silent.

Taking the flashlight out of the glove compartment, I made my way to the front door. Locked. I didn't knock. I couldn't see anything in the windows but pitch black. Making my way around to the side door, I found the knob and turned it. As the door gave way, it registered briefly on me that the knob had something sticky on it.

I was in the kitchen. I could hear the clock on the wall and see the tiny digital glow of the microwave.

"Gordon?" I called softly, doing just what I'd told many TV characters they were idiots for doing—from the safety of my couch. "Are you . . ."

My foot hit something soft. I didn't want to look down. I really, really did not want to look down. But I pointed the beam of light at the floor.

My uncle lay sprawled face downward on the ceramic floor, eyes closed. There was something dark on his head and neck, and beside him on the floor.

Trying to swallow my panic, I reached my hand out toward him and the flashlight picked up what I'd touched on the doorknob coming in.

Blood.

Chapter 13

Washed Away

᱐T ALL had a terrible familiarity to it—riding in the ambulance to the hospital, listening to the reassuring small talk of the paramedics, gripping my whole family in one hand while I tried to keep the panic down. Gordon never stirred, except once to call Ruth's name. I told him he was safe with me and squeezed his hand. I thought I felt him squeeze back.

At the Cornwall General Hospital, I followed the stretcher through the ambulance entrance and was promptly intercepted by the triage nurse. The paramedics had reminded me to bring Gordon's wallet, and somehow I answered all the questions. Then I was gently steered toward the waiting room.

"I can't leave him," I insisted.

"You'd just be in the way," the nurse said, not unkindly. "Your uncle is in good hands. Dr. Barkley is our Chief of Emergency Medicine. Do you have anyone here to wait with you?"

I shook my head. "You don't understand. It isn't safe. Someone tried—"

"She can wait with me."

We both stopped arguing and fastened our gaze on Inspector Strauss.

"Where the hell did you come from?" popped out of my mouth.

Strauss ignored me, and showed his badge to the nurse. Then he pointed to a female officer behind him.

"Constable Taylor will stay with Mr. Leonard for now. I'll be in the waiting room. Tell Barkley I want news as soon as he's got it. Mackenzie, you come with me."

We all followed orders, Strauss taking my arm and seating me firmly.

"I'm going to get you a hot coffee from the machines," he said curtly. "Be here when I get back."

I really couldn't have gone anywhere else. I had no motor skills left. The last twenty-four hours had drained me, and it actually felt nice for a moment to have someone tell me what to do.

"Nine-one-one got hold of you, I take it?" I accepted the coffee gratefully, vaguely remembering my babbling something to the operator about murder again and tell Inspector Strauss.

He took the seat opposite me. It was very quiet in the waiting room, the two of us having it almost to ourselves. I looked over at the doors and wondered what was going on in there.

"Word got through, but I was already here. We found Ruth."

The coffee stopped halfway to my lips. "You did? Is she . . ."

"She's alive, but it's a miracle. She drove her car into the river this evening. Would have drowned, but there was a couple parked nearby. He fished her out in time. She's in the ICU here. Coma. The daughter is with her."

He let me digest all this for a moment. I felt sick, thinking of how I'd set Ruth off. Then Strauss set his coffee down on the little table and looked at me.

"Now," he said in a voice that probably froze the stomachs of trained officers, "I am going to listen while you tell me everything that happened. Begin at the beginning, and don't leave anything out."

I took a good gulp of coffee, and began. I started with the bad dream and my growing unease about Gordon, finishing up with finding my uncle bleeding on his kitchen floor. When I came to the part about my face-off with Ruth, I hesitated but continued. I didn't want to reveal any personal secrets, but I knew it was time to get out of Strauss's way and let him do his job.

"So Ruth followed you to the sanctuary after you left her house and was going to kill you," he mused. "Failing that, she went after Gordon. Then tried to kill herself."

I shook my head slowly, rubbing my knee. It was still throbbing from my sprint out of the maple grove. And something else, too. Something was tapping me on the shoulder again, and then slipping away.

"Ms. Mackenzie?" A man in a white coat stood over us with a clipboard. We rose to face him. "I'm Dr. Barkley. I thought you'd like to know that your uncle will be just fine."

"Oh, thank God," I sighed with relief.

"He's had a nasty cosh on the head but, other than a slight concussion and some stitches, there are no problems. I'm sending him in for a CAT scan just to make sure, and we'll keep him overnight in Observation."

"When can we see him?" Strauss asked.

"In about an hour and a half. I'll have a nurse come to get you. But trust me," Barkley added, "he's out of danger."

"It seemed like there was blood everywhere," I said.

"Heads are good bleeders," he explained. "Heads, ears and fingers. But he's healing quickly. We had to take away his cell phone."

Just over an hour later, the three of us (sans Officer Taylor) were catching up on each other's news. Gordon looked grave.

"I just can't believe it, Jerry. I've never been close to Ruth, but she always seemed like a nice woman. She was so upset when she came to the door that she wasn't herself. Still, it's going to take a while for it to sink in that she killed Hal."

"We haven't taken her statement yet, Gordy, but it certainly looks that way. Did Ruth say why she was so upset?"

"No," said my uncle. "I just tried to calm her down, offer her a chair. She wasn't making sense. Kept talking about taking Farran's father away. I turned to get her a stiff shot of something and that's when she hit me."

"I'm just glad she didn't kill you," I said. "I set her off. I would never have forgiven myself." Strauss hadn't mentioned our suspicions about Ruth having Hal's baby and I followed suit. Gordon didn't seem to know. "I guess I just asked the wrong question, and she felt threatened."

Gordon slowly reached out for my hand. "I'm glad she didn't kill you, either. Not when we've just found each other."

"Mr. Leonard needs rest." A nurse you didn't argue with came in and shooed us out. I turned to Strauss.

"Any chance I could look in on Ruth before I go home?"

He nodded and headed down the hall with me in tow. Flashing his badge at the ICU nursing staff, we went through and paused at the door to Ruth's unit. Ruth lay still, looking younger and fragile in the bed. The sound of the machines around her pushed me back to that day months ago after the fire. I almost turned and walked away. The daughter I had met just a few hours ago looked up from where she sat next to the bed. She wasn't happy to see me.

"What are *you* doing here?" she said in a low voice, rising to her feet.

"I . . . I came to see how your mother was," I faltered.

"Haven't you done enough for her already?"

No, I wanted to say. No, I haven't. This shouldn't be happening. I retreated and waited for Strauss. He went over to the nurses' station.

"Keep that on your desk," he told the two women working there, passing them a card. "If there is any change, any at all, I want you to call me immediately."

I felt like crap inside and out, and all I wanted was my bed. I asked Strauss if he could take me home. He obliged, and we drove almost the whole way in silence. Just after Ingleside, one of the smaller nickels fell through the slot.

"Inspector," I said suddenly, "I've been wanting to ask you something. In the newspaper reports about my father, they called you 'Detective Inspector' but no one uses that title here. Why not?"

"I was in stationed in Kingston when they found your father. Dave Lewis, the inspector here at the time, asked me to give him a hand because he knew I had come from the villages and he wanted someone with that background for obvious reasons. When Lewis retired last winter, I transferred here. The highest rank in Long Sault is inspector."

"So you took a demotion to move back home?"

"Not really. The detachment here just isn't big enough to support a detective inspector. I still have the same responsibilities."

And authority. Nice way to keep things you want quiet under wraps. But then, there was Ruth lying in a halo of machines, and Gordon under observation. Why did I feel like I was missing something obvious?

"Gordon's retirement celebration is in three days, at the end of the week," Strauss changed the subject. "I understand they're having some official change of management ceremony in the Village with the minister of tourism, and our local MPP. They'll probably postpone it till he gets on his feet."

"Sounds like Gordon has friends in high places," I commented.

Strauss shrugged. "Your uncle pretty much devoted his career to the Parks, not having family. He's been there for almost forty years and is well respected. They should do something nice for him."

"Thank God he made it to retirement," I said dryly.

I brought Gordon home the next day and got him settled in with a nurse for the next few. I considered taking care of him myself, but felt it would be awkward. We were still relative strangers (very appropriate term in this case) although we'd been through a lot in the few weeks since I'd arrived.

Ruth stayed in her coma. Strauss put a guard on her after Gordon left the hospital, maybe worried she would try suicide again when she woke up. The Hoffmans decided to go ahead with Alice's funeral, but I would not attend. I didn't know if I could ever make all that right again.

Friday morning after breakfast, I walked (okay, hobbled) over to Gordon's house. Even with two days on the sofa, my knee was not backing down. I was told last year that knees never really heal, and that I would have to baby my recovering tendons for some time or have corrective surgery. Traipsing around the Seaway Valley and mad dashes for survival don't qualify as babying, and I was paying the price. Swollen and angry, the knee forced me to dust off my walking stick. Time to get it looked at.

"You better get that looked at." Gordon's nurse, an older woman that reminded me of Meredith, crossed her arms and frowned.

"I am," I said meekly. "Probably today. I looked up a clinic in Cornwall. I just thought I'd look in on my uncle first."

"He's not here." Her frown deepened, if possible. "He's at the Village."

"What? He's supposed to be resting for the week."

"I told him that but he wouldn't listen. Seems the minister can't make it next week, so Mr. Leonard said he could do it today. Stubborn, that man. I was to tell you that the ceremony will be at 11:00 a.m."

I shook my head. "I'll bring him home as soon as it's over," I promised.

I went straight back and changed into something less casual. Then I drove right over so as to give me lots of time to find him. Hobbling takes twice as long as walking.

"He was here, Dr. Mackenzie," said the receptionist at Operations, "but he left about ten minutes ago. I know they're setting up for the ceremony in front of Crysler Hall. Maybe he's there."

I thanked her and headed out. Sheep were grazing in the field just down across the road, and a wagon with two men in the uniform white shirt and breeches went past. I decided to take the back route to avoid the sawmill, and had my season's pass ready if anyone put me in a neck hold for not paying at the front gate.

The people setting up pointed me in the direction of the Physician's Home. I walked on, turning back to look at the little stage they were setting up for the ceremony. I thought of what my family had been through, and how much Gordon had lost; and I was glad they were making a fuss over him. Glad I was there to be part of it.

The "physician" was doing his spiel with a group in the front room, but Gordon was nowhere in sight. I carefully went upstairs and found him in the main bedroom looking out the oval window, a small bandage still on the back of his head.

"Gordon?"

He turned and smiled. "You got my message. I hope you're not angry I came today, but I felt up to it. And I'm having a hard time being fussed over."

"My instructions are to take you home as soon as it's over," I smiled back. "Then I'm going to be a good girl and get this knee looked at."

"Fair enough." He turned back to look out the window again. "You know, Farran, I haven't been in this house since the day they moved it from Aultsville. Too many bad memories. But I thought perhaps I could today, it being my last day, and feeling like this whole mess is finally over.

"The view out this window sure has changed," he continued. "After they moved the houses, a lot of the older folks found it very disorienting to have a completely different view out of windows they'd lived with their whole lives. It was depressing to them. I never thought about that until now, and now I think I see what they meant."

"Does the house look much like it did when you and my father lived here?"

"No," Gordon looked around at the room. "This house is furnished circa 1860. We might have been a little behind the times in the villages, but we weren't that bad." He shoved his hands in his pockets. "I'm glad you're here. I mean that. It's been a roller coaster since you arrived, but it also seems to make up for things. I only wish we could have found each other years ago. If only Hal would have told me about his having a child that last time I saw him, it might have changed things. At least I could have tried to find you. Why he didn't, I'll never know."

Just like Ruth didn't about her baby. Even when she was losing it.

Your father was a good son to his mother. Lynn talking about the river. The third picture on Wiley's fridge. Why Hal couldn't come home. Why my mother never came back. The fawn and the doe. And the only reason in the world Hal never told Gordon about me. I blinked. I thought I heard the words only in my mind, but God help me they came out of my mouth.

"Because he knew you'd kill me too. He was my father and he was saving my life."

For a full minute, no one said a word. Then Gordon looked confused.

"What did you say?"

A thought flashed through my mind that maybe I could laugh it off as a joke and then get the hell out of there. But I had just seen something new in his eyes—a black, soulless look. What Meredith probably saw in her final moments. And my father, too.

The pieces were coming together in my head with brutal speed, and I tried to sort them out.

"Ever since I got here," I began slowly, "two things have bothered me. That everyone thought my mother was dead, and that my father seemed like two different people. A good son to his mother. A hard worker on the *Emerald*. A surrogate brother to Jerry. A chaperon for Emme on her evening walks home. A man who pulled any string he could to have even just a few hours home to see Leslie when he heard Harper had died."

"A man who forged cheques, stole money, ran around with our foreman's wife, and possibly killed him," Gordon reminded me.

"Exactly. Like two different people. And one day Lynn said something to me about the river. About how she could see the artificial lake in front of her but she knew in her heart *it wasn't real*. That thought started to bother me deep down. Something here wasn't real.

"And I am finally understanding that the reason Hal Leonard seemed like two different men was that he *was* two. The real Hal—and you. When he was on his own, he was fine. But when you were involved, things went wrong. There you were, one step behind him, being to the world the supportive brother. Alice put her finger on it when she said Hal brought the wickedness with him. He brought you."

"You don't know what you're saying," said Gordon, shaking his head. "You weren't there."

"I was there when Meredith died," I said quietly. "When I told her my mother had lived, she wasn't just shocked. She was angry. Why? Did she hate my mother so much after forty years? Can hate run that deep? Yes, it can. But so can love."

"Love?"

"Yes, love. Everyone believed absolutely that Leslie was dead. Why? Because Meredith said so. *Meredith didn't lie.* Obviously, she had no proof, so she must have heard it from an impeccable source. That source was you. The man she loved."

"Meredith loved Hal," Gordon snapped.

"No. She wasn't hanging around the store and the lumberyard to see Hal, she did it to see you. The young man with the movie star good looks. The man she stayed close to for forty years, hoping someday you'd want to remarry. The man she believed in absolutely."

"You're not making any sense. Why would I tell her such a lie?"

"It probably just slipped out one day. And you believed it because Hal told you. The night you killed him."

My uncle no longer replied. The murmur of voices downstairs had faded. They must have moved into the kitchen. I wondered if they would come upstairs.

"It took me a while to pick up on the discrepancies in the stories." I leaned on my stick for support, longing to sit down but not daring. "But they were there. Hal said you wanted to leave Lila in the old cemetery; Meredith told Lynn you said it was Hal who felt that way. You said Hal asked to meet you in the remains of Aultsville because he wanted to see what the old neighbourhood looked like. Then why go at night when you can't see much? You said no one was around, but men worked late every night for the last two weeks burning and destroying what was left at the end. You must have met where you could avoid everyone. And why go there at all? Because Hal wanted to see the old neighbourhood? He'd already been there on his way to Casselman's Dance Hall, remember? And again the following December.

"Why not just go home and see Eric? Eric who was wasting away because he thought he'd driven his son away. Because *you* kept getting in the way. Hal must have called home because you knew he was coming that September night. You made sure to get everyone away—your father wasn't at home, and you had taken Leslie and the girls to Morrisburg. But you forgot about Lynn.

"My mother left with Hal in December. They married and she became pregnant. He wanted to come home, to mend fences and raise his family where they belonged. The prodigal son was going to return but you couldn't let that happen. You took the call and asked him to meet you in Aultsville. My mother probably didn't like it. I'm sure her gypsy blood sensed the danger and she begged him not to go. But my father probably saw it as a chance to clear things up with you, things that bothered him because *he* knew he hadn't done what the people believed. He hadn't yet followed it through to the right answer because he loved you. Just like Meredith did. And they both paid for it with their lives."

I fell silent and waited. Gordon said nothing. Finally he shrugged and smiled.

"What a shame. And I had just changed my mind about killing you."

"So you were there in the maple grove, watching me."

He nodded happily, then frowned. "I was going to bury you roughly where we found Bill, but you ran out of there too suddenly."

"And you were the only one who could have killed Meredith," I continued. "You returned her call from Toronto and heard the unbelievable news about me, about Leslie. After you got angry, you got scared. You knew Meredith was already on her way to piecing it all together—that's why she was angry, too. So you arranged to meet her, you drove like hell from Toronto and killed her in the sawmill before she could spill it to anyone else. That's why she said she had an appointment with administration—she didn't want to tell me it was with you, but she didn't want to lie, either. And that's why I didn't see anyone entering or leaving the mill at the time of the murder. You easily slipped into the employee locker room with your pass key, put on the shirt and breeches all the men wear, and topped it off with a straw hat. I saw you but didn't see you because you blended right in." And why, come to think of it, he hadn't been all that upset to find out about me at the police station—he already knew.

Gordon was nodding. "It was easy. It's always been easy. People are so easily manipulated, you know. I took the cash from Hal's boxes. I forged some cheques and then slipped them into the batch Hal gave me. I would try to "settle" fights for Hal but I really made them worse. I knew a guy named Desmond Shaler would be in the park at Farran's Point one Saturday night not long after I'd given Hal a bad cheque for Desmond's father. I knew Shaler's temper and counted on there being a fight. I got quite good at it after a while.

"Like with Bill Strauss. I got everyone—including my father—to believe the worst about Hal and Emme. I'd set my brother up by sending him to the train the same time she'd go so they'd come back together. If Meredith was there, so much the better. Word got around fast. And I would tell Hal only half of what Bill needed done around the lumberyard, so Bill thought he was goofing off. It built the tension between them. Just to spice things up, one day I timed some bad remarks about Hal and Emme just when Bill walked into the yard office. Perfect. Because it doesn't matter if something is true, as long as people believe it to be true."

"Did you murder Bill?"

"Oh, no. Didn't have to. He did that himself. Took the gun out of my father's desk that night and put a hole in his head. Said in his note Dr. Burns had recently diagnosed him with Lou Gehrig's disease. Couldn't face dying that way. I found him, decided I couldn't pass on such an opportunity, and set the fire in the office. Didn't mean to lose the whole yard, but it couldn't be helped. He was burnt so badly they couldn't trace the cause of death. One bad moment, though," he added with a smile. "When I got home, I saw blood on my hands. I was still washing it off when Hal came into the kitchen. Thank God he was too upset to notice."

A smile. Not a word about Jerry's pain all these years. My uncle spoke easily, coldly, with that absolute calm only the truly crazy can achieve. The most dangerous crack in human existence is the gap between who we are and who we think we are—and Gordon was sliding down that hole.

"So that's all it ever was," I said softly, feeling my throat tightening. "Hal was just Hal. A boy from Aultsville who fell in love with the girl next door. But you had to destroy them. God, it must gall you about me. You thought you were so smart, but Leslie knew enough to trust her feelings. When Hal didn't come back, she knew something had gone terribly wrong and with whom. But she had no proof, and she had to protect her unborn child from someone deadly. So she left forever, disappearing without a trace and never speaking of the past to me. And my father," I tried to swallow the growing lump in my throat, "my father, suddenly seeing you for what you were, knowing he couldn't reason with you, didn't use Leslie and me to talk his way out. He couldn't take the chance, so he did what any good father would do. He lied to protect his family, to send you off in the wrong direction, taking the secret of his marriage and child to his grave." My eyes blurred and I blinked it away.

"Oh, Dad. *Dad*." The dam blew after all these months and a wave of grief smashed into my eyes. Tears. Lots of them. Goddammit, not now. I started wiping them away frantically. "Why, Gordon? Why?" I played for time. "What have you done? He loved you."

"*He* was her son!" Gordon's sudden fury made me stumble back to the wall behind me. He came up and kicked the four-poster bed in the middle of the room. "Her *real* son! I sat with her, right here, feeling like I was dying too. And she asked me to get her real son! Can you believe that? What the hell was I? Lila was the only mother I'd ever known. But in the end, I was only Eric's son to her."

Gordon was breathing heavily, as though he'd been running. I took advantage of his distraction to move toward the door. Where the hell were the tourists when you wanted them? Suddenly, a small pistol appeared in his hand.

"No," my uncle said quietly. "I can't let you get away a second time. Recognize the pistol, Hal? It's Dad's from the yard office. I kept it when I found Bill. That's why they never found it. This time, you'd better stay dead. And at least I won't have to wait four goddamn days for the river to cover you."

I tried not to let the full horror of the moment get to me. I had to think. The silence in the old house seemed like a vacuum. Time seeped out of the walls like dust motes, swirling, pinning us there in that moment. We stared at each other across the years—He was the last piece of what I'd lost, I was the face of what he'd risked everything to destroy.

Now I would have to destroy him to stay alive.

His eyes were black and empty, even the light of pain having gone out long ago. He was absolutely still, watching me, waiting for just the right moment to strike again. Life would grant him only one try and he knew it. He would not miss . . . my beautiful killer.

I grabbed at a straw, and lowered my voice. "We're not alone this time, Gordy. People will hear the shot and come runnin'. And there's nowhere to bury me here."

He seemed to think about that, so I kept going.

"I brought my fishin' rod." I held up my walking stick. "Why don't we just go fishin' and talk about it like we used to. I miss that."

Gordon's mouth worked, and he shook his head slowly. He seemed suddenly a little dizzy. One hand went up to touch the bandage; the other lowered the gun a couple of inches. I moved. Taking a step forward, I brought the stick down as hard as I could on the pistol. It flew out of his hand and spun across the floor, along with my walking stick.

"Damn you!" Gordon lunged at me and I dove through the doorway into the hall. He turned back and I heard him scrabbling around for the gun.

With what was left of my legs, I stumbled quickly down the stairs and out the door. One thought kept running through my head: One of us is going to die today and it isn't going to be me.

Queen Street was full of people milling around where the platform stood ready. A group of Village musicians was warming up with some cheerful fiddle music, a soundtrack for the crazy movie I was in. And some man was checking the microphone, the chairs behind him still empty. Would he believe me that the guest of honour was a murderous lunatic?

Like my mother before me, I had no proof of anything about Gordon. It was all gut feeling and conjecture based on memories— some of them lost now in death. And Gordon was a highly respected man around here. But in his current state, my uncle would give them all the proof I needed. If he didn't kill me and some bystanders first.

I started to zigzag through the crowd, putting enough people between me and him. But I knew I was running out of time. I had to get someone who could help. And I had to draw Gordon away from the crowd with that old gun. He wasn't flying with both engines and I didn't want him to start taking potshots at me in frustration. I had enough innocent blood on my hands.

Shouts started behind me and I turned to check my uncle's progress. Someone called his name. He broke free of the crowd and some parents began pulling their children close, uncertainly. I reached the corner of Queen and Church Streets, almost ending up under the hooves of the tour wagon horses. They weren't pleased. I saw Gordon raise the gun but the wagon cut him off. Someone screamed.

I cut past Cook's Tavern, and pushed past a small crowd of what looked like reporters milling around some guys in suits. Queen's Park. By that time my knee was having a meltdown, and I didn't know how much farther I could push it.

Security. The admissions office. It was probably my only chance. It was also the worst place to get to—an open area down Queen Street leading to the bottleneck of the bridge. Talk about a sitting duck.

Then, in the heat and the dust, I saw Strauss and Wiley appear at the end of the bridge. They were in suits, too. I wondered fleetingly if I were making them up. Behind me I heard someone yell about a gun and I knew Gordon had arrived. Time was up.

"Farran!" Strauss called out. He was looking past me, reaching for something in his jacket. "Gordon, don't! It's over."

I turned and faced my uncle. For one second, our eyes locked. Then he fired.

It felt like a blowtorch cut through my earlobe and instinctively I put up my hand. It came away full of blood. People began screaming and running for cover. There was none. Gordon took aim again and I heard the louder, popping sound of a second shot.

But the soundtrack was beginning to fade. The crowd was coming through as a muffled roar, with the banging of that cursed sawmill sounding like the beat of a human heart. I saw Gordon's arms fly up, taking his body with them, puppet-like, to the ground. I felt a hand on my shoulder shaking me, and noticed my shirt was covered with blood. Why didn't I feel the pain?

Jerry grabbed my other shoulder and shook me again. He was yelling something, but I could only see his lips moving. I pushed his arms away and stumbled over to my uncle. He was clearly dead, with a red hole in the centre of his chest. Blood was beginning to pool beside him in the dusty road. He lay on his back, face up, sightless eyes trained heavenward.

The knee gave up screaming and let go in disgust. My legs buckled and I fell on my knees in the dust beside Gordon. And then the picture faded, too.

Part Three

I've kissed the ground from
which I came
And someday will return again
For I am just a messenger
you know

Love lives on
So they say
It's the one thing we cannot afford
Not to give away

Love lives on
So it is told
Worlds will rise and fall
And come and go

But love lives on.

Bruce Guthro
Love Lives On

Chapter **14**

Mosaic

⊘HE ST. LAWRENCE RIVER runs wide and deep, carving Her name out of the heart of North America. She continues to be the lifeblood of three peoples—Canadian, American, and Mohawk—at once dividing us physically and joining us forever in a common destiny. By the villages of Long Sault, Ingleside, Morrisburg and Iroquois, She is forever changed but continues to shape our lives as She has always done here; even if for the most part we can now only admire Her from a distance. For it is really the River—more so than the land—that is our home.

I buried Gordon in the cemetery on the rise, beside the wife and child he lost and near the father and brother he destroyed. The bigwigs didn't attend but pretty much everyone else did—which I found comforting for Gordon's sake. I thought of my mother the day she buried Harper in that same place. I expected to be standing alone for the service at the graveside considering the situation, but I guess people came out of respect for my father's family . . . of which I am all that remains.

When I regained consciousness that morning at the Village, I remember many voices at once, including Jerry's. He sat me up and somehow got me a glass of water. There was blood on his shirt, too. The sight of it reminded me what the hell I was doing there and I turned to look at Gordon. Someone had covered him with a blanket, security had arrived and Wiley was keeping everyone away. Press cameras flashed from a distance. The Queen's Park alumni were nowhere in sight. Then the paramedics arrived.

249

Dr. Barkley checked me out at the Emergency, asking me how my uncle was doing. I had to tell him. My ear was stitched, and my knee packed in ice again. They sent me in for X-rays, with dire predictions about pending surgery. A constable stayed with me until Jerry arrived, about an hour after that.

When we were finally alone, for several minutes neither of us spoke. It was all a lot for me to take in, and Jerry had just shot an old friend in the line of duty.

"When I saw you at the bridge," I said finally, "you didn't seem surprised to find Gordon chasing me. Why?"

Jerry rubbed his eyes and sat back in his chair.

"We were already on our way to have a talk with him after the ceremony," he replied. "I haven't liked the feel of this thing with Ruth. There were gaps in Gordon's timeframe the morning of Meredith's murder and I had been looking into it—not seriously, because they had been friends their whole lives and I couldn't see any reason why Gordon would kill her. Still, the gaps were there and I couldn't forget that; although I still can't explain Ruth's actions.

"I guess that started me thinking about the old days again and what went on. I had done that many times before but put it all away for years. Then I spent time with you, answering your questions and looking at things from new angles. Especially about your father. And I realized that what had always bothered me about it was not that Hal had become someone I didn't know, but that he'd *stayed the same*. Friendly, outgoing, likeable. Yet all these things went on.

"And this morning," he finished, "when I stopped in to pick Wiley up for Alice's funeral, I saw the drawing on his fridge door and it finally hit me. *It was Gordon that changed.* Moody. Solitary. Quiet. Even long after Lila passed away. And then all the pieces began to fall into place and we took off for the Village."

The prodigal son. The resentment on his return. Made deadly in the face of four years' work to drive him away.

"Meredith sensed the wickedness," I nodded, "but always thought it was Hal."

"Until you showed up. Then she finally started to question the man she thought she knew, and listen to her real instincts. She gave him a chance to explain himself and it cost her her life."

"She loved him, you know," I said softly. "For over forty years.

And he threw her into those gears like . . ." I covered my face with my hands.

"Farran." I heard Jerry get up and come over to the side of the bed. "Don't." He sat down on the mattress facing me and pulled my hands away. "You couldn't control his actions. Gordon had become what he was even before you were born. Start letting it go. Right now. It's the only way to make it through something like this."

I looked in his eyes and knew we weren't just talking about my uncle. Jerry had said the pieces fell in place for him that morning, but so far had not mentioned his father's death. I said nothing. This was not the time or place for me to tell him the truth.

Barkley kept me overnight for observation, and I found out later that the constable stayed to keep the press away. Gordon had been a bigwig in this area. The violent end to his life made great local headlines.

I wanted to see Ruth while I was in the hospital, but she remained in a coma. I was sent home with a day nurse and medication to help with the swelling and pain of my knee. Surgery was the prognosis, and I was given an appointment with a local surgeon for an interview in July.

The day I came home, the church ladies of Ingleside began to drop by with condolences and food. This unexpected kindness for an (almost) complete stranger, coupled with the shock of Gordon's dark side and death, broke the last of my reserve. The crying jags would settle in for sometime, waking me up in the night or greeting me in the morning. Sometimes it just took a memorable song on the radio. But the tears were washing me clean, and I welcomed them after such a long dry spell.

At the time of the funeral arrangements, I met with Gordon's lawyer. My uncle's will left everything to Meredith, a succession that lapsed with her predeceasing him. There was no other extended family, but it was up to me to petition the courts as rightful heir. I said I'd get back to him.

I took a week at Shad's and buried myself in her company. For seven days, I pretended to be the Farran I was last year, before my world blew apart. Then I returned home, and reluctantly filed my petition. A week later, Jerry called to say that Ruth had come out of her coma. Amazingly, she wanted to see me. Jerry drove me to the General that evening.

"I thought you'd like to know," he said after several miles of silence, "that Alice did die a natural death. Heart failure. Nothing more."

"Thank God for that," I said. "At least Ruth doesn't have that to deal with, too." And neither did I. "Has she said why she wants to see me?"

"No, but I hope it's to clear up what happened that night with Gordon. She hasn't been too forthcoming about that yet. Says she can't remember much."

I expected a tirade on my thoughtlessness and hoped I would be given a chance to apologize when it was over. When I hobbled into Ruth's room that night, however, she seemed more sad than angry while she shooed her family out. She looked pale but composed, with a large patch on her forehead and one wrist in a cast. When we were alone, Ruth indicated a chair beside the bed.

"First of all, Farran," she said as I sat down, "I want to apologize for all the trouble I caused and tell you how sorry I am about Gordon."

I blinked a couple of times while this set in. "But Ruth," I protested, "I'm the one who owes *you* an apology for what I said. If anything had happened to you, I would never have forgiven myself. You might have been killed—"

I stopped when Ruth held up her hand.

"You came here, Fan, for answers you deserved. It would have been one thing if you'd simply shown up as a surprise to all of us. But Hal was dead—murdered. We knew that. And then someone killed Meredith. I should have told you the whole truth, but I got scared."

I started to speak, but she silenced me again with her hand. "Please let me say this. It isn't easy." I duly shut up.

"Day after day," Ruth continued, "Mother and I talked around the issue, but avoided coming right out with it. At the time, I thought Mother had killed Hal or that she was covering for my father. She, I believe, wondered if I were guilty, and then killed Meredith to protect myself."

She struggled with something for a moment.

"Because you'd become pregnant years ago and Hal was the father?" I prompted gently.

Ruth closed her eyes and tears began without a sound.

"No," she managed, and took my hand. "That was the hell of it, Fan. Not Hal. *Gordon*."

"Gordon?"

"Yes. I told my parents it was Hal because he was gone and I wanted nothing to do with Gordon ever again. I had my baby in secret in Montreal. And that's how things stayed for forty years—until they found your father. I've spent all the time since thinking that my cowardice killed an innocent man. A man, I discovered when you arrived, who had left a daughter behind."

I let this sink in for a minute.

"But you two never dated," I said. "No one said you spent time together, except that Alice was hoping you would."

Ruth looked away to the window and absently smoothed her blanket with her good hand.

"The night we went to Casselman's Dance Hall, Gordon drove me home. Meredith was gone and Leslie had left with Hal. I could see Gordon was in a bad humour, and we didn't speak at all part of the way home. Then he started to mutter about Hal coming and going like that, and how Leslie shouldn't have gone with him. I put my two cents in, and then he got angry."

She swallowed hard. "He pulled off the road. Started yelling like a crazy person about his brother not caring and he cared and why couldn't she see that?"

"She?"

"Your mother." The tears were falling freely now, and she spoke just above a whisper. "In his fury, he called me Leslie. Then . . . then he raped me."

The ugly word sat between us for some minutes. I moved to sit on the bed in front of her and held both her hands in mine, crying a little too.

"Ruth, I'm so sorry," I whispered.

"You are the only person in the world, besides Gordon, who knows the truth. I've never told anyone, least of all my parents or Leslie. My father would have killed him. Leslie would have seen it as her fault, and I couldn't tell her that Gordon loved her. It was all just too awful, so twisted and strange. I was seventeen," she added, "and I thought it was my fault."

"And the baby?"

"I gave my son up for adoption in Montreal," Ruth reached for a tissue. "We never spoke of him. Leslie never knew. I didn't want Gordon to ever find out. I didn't want him near my son."

I thought of Gordon staying alone all those years after losing his wife and child. Of the pain he had caused Ruth, and of the son he never knew he had. The waste of it all. Like the waste in my own life.

"Where is your son now, Ruth?" I asked. "Have you looked for him?"

She shook her head.

"Never. What would I say to him? That he came from rape? And that now we know his father was a murderer?"

"Tell him who you are and that you never stopped loving him. Give him the missing pieces he needs in his life." I got up and walked over to the window. "I don't mean to stick my nose into something so personal, Ruth. But first of all, you realize that if Gordon has a son out there somewhere, that man would be the rightful heir to his estate." I turned back to her sitting on the bed. "I'm also speaking as a mother who never knew her child. I gave my daughter away when I was in university. I've never talked about it, either. And I know I have to find her, to tell her the truth she needs to hear—even if all she does is turn and walk away. Because I can tell you, as Hal's daughter, that knowing the truth—even when it looks pretty grim— is better than knowing nothing at all."

"And tell him that I might have been a murderer, too?" she said softly. "Don't forget, Fan, that I almost killed your uncle. After you asked me about my baby that day, it all boiled up to the surface and I drove out to Ault Island. Gordon's door wasn't locked, so I went in and waited for him. I was determined to have it out with him, face him as I should have done in the first place. I saw you walking the bike path in the sanctuary. About half an hour later, Gordon came home. I admit it was my turn to act the crazy person."

"You said nothing about your son?"

"No. We never lose our instincts to protect our children, do we? And I've never regretted not telling him. When we argued that day and I told him the pain he caused me, he had no remorse. He just laughed. He said it was my fault. That I was a bad person." She shook her head. "That's when I hit him. Then I drove to the river to let go of it all."

"I know now that's why Mom never told me about her life here. She was protecting me from Gordon, too."

Ruth wiped her eyes and sniffed.

"Yes, I'm sure she was a good mother to you. The Leslie I knew took family seriously. I've always regretted closing the door on that friendship, never stopped missing her. When I thought she was dead, I always felt guilty for not being there when she left. And when you came, I can't tell you the feelings I went through to know that Leslie had been alive all these years. With that and Hal's murder, it felt as though the past was no longer as I remember." She sighed and shook her head. "I guess it's true that you can't go home again."

"I don't know about that." I returned to the chair beside her and sat down. "When I first got here, I certainly would have agreed with you. Now I'm feeling that perhaps we never really leave."

She took my hand again, saying, "Maybe you're right, Fan. Maybe you're right."

We sat together for a few minutes in a comfortable silence, knowing without saying that we'd both just turned an important corner. The healing must go both ways if it is to work at all.

"Excuse me." A man appeared at the door. He seemed about Gordon's age, with greying hair and a nice smile. I was afraid he was a reporter who'd slipped through, and I got to my feet. "I'm looking for Ruth Hoffman."

"And you are . . .?" I spotted some flowers he held a little behind him.

"Ernie. Ernie Black." He shook my hand and looked at Ruth. "It's Ernie, Ruthie. Remember me? We met at Casselman's one night a long time ago."

Ruth's face took on a beautiful smile, and she held her good hand out to him.

"Of course I remember you, Ernie," she said as he came over. "You were quite the dancer back then."

"I hope you don't mind my dropping in on you," he said shyly, giving her the flowers. "I'm back home for a bit. New grandchild. First one. I saw your name in the paper about your accident and thought I'd come see how you're doing." He looked at her a moment. "It's good to see you, Ruthie."

Ruth blushed like a teenager.

"It's good to see you, too, Ernie."

I took the flowers to find them water and left the two of them to it. Not that they noticed me leave.

"Hi, Fan," said Lynn on my doorstep several days later. She held out a large envelope. "Peace offering."

"For what?" I held the door open to let her in.

"For not going to Gordon's funeral." She sat down at the kitchen table and put the envelope by my teacup. "I should have come by before. I should have been there with you at the funeral. I'm sure it wasn't easy for you. But he killed Meredith and I guess I'm still coming to terms with that."

I poured her a tea without asking and sat down. "We all are, Lynn. I've always felt responsible for your cousin's death and I still do in some ways. My uncle was a sick man. I don't ask you to forgive him but I hope you'll forgive me for walking in blind like that."

Lynn slowly stirred her tea. "I should have seen the truth forty years ago. Instead, I chose to see what Gordon wanted me to see." She pushed the envelope at me. "Like I said, peace offering."

I opened the envelope and pulled out a stack of photocopies. They were news articles from *The Ottawa Citizen*, going back several years. The top one sported the headline "Study Condemns Cornwall Dam."

"They go back about three years, when the Ottawa U study was first published," Lynn explained. "If you want the whole story, you can call the name and number on the last sheet."

"Doesn't look good, does it?" I commented, giving the articles a quick scan.

"No. I think in some ways they bit off more than they could chew with this project. You can't screw around with Mother Nature and not pay a price. But that was the arrogance of that era—and the Power Project certainly didn't have a monopoly on it."

She pulled out a pamphlet and passed it over.

"That's about the St. Lawrence River Institute. They're an environmental agency that's been working with Ontario Power Generation, the Mohawk Council of Akwesasne, government and local business to keep the river healthy. I've been talking with them about setting up an internship program or scholarship fund in

Meredith's name. Something positive to remember her by. What do you think?"

"I think that's a great idea." I considered my tea for a moment. "You know, I've thought a lot about Meredith since Gordon died. About their relationship all these years. She loved him her whole life. Things could have been so different here if . . ."

"Yes. So many times Gordon used my cousin to spread rumours around about Hal. Saying things when she was in the store, or dropping hints in their conversations. She was so careful about anyone else's stories but she believed him always, because she loved him. And I believed her because I didn't see it."

I didn't see Jerry for three weeks after I gave my statement about Gordon's death, and in a way, I was thankful. I still had to tell him about his dad and the night he died—something I definitely wasn't looking forward to. Part of me thought that the good cop he was would already be doing some basic math about it, but still would have no idea about the suicide. And although he called almost every day to check up on me, he never asked about it. Perhaps he knew he didn't want to go there until the investigation was tied up. It would be a loaded charge waiting to go off.

And then my petition was granted, and the process of handling Gordon's estate fell to me. I spent one afternoon in the big white house sorting out his papers in his office, trying not to let the silence get to me. There, in a cubbyhole in plain sight, sat an envelope yellowed with age. It was opened. I think I knew what it was even before I read the 'Emme and Jerry' scrawled on the front. I looked at it for a long time, and then slid it into my purse unread.

That night I called Jerry and asked him to stop by after work. I made supper but couldn't eat, wondering how the hell I was going to tell him. When he finally knocked on the door, I jumped.

"Come on in, stranger," I managed a smile. "Have you eaten?"

Jerry looked tired.

"Yeah, I think so. How's the knee?"

"Hanging in." I pulled a chair over for him and he sat down. "I've seen a doctor here and she wants to cut me open. Replace the kneecap. It's never healed properly since the fire."

"A bionic woman?" he said with a small smile.

"Yep. Better, stronger, faster."

"Ruth went home today. We had a long talk yesterday and she told me about the baby. About Gordon. She said she feels a great relief to let it go."

"I hope so. She's been through enough."

I poured him a coffee and placed a brandy beside it. He downed the brandy and let the coffee sit. Feeling something coming, I waited.

"The gun, Farran."

"The gun?"

"The small pistol Gordon used to shoot you. We ID'd it positively as belonging to Eric Leonard. Only a handful of people knew he owned it and kept it in a drawer at the lumberyard office in Aultsville. Eric, Gordon, Hal, my father, and me. They never found it—or its remains—after the fire. No one brought it up at the inquest back then, so I didn't either. It seems that Gordon had it all along."

Still I waited, letting him take the lead. He looked at me for a moment, picked up his spoon, set it down and folded his hands.

"Did Gordon say anything to you about the night the lumberyard burned? Anything that we didn't know before? If he did, please tell me—whatever it is."

I took a deep breath, then let it all out. My heart was pounding and wouldn't slow down.

"Gordon said he was at the lumberyard that night and found your father on the floor. He was . . . dead. Shot. With the pistol. Gordon must have read the suicide note because he said that Bill had killed himself. Said your father had found out he was dying of ALS and couldn't face it.

"Gordon saw it as a chance to make things worse for my dad and set the fire, knowing they'd find Bill and assume the worst. He'd just made it home when Hal came with the news of the fire."

Jerry sat as still as a sphinx, with his face as unreadable. Then he shook his head.

"Gordon must have killed him then, to frame Hal."

"No." I went to my purse and pulled out the envelope. "That much is true," I said, holding it out. But Jerry didn't take it.

"What's that?" he asked in a low voice.

"I haven't read it but it's old and has your name on it. I'm assuming it's the suicide note. Gordon must have opened it and read it when he found your father that night. I found it today in his desk just sitting there, as though he'd left it for me. I can only say how sorry I am that you had to wait forty years to read it."

Jerry continued to look at the envelope in my hand for another minute, then slowly reached for it.

"It's his handwriting," he said in a husky voice. Then he got up suddenly without a word and left.

I closed my eyes and felt the tears return, this time for the boy who, in his confusion and pain, took on the guilt for his father's death so long ago. Another thing made wrong that probably could not be made right.

I spent the evening on the porch, nursing a drink. Concentrating was out of the question and I couldn't tolerate TV at this point. I wondered if I'd see Jerry again beyond professional duty. If not, I couldn't blame him. Every time he'd look in my eyes, he'd see the terrible cheat Gordon had played on him.

Then I thought about my uncle and the relationship he'd had with my grandfather in the last years. How deep does hate run? The twisted logic that made Gordon turn on his father after driving his brother away. The pointed remarks, the constant suggestion that Eric had told Hal to leave, the seeding of the thought that Hal had indeed killed Bill and then the use of the guilt it engendered in Eric. Wearing him down slowly, ruthlessly, with a terrible precision. Hadn't Gordon said it all came easily?

But were there never any moments of doubt, triggered by memories of the loving family they'd started out as? One hesitation before striking down his only brother? They had once been close, only to be shattered. But I know time is a ruthless healer. And somewhere in me then, despite myself, grew an infant hope: That out there, in whatever awaits us when we cross the river for the last time, those two wounded souls might find each other again.

I'd gone to bed and was in a restless sleep when the knock came at the door. My alarm clock read 3:15 a.m. as I stumbled into my housecoat and made my way to the kitchen, snapping on lights as I went. When I opened the door, Jerry stood there. I moved aside to let him enter and he came in without a word. Once he was in the light, I could see that his eyes were red and his face was etched with lines. He stood by the door uncertainly, with his hands in his pockets. He was suffering terribly with this and I waited for his anger.

But it never came. We played a different kind of eyeball game, soundlessly, until I reached out to take him by the hand. I held him close until morning, not a word exchanging between us. When I awoke, he was gone.

Not long after, I got a phone call from Bick, saying he'd read about Gordon.

"Are you sure you're all right, Farran?" The concern was audible, even through the phone. "The report said you'd been injured, too."

"I'm fine. My knee isn't happy with me and I won't wear pierced earrings for a while," I quipped, "but other than that I'm fine."

"But how about you yourself?" he persisted. "It's a terrible thing you've gone through. Are you sleeping all right?"

I smiled, seeing why Dad had considered Bick a trusted friend all those years ago.

"Yes, Bick. Some nights are better than others, same with the days. At least I have some resolution to it all. Now it will just take time."

"You're right there. Now that Hal has peace, maybe you will, too."

That thought stayed with me for the day, and as I spent the evening on the porch that night, I began to settle a few things in my mind. Watching the geese on my lawn, I realized we now had something in common. In the fall, when the first cool winds would tip them off, the geese would leave. So would I, when the cottage got too cold for comfort and I had no excuse to stay longer. But in the spring they would return here, to their real home, as they have done for a thousand years. And I suddenly understood looking at them that I would find my way back, too.

I will come back in the spring, to bring Mother home again. I will lay her in the earth near the man who was more father to her than any flesh and blood could replace, beside her one true love, and in sight of the great river she never forgot. And then, I think, we will both have peace.

My peace with Gordon will take more time, of course. I understand his pain and the twisting that happens to our souls when they cannot breathe. There were two deaths in the little red brick house that day so long ago. The careless words of a dying woman killed the spirit of a young man named Gordon Leonard. Still, he destroyed the lives that matter most to me and it will take a lot of healing on my part to forgive him. I continue to work at it still.

I stayed for the summer, to finish the research in the Seaway Valley, to tie up Gordon's estate, and to have the surgery on my knee. All three went well, more or less. I spent many evenings crying, angry, depressed. I spent many more mornings on the porch, letting the river wash it through me. Grief was moving forward and I was alive again.

It took two weeks to pack Gordon's life into boxes. Almost all of it went into storage. Shad came to help me and just be there for that particular gauntlet. We brought back the store sign and the doll carriage. We sat up several nights talking about my decision to find my daughter. In September, I put the house up for rent for the winter I didn't want to do anything final until I had talked to Ruth again about searching for her son— my cousin.

My plans upon leaving the area were to look into the wartime expropriations with the Japanese on the West Coast and the German populations of Pembroke and my hometown area of Cambridge, Kitchener-Waterloo. But first the knee just before Labour Day weekend and then two weeks off my feet. I considered taking up rug hooking.

Fortunately, my second convalescence attracted more visitors. Wiley and Diana came once, with flowers and books. Diana came for several visits on her own after that, spending the day to keep me company on weekends. I cherished the time with her, framed— naturally—with thoughts of the years I lost with my own daughter. Once she brought a stack of her favourite teen magazines, pointing out the young men and boy bands she judged to be "hot." I later found one she'd left behind and casually leafed through. It hit me suddenly how young these heartthrobs were (at least the Monkees had been in their twenties), and that most of them were the same age my father was when he died.

Ruth stopped in several times and we had afternoon teas on the porch, enjoying the early fall break from the heat. Our conversations usually turned to memories freshly recovered of my mother and my grandparents. Once she brought an old photo album, and we spent the afternoon lost in Farran's Point. On her last visit before I left, Ruth was accompanied by Ernie Black, who lugged in a large box and set it on the living room floor. When he left to get the second one, I elbowed Ruth and gave her a "look."

"So what's the scoop here? You two an item?"

She blushed like the schoolgirl she still was, deep down.

"Oh, for heaven's sakes, Fan. He's just an old friend. Ernie's retired and widowed, and he's decided to stay in the area with his daughter for a while. So we go for drives or a coffee sometimes. That's all."

"Well," I said, as Ernie made it through the doorway, box in hand, "I like him."

Ruth smiled as he came over to set the second box beside the first, but she wouldn't meet my eyes. "So do I," she said.

"What's in the boxes?"

"Ruthie wouldn't tell me on the way over," Ernie laughed, "but from the weight I'd guess large rocks."

"Something I couldn't believe when I found it," Ruth answered with a shake of her head. She leaned over and opened one of the boxes, pulling out something wrapped in paper. She handed it to me. "Be careful. It's fragile."

I slowly unwrapped the bundle and held up a white china teapot, gilt-edged and laced with a beautiful pattern of blue forget-me-nots. "Ruth?" I whispered.

She nodded her head happily. "Your grandmother's china. Leslie brought it to our house from Harper's that day we closed her home. I always assumed she'd taken it with her, but I guess she couldn't. Mother must have forgotten about it. It's been sitting up in the rafters of her garage all these years." Her voice caught for a second. "I'm just so happy that I found it and that I can give it to you."

I ran my fingers along the edge of the spout. The pattern blurred in my eyes.

"Do you know," I said softly, "that this is almost all I have left of my mother? Thank you for keeping it safe for me."

Ruth came up to give me a hug. We held each other for a moment. "Just remember something, Fan," she said firmly. "The villages are gone but this is still your home. You come from here.

You have roots here. And your mother was my best friend. You'll always be welcome in my house."

They stayed for tea, bringing it in a hamper. We had a wonderful time, with Ernie telling us tales of Old Morrisburg and some of the tears he and his pals would get into. When they were getting ready to leave, Ruth put her arm around my shoulder.

"I thought you'd be happy to hear that I've made up my mind to find Steven."

"Steven?" I echoed hopefully.

"My son. That was the name I gave him for his birth certificate."

My eyes rolled for a second in Ernie's direction. Ruth smiled and shook her head.

"Ernie knows. We've had some good talks about it, and I value his advice. It's going to take time, but I'm going to find him. Ernie's right," she added, giving my hand a squeeze. "I was young and I did the best I could. I've got nothing to be ashamed of."

Good for you, Ruth, I thought as I waved them goodbye. This much I now know: There are no skeletons in the closet—only the ghosts we choose to haunt ourselves with.

Speaking of ghosts, after the night I gave Jerry the envelope, I didn't hear from him for several days. I could guess he had a lot to chew on, plus work, plus not knowing what to say to me. I knew enough to let him resurface when he was ready. After about a week, he did.

"You're just in time for breakfast, Inspector," I said when he pulled into my driveway one morning. I was sneaking out in my housecoat to get the paper, bedhead in place. Mornings have never been kind to me.

"Then I timed it right," he said dryly, unfolding himself from the front seat. He was out of uniform, looking and smelling great. Damn him "I . . . brought these," he added uncertainly, holding out some flowers. "I thought you might like them." Roses, to boot. White—my favourite. For the first time in months, I longed to slap on some makeup.

"They're beautiful," I said sincerely, taking the bouquet. "Thank you. Come on in. I was just going to start some eggs. Can you give me five while I get some clothes on?" I added as we reached the kitchen.

Jerry walked over to the fridge and opened it. "You get dressed," he ordered. "I'll cook."

I followed orders. By the time I got back, he had the meal well under way. I put the roses in water and we sat down together awkwardly.

"So when's the surgery?" he asked after a minute.

"Friday before Labour Day weekend," I said. "There was a cancellation so she fit me in. I got the impression she wanted to get me under the knife before I manage to slip away."

"Smart doctor," he grunted. Then he set down his fork. "About the other night, Farran," he began.

I cut him off with a shake of my head. "Jerry, I'm a grown woman. No one said anything about assuming things. I don't. But I don't regret it, either."

"Neither do I." He looked me straight in the eye, but this time there was no struggle. "What I wanted to say was that . . . well . . . with everything that went on, our . . . relationship . . . got off to . . ."

"An odd start?" I finished. "It sure did."

"That doesn't mean I would change it," he continued. "Just that I'd like a chance to start over, if we can."

I nodded slowly. "Get to know each other the normal way. You're right. I know the boy that was my father's friend, and I certainly know the cop," I smiled, "but I don't really know you. Just you. I'd like to."

For the first time, Jerry gave me a real smile. It was a nice smile, too. And that, to paraphrase Alice, is how it all started again. For what was left of the summer and into the fall, we went for drives and did coffee. Jerry showed me all around the United Counties, and checked in on me every day that I spent mending from the operation. He said the new kneecap looked good, scars and all.

On my last day on Ault Island, I bundled up to watch the sunrise one more time. It was the end of September and fall was truly under way. If I thought Lake St. Lawrence looked spectacular in May, it couldn't hold a candle to its autumn incarnation. The trees, going as far as the eye could see in either direction, were in full colour blaze. The river, quietly listening for the first whispers of winter coming, seemed like glass—doubling the panorama on the shoreline. The birds no longer sang and the morning was still. No bees, only the odd wasp. Mr. Heron had disappeared around the end of August. But the geese still came. They had spent the day before in groups filling the river, squawking and working out the fine details of flying south. Every once in a while, one group would fly up over the lake in V-formation for practice. This went on all day, with the honking coming through my windows long after I'd turned out my light for sleep. Union problems, maybe.

I thought of how much had changed since the first morning I'd spent on that porch. In my hand, I held a photograph—the two halves of my father and my uncle—that I'd joined back together. The story behind its being torn asunder I'd never know, but I didn't have to. My mother had kept her secrets to keep me safe, not because she didn't trust me. And my father had given me life twice—perhaps three times. I had all the pieces I needed.

Jerry came by that afternoon to help me load the car. I would leave first thing in the morning, and he instinctively knew I wanted my last night alone. When he was done, we sat out with coffee and brandy, talking about the river.

"So much history was lost," I said. "A culture. Alice said you lost your river and your ways. What do you think?"

"I'm not sure, really," said Jerry. "I shut it all out for forty years. Now I'm just beginning to size it up. Off the cuff, if I could have a choice, I'd go back to the way it was. Find some other way to do it without losing the villages, if there was one. But it's done, and it does what it was designed to do. You can't take back the river."

"Don't forget entropy," I put in.

"Entropy?"

I nodded. "The tendency in the universe for increasing disorder. It's a necessary part of the balancing act. And nothing is safe from it, not even the Front. You know," I added, "when I first got here, I was angry that I was cut off. That such a sweeping change had come and I couldn't see the villages as they had been then. I still feel that it's an irreparable loss, but I have to realize that I'm missing the villages as they were almost a half century ago. They wouldn't be that way now, anyway. Change would have come. But what hurt, of course, is that it was so massive and so fast because of the Power Project. Maybe they did it in four years, but it's taken people here a generation to deal with it."

"Change seemed to come very quickly in that era," he mused. "We thought we were building the Brave New World."

"What we should have done is pay attention to the man behind the curtain," I said. "It was our own fault, really. But in retrospect, you could see it coming. After running out of new worlds to conquer, we ended up colonizing ourselves."

A tanker slipped by in the channel, and we silently waited for the ship's wake to roll in. The size and speed of a ship, you know, are only variables. Sooner or later, the waves always reach the shore.

Out on the river, the geese began to call. I'd listened to them all season and could hear the difference in their cry. Whereas before it had sounded like a greeting, now it was tinged with goodbye. Jerry must have heard it, too.

"Will you be back sometime?" he asked quietly. "I know you have to finish your book, and you do have a life in Cambridge. But would you ever come back for a visit—or longer?"

"Do you know that's the first time you've asked me in all these weeks?" I turned to look at him, but he kept his eyes on the river.

"Maybe I wasn't sure I wanted to hear the answer."

I looked out at the St. Lawrence, doing what it has been doing since the last ice age—going home to the sea.

"Hear the geese, Jerry?" I smiled. "They know. The prodigal always returns home."

The sun was just dipping below the trees behind me that evening when I went to the river.

A sweater kept the autumn chill off my shoulders, but I found the water warm when I waded in. At first I thought just to stand there, but I kept going. The river was in its end-of-season ebb and I was only to my knees when my feet found the old highway. The road used by a thousand vehicles bound for the dam. The road they'd pulled the old church along to Upper Canada Village. The road my grandmother had been crossing when she was struck down. Now it was forgotten under the water, decayed and breaking down, but still there. I stood on it.

Feeling rather heron-like, I remained very still. Thinking nothing, watching, waiting—for what, I wasn't sure. I listened to the river, to the intermittent call of the geese from somewhere out of view, to the rustle of the leaves as the evening breeze picked up.

I checked the sun over my shoulder. It was below the treetops now, and the sky above it was tinged with red. The promise of a good day. Turning back, I breathed in the scent of the river's dusk and closed my eyes.

Minutes passed and I felt a great calm come over me as the wind played with my hair. It came at first faint, as though a trick of my mind. Then clear, sharp. The distinctive shriek of a steam locomotive. The Moccasin.

I opened my eyes. "I've come to say goodbye," I said softly.

Whispers, mingled and scattered by the wind. Many voices, snatches, pieces mixed together. Then the odd one over the rest.

. . . tell the neighbourhood. I'm not here to stay, just makin' a scheduled . . .

What else can you do? You need him . . .

. . . that sign up myself in '33 . . .

"Dad," I whispered, "if you can hear me, I'm okay. Thank you. For what you did." Tears pricked my eyes.

Yer pa was a good man. As good as they come.

It's the only home . . . else would you want me to be?

Will you dance with me one more time?

I let her go then. "Goodbye, Mom." The tears began in earnest, but the grief was different. A warm, enveloping sadness. "I'll love you for the rest of my life."

The sound of a church bell, tolling.

He's gone . . . think you know that . . .

Harper Mackenzie is a dead man walkin' . . .

. . . all of us from the villages of Farran's Point and Woodlands . . .

The wind picked up, whipping my hair into my eyes. I pulled the sweater closer around me for warmth.

. . . covering for Emme. They are . . . good friends, I think . . .

I still think you're a brat, but sometimes . . .

The light was going fast. The voices were beginning to fade. It became harder to pick out the words.

. . . came to dance . . .

. . . this here's a game . . . of you and me . . . table . . .

I closed my eyes to concentrate, to pull them back, but it was no use.

. . . Point . . . seen you . . . park . . .

Then I was alone.

It was almost dark. I turned to go into the cottage, framed as it was by the red glow of sunset now quickly melting behind the trees. I picked my way carefully over the stony riverbed, made it to the sand and then onto the lawn.

A final breeze brushed my ear and for some reason I momentarily turned back.

And then, in the fading light, I heard it.

The sound of two young brothers

laughing

racing

toward the river.

The Physician's Home—Upper Canada Village

The house known as the Physician's Home at Upper Canada Village did indeed come from Aultsville. Once named Forget-Me-Not Cottage, the house was built circa 1845. A cottage-style design in the Neo-Grecian tradition, its details speak of romantic influences from the 1840s: the concave roof, the trellis supports of the verandah, and the oval window in the upper front of the house.

One of the real inhabitants of the home was Michael Urias Cook (1824-1912), a prosperous farmer who was the first man to import Holstein-Friesian cattle into Ontario in 1881. When the cottage became part of Upper Canada Village in the late 1950s, it was decided to restore it as the home of a typical nineteenth-century doctor. Although two of Cook's sons later became physicians, neither ever ran a medical practice from that house.

Forget-Me-Not Cottage is one of the smaller buildings in the historical village, but it is my favourite. In my heart, I will always see it as Hal and Gordon's home—the little red-brick house from nowhere, with a distinctive oval window upstairs.

The Brother of Sleep

A ST. LAWRENCE SEAWAY MYSTERY

Farran Mackenzie couldn't have been more surprised when Alison Perry walked into her University of Waterloo office. It had been thirty years since she had last seen her best friend in high school, and thirty years since her best friend's father, a police officer, had been killed in the line of duty. And now Alison was asking for help in discovering who had really killed her father.

Farran has doubts about helping her long-lost friend. A lifetime has passed since Alison walked out of her life with no explanation but doubt fades when a car bomb results in the death of Sergeant Perry's old partner, nearly killing Alison and Farran, as well. Someone obviously doesn't want them to dig up old skeletons, so Farran takes them to the only place she feels safe—the St. Lawrence Seaway. But the past keeps catching up with them there, too. A fated meeting in the local cemetery with Paul Vaughn, a police officer from Newfoundland, has Farran revisiting the origins of the St. Lawrence Seaway, a journey that turned her own life upside down only a year ago, and threatens to do so again. She feels a strange attraction to Paul, whose life seems to mirror her own, but what about Jerry Strauss, the OPP inspector to whom she owes so much? Too many police officers in her life, both past and present, and too many coincidences. Farran's heart is playing havoc with her instincts, which could prove dangerous, if not deadly. Whom can she trust? And is the truth worth the price of knowing?

About the Author

In the three years since the successful publication of her first novel, *A Violent End*, Maggie Wheeler has established herself in not one, but two, Canadian literary genres. By seamlessly merging the craft of the mystery novel with her passion for Canadian history, Maggie has become a prominent voice in the growing contemporary movement to preserve and celebrate the stories of this country.

As well as her literary endeavours, Maggie continues to travel and meet with people to talk about not only the novels and the writing process, but also the emotional and cultural cost of the St. Lawrence Seaway. Her classroom lectures, symposium presentations and media interviews have sharpened the focus on Canadian history in general and the Lost Villages in particular.

Maggie and her husband Robert Childerhose, a Seaway pilot, live on Ault Island, with their three daughters, ten-year-old Anna and eight-year-old twins Evan and Lindsay. They also share their home near Ingleside, Ontario, with Bagel the Beagle.

www.maggiewheeler.com

To order more copies of

A Violent End

The Brother of Sleep

Contact:
**General Store
Publishing House**
499 O'Brien Road, Box 415
Renfrew, Ontario Canada K7V 4A6
Telephone: 1-800-465-6072
Fax: (613) 432-7184
www.gsph.com

VISA and MASTERCARD accepted.